MELT

ARLAN ANDREWS, SR.

WOODS
PUBLISHING

CONTENTS

prelude	vii
Chapter 1	1
Chapter 2	7
Chapter 3	13
Chapter 4	19
Chapter 5	25
Chapter 6	33
Chapter 7	41
Chapter 8	49
Chapter 9	61
Chapter 10	69
Chapter 11	75
Chapter 12	81
Chapter 13	91
Chapter 14	101
Chapter 15	105
interlude	109
Chapter 16	111
Chapter 17	119
Chapter 18	131
Chapter 19	143
Chapter 20	149
Chapter 21	153
Chapter 22	163
Chapter 23	169
Chapter 24	173
Chapter 25	177
Chapter 26	189
Chapter 27	195
Chapter 28	201
Chapter 29	207
Chapter 30	211
Chapter 31	225
invasion	231
Chapter 32	233

Chapter 33 241
Chapter 34 255
Chapter 35 261
Chapter 36 265
Chapter 37 271
Chapter 38 277
Chapter 39 281
Chapter 40 285
Chapter 41 293
Chapter 42 301
Chapter 43 305
Chapter 44 309
Chapter 45 311
Chapter 46 313
war 317
Chapter 47 319
Chapter 48 329
Chapter 49 335
Chapter 50 341
Chapter 51 343
Chapter 52 347
Chapter 53 349
Chapter 54 351
Chapter 55 357
Chapter 56 363
Chapter 57 365
Chapter 58 371
Chapter 59 377
Chapter 60 381
Chapter 61 387
Chapter 62 395
Chapter 63 401
Chapter 64 405
Chapter 65 411
Chapter 66 417
Chapter 67 427
Chapter 68 431
Chapter 69 435
peace 437
Chapter 70 439

before 447
Chapter 71 449

About the Author 491

Melt

This is a work of fiction. All the characters and events portrayed in this book are fictional, and any resemblance to real people or incidents is purely coincidental.

Copyright © 2022 by Arlan Andrews, Sr.

All rights reserved, including the right to reproduce this book or portions thereof in any form.

Physical printed format by Woods Publishing

ISBN Paperback 978-1-946419-58-3

ISBN Hardback 978-1-946419-59-0

Note: Distance units used herein—miles, yards, feet, kilometers, meters, centimeters—refer to roughly equivalent values in the societies they are used in. Those different societies will use their own names for these units of measurement.

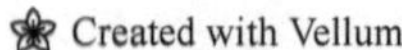 Created with Vellum

PRELUDE

CHAPTER ONE

There will be war, Wakan Kech, High Priest, thought as dawn light broke over the far horizon, *war across this beautiful land, a war that* I *have brought upon us!*

The tall olive-skinned priest, a striking figure in his scarlet godscloth robes, stood on the raised stone platform at the base of the carved Arch of ShadowFall, looking out over the gathered crowd below. Glancing over his shoulder, he looked up briefly to note the beauty of the recumbent ancient rainbow-shaped stone sculpture behind him. But today his thoughts were not of beauty, but of doom. He dared not share his dark thoughts with the thousands of citizens and nobles who were anxiously gathering to watch the ceremony. Wakan Kech kept his visage noble, yet stern, as benefitted one of his stature. The Princess would not be attending; she only honored this site once a year, with an appearance on the longest day, the beginning of Season Warm, when she would personify ShadowFall's coming prosperity. That was six months from now. No, Wakan alone officiated over the rituals at this opposite end of the year, Season Cold.

On the far horizon to Wakan's left, the ominous black wall of the Dark Highlands slumped like a low, dark shadow across the northern edge of the Sisterdom of ShadowFall, stretching from sunrise to darkness, cleft only by the kilometers-wide waterfall that birthed Mother's River, the wide, mirror-flat channel east of the city that flowed south, just two kilometers distant. Directly in front of Wakan, the newborn sun was just rising above ShadowFall's wide plains and colorful crop fields, which seemed to stretch endlessly from the Mother's River on to infinity. And to Wakan's right, high in the southern morning sky, boiled a stormfront of anvil-shaped gathering gray clouds. *An omen of the armies of Motherland*, he thought, *coming to invade ShadowFall and depose its rightful ruler Princess Perneptheranam. And to kill me—slowly!*

He paused to look behind himself again, up at the Arch, noting how the earliest shadows were playing out their destined calendric roles. Carved in high relief in the living stone of an outcropping of limestone rock half as large as the nearby Princess's palace, the Arch itself reached up twice Wakan's height and stretched twice *that* in width, a sloping relief sculpture with a hollowed-out center below the bottommost arc.

For all its unblemished appearance from the viewpoint of the assembled crowd, up close Wakan could see that the sculpture had been chipped out by ancient stone carvers. From the keystone-shaped wedge at top of the Arch, to the three successive tilted wedges arranged down each side, their different slopes giving rise to radial triangular shadows, to the smooth back side, the entirety of the Arch was a "shadow machine" of incredible sophistication.

In all, the Arch was the powerful symbol of ShadowFall, even to the ignorant who did not know its true astronomical functions. *But for those who understand its use, like me,* Wakan thought, *it lets us observe how the sun creates shadows, so we can forecast events in the heavens. Such as today, the shortest day of the year. And most probably the day of our impending doom!*

For this specific day, the changing of the seasons, the ancients had provided a signal in light and shadow that all could see, a sudden horizontal shaft of light, framed by shadows of intricately positioned overhead stones, would appear: the Arrow of the Sun, its sharp end stabbing a wedge on the south side, indicating the death of Season Wet. And the birth of Season Cold.

Wakan thought that the Arch had been a magnificent achievement by those unknown artisans, and was now a beautiful symbol of the new Sisterdom of Princess Perneptheranam. But a reminder of ShadowFall's still-savage society remained here, impaled on a horizontal spike: the now stripped-clean, bony skull of the last Season Warm sacrifice, once the head of a handsome young man, stared out with lifeless sockets and a wired-on dangling jaw.

And I myself reinstituted this ancient custom here, he thought grimly, *as a way to demonstrate Princess Pernie's absolute dominion over all of us. It has succeeded in that, at the cost of an innocent boy each year. But there's no shortage of volunteers, not when a night with Pernie is the incentive!*

Wakan sighed. *We have a long way to go, to civilization.* His own place of origin, the High Antis, fortunately lay thousands of kilometers south of Motherland; he was only in Mother's empire by virtue of being captured by Mother's Army some twenty-three years before, during an ill-fated archeological expedition to study the ancient and mysterious crystal domes of Chi'a. Mothersmen had slaughtered his High Antis guards, saving only himself and two dozen other Kech scholars. *Just because luckily I could speak a pidgin they understood.* Involuntarily, the High Priest shuddered at the memory of the vicious castration that he and the other male captives would have suffered, if indeed they were allowed to live.

But like the enigmatic Arch, the whole of ShadowFall itself was equally mysterious, Wakan knew. Mother's scribes had no records of why the large stone-built city, its magnificent palace, this enigmatic yet useful sculpture, and in fact, the thousands of square kilometers of fertile croplands on both sides of the

Mother's River hereabouts, had all been abandoned in antiquity. Only a few small, scarcely populated villages and the vast, abandoned stone city had awaited the new Princess's coming to take possession. Wakan often wondered, too, why none of the neighboring Sisterdoms had tried to reclaim the whole region for themselves long before. *Just one more ancient mystery of Motherland,* he mused. *One more among many in this strange empire of the vast bottomlands.*

As the sun climbed into the cloudless sky to the east, Wakan carefully noted the positions of the shadows crawling across the Arch. When at last the golden arrow of sunlight penetrated the carved pathway hole and illuminated the stone tile on the south side, he would announce to the gathering crowd that Season Cold had officially begun. He was grateful that no tradition called for beheading another young man, as was done six months before, the day…*the day that little Rist, the brown dwarf from the Dark Highlands, arrived, and changed our lives.*

As the sun rose to a specified angle, its rays aligned with the carved opening; suddenly the shadow across the face of the Arch was split by a spear of sunlight just centimeters across, illuminating a dark triangle on the south side. As expressions of wonder, the *oohs* and *aahs*, wafted through the assembled crowd, Wakan Kech spoke. "It is now Season Cold, citizens and nobles," he announced in the deep, sonorous voice for which he was well known. "Let us prepare as tradition demands, by turning over the soils in our fields, putting back hay and feed for our animals and birds, and the dried meats, fruits, and vegetables for ourselves." Bowing toward the Princess's palace, where he saw a doorway opening above a high balcony, he continued, "And let us all give thanks to our beloved Princess Perneptheranam, who brings us peace and prosperity!" At that, the red-tressed Princess appeared on the balcony, waving her arms and spreading her radiant, rainbow-hued godscloth sleeves, acknowledging her subjects' cheers before bowing and retreating amidst the wild cheering and applause.

Wakan allowed himself a smile. As did the loudly shouting crowd, he truly loved the Princess, and she loved them. And he also knew, as they all knew, to the core of their being, *We are all her slaves, her personal property.*

CHAPTER TWO

"Watch out!" Tunneler Jolan Keesh yelled at his dig crew. "The whole thing is caving in!" Throwing his Eternal Machine into reverse, Keesh felt it tremble as the growling melter's treads slipped, then caught hold of solid ground, lurching backwards out of the way of the imminent collapse of the excavated tunnel in front of them. Through the cloud of dust and dirt, he counted off as *one, two, three, four—all five!—* of his men stumbled out of the falling dust and debris. A quick glance behind him showed that the main tunnel had not suffered any cave-in, thank the Creator! They would not be trapped in Infinite Rock, but still had a way back to Community.

"Close, boss," Ledd Mernan yelled up to him, "but Creator be thanked, we are all alive." Keesh clambered down from his operator's cabin, waving his hand to clear away the dust cloud around himself and his crew. "What happened, anyhow?" he asked between coughs.

Ledd explained that although their ultrasonic instruments had shown only solid strata directly in front of them, they had run into an unseen upward-angled void that caused the collapse. "The way ahead into Infinite Rock was pure and clear, no voids, boss," he was telling Keesh as his supervisor went around to each crew member to reassure himself that every man was uninjured. "But at the last melt, we hit a void coming from a down angle, perpendicular to the direct of our melt. Somehow, that let the tunneler surge forward just enough to make the cut unstable."

Keesh nodded at that; he had felt the Eternal Machine jerk forward at the last instant, causing him to yell out that warning to his crew. *Just seconds more and —!* He didn't want to think about the loss of men and maybe even the Eternal Machine. And himself. But thank Creator that they were all in good shape!

"*Mee—mee!*" a faint sound came from the rubble. Listening closely, the men heard it again. Mernan and Keesh dropped their jaws and ran with the other crew to the source. "Nothing could be alive in this collapse, boss," Mernan was shouting, as he shoveled stones and loose dirt away from the pile of debris. "I know, Ledd," Keesh said through clenched teeth as he removed loose rocks from the pile, "but somebody—or somet*hing*—is trapped. We gotta get it out!"

Ten minutes of rock and dirt removal by all six men, working furiously, uncovered the *someone* in the pile—a tall, thin person, dressed in a dim-red skintight suit of some kind, which covered even the head, leaving visible only the face behind a transparent plate. That person was whimpering and mewing like an injured catimal, its slanted eyes wide in panic. "Take off that face covering!" Keesh yelled. "It is suffocating!"

Keesh felt around the skinsuit, trying to remove the clear plate covering the person's face. After a few frustrating minutes, the plate softly popped off, and the person inside gasped for breath. Keesh's nostrils were offended by the pungent odor that accompanied the breaths. *What gives off such a smell?* he wondered. But that was a minor concern: he was grateful for the rescue, but who was it? In that strange suit? That smell? So tall! And emerging from Infinite Rock?

"Who are you?" he asked softly. "And how did you get here?"

As Mienne herself related later, right before that cave-in she was trapped! She had been running for hours, her oxygen running low, she knew. Mother had placed her own emergency breather supply on Mienne's chest, turning away and going back upward into the darkened tunnel. Somewhere along the way, Mienne heard a hissing noise behind her, and her skinsuit displate told her that she was in breathable air, that it was switching from the hormone-saturated membrane breather pack to open atmosphere. But in constant panic, with no known destination, Mienne had kept on running, the way lit by her skinsuit's lamps, until—until the floor of the tunnel collapsed from beneath her!

Buried alive in a jumble of rocks and dirt, she had screamed until there was no more breath left. Then miraculously she heard the growling engine of a large machine. And—were those *voices*? *Human* voices! Gathering her last, hopeless breath from the breather, she screamed again. *"It's meee! Help meee!"*

Someone did hear her, and minutes later, she was unburied and breathing again. But the new air was strange—*No additives? No hormones! And where is this?* There were half a dozen very small people gathered around her in what were obviously work suits with lighted work caps, but she could barely make them out in the dim red glow. The strings of almost-dark reddish lights strung from the low ceiling of the tunnel behind them did not provide much illumination. Even the headlamps on the big digging machine taking up half of the tunnel were dim-red.

"Where am I?" she asked, as one of the strange men stood her up and brushed the dust from her skinsuit. "And who are you all? Why do you smell so funny? And why is everything so dark and red?"

Brushing the dust and dirt off the dark skinsuit, Jolan Keesh had the impression that it covered a girl underneath, though one much taller than himself and his men, and obviously well fed. But from her build and undeveloped feminine shape, she was obviously still a child for all that. She was talking in a rapid, high-pitched voice, giving him final confirmation of the sex. Though she continued to jabber, neither Keesh nor any of his men could make out even one recognizable word. "You speak Rin?" he asked. No response. Keesh then went through the half dozen pidgin languages he'd learned about from the Teacher Elders, some from the few surviving audio recordings of the Old Lost Ones, without success. Finally, in frustration he tried the forbidden tongue. *"Glish?"* he gestured with the V-sign of two fingers of his raised hand, inviting her to speak. The child—the *girl*, he knew—opened her eyes wide and made the sign of the X.

"Glish!" she whispered loudly, erupting into a chant of some kind, and making the X sign again. Clearly the mere mention of the ancient cant upset her.

Keesh and his men smiled at her reaction. "Well, she knows enough of the ancient curse and the sign of the X," he laughed. "I think we ought to keep her!" The men all laughed. At that, the tall girl stood up and ran away from the group—*smack!*—into the tread of the melter. Stunned, she turned around and tried to run into the finished tunnel behind them, but stumbled and fell. As Keesh and his men watched, she crawled her way to one wall, stood, and waved her hands in front of her.

"Blind!" Ledd said. "The poor girl is Blind!" Keesh sighed at the fate of the poor child, wondering what would come of her. Community would not Reprocess her right away, but if she didn't show some promise by her Thirteenth Motherth Year, she might be doomed. In resignation, Keesh instructed Ledd to escort the tall child back to Community, to Shinyeen City, newest of the Five Cities, where she would be taken care of by an Elder in the Niche of Disabled Children. Keesh estimated that the abnormally tall child had a year or two, at most, to find something worthwhile to contribute. *But Blind? What a shame,* he thought, *just a shame!*

But, Keesh wondered, where had she come from? Obviously even though she was tall she was not an Old Lost One, because all of *those* tall people were only found in ancient Tubes, long dead, most of them mummified or horribly rotted away to bones or even dust. He shuddered at the memory of discovering the intact Vac suits of such large ancient ones, their occupants now just unrecognizable ash-like debris. *Hundreds of them,* he recalled. *And nobody knows who they were or how they died. But their Tubes do provide us with living volume and physical resources. Surely must be part of Creator's plan?* Unaccustomed to worrying about the mysteries of the Creator, a pastime frowned upon by the Elders, he tried to draw his mind back to the task at hand: his schedule called for tunneling a quarter of a kilometer a day, so he would not have time to investigate what kind of other tunnels may have intersected with this new one he was excavating, or what kind of People might be living there.

As Keesh fired up the Eternal Machine again, signaling for his remaining crew to stand by while he melted a protective layer through the collapsed overhead debris, his unwanted thoughts intruded. *We know Creator has provided us Infinite Rock in all directions—save Up!—for us to explore and expand and exploit,* but *what if, like the Old Ones who once lived in the abandoned Tubes, we are not the only ones still left alive in Rock? This strange child, this tall girl, had to come from* somewhere! But thinking on such things did not melt rock, did not produce volume. *I've got another hundred meters to go to get to those vertical voids that Ledd discovered, to try to send my test probe up toward Vac. After I bring back actual proof of Vac, then the Elders can decide all of that philosophical stuff!* With that thought, putting his mind back to his original task, Keesh melted over and smoothed out the opening to the collapsed overhead void, and continued melting Rock.

CHAPTER THREE

Reporting directly to Mother Messinex, Chief Advisor Miran Kech was the highest-ranking appointed person in Motherland. And at the moment, the angriest. Like his High Antis countryman Wakan Kech up in ShadowFall, Miran also bore the title of High Priest. Unlike Wakan, Miran was short and obese. Like Wakan, he also welcomed the rising sun, but briefly and without public ceremony, before returning inside Mother's Palace to attend to the day's business.

Back in his spacious white marble-tiled courtroom, Miran smelled with approval the morning's new incenses, a daily aromatic experience expertly crafted by his chief concierge. That white-robed worthy then approached the High Priest, whispering briefly in his ear. The High Priest was not amused at the report. "Bring him in, now!" Miran Kech roared. "I want to see that soldier!" The concierge bowed, backed away, and left.

Furious at the soldier who now stood before him, Miran Kech waved his flowing blue robes around like a bird in battle. "What do you mean, Colonel Creesile, that you 'believe' you confiscated all of the godspheres and ancient books and springbow weapons at ShadowFall? My specific orders from the Mother were to take them *all*!"

The tall, bearded, black-leather-clad soldier stood at

attention before Lord Kech, erect but nervous, brass helmet in hand. A simple word from the Kech, a gesture, and Creesile knew he would face the tender mercies of the torture chambers that Mother Messinex's advisor had set up below the palace to deal with members of the deceased Lordess Mother's court. Rumored hundreds had already met their protracted deaths there, and Creesile was determined not to join them. *Not this day, you overly perfumed toad!* he thought. *You soft, fat slug of a man!*

"Lord Kech," Colonel Creesile said without hesitation, "I had the word of Wakan Kech, the High Priest of ShadowFall, that his Princess had turned over all those items to my men, for transport back here, as you ordered. Furthermore," he said, pulling out a hefty scroll, "I have here the inventory that the Princess ordered. We now possess every item on it."

Miran Kech calmed himself down, taking the document and pretending to inspect it closely. "So I see, Colonel, so I see." He handed the inventory to a hooded scribe who scrambled up to receive it, running back away from the Kech. "So why did you *first* say you only 'believed it to be accurate'?"

Creesile turned and snapped a finger at guards behind him. One brought forward an attractive, dark-haired young woman in dirty robes and tattered sandals, her hands and feet bound in light chains, who now stood before Miran Kech with a defiant look on her pale face. "Because of this woman, Lord Kech. As we departed from ShadowFall, we found her being transported on the Main Road, near the southern border of the Sisterdom of Stone Pyramid. We had not encountered her escort cadre en route to ShadowFall because they were staying at a lodge while we were riding north at night. But on our return trip we overtook them in daylight and assumed responsibility for her. You need to hear what she says."

"Bring her to my private chambers," Miran Kech said, "but keep her chained, and station a guard outside my door." When they arrived at the ornate white marble archway of his chambers, the Kech dismissed the soldiers with a sneer, making mental notes as to the colonel's attitude. That soldier's fate, his life, depended upon what the prisoner had to say.

In his secure private chambers, its shadows a welcome relief from the distracting light of day that permeated the ceilings of the palace's meeting rooms, Miran Kech sat in a stuffed chair while his captive remained standing, still defiant though in chains. *She needs a bath*, he thought, sniffing her sweat and fear. *Maybe with that road smell gone, and some perfumed powders, she might be acceptable for a night's entertainment in bed.* "What is your name, woman? Where are you from, and what do you want to say to me?"

The woman bowed gracefully toward Miran Kech, taking the appropriate three intermediate positions as she did so. *She has been in court*, he thought. *She is cultured. More interesting all the time!*

"Lord Kech, my name is Rumi Similla. Until a month ago I acted as temporary administrator of ShadowFall, whilst Princess Perneptheranam was here in Mother's City for the Game." Catching her breath, she said, "And of course, for the coronation of our new Mother Messinex." Miran Kech was even more impressed; the girl knew the proper titles, the preferred inflections of tone, even the subtle hand gestures of loyalty acknowledged only among the High Court. And besides, standing upright revealed that she was curvaceous and rather attractive, dirty robes and feet aside. *Yes, I will have her tonight! Whether I keep her alive after that, well that depends on what she has to tell me.*

"But why are you in chains, Rumi Similla? And why were you with Colonel Creesile and his troops? A six-hundred-kilometer journey from Stone Pyramid Sisterdom is not just a nice visit to the Blue Salt Sea." His own statement suddenly brought back memories of his last truly relaxing vacation on the white-sand beaches of the Mother's private resort, just fifty kilometers south. *Has it been three whole years now? I really need to get back. But—there are so many enemies of Mother Messinex that need...attending to.* That thought brought back other more recent memories, pleasant ones for him. *Not so pleasant for the stubborn traitors remaining loyal to our former Lordess Mother, though!*

Rumi Similla looked at Miran Kech with her large, deep blue eyes, an appeal not only to her judge but also to a powerful male. In his positions of power over the years, Miran Kech was quite aware of such tactics. *But they do work, girl,* he thought, *they do.*

"Lord Kech, the Princess's advisor, Wakan Kech, falsely accused me of usurping her power while she was away. He sent me to exile; I was to be banished to a penal colony in the Western Dry Highlands." Tears ran from her eyes and she bowed her head. "But Lord, by good fortune Colonel Creesile and his men found us on the Main Road from ShadowFall. They forcibly took me from Wakan Kech's guards and brought me here. I am innocent. If you would release me, I can tell you of many of the secrets of ShadowFall, things no one else knows."

Being used to pleas of true innocents begging for mercy before being relegated to the bloody terrors of his dungeons, Miran Kech was only interested in one thing. *Two, if she is a willing partner in bed,* he thought. "Rumi Similla, I can find out everything you know, and more, within a few minutes if I just call in my inquisitors right now." The woman didn't flinch; he liked that. *She does have the class of someone raised around royalty.* He was growing weary of the promiscuous females around the palace who, though physically attractive—at least until he grew tired of them and had them...adjusted—had shown little in the way of brains or intellectually stimulating behavior. Maybe this feisty one would be different? Something interesting to be found in her brain as well as her other parts?

"Lord Kech," Similla said, "I told Colonel Creesile a few of the secrets. They were enough to make him bring me here, to risk his career, his life—and *my* life—to incur your displeasure about the confiscated globes and books and springbows. I told him that while I was still at ShadowFall, I discovered that there were two sets of inventories of those books and globes and weapons. Wouldn't you like to know the rest? I give these secrets to you willingly, and ask only for your mercy and the opportunity to serve you here in Mother's Palace."

Miran Kech arose and walked around the young woman, noting her attractive body, her face, her long hair. *Beautiful. Courageous, too,* he mused. *Confident, cultured, intelligent. Worth a few nights at the least.*

As the Kech rubbed his chin as if trying to decide her fate, Rumi dealt her final card. "Lord Kech, did you know that the little dwarf Rist, the Lordess Mother's Champion in the Game, has a twin brother who flies a giant green god-machine? One from the ancient gods that he retrieved from a glacier in the Dark Highlands? Wakan Kech himself has flown in it." At Miran Kech's shocked face and dropped jaw, she added: "And I know how to capture it!"

CHAPTER FOUR

"Tell me again, Wakan," Princess Perneptheranam said, slurring her words slightly after several glasses of wine, "what do you think happened to my little Rist and his twin? I rode in that marvelous Una machine for only a few minutes, up in the sky and invisible. He said he could have flown me here to ShadowFall in half an hour, but we thought that I shouldn't let anyone else know about the machine." With a grimace, she said, "So I had to spend another week on the road in my miserable, bouncing horse-drawn coach before I got home."

The Princess waved an arm to encompass the stark surroundings of the gray stone walls of her private chambers. "Wakan, do you think ShadowFall will ever be our real home?" She concluded that she needed more tapestries to stifle the echoes of her conversations and to add more insulation against the oncoming Season Cold. *This place is no Mother's Palace*, she thought, *but after five years it ought to be more plush than I've made it.*

Wakan Kech looked at his Princess with respect, devotion, and not a little fear. At nineteen years old, she was already wiser than most of her half-siblings. *Much because of my own influence, I like to think. She is level-headed and wise beyond her years, having turned down the opportunity to become the new Mother, instead yielding that opportunity to Messinex.* He had mixed feelings about that decision; if Pernie were now *Mother* Perneptheranam, then he, Wakan Kech, would be the most powerful appointee in Motherland, and the two of them could begin their hoped-for improvements to the Motherland.

But now such reforms would have to wait: education in writing and maths and geoms for all citizens, a reduction in royal powers to include fair trials, only minimal torture, and all the rest. He did have reservations about his High Antis countryman, Miran Kech, now chief priest for the new Mother Messinex; rumors of Miran's numerous executions and imprisonment of the late Lordess Mother's courtiers and local nobles were disturbing. *But all of that is far away in Mother's City. For now. If only Rumi Similla were not there to speak to Miran about Una!*

In answering the Princess's question, Wakan hated to have to lie to her; first, because lying to his best friend and confidant felt like a terrible thing to do, even though he was doing it to protect her from Mother Messinex's likely vengeance. And second, because by Motherland traditions and law, the punishment for such treason was the slow removal of the liar's tongue, a small slice at a time, followed by the sewing up of the mouth and then a slow death by starvation in the stocks, unless one was lucky enough to first die by bleeding out.

Shaking off such thoughts, Wakan said, "Princess, looking at our timelines, our calendars, you must have encountered Rist and Rusk and their Una machine along the Main Road somewhere in the south of the Sisterdom of Trader Plains, in Princess Desmeen's domain, about two months ago. I had only arrived at ShadowFall shortly before that, on your fast horses." Sighing, he lied, "I saw that marvelous flying Una once at our training facility in Mother's City prior to the Game, but not since." His face grew grim. "I did not discuss the machine in Mother's Court at all, for fear of being overheard. The consequences for yourself, for ShadowFall"—*and for myself,* he added silently

—"would have been disruptive and maybe fatal, what with the shock of our Lordess Mother's unfortunate passing. Adding to the succession turmoil then, some Sister or other may have initiated violence to try to seize the Una. It was only for that reason I did not tell you about Rusk and the god-machine at that very moment.

"As for what happened to our little friends after they left you along the Main Road down there, I fear that they must have crashed somewhere or perhaps they flew the Una back to their Tharn's Lands. Rist talked about their parents being in some kind of trouble up there, over two thousand kilometers upriver."

In actuality, Wakan knew, the dark dwarves Rist and Rusk had flown their Una machine, powered by some unimaginable magic—*No*, technology! *Not magic!* he reminded himself—from their meeting with the Princess, directly here to ShadowFall, in less than half an hour. Rist had brought with him the shocking news that Miran Kech, Mother Messinex's High Priest, had ordered the seizure of all of ShadowFall's godspheres, bound ancient books, and unique springbow weapons. For what reason, Rist didn't know, but had speculated, "After I told Mother Messinex in her courtroom that some of the godspheres from the bottommost libraries under the palace said that Motherland had once been a sea in ancient times, she became agitated and threw us all out. Next thing I knew, a Mothersman came out to the atrium area where the godspheres were soaking up sunlight, and ordered them all confiscated. And the ancient books, too."

"Wakan," the little man had told him, "so Rusk and I came here to ShadowFall to save all that we could before anybody from Mother's City arrives. We will leave some godspheres and books here, but we will take the bulk of them with us. And all of the carved spindles that only we Tharnslanders can read. We can't allow them all to be taken back to Mother's City and destroyed or sealed up forever. They are too important to us for that, all that ancient knowledge, the history."

Both Rist and Wakan knew that the Una machine

possessed an incredible archive of stored text, drawings, and videos from ancient times, but they also realized that nothing new had been added to that collection of information since the flying machine was trapped under The Ice, back when that ancient world ended. Only the books and spindles would have any more recent history, things that had happened in the thousands of years since. Wakan had reluctantly agreed with Rist's and Rusk's plan, and they decided not to tell the Princess, lest she take immediate vengeance out on Wakan for his part, or for complicity should Miran Kech discover their subterfuge. So the priest had continued with the deception.

"Princess, as you witnessed within a few days after your arrival, Colonel Creesile's party of horsemen showed up, demanding our godspheres and books and even our springbows. Of course, though reluctant, you saw that we yielded and surrendered what was asked of us." The Princess had not been aware of the two sets of inventories that Wakan had always kept, lists of possessions that Mother's occasional tax auditors would be shown. The inventory given to Miran's men was one that did not show all of the spheres and books, or the hidden caches of springbow weapons, ShadowFall's last-ditch means of arming thousands of the Sisterdom's adults in the case of another invasion. Even Pernie had to be kept in the dark on some things, *for her own good. And mine!*

"Yes, Wakan, I saw," the Princess said. "I had no choice but to give Mother Messinex what she demanded, but I still wonder at her motivation." Nibbling on a ripe yellow fruit just arrived in a delivery from Three Rivers, Perneptheranam licked her lips and said, "Now that Messinex has had several months as our new Mother, do you think she might be trying to consolidate her power over all of Motherland, to make sure that none of those ancient technologies can be used against her?"

The Princess had long been friends with her biological half-sister Messinex, and the recent death of their previous Lordess Mother, blood mother of twelve of the thirteen Princesses, had elevated Messinex to the position of supreme ruler of their nation. Alone among the half-siblings, Messinex had maintained loving and friendly relations with Perneptheranam, for as long back in childhood as "Pernie" could remember. So surely, Pernie maintained, whatever her Sister's reasons for confiscation, Messinex meant only good for ShadowFall and its Princess.

Wakan was not so certain; his last few interactions with Miran Kech at Mother's City had been less than pleasant. After his old acquaintance became High Priest and chief advisor to the new Mother, his latent arrogance and previously controlled lust for power seemed to increase exponentially. *And those terrible rumors...*

Wakan replied, "Princess, I am sure that it had nothing to do with our Rist and his twin's Una machine." He hesitated, then said slowly, "But there may be a problem. I returned here from Mother's City because your maid Anklya, who flew there with Rusk on the Una machine, told us that Rumi Similla, your administrator in absentia, had tried to seize the flying Una from Rist's twin. Her actions were suspicious to say the least, and maybe even treasonous." The Princess nodded thoughtfully but said nothing.

Wakan continued, "So I sent her away south on the Main Road with two armed guards, with directions that they find the next company of troops or traders who were leaving for the Western Dry Highlands, and send her with them, in official ShadowFall chains. Banishment rather than execution, as you and I have agreed, is a more humane way to deal with potential crimes less than outright murder or treason."

"So, my wise priest, what is the problem with that?" Pernie was getting bored, the Kech could tell. Slowly peeling another yellow fruit, she was obviously uninterested in personnel details. Wakan sighed; he constantly did his best to shield Pernie from the day-to-day minutiae of managing a Sisterdom of the sixty-five thousand citizen-slaves who inhabited ShadowFall's forty thousand square kilometers. Given their responsibilities, Wakan and the dozen lesser nobles under him had little free time, what with the continuing urgencies of crops, animals, birds, fisheries, manufactories, and mills, not to mention educating the populace and maintaining the defense of the realm from predatory neighboring Sisters. But this one person's whereabouts was worth mentioning.

"Princess, my returning guards reported that Colonel Creesile and his men encountered them and Rumi along the way back to Mother's City. Apparently on the way here they had missed my guards and their prisoner, passing in the night. But upon returning, they insisted upon taking her, guaranteeing that she would be transported to the Western Dry Highlands colony as required." At the Princess's perplexed reaction, he delivered the bad news. "But if the Colonel does take Rumi to Mother's City instead of that colony, she may get the attention of my brother Kech, Miran."

Wakan spoke slowly, realizing the import of his words. "Rumi knows all about Rusk's flying god-machine. And how our guards were able to shoot it down." If the woman were to tell Miran Kech about Rusk and Una, he would report it to Mother Messinex. Then the withholding of that information would be viewed as treason, by any rational definition. *Even if Miran Kech himself is irrational!*

Pernie dropped her half-peeled yellow fruit and put her hand to her mouth. "Keeping that Una machine a secret from our Mother means that ShadowFall could be declared in rebellion, treasonous. There will be war, Wakan. We—we—*have* to find Rusk and Rist. And, and, *our* Una machine!"

CHAPTER FIVE

At the moment the Princess and Wakan Kech were discussing their probable fates, the two small young men whom they had known as Rist and Rusk were leaving their cold, glacier-bound homeland two thousand kilometers to the northwest. Until recently, that nation had been called The Tharn's Lands, but was now renamed The People's Lands as a direct result of the revolution the two had initiated. Half a year ago the twins had both been mere unsophisticated bird-riders, small men traveling astride their emus with their Sire Thess, learning from him the business of identifying and then selling icebergs that split off from The Ice at the End of the World. Circumstances beyond their wildest dreams had brought them down to the Warm Lands in the south for legendary adventures in the places called God's Port and Motherland. Having led a revolution in their newly-named homeland, they were now on their way back south, hoping to introduce similar changes to another nation, Motherland, the ancient and fertile country spread across a vast bottomland basin. They had learned from their craft's video archives that the ancients, before The Ice came, had called this place the Gulf of Mexico, then a vast salt sea.

Comfortable inside the spacious cabin of Una, the ancient flying god-machine that Rusk and their late Sire,

Thess, had retrieved from The Ice, the twins—now bearing the man-names Thist and Thusk—viewed the various video wall screens inside the craft's cabin. Una's Developing Intelligence system (DI), comprising uncountable numbers of invisibly small quantum computers (qomps), had repeatedly attempted to explain its ability to fly. But neither man had understood terms like *microfusion, magnetohydrodynamic fields* and *micronozzle arrays*. All they knew was that their Una— short for United North American Survey Craft #201— said it had enough internal fusion power to fly within the Earth's atmosphere for years to come.

In preparation for their two-man invasion of the Warm Lands, Thist and Thusk had taken out the front seats in the cabin, reducing those from large god-size to accommodate their own stature. The toilet facilities in the rear chamber, unfortunately, could not be replaced with any materials known in The People's Lands, and so footstools sufficed for the required extra verticality. The spacious interior, some eight meters in length and three in width, easily accommodated the two small men and their cargo of food and weapons. Weapons they intended to use for war.

The twin sons of the late Reader Thess had been man-named by their late Sire, as was the custom, a status earned for their extraordinary exploits during their months in the Warm Lands. Together with Thess, the twins had returned in Una to the capital city of The Tharn's Town where they inspired a popular rebellion that overthrew the former despot called The Tharn. But during The Tharn's capitulation, that tyrant murdered their Sire, and Thisk retaliated instantly, putting a springbow arrow in that murderer's eye. To assuage both sides of the surprise revolution, the remains of The Tharn were publicly immolated next to those of their murdered Sire just a month before. All business in their homeland now settled, the twins were on their way to the Warm Lands, the country of Motherland in particular, starting with the Sisterdom of ShadowFall, where they were hoping for a welcoming reception.

"The Princess might yet be friendly, as long as Wakan Kech has not told her of our thefts, if she does not know of the godspheres and books and spindles we took," Thusk said. All of those potential treasures of ancient knowledge and modern weaponry were now safely stored in The People's Palace back home.

"And if Wakan himself does not know how many springbows and arrows we stole," Thist replied. Some of those weapons were now with them, stacked aboard the Una machine; hundreds of others remained in the hands of The People's Lands defenders. Rist had figured that Wakan Kech might not be aware of a shortage of a few hundred weapons and their arrows, not when the secret ShadowFall armory he unlocked had contained many thousands more.

Just six months before, Rist—now Thist—had ridden a sold iceberg down the Mother's River to WarmLander customers in the Solar Priesthood–controlled city of God's Port, in the nation they called God's Country. After nearly being captured by Priests' Men for the theft of a spool of their near-magical godscloth, in a miraculous escape over the cliffs at the New River's southern end, he had literally landed with his precious square kilometers of wispy material down in the bottomland nation of Motherland. Months of adventures there left him with fame as the surviving champion of the deadly Motherland Game, where his emu-riding and fighting skills brought bloody glory and a significant fortune of tribute for ShadowFall's Princess. *Costing me my damned left foot!* Thist felt that he would never become used to the dead weight of its ivory replacement. *And the itch! If only that would stop.*

For his own part, Rusk—now Thusk—had helped their Sire retrieve the god-machine Una from The Ice. Flying in the marvelous green cylinder, he had searched for, and eventually found, his twin far south at Mother's City, helping him escape from the clutches of a devious Miran Kech, High Priest for the newly crowned Mother Messinex. Princess Messinex had replaced the Lordess Mother after a fatal stroke during the Game, and her longtime advisor Miran Kech accompanied her as the second-most powerful person in the country.

As his twin told Thusk, "That was three months ago. For a month after I lost my foot, Mother Messinex let me recover from my injury while her Healer, Insart Fyth, tended to my needs. When I could walk again I explored a few of the vast catacombs and libraries deep below Mother's Palace. I brought up godspheres and ancient books that had just lain untouched for long centuries or more. Placed in sunlight, when I touched them, many of the godspheres poured forth stories about the ancient past, wonderful things."

Pointing to the large forward screen in their cabin, he said, "Much like the things—the 'history'—that Una shows us. But when I started telling Mother Messinex what some of the godspheres said, about the ancient ocean that once covered Motherland, she became nearly hysterical, demanding that all of Motherland's godspheres and ancient books be confiscated. I asked her to spare those at ShadowFall, but she wanted those brought back first. I was afraid she would bury them so deep that they could never be found again." Thist did not understand Messinex's motivation, yet still respected her position, but was fearful of her Kech advisor; rumors were rampant in the palace that Miran Kech was torturing and killing everyone whom he deemed a risk to the new Mother or himself. Hundreds of people, maybe more.

Una itself was Thusk's own discovery out of The Ice, and its video archives of technology and history were a daily revelation about the ancients and the Solar Event and the ice age that wiped them out, thirty thousand years before. *Una is the most wonderful thing I have ever experienced,* he thought, *but I will never feel totally comfortable talking to a Developing Intelligence, a DI, a machine that talks back, that flies, and still seems too magical to be real.*

Una itself, as a DI designed for scientific survey, stayed in constant scan mode, always probing for any remnant sensors and data caches that may have survived the environmental apocalypse of thirty millennia past. By the protocols of its original programming, the DI did not volunteer the extraneous information it collected unless specifically requested by its human crew. Without comment, Una did not relate the fact that the soccer-ball sized "godspheres" it had transported from ShadowFall north to their People's Lands had all responded to its radio inquiries, uploading all their data for Una to collect, correlate, and analyze.

The flying craft was conveying Thusk and his twin at an altitude of ten meters above the south-flowing Mother's River, at a leisurely pace. "Thist," he said, "soon we will be approaching the city of God's Port. I still have this strange note brought up from there by the last berg-men who returned, right before we left home." He pulled out a palm-sized leaf of soft yellow paper bearing stylized black marks and a line sketch. "All I know is, some large redheaded fellow at the docks down in God's Port gave it to Cruthar and said it was important that I read it." Thusk had not yet bothered to learn to read printed writing, as he still preferred to use his lifelong skill of carving and reading spindles, the ancient mode of recording and retrieving writing. Looking toward the front wall screen, which portrayed an attractive tall blonde woman uncannily resembling their mutual lover, Anklya, he asked, "Una, can you read this writing? Is this drawing a kind of map?"

Through the woman's image, the DI answered, "Yes, Sire Thusk. The script is readable. It derives from the writings observed and analyzed during your visit to the city of God's Port. The sketch contains enough graphic and notational information to locate the specific destination, which is a stonecutter's camp and quarry adjacent to a 'bald knob' mountain, approximately one hundred fifty kilometers due east of the city of God's Port."

Thusk wondered at the manner of speech that Una seemed to be acquiring. Ever since the first day he had flown in the craft, the answers to his inquiries had always been terse. But after his trip to God's Port and ShadowFall and Mother's City while searching for Thist, and in the months since, Una had begun changing in subtle ways, mostly its speech patterns. *I'd say the DI is becoming more like a human*, he thought, *developing a personality. It keeps saying it's not, but Una sounds more like a real person than some flesh-and-blood people I know!*

Una continued. "The text of the writing says: 'Little dark man, I give this paper to the iceberg man. Hope you see it. I watched you and your big green flying machine in the sun priest plaza. How it walked away like a big bug, dragging away that godscloth net like a bug-web, made me laugh. I, too, can fly, but in a different way. Find me and I will show you.' The note was signed by one Odel M'ridge, quarry owner and chief stonecutter."

Thusk thought over Una's comment. "Thist, is there any reason we shouldn't stop there? Could we possibly find allies with this stonecutter? He doesn't sound too much in love with those sun priests. And I would like to know what he means by flying 'a different way.' Could he have his own Una?" The twins had often wondered if other ancient craft might be discovered some day, and what that might mean. "We don't really have to stop in God's Port itself, do we?"

Thist made an obscene gesture, laughing sardonically. His miserable days in the city of God's Port had ended when he was forced to escape by sailboat down the river, almost losing his life at the great waterfall that dumped into the Motherland bottoms. "Thusk, I had to watch those Solar Priests roast a poor man alive with their big sun-mirrors. And don't forget, I also stayed overnight in a shit-pit, up to my neck." He shivered at the recollection, wishing he could erase those images—and those *smells!*—from his memory.

Thusk laughed at his twin's reaction. He had also been in that great city of tall stone buildings himself, searching for Thist. While flying Una overhead, he had admired the stupendous structures and temples, but upon landing immediately ran into trouble with the same troublesome Solar Priests. "I had a fun time there, too, Thist."

Thist grinned. "Your escape from those priests must have been something to see," he said. "I can just imagine Una sprouting its big legs, walking away from the sun temple, and dragging that godscloth net through the narrow streets, all those kiosks and banners and carts entangled. People running everywhere. Like that Odel wrote, Una must have looked like a big green biter, pulling its web along, scooping up prey."

Thusk smiled at the memory, and looked again at the written message that Una had translated. "Yeah, I'll bet those stories get told and retold. This Odel guy seemed to enjoy it." To escape the confining godscloth net, Thusk had ordered Una to walk to the city's river harbor and drop off a high pier into deep water, then dive away from under the floating blanket of impenetrable material that had kept them immobile for over a day. After that escapade, he had flown in Una down to ShadowFall, where he inadvertently learned of Una's unique vulnerability to borophene arrows.

"Una says about those borophene arrows being shot from the springbows, that their 'nano-qomps' interact with the shielding and paralyze it. I don't understand that but it is something left over from ancient times, 'noninterference programming,' Una calls it. If ShadowFall still has those arrow defenses now, or if that Rumi Similla woman has told anybody about us, we have to be very careful." Fortunately, as they had experienced, Una could make itself almost completely invisible. Thusk thought, *I can't comprehend Una's explanation, all about* nanophases *and* multilayered borophene refraction, *but as long it works, I'll use it!*

Overwhelmingly curious about that Odel's meaning of "a different way to fly" and having no set schedule or obligations, the twins decided to visit the stonecutter's camp in God's Country first before going on downriver to ShadowFall. Staying invisible and many kilometers away from God's Port was an easy choice. They had no desire to cross paths with those big burning solar mirrors. Even Una agreed.

CHAPTER SIX

Three hours after he and Jolan Keesh and the others had rescued the strange tall child, Ledd Mernan arrived at Shinyeen City and escorted the new-foundling to the Niche of Disabled Children. Elder Myuk, a short, elderly woman of uncommon unattractiveness, dressed in thick red robes, welcomed them.

"Elder," Ledd said, "we found this smelly child after a cave-in way out in Foremost. She speaks in an unknown tongue, though she does respond when you say 'Glish.'" At that word, the child again made the sign of the X and made her chant again, finishing with the obverse X sign.

"My," Elder Myuk noted, "she knows some of our traditions at least." She smiled. "I should be able teach her our language based on that. But," she asked, "where is she from? And why bring her here? Though she is quite the tall sprout"—*Almost like an Ancient One,* she thought but didn't say—"she does not appear to be Disabled, not like some of my other charges here."

Ledd nodded; in the niche behind the Elder, he could see a young girl, blonde and pretty—except that she had no arms. Behind that one, in deeper shadows, lurked younger children with physical deformities he would not have believed possible. "Well, Elder," Ledd gulped, "it's not just her language that's her problem. The girl is *Blind!*"

Elder Myuk grimaced. Many other disabilities could be adapted to perform useful chores, or even overcome totally. But Blindness? The poor thing was a certain candidate for Reprocessing unless she could prove herself otherwise! From the looks of her, so tall and well fed though she appeared to be, she was obviously close to Decision Age, and soon Elder Myuk would have to recommend either life or Reprocessing. She hated to make that latter decision; at least a dozen unfortunates had been terminated in just the past five Motherth Years. At those woeful memories, she shook her head sadly.

THE FIRST LONG DAYS—*NIGHTS?*—CALLED "WAKE Periods" and "Sleep Periods" by the short people in Shinyeen City, had been the worst for Mienne; surrounded by near darkness cut only by dim red illumination, she huddled in blankets against the cold. When the Ugly One was awake and paying attention to her, the old woman seemed insistent that Mienne understand her, gabbling in a cough-like grunt. Mienne tried her best to understand the guttural language; she truly wanted to communicate with the short people who had saved her, who were treating her with kindness. But all she and Ugly had in common was the forbidden word "Glish" and the two versions of the sign of the X.

"Ekks," the Ugly One would say, making the sign. "Ekks," Mienne would repeat, both by voice and hand motion.

Ugly pointed at Mienne: "U." When Mienne pointed back and repeated "U," Ugly smiled, followed by more gibberish.

Then Mienne had a thought: *We all have five fingers; why not start by counting?* Holding up one finger, she said, "Yi."

Old Ugly apparently caught on: "Yi."

Mienne followed by holding up two fingers: "Err." Old Ugly followed suit, and within minutes the two were counting up to ten.

"Shee," they both said together, nodding heads and smiling. Their numbers were pronounced the same way; they were on a path to understanding!

Weeks of long, frustrating days—Wake Periods—followed, but Old Ugly was as patient as Mienne, and eventually rudimentary conversation became possible. Through the continued ministrations of the woman called Elder Myuk, Mienne picked up the speech of the city. But, as she was frequently informed, her thick accent was unknown anywhere in Shinyeen City or its neighboring Tubes of the Community. Novelty was not of interest to most of Community's industrious but unimaginative citizens, so few ever cared about her origin. *Only* I *do*, Mienne thought, *And someday I will find out!*

Mienne learned from the Ugly Elder that her new home was in a Tube called Shinyeen City, District Cho, in a decrepit warren called the Niche of Disabled Children, where she and several dozen younger children lived. She had no idea where this city was, but she knew that it was in the Deep Down, probably in an ancient Tube, one not explored by her UpTop people. She recalled her father and mother arguing about whether UpTop citizens in Zhee City should ever expend the resources to explore the Deep Down. "Nothing lives down there," Father had said. "Even in the legends, all those supposed underground demons died Back When. We should let sleeping Tubes die. Retrieving ice, raising crops, securing solar, observing Motherth, those are our goals, our survival." Puzzled, she always wondered what Father had meant by all of that, but had never asked.

One of Mienne's other puzzles was why the air itself was so different in this city as opposed to what she remembered as home, Zhee City. Once she had grown used to the atmosphere of her new city, she discarded the heavy breather pack from her increasingly ragged skinsuit, along with the unnecessary helmet. For some reason, that pack provided what she had known as "additives" and "hormones," things she apparently didn't need in Shinyeen City. *Just another mystery!*

Though safe and fairly well fed, Mienne hated her situation; unlike the able-bodied Sighted, she and all the other Disabled children in the Niche had no other choice of habitation and no freedom to roam. "Mienne, my child," said the Ugly Elder (the Niche children's name for Elder Myuk, behind her back), "you must be only a short time from your Thirteenth Motherth Year, your Decision Day. Though you were apparently and unfortunately born Blind, wherever you originated from, you still retain all of your other human senses, and if you live someday you will be Woman. Be grateful that Community shelters and feeds you, child. Other cities in Community often Reprocess their severely Disabled and their Blind, at birth."

Mienne had heard that disturbing rumor from the other kids, but thought it too cruel to believe. *How could anyone as loving as this Elder ever harm a child? Even kill one of us?* The upsetting thought then occurred: *Maybe not all adults are as loving as Ugly Elder?* Her own home in Zhee City had not been that way, she was sure. Her memories of it were all loving. Well, most of them. Until the end. That last day had been frightful! She shook her head to dispel the horror, the memories of that frantic flight in the dark tunnel.

Ugly Elder continued, her voice calm and reassuring. "We will begin now to find you some useful endeavors. But someday, as you approach your Thirteenth, you must visit the Hall of Whispers. There, the Voices may help us determine which station you are most suited for. We trust you will find a calling there. Some few do understand the Voices, and discover their destiny." Left unsaid was the fate of others in Community who had been so terribly Disabled, so malformed, that they would have never found a calling, would always have been a burden on Community.

Reprocessed was the term the Elder used, but as Mienne understood it, that term meant only *Death.* She was determined to learn enough "useful endeavors" to save herself from that fate. Reluctantly, she revisited her early memories, trying to make sense of her life so far, to find something she could do, any skill to avoid dying. Her memories, she knew, went back at least nine or ten Motherth Years, back to when she was a tiny girl.

Mienne's favorite recollections were of the strange, wonderful place, the city called Zhee, where she had been birthed by a Woman named Mother. That Woman, Mother, and a big male Mienne remembered as Father, had worked in Zhee by harvesting solid water from Outside and bringing it into their city where others used it for marvelous purposes—to grow strange crystalline devices of some kind, and also green plants and colorful flowers and marvelous foods. Through the transparent walls of Zhee, she remembered, on the vast gray plains outside, she saw other huge, clear hemispheres in which those same miracles of color were commonplace, unlike her present dim-red prison. And most wonderful of all, arching over everything, was a vast black dome called "Sky," its darkness graced by the whiteness and blueness of the small disk of the goddess, Motherth. And at times, Sky was sprinkled with myriads of tiny lights, splayed across the darkness.

In memory, Mienne's life in Zhee had been nearly magical. But some disaster had struck their home, and she and her Mother alone had survived, as far as she knew. She recalled a strange, scary, running trek through endless kilometers of dark tunnels, with Mother crying, dragging her along. And being hungry, and so very thirsty. Her last memory of Mother was of that Woman applying her own breather to Mienne's skinsuit, and then turning away into the dark, gesturing for Mienne to keep running, her skinsuit's glow torch lighting the way through nameless, endless dark tunnels.

How long she had kept going, Mienne did not remember, except for the unexpected discovery of air around her. Nor did she recall the details of encountering the team of tunnelers from Shinyeen City who found her under a collapsed berm of rocks and dirt, near death, gasping for breath. Her rescuers immediately found that Mienne could not navigate through the dim red-light-lit tunnels and caverns that were normal illumination to them, and so decided she was Blind, a rare but not unknown birth defect among Community's children.

On the day of her rescue, taken to her new home in the niche, Mienne had met Wayer, another female child about her own age but much shorter in size, whose obvious disability was a lack of arms. The two girls had been friends ever since, sharing the menial housekeeping tasks in their niche (Wayer could use a whisk broom tied to her leg, for sweeping), playing together when they had a few precious moments alone, and telling each other stories. Born in the Crèche Tube and tended till toddler-hood by birthers, Wayer had no parents. As such, she was fascinated by Mienne's stories of the domed city of Zhee, and of Father and Mother and of the strange colors that her tall friend could not describe.

"Wayer," Mienne told her friend one evening after bed time, "in my dream, there was sometimes a brightness in that dark Sky, so intense I could not let my eyes rest on it."

Wayer replied, "But you are Blind, Mienne, so how could you tell?"

"I don't know how. But I remember Mother and Father telling me never to look at it without my shaders."

"What are *shaders*?"

"I don't know what they were, I just remember the strange name. I think they were coverings that went over my eyes."

"And what about those 'domes' and 'flowers' and 'colors'?"

"I can't tell you about those, either. You would have to be there to understand. There is nothing at all here in Shinyeen City that I experience that way. Everything here is so dim and red."

Wayer sneered, "Mienne, you are just Blind and cannot see the beauty around you. Shinyeen City is bright and beautiful. There are lots of colors painted on the walls—many kinds of pinks on the ceilings, and patterns of scarlet, carmine, vermillion, crimson, umber and glorious IRed. I mean, there's all kinds of colors, everywhere—the walls, the floors, the machines, people's clothing, our food. And of course, white and black. I am so sorry you are Blind and can't See them." She giggled. "But I do love to listen to your weird stories."

The Ugly Elder often gently chastised Mienne for her outlandish tales about the imaginary Tube of Zhee City, saying they were merely childish dreams arising from the trauma of being lost in the tunnels for many days from her home somewhere far away in Infinite Rock. But Mienne still shared the stories secretly, and her new friend believed her, she felt. Nobody could explain why she was so much taller than people of the city; it seemed no one cared. But Mienne did. *In Zhee City, all the other people were taller than me!*

Telling and retelling her memories also helped Mienne re-experience what she thought she remembered from her childhood. *But there is nothing like those memories here in Community,* she thought sadly. *No matter what Wayer says, everything here is dim red at best, and many times just dark. The Sighted here all move around gracefully, but I run into walls and chairs and posts if I am not careful.* Occasionally, though, she doubted herself; around her was Reality—dark, dim and red. *Why do I think I witnessed all those strange things? Were they only imaginary, just dreams, as Ugly Elder says? No, my own height, so much different from all these short people, tells me that I am not of them, that my memories are* real!

CHAPTER SEVEN

O del M'ridge gave the signal and his men began to grunt, putting their bare backs into pushing and pulling the wooden framework that lifted their large finished granite blocks into place aboard the ox-drawn wagon. A Solar Priest looked on with disdain as the crew strained at the load. "Back in God's Port, we have much better hoisting equipment than your primitive affair here," he said. "You ought to come and learn from us. We won't charge much copper for the learning." Then he looked from under his dark hood directly into the big red-bearded man's deep blue eyes. "It would do you good, too, to learn the truth about the Shining One and the Pale Lady. I know you escaped here to God's Country, away from those heretics in Old Country and all their despicable lies. You should come and see the truth."

"I will take your advice, Brother Priest, next time I'm in your city," Odel replied. *Which will be* never *if I have my way!* He hoped his gentle tone of voice was hiding the rage he was feeling toward the wrinkled old man in the wrinkled old once-white robe.

The priest took out a small tube of rolled material from one of the pockets in the dirty robe and handed it to Odel. "And you may wish to purchase your godscloth from us from now on. Our temple godscloth has the sharpest edge ever known," the priest said. "It can slice off a finger—or a head—just as easily as you can pop a soap bubble."

Odel told his men to stop, that they could finish the loading job later. He had received the priest's declaration as the unconcealed threat it was meant to be, without objecting that not all godscloth was so fine on the edges. He wanted to say, "I have pieces of it that won't even slice a throat—like I'd like to do yours, you wrinkled piece of asswipe." But Odel hadn't and wouldn't say anything. What he *would* do, once the temple priest had left payment for the next month's quarrying quota, would be to toss out the priest's dull material (*Holy temple godscloth, my ass!*) and bring out his own stash of truly sharp-edged godscloth. *Having my own supply of spools, the spindles to spin it into wire, and the means to cut it, lets me haggle all I want with these worthless crawdads. But they don't know it!*

Acknowledging the gift of the useless material, Odel bowed slightly. The priest then handed him a purse full of coppers, which the stonecutter quietly weighed on a balance scale, finding the amount to be sufficient, if not overly generous. The two men shook hands, and the priest departed on a broken-down mule. *A miserable old man*, he thought, *riding on a poor, miserable old donkey. Which is the worse off?*

Rolling some shredded ginseng into a paper, he lit a stub of his roll-smoke and sat down at a rough-cut wooden table to collect his nerves. A big man, his oversized white cotton work shirt was now wet, sticking to his chest and back, sweat pouring from his brow to his bushy red beard. Damn, but he hated those priests. *Ever since they roasted my bud, Razzo, with their damned mirrors. If they didn't pay me to provide my granite for their big buildings, I'd, I'd*—Even in his mind, Odel was realistic—Nothing, *that's what I'd do. I got nothing, can't do nothing. Shit!* Hefting the bag of coppers, he thought, *At least the sun-suckers pay well, and in advance!*

As the priest and his mule disappeared from sight from M'ridge's quarry, Deen M'lorin, Odel's stonecutter foreman, came over to join him. "Odel, I seen you don't like that old guy." Odel grunted but didn't say any more. Deen said, "But he does bring us a lot of coppers, for us cutting him some big stones. Shouldn't we oughta keep 'im happy?"

"Deen, my boy," Odel said with a crooked grin, blowing out acrid smoke, "You are most correct. Copper is copper, even if the payer himself is a worthless sliver of oldiron." Oldiron was a worthless metal, one most always found in sharp slivers that fell apart at the touch; no use had ever been found for it. It couldn't be melted, and its powder form was poisonous to breathe. In his years of digging in quarries, Odel had come across lots of oldiron pieces and many other strange objects, and occasionally wondered what the ancients had made them for, and how. Then again, at times he didn't believe there *were* any ancients, that the pieces of oldiron and porcelain and unbreakable glass might just be natural, like rocks and roots.

But digging up godscloth? Now, *that* stuff was indeed a problem. How could it have been made, and why was it found underground in some places—*like back home in the mountains and my cave*—but draped across square miles of bald hilltops in other places—*like up the hill above my quarry?* And who had made those tools for cutting it, those gloves for handling it—and *how*? Blowing out another puff of smoke, he told Deen to take all the oversized gloves and scissors back to the tool safe and make sure they were securely locked up. Along with his secret stashes of godscloth, those were his living—*spools and tools!*

In the days before the priest had arrived with his outrageous offer to sell the dull, priest-approved godscloth, Odel and his men, working with his custom-made sawblades—godswire spun invisibly thin from his godscloth—had finished off a total of twenty finely cut and smoothly finished granite blocks of specified sizes, today stacking them aboard three ox-drawn wagons. "A week's work, all done, Deen," he said. "In the morning, you take a week to deliver it to God's Port, then two days of rest and wreck there, then a week back." He gave each of his teamsters their full pay in coppers, knowing that they would return skint. *But the pubs and brothels in the city will be all the richer for it.* He knew his crew; they'd never save, never have anything but the clothes on their backs and the hovels he provided them here at camp. No woman would ever settle for such a life, he knew, so they'd purchase some temporary female company in God's Port.

NEXT MORNING, DEEN AND THE BOYS LEFT WITH THEIR moaning oxen and groaning wagons, en route to the city. Odel knew that their first few miles of road would be pretty rough; he and his men had cleared it of trees and stumps and graveled it years before, keeping its ruts cleaned out and rock-filled after the spring rains. Down at the base of the mountains, the barely usable dirt road would connect with smoother wide paved roadways that the priests kept in good condition with the forced labor of large press-gangs of heretics and other troublemakers. Odel didn't like that part of the priests' activities, either. *But at least they keep the highways in good shape!*

Having seen his men off, Odel climbed ancient rock-cut stairs up two hundred feet above the quarry he operated, all the way up to his log cabin on the "bald knob," a bare granite outcropping crowning the small mountain. He thought that back home, a few hundred miles farther east, his people would call the place just a little hill, but around here it was a "mountain." Whatever, for Odel's purposes it was a perfect location, for privacy, for living—and for flying. Walking over to the barn beside his cabin, he opened the large hinged door to look over his flying machine, remembering how he had come to build one like it, years ago. *Back in another life,* he thought. *When I was too young to know you don't want to be* too *creative,* too *disruptive.*

As a young teen in the Big Blue Mountains in the east, in the loosely organized nation called Old

Country, he had discovered a cave full of godscloth spools the height of a man, and an assortment of tools and fixtures for cutting and sewing the usually unscissable material. Using spindles to spin the wispy material into a thin wire form, and then using it as a cutting blade, he had revolutionized his family's traditional quarrying and stonecutting business. No more using hammers and chisels except for particular details and finishing; the godscloth-based hand tools provided fine stones for buildings and fortresses all over the Big Blue valley region, everywhere in the Old Country that rivers would take his family's barges. Over the next ten years the M'ridgers became the wealthiest clan in the region, buying up granite and limestone sites for miles around.

But then one blustery day, while working with several square yards of the wispy material, it wafted away in a sudden wind. Odel had watched it sail upward like a leaf until it wrapped itself around a crow, bringing the bird down in a tangled net.

A thought occurred to him at that sight: *If it flies like a leaf, and can catch up with a bird, then what if I could use it and fly like a bird?* Stretching out a yard of godscloth over a thin sapling frame, Odel had experimented, adding layer upon layer of material until he could feel air resistance when swinging the frame around. Somehow, he knew, it was the resistance of the air that gave bird wings a way to fly. Weeks of playing around gave him the semblance of a kite; adding a tail for balance gave him a nice toy, but nothing practical. His family thought that the kite was a fine invention of a toy, and even handcrafted hundreds of them for the better-off families. Some clans even took to using the kites as totems, decorating them with sigils and symbols. Odel made several varieties, a large one of which could carry a child or a small man when the wind was high enough. That demonstration alone made him famous in communities far and wide. But a few gospielers took him aside and gave him friendly warnings that toys were one thing, but a human trespassing in Shining One's sky domain was another, and urged him to stop.

But Odel had been determined that if a bird could fly, then so could he. Within a year he had fabricated a large, triangular winglike contraption that he could hang beneath. The terrain of his homeland provided wonderful hills of all sizes from which he secretly launched himself, developing the knowledge and skills to control the glider. After a dozen trial flights in secret of his final design, he announced to the town that he would show them how to fly.

The day came and the residents of M'ridge Town, all few thousand of them, gathered at the bottom of Noog Hill, a cleared hilltop overlooking the wide Ensee River. Odel trudged to the top, wheeling on a cart behind him his flying machine, a godscloth-covered triangle some ten feet on a side, with a leather harness dangling below. He stopped at a protruding stone ledge some fifty feet above the sloped-hill surface, strapping himself into the harness. Feeling the updraft of a breeze, as the townspeople stood disbelieving, he jumped. Airborne, the craft lifted him up; catching an invisible current he called "the warm", Odel guided his tri-wing higher and higher, up to three hundred feet. He was ecstatic; now the family, even the gospielers, could see that a man could fly, that it was not an impossible dream!

"That boy is a bird-man!" somebody shouted. "He kin fly fer sure!" "Hey, Odel, why'nt you say hi to the Shining One up there, from us'ns down here!"

Feeling that he had proven his point, Odel twisted his harness this way and that, pulling control cords and slowly descending the tri-wing in a wide spiral, with the crowd below him running to stay underneath the miraculous flying man. People cheered as he landed with a fast walk, allowing the tri-wing to gently settle on the grass behind him. It was a glorious day!

Yeah, glorious, he thought. *And my last day at home! Dad and my brothers had to smuggle me out of town right after that, before the gospielers and their whipped-up mob of crazies came to burn me for heresy. They* did *burn my tri-wing!* He had hidden out in his secret cave, miles from town, until Dad brought him horses and a wagon. With his spools and tools Odel then traveled over three hundred miles west, believing it was a safe distance from the Old Country. He found out from God's Country traders that the gospielers there were a separate sect from the Solar Priesthood at God's Port, and the two were often at odds—and sometimes at war —with each other. He'd never had much use for those gospieler priests, anyhow. His philosophy was, *If you don't work, you shouldn't take coppers from those who do.* And he didn't see anything the gospielers ever did in the way of real work, just making people afraid of the Sun and Moon and stars. Other than their old stories about horrors in the skies and mountains of moving ice, they had nothing to offer. For himself, he would worry about the heavens only after he had no more worries here on Earth!

After weeks of travel, Odel had located this unclaimed bald knob hill, recognizing its untouched trove of rare pink granite. In this mostly unoccupied frontier, all he had to do was map out the land he wanted, set up some border posts—*and be prepared to fight for it if somebody else intrudes!* The nearest authority site, actually two dozen men and their families in a wooden stockade fort, was twenty miles away to the west, and the rocky terrain spread out in all directions discouraged all but subsistence farming. Registering his staked-out land claim with the scribe at the fort, Odel built a log cabin for himself atop the bald knob, then opened a quarry at the base of the hill. With his spools and tools serving him well, and having hired a few travelers from the main road that ran at the edge of his property, the business with the God's Port Solar Priests and others provided a good living, and in a few months he felt himself a success.

And then one day in God's Port, he had seen the giant green flying machine come out of the sky, become trapped in a godscloth net, and walk away the next day like a big green bug. Inspired by the big bug's flight more so than its walking, over the next months in the privacy of his new homestead at the top of his bald mountain, Odel M'ridge built himself yet another tri-wing glider and flew it in secret. Today, after his crew left, he would fly it out again, launching from his little mountain, flying over his property and the surrounding countryside.

CHAPTER EIGHT

"Sires," Una announced through the Anklya-image on the front wall screen, "the destination is near. Shall we land? Become visible?"

Thist and Thusk both looked at Anklya on the front wall screen. They had been engrossed in the view through Una's transparent walls, flying over towns, villages, and then small settlements, as the distance from God's Port grew. The pine-green hills and the occasional river and smaller streams were refreshing; as Season Cold was now beginning, most of the leaves of color had already fallen from the trees farther north, leaving many square kilometers of bare branches, seemingly lifeless dark hills. A wooden stockade next to a paved road was the final testament to human occupation, its few dozen simple buildings proclaiming little official interest in the endless pine forests beyond.

"Sure, Una." Thusk said. "We haven't seen any signs of dangerous weaponry since we left the river north of God's Port, none at all in the smaller towns and villages we've been over. If you don't scan any of those dangerous arrows ahead of us, then we should be safe enough." Thist nodded, taking down a springbow and a quiver of arrows. They weren't sure about wild animals in the area they were going to land in, and not totally certain that the note writer, one Odel, was trustworthy.

But they expected him at least to be an interesting sort—nobody else from God's Port had ever written to them.

A kilometer out, Una said, loudly, "Sires! There is a flying craft of some kind, immediately ahead of us, and below. Please be warned!"

Rushing to look through the transparent walls, the twins saw a dark triangular shape, slowly spiraling downward, then upward, almost as a leaf caught in a whirlwind. Thusk yelled out, "What is that thing, Una? Is it a bird—or another god-machine? Can you get closer?"

As if in answer, Una stopped forward motion, hovering in place and zooming in with a display on the forward cabin screen. "It appears to be a man, hanging from a triangular glider. He is guiding it by moving his body. He is *flying!*"

Both men laughed at Una's shocked voice; that was something new, but their DI was constantly surprising them. In the close-up view they could see a broad-shouldered, red-bearded man in the hanging harness, deftly moving his brown-cloth-covered body, pulling cords with his arms, controlling the strange flying craft. "Almost like a bird," Thusk said. "I've never seen anything like it."

"Not at all like our Una, but it must be that Odel guy," Thist agreed. "Take us down, Una, to where he is going to land. And don't run into him; we don't want to knock him out of the sky."

As Odel M'ridge touched down onto the level field near his quarry site, he ran along, gently pulling overhead control cords that brought his tri-wing glider to a soft landing behind him. It had been a glorious half hour, catching the warm winds off the hillsides, climbing up hundreds of feet to view the surrounding countryside, its valleys and small mountains, the several rivers in the distance. *Someday, given enough copper to hire men and bring in settlers, I will own everything I can see from up there.* He watched as a flock of honkers flew south, much higher than he dared try to fly. *But if I could have a way to power my tri-wing, not just glide with it, I might could get up there, too.* He had a momentary flash of a vision, of a huge tri-wing carrying loads of finished stones to God's Port. *If I could really do that,* he thought, *who's to say that I couldn't just drop them instead of landing with them?* The concept of squashing some of the gospielers back home made him laugh. *But the wrinkled, murdering old priests in God's Port, they get squashed first!*

While storing his harness on the glider for transport back up the hill to his barn, Odel felt a light breeze from above. Looking up, there was a shimmering in the air above him, a greenish mist that took shape as an emerging large green cylindrical object, the shocking appearance accompanied by a slight acrid odor. Thirty feet long by ten in diameter, he estimated, the now-solid cylinder was domed on both ends, a black elongated bubble situated atop near one end. He had never believed in sky-gods, but Odel was frightened like never before in his life. He stepped back in fear, until suddenly the memory of the incident in the priests' plaza in God's Port months ago returned. "This is that big green bug!" he shouted. "You got my message, little man. You came to see me!" Standing with arms open wide, he grinned and waited to see the dark little visitor.

As Una settled in the grass, the side door opened, and Thist walked out, slowly, carrying the springbow at ready. He still didn't trust the big redhead who was welcoming him. "Who are you, Red?" he asked in Peoplespeak. "Why did you ask us to come here?" Pointing his springbow at the tri-wing, he asked, "And what kind of god-machine is that?"

Before Odel could answer, Thusk walked out beside his twin.

In a thick but understandable accent, definitely Peoplespeak, the big man said, "There's *two* of you? I reckon I do recall one of you flying that green machine of yours over to the plaza at God's Port. Is that right?"

Sensing Thist's unease, he raised his hands to show he had no weapons. "Here, boys, I invited you. I got no arms. Let's just talk."

After shaking hands, Thusk invited Odel into Una for a short tour of their flying machine, while Thist kept his springbow loaded, though pointed downward. "All of this is god-machine, made by the ancients," Thusk said. "Nobody today knows how to build anything like it." Odel marveled at each fantastic feature of Una—the smooth, hard walls, the materials of the seats and toilets, and especially the wall video screens with full color and three-dimensional images.

"This craft only responds to the two of us," Thusk said, as a friendly warning to their as yet not completely trustworthy acquaintance. "We have set it up that way." Odel nodded, acknowledging his host's intent.

But Odel's enthusiasm only increased as he touched the variety of surfaces, appreciating the finishes and the variety of seamless materials making up Una's interior. "Nothing like nobody has ever seen. Boys, them ancients really knew their stuff. And how about that white talking thing up on top? That one liked to have scared us all to death?" Thusk took Odel out the door and asked Una to activate the white pilot. As the black bubble retracted backward on its hinges revealing the expressionless manlike pilot, the big man spoke, laughing again. "You boys have got the durndest piece of machinery this world has ever known. Think you could take me for a ride in it?"

An hour later, the three had flown over several hundred kilometers in all directions, even over Odel's former home—"Dang! There's my ma and pa, my bros, down there! I wish we could land and see them"—at which outburst Thusk and Thist both shook their heads: *too dangerous!*—"Their houses, the quarries!"—and high over Gods Port—"It sure looks different from up here, like a little toy town"—before returning to Odel's camp.

"Boys," he said, "My little old tri-wing over there, your Una puts it to shame."

Thusk said, "But Odel, I only found our Una in The Ice. You built your flying machine all on your own."

"There is that, I guess," Odel said in a quizzical tone. "But I guess not one of us could even begin to build a Una, you think? I do have a question, though: Does your Una have any ideas about how I could make my tri-wing fly better? I'd sure like to have some power, a way not to just depend on winds and warms."

"Let's ask," Thusk said. "I'll bet Una can help."

ODEL TURNED OUT TO BE NO FAN OF THE PRIESTS OF God's Port. In his spacious log cabin, with a roaring fire in the hearth, over a delicious dinner of venison stew that he made up for them, and hoisting a porcelain mug of home-brewed "shine," he said, "Two times. Two times those old wrinkled robes totally infuriated me. I was there when they turned their damned mirrors on my old buddy, Razzo. I used to trade spools of godscloth and other stuff to ol' Razzo. Burnt him alive, the bastards. All I could do was stand there and watch him die." The big man clenched his fists in remembered rage, quickly followed by a deep frown of grief.

Thist held his tongue. His theft of godscloth from that man's warehouse, Razzo's, had been responsible for that execution by concentrated sunlight, and he himself had been there, had witnessed that same gruesome event. He didn't want Odel to hold that against him. He couldn't trust a stranger, even a friendly one, with that knowledge. "And the second time, when one of you— Thusk, was it?—was caught in that godscloth web and held down with rocks. By the way, with this big Una of yours, how come that flimsy net held it—and you— down? Don't seem possible."

Thusk stayed silent. He, too, didn't want to share

secrets with the redbeard, especially about their vulnerabilities, no matter how personable he was. The man was a genius of invention and no telling what he might conceive of to capture Una. *And us!*

Sensing his visitors' reluctance to discuss their unique experiences, Odel took another swig of his "shine" and continued his stories. "When ol' Una there sprouted those big old spider legs and started walking away like nobody's business, I liked to have whooped up a storm, laughing. I was on your side. But when your white pilot-thing shouted out that the priests had violated the will of the Shining One, their sun god, some of that crowd took it serious-like. They run back and beat up a few of those priests, and tore down one of those big burner-mirrors.

"If you'd'a turned around and charged the other way right then, Thusk, why you'd'a had that mob with you." He stopped talking and finished off his mug of brew, staring intently at the twins. "I have thought right much about that day, ever since. Some folks, lifetimers there in the city, told me they'd never seen such outright opposition to the priests. Funny thing, too, them Priests' Men, they never did go out and punish anybody for that riot. I think they were too scared to rile folks up again. Been a while now, but I bet if you flew ol' Una back there now, you could get yourself another revolution, like you said you did back to your home country."

M'ridge regaled the northerners with tales of God's Country, where he now lived and worked, and of Old Country, his homeland to the east. "I figure God's Port to have a hundred thousand people or so, with another fifty thousand in the farms and ranches around it. Coupla other cities up the tributary rivers, half that size. The whole country run by the Solar Priests, all the cities and towns? Maybe a million." He quaffed another mug of shine, keeping his visitors' mugs full as well, tapping a cask at the end of the feast table. "My Old Country, a couple hundred miles east of here, don't have that big of a capital city, but's got dozens of small towns in the hills and hollers, all the way to the Cold

Sea. I believe there's a couple million people over there in Old Country, scattered between the Big Blue Mountains and the Cold Sea, and up and down the coast."

Thist brought up a topic of continuing interest to him. "Odel, how do people run things around here, and over in Old Country? Are there Tharns or chiefs or Mothers that tell everybody what to do? I've been in three different places now, and nobody seems to do it the same way." He didn't add that he hadn't cared for any of them, and was happy to bring about political changes back home. He was hoping The People's Lands would turn out better for those changes, but there was no way to tell, yet.

Odel laughed heartily, trying to catch his breath. "Well, boys, I think you both saw God's Port. It don't have a chief but the gang of Priests' Men there keep a kind of order, so long's you don't get in their face or put down their superstitions. Out here in the hinterlands, the priests keep the roads fixed up. I think, so's they can send their men out fast in any direction, if needs be. It also helps them know where any invaders might come in. I've heard stories that they have laid traps at places, but I don't know of any. The smooth roads do make transporting my finished stones to them easier since I don't have a river nearby. And the few farmers out here, it's good for them, too. So the Solars are not all bad." *But I still hate them!* he didn't say.

"Over in Old Country, every town of any size elects its own folks in an Elder's Council to get things done—build a bridge, whatever."

"The *people* do that? They vote?"

"Most near all do vote. Then, because some things affect everybody, all towns, then they have a one-week Congress at the KayEn Ruins, in the Big Blues, once a year, one man from each town."

Thist said, "Sounds complicated, but whatever works, works, I guess." Actually, Odel's description paralleled much of what the people of The People's Lands, back home, had agreed to. *At least his Old*

Country has no Tharn, no murderous Game, and no all-powerful Mother!

Thusk was mildly interested in Odel M'ridge's stories, but since their host's Old Country was far away and no particular threat to their People's Lands or even Motherland for that matter, he had more urgent considerations. Thist, though, had another thought, much more strategic. "Odel," he said, "you said that your 'gospielers' had warred with the Solar Priests at times? What was that about? Who won, or what happened when it was over?"

Odel sighed. "Them gospielers claim to be the true religion, speakers to Shining One and the Pale Lady. Though they could never show *me* what they heard from them gods, at least nothin' that made any sense." He laughed. "I once saw a debate of a kind, when one of the Solars came to my town, donkey and cart and all. He set up a tent and started preaching how Shining One was gonna strike us all down like He did the ancients, only he said, 'No more Ice; the Fire next time.' Well, our local gospielers outshouted him, calling him a heretic, that Shining One and the Pale Lady were equal gods; they balanced each other out. To prove it, they showed us how the Lady could totally eclipse ol' Shiny whenever She wants.

"Unfortunately for ol' Solar guy, the next day the Lady did just that and for a few minutes the world went dark as night. Right much impressive, let me tell you. Couldn't really argue with that demonstration." He took another swig. "'Course I never figured the gospielers did it; it was just they knew it was gonna happen. I had seen several partial 'eclipses' of the Lady over the years, and nobody ever said anything about any gods ahead of time."

"Wow," Thist said, "I've heard Una talk about eclipses, where the Moon does go in front of the Sun, and blots it out for a while. So what happened then? Did the Solar Priest admit he was wrong?" Thist knew he needed to have Una show this big man a video on what the Sun and the Moon really were and how eclipses occurred. But he would save that for another time. Odel was already learning a lot from them without offering anything in return.

"Never got the chance," Odel said with a loud burp. "Folks there nailed ol' wrinkly to a post and burnt him up." He gave a grim grin. "My kinfolks are a right much intolerant bunch."

With that, he walked over to a strange instrument hanging on a paneled wall away from the fireplace, pulled it down and began to strum its tight strings, producing melodic sounds.

Thusk's and Thist's homeland had no musical instruments, the very concept of music being unknown to them. Thist had heard a sort of singing, more of a musical chant, from the lesser priests in the sun temple at God's Port, and in the stadium in Mother's City a chorus of voices had praised the Lordess Mother before the Game began, but to Thusk, the intonations he heard now were completely new. So both twins were enraptured when their big redheaded host began strumming and singing softly, accompanied by the sounds of his "guitar."

"IN ANCIENT TIMES WHEN THE WORLD WAS NEW
    The ancient ones, you know they flew
    Around the Earth and up in the sky—
    Some to live and some to die.

"OLD SUN HE SWOLE, OLD SUN HE BLEW
    And burnt Hisself a world or two
    But barely bussed ol' Mother Earth—
    'Cause He knowed what She wuz worth.

"THE ICE IT CAME AND THE ICE IT GREW
    Till it reached a mile or two
    But favored folks it left alone—
    Like all us down here in our home."

. . .

ODEL STOPPED SINGING, BUT KEPT STRUMMING A melodic background. Encouraging his guests, he said, "Come on boys, get into it." Thusk tried to reproduce the sounds Odel had sung but his throat and larynx wouldn't follow his efforts. Thist just laughed at his twin's croaking, waving off any temptation to try. Instead he poured more of the honeyed 'shine.

THE NEXT MORNING ODEL WHIPPED UP A DELICIOUS medley of fried eggs, strips of roast boar, and a sweet bread much tastier than the monotonous peat-bread back home. "Fresh water from spring, boys," he said, filling two tall glasses. "Healthy for ya."

During the night Thist had questioned Una about ways to improve Odel's tri-wing craft. "Is there any way to power it?" He didn't think Odel or anybody in today's world had the ancient tools available to make powered craft, but anything that would keep the big man aloft for a few hours could conceivably be helpful, if and when a rebellion in God's Country might be planned. Spying from overhead, for one thing. Without an Una, such a tri-wing could prove very valuable for observation.

"Sire Thist, during our flights yesterday as a matter of course this DI performed ground penetration scans of the immediate area. There are mineral deposits that may be of such use." To Thist's surprise at Una's action at its own prerogative, the DI went on to describe a possible method whereby Odel could produce improved tri-wings and provide them with short-term booster devices. "If carefully fabricated and installed and safely utilized, a tube of godscloth packed with an appropriate chemical mixture could boost an airborne tri-wing and its pilot to high altitudes, and then for propulsion once at altitude. Of course the pilot would have to be trained in its use."

Thist and Thusk called Odel into Una's cabin for

videos that showed how such boosters could be made from specifically wound tubes of godscloth, how the propellant minerals could be mixed, and other fabrication details. Thusk was amazed. "Una, you have never shown us any of this before. Why not? And what is the compound you are showing us?"

"Sire Thist, first, you never asked. Second, the propellant compound is a highly refined version of a chemical compound that was already old in ancient times when this DI was assembled.

"It is called firepowder."

AS THE DARK CAME AGAIN, THIST ASKED ODEL IF HE might want to assess the mood of the people in God's Port, maybe elsewhere in the countryside. "Maybe even make contact with the people in your homeland, if they are really hostile to the Solars." Having seen how successful their rebellion back home had been, Thist began to imagine stirring up resistance to the Solars.

Odel said that, based on his own anti-flying experience, he wasn't certain that the gospielers were much better at noninterference than the Solars, but at least back in his part of Old Country those preachers didn't control every single aspect of life through superstition and fear. As long as people didn't outright challenge their religious beliefs, they were mostly let alone to have their businesses and accrue wealth. He did say, though, that the idea of overturning the God's Port priests was intriguing.

"Things would be better if those Solar parasites were out of the way. They're like bloodsucking ticks," he said, grimly. "They don't work, don't do anything, just take from those who do. If you boys were able to change things back home, then maybe I *can* do it here, too. 'Course if what you tell me is true, the city alone has more folks than your whole country, right?"

The twins nodded. After talking between themselves, they had decided this wasn't their fight at the moment, though they would be happy to see the WarmLanders in God's Country weakened so that they could never try to invade Coldward again. Three wars between their People and God's Country in the last hundred years had left permanent distrust in their wake, even though the WarmLanders still bought Ice from the north. The twins knew they might never understand the motivations of WarmLanders, but they also realized that they themselves were no longer the naive innocents they had been just half a year ago. They had done things—and were planning to do even more—that would have been inconceivable to them before their trips Warmward.

For his part, Thusk was anxious to get back to ShadowFall, among people they knew. He told Thist as much as they went to bed inside Una that night. "First things first. Odel is smart enough to know what can be done and he's the one to do it. After we finish things down in Motherland—if we do—then we can think about God's Country and Odel and Old Country and those Solar Priests."

CHAPTER NINE

With growing alarm and anger, Mother Messinex —until three months ago, merely Princess Messinex of the Three Rivers Sisterdom, one of the thirteen Princesses of Motherland—listened intently to her High Priest and Chief Advisor, Miran Kech. Seated on her royal blue sapphire throne, she looked down upon the High Antian in his blue godscloth raiment, and the dowdy but pretty young woman standing next to him. And of course, around the twenty-meter-square throne room, stood the ever-present half dozen Mothersmen in their black leather armor, their shining swords and spearpoints at the ready for more than decoration if needed. The bright overhead lighting, Messinex was assured, was provided by an ingenious array of sunlight reflectors from the palace roof, hundreds of meters above them, down through passageways onto the translucent ceiling some four meters above her. The highly polished white marble floor completed the austere yet expensive milieu that Messinex preferred.

Miran is very efficient at arranging some things, she was thinking. But as he droned on about this young woman with him—*not so much at other things. What is he trying to tell me that is so important it couldn't wait until after I visited the Crystal Throne this morning?*

"And so, Mother Messinex, Rumi Similla has not

only revealed the criminal act of withholding inventory from your confiscation orders, but most importantly has told us that Wakan Kech, and perhaps your sister Princess, have in their possession an ancient god-machine. One that can fly. And talk. And vanish into thin air. And it was found and operated by the identical twin of your own champion of the Game, ShadowFall's little Rist, the bird-riding warrior of the far north Dark Highlands!"

Her attention now focused on the Kech's last statements. Messinex was speechless, trying to absorb the unbelievable information that the priest had just disclosed. *A flying god-machine? And invisible? Little Rist, Motherland's champion warrior, has a twin?* But Rist had disappeared from the palace months ago, nowhere to be found. He had been last seen in an inner courtyard atrium, but vanished from there without a trace. The only thing that all of Miran Kech's inquisitors had been able to conclude, after exhaustive searches—and tortuous questioning of palace staff, which left some dead, unfortunately—was that the little man must have been kidnapped by Mother's enemies.

Messinex knew that Rist had been upset by her orders to confiscate all those cursed godspheres, the blasphemous ancient globes, but that would have been no reason for him to go into hiding; as a honored guest, he wasn't threatened. And whatever little Rist's feelings or his status as Pernie's champion, she could not chance having those globe things spread their heresy of a giant sea once covering all of Motherland. The Sisterdom of WaterEdge was already reporting more and more attacks by the big blonde men of the Cold Sea, using as a public excuse for their plundering the absurd claim that all seas, even dry ones, belonged to them. She had refused to listen to such outrageous assertions from the presumptuous emissary who had made his way from the Cold Sea to her palace last year, that albino pirate Noor, whom she had dismissed immediately. *I should have let Miran have him,* she thought regretfully, *but I didn't want to a precedent of torturing foreign messengers.* She would not have her subjects hear such tales, or suspect they were true. And even if the Earth had been different in ancient times, so what? Legends also said that the Cold Sea itself once was all ice!

But now, a magical, invisible flying machine, flown by little Rist's identical twin? If the woman Rumi were telling the truth, could that twin have rescued Rist with it? Even the most ancient golden tablets in her secret Mother's Sanctuary did not mention any kind of flying devices, god-made or otherwise. Shaking her head, she said, "You, Similla. Is this true? What evidence do you have? And why have I not been told before of this, this, extraordinary machine?" She glared at Miran Kech, disturbed that he had not known of it before now. *Or had he?* She didn't think she could always trust her priest, even after all these years together. Lately he had shown a vengeful side of his character she hadn't witnessed before, with dungeons full of her own late Lordess Mother's former administrators and courtiers. *But if not Miran, then who? This is most confusing!* To her court, however, the uncertain and distrusting Messinex remained regal, stern-faced, demanding. *A Mother must remain calm, stable, even when all others are in panic!*

In the bowing ritual required of nobles, Rumi Similla first bowed her head, then her shoulders, then at the waist, keeping her eyes lowered as she spoke. "Mother Messinex, while Princess Perneptheranam was away from ShadowFall, for the Game and, and, your coronation, I was acting administrator. In the performance of my duties, I discovered two separate inventories in the hidden files of Wakan Kech. Apparently these were kept for tax purposes?" Rumi did not allow herself a smile. Such charges alone could bring about severe punishment to Wakan, but not necessarily to the Princess. No, for that to happen, real treason must be proved. Such as—

"And Mother Messinex, during that time, the strangest thing I have ever seen flew over the plaza outside the palace. A huge green cylinder, probably eight to ten meters long, about a third of that in diameter, appeared in the air, right outside the palace balcony." Hesitating for dramatic effect, Rumi watched as the Mother's eyes grew wider and wider, her mouth a perfect O of astonishment.

"Then Mother Messinex, the walls of the flying machine became as clear as crystal, and I beheld a dark little man inside. At first I thought it was little Rist, but I knew that he was on the way to this city for the Game. Then the little man spoke to us in a loud voice."

Messinex sat silent, absorbing the incredible story of what happened next. "As the machine descended close to the ground, a door opened, and the little man—Rusk, he called himself—stepped out. The palace guardsmen thought we were under attack, and fired their springbows. The big green machine fell the last small distance and went silent."

Similla's story continued, as Mother Messinex drew out more and more detail. "So, when those arrows were pulled out, the machine was able to fly again?"

"Yes, Mother Messinex. But then the little man tricked us, escaping with a handmaid, the treacherous Anklya. She who had been the kept mistress of the other twin, Rist." Rumi did not care to mention that she, herself, had also slept with the enchanting Rusk during his stay at ShadowFall, and that her trust in him had been the reason for his opportunity to escape, kidnapping Anklya—*if that bitch didn't go willingly!*

Messinex told Miran Kech to make sure that his captive, Rumi, was well cared for and given a room and certain privileges for her report. "Then come see me, in private, later, Miran. We must decide how to deal with this, this, *treachery*!"

THE UPSETTING NEWS ABOUT PERNIE'S POSSIBLE treason notwithstanding, Mother Messinex was experiencing another apprehension, as she had every morning for the last months: her daily visit to the

Crystal Throne. Preceded by a dozen dancing maids playing their lutes and tambourines, she strode into the vast domed hall where she received daily communion from the goddesses. *Or where my subjects* think *I do,* she thought. *So far I can't make any sense of what the goddess is trying to tell me. A goddess who speaks nothing but gibberish?*

Stopping before the walkway of stairs leading up the pyramidal dais to the Crystal Throne itself, she paused as she always did, looking up with reverence at the painted ceiling a fifty meters above, the largest dome in all Motherland. There in magnificent glory, the sky blue ceiling was painted in a realistic portrayal of ancient gods, giant female figures with the purest of white skins, large blue eyes, waist-length braided red hair, clothed in flowing white robes. The largest figure, the slender and beautiful First Mother, held in her outstretched hand a scarlet scroll to the figure of Mother Messinex, the ruler who was accepting authority from the First Mother Herself. Miran's painters had replaced the likeness of the Lordess Mother—her biological mother—with Messinex's own portrait, a flattering visage that now also graced posters and walls on every building, in every public square, all across Motherland. Each citizen now knew the beauty of their new platinum-haired Mother by sight.

In the painted background, much smaller male figures in gray robes stood by, wistfully observing but obviously ineffectual. Overall, the story the painting presented reinforced Mother Messinex's goddess-given power in a manner that even illiterates—*especially* illiterates!—immediately understood.

Then Messinex's gaze dropped down to the breathtakingly beautiful Crystal Throne itself, an outsized chair sculpture made of a transparent stonelike material, a magical god-stone that would emit a myriad of colors, but only when a Mother sat on it. Its arched back pointed straight up, toward the vast domed ceiling and its tableau of history and power. A hidden aperture somewhere in the dome ensured that the light of the sun would fall upon the Crystal Throne during the day.

As part of the ritual, two maids lit incense urns, the smoke from them wafting heady fragrances upwards, as if in an offer to the throne and the Mother. Messinex breathed in deeply, and wondered once more whether the burning herbs were supposed to prepare her for the experience to come, her alleged communion with the goddess. Slightly dizzy from the incense, she scaled the stairs leading to her translucent throne. As she stepped, internal lights illuminated each of the risers along the way—green, red, violet, blue—presenting an ever-changing pattern, as if traveling up and down the staircase. Though most subjects thought that Mother was orchestrating the lights, Messinex knew that the patterns were apparently random and under no human control. Even her Kech scholars had not been able to determine why and how they lit, why they seemed to move in such a manner, and why they only responded to a specific Mother and no one else. Messinex sighed. *More secrets of the ancients.*

Messinex hoped that this day's communion with the goddess would be more insightful, more enlightening. So far, for three months now, every day's session had been identical. But she could not confide her doubts or fears to anyone, not even Miran Kech, lest her absolute Mother-given powers be suspect. *That would lead to chaos,* she thought, *not to mention my own death and a nationwide civil war.* The golden tablets in her secret Mother's Sanctuary Room told tales of unending unrest, invasions, and slaughter in previous centuries, miseries that prevailed even after all of Motherland was pacified millennia ago by First Mother.

Messinex thought, *The charming story that First Mother peaceably brought all of Motherland's various warring tribes together from nothing is simply a fae tale, fit only for children and the simple.* Even though, when in the ultra-private Sister school she had first learned of her nation's true founding, Messinex had been shocked. *Sisters still war upon their neighboring siblings until Mothersmen are sent to quell disorders and restore order and borders. I can't let that happen again! Please, Goddess, give me the wisdom to manage this vast nation, my empire, my millions of, of, of slaves!*

But as she placed her bare buttocks on the throne, the same meaningless noises once again saturated Messinex's being, taking over her senses. First came the cacophony of whispers, almost like a person talking, overlaid with crackling noises like green tinder burning in a fireplace. Messinex could again *feel* that it *was* someone speaking to her. She could not understand the words, but knew they *were* words. "Goddess, I hear you, but I do not understand you," she whispered, hoping that the distant being would hear her. The voice answered in nearly recognizable Motherspeak, but in inflections carrying no meaning: *"—qomp translation algorithms—"* *"—accommodating tonal shift variables—"*

Disappointed, Messinex begged aloud, as she always had, but not so that her maids or guards could hear, "Goddess, what language are you speaking?" As before, the other voices went silent for a minute, followed by whistling noises and sounds like rushing waterfalls resounding in her ears. Then more words came through, in the midst of a staccato series of broken phrases, obviously not in human voices, but more like priestly chants echoing in a closed chamber: *"Translation complete. Archived variation of evolved Diníglish at Earth terminal. No operator present at local lunar terminal. Ending session."* Messinex heard the familiar sounds of the unintelligible words, the almost-recognizable cadence and inflections, but the Goddess's message was still not understandable.

As the contact faded into meaningless noise and shrill whistles, Messinex was so disappointed that she was shaking. *I have tried so many times*, she thought, *and still the Goddess is not speaking to me in words I can understand.* Unable to hide her tears, she stood up from the Crystal Throne, shaking her head, her arms trembling. Casting her gaze upward to the painting of many of her predecessor Mothers, she thought, *If they learned wisdom from the Goddess, then so will I!*

Collecting her composure before descending the color-changing staircase, with a smile Messinex acknowledged the maids and Mothersmen who were bowing in her direction. Feeling a sudden tremor and a flash of light, she recoiled at the onset of another migraine, catching herself before she could stumble on the way down; the open staircase had no handrails. *That would be a disaster, showing weakness in front of these, these, smiling faces, these subservients, these...* She couldn't finish the thought as a blinding pain shot through her head, temple to temple. Her vision *fractured*, sharp shards of golden spikes seeming to stab her eyes; she couldn't see!

As she stumbled, in her pain Messinex was thinking, *Miran Kech has told me I have unseen enemies, all around me.* She looked around at the shocked faces of her maids, who were running to catch her from falling on the last step. *Which of these subversive heads must roll until we have eliminated all threats?* Regaining her sight and her stride, with a slight nod and thumb gesture she directed a Mothersman to seize the nearest maid, the one holding her arm. *I will start now, with this one. She didn't reach me quite fast enough. Is she a threat? She will pay!*

CHAPTER TEN

Miran Kech drew himself up to his full height, smoothing his blue robes as he turned toward his assembled audience of black-leather-vested military officers, all much taller and more muscular than himself. Clearing his throat—*That damned incense is overpowering today, and the wrong aroma for a serious meeting!*—Miran said loudly, "Colonel Creesile, how many men do you need to subjugate the Sisterdom of ShadowFall? And how quickly can it be done?"

The priest stood before a wall-sized map of Motherland, pointing out the target area located at the northernmost border of the empire, a relatively flat, lightly forested domain, split by the slow-moving Mother's River formed by the huge waterfall flowing down from the Dark Highlands.

"Lord Kech," answered the tall colonel, "There may be difficulties. In the last four years, ShadowFall has successfully fought off invasions from its two neighboring Sisters. My spies tell me that their citizen militia are again heavily armed with those deadly springbows. They must have kept the majority of the weapons for themselves; they only surrendered a few dozen of them to us, and a couple hundred of those arrows, but we don't know how to make any more of them. That Wakan Kech knows the secrets to forming godsmetal, but he is loyal to the Princess there. We've tested them; those damned things can kill at three hundred meters, even through our leather armor, and—"

"Damn it, man!" Miran shouted, red-faced, "don't tell me your *problems,* tell me your *solutions*! I want ShadowFall torn down, reduced to piles of rubble. I want all the men peasants killed and their women and children turned over to the other ravenous Sisters for slaves; they can divide up the lands of that festering pustule of ShadowFall any way they want." He figured that the resulting northern internecine war would spread and go on for years, weakening each Sister until he could persuade Messinex to replace them all with women of his own choosing. "I want that Wakan Kech killed slowly, that Princess Pernie brought to me, in chains; I don't care how many of those peasants you have to kill to do it." Calming down, he repeated the question.

This time the Colonel answered directly. "Lord Kech, in anticipation of your resolve, I have already arranged for troop transport barges to rendezvous at the docks at Lake Roos. And I have made plans that call for six thousand experienced soldiers to accomplish the mission. Give me three weeks and I can assemble four thousand men from here at Mother's City and begin their march toward ShadowFall. Once at Lake Roos, we will board them on rowed barges and tow several spare barges with us for supplies and weapons. Because of these two sets of rapids"—he pointed toward the map features—"we will have to portage around them, delaying the northern passage. However, my chief engineer has been constructing special swivel ramps for quick debarkation and re-boarding. We will proceed upriver and arrive at ShadowFall at the same time as our force on the Main Road. We will flank them from the river and attack together. Convergent force, if you will."

Miran Kech nodded; those damned rapids were the reason that river transportation had never developed, the Main Road being by far the easier pathway. *I will have to think about locks and dams at those places*, he thought. *They would stimulate trade throughout half of*

Motherland. He sighed. *But only after I erase ShadowFall and that damned Wakan!*

Creesile was still speaking: "With written orders from you, I will requisition another two thousand militiamen from the northern Sisterdoms, and will have your authority to commandeer supplies along the way, from those princesses." He pointed toward the other Sisterdoms as he named them. "Eighteen Stones and Trader Plains will provide me their troops only under those written orders. They are somewhat obstinate about fighting outside their own borders." Miran made a mental note of that; all of the Sisters would have to be taught a lesson about their Mother's absolute authority, once ShadowFall had…fallen.

Creesile continued, "But High Tables, Stone Pyramid, Four Peaks, and RidgeBack will all willingly jump in for a share of the spoils, if they see us as potential winners." Miran was pleased that those Sisters yet were driven by greed and, perhaps, jealousy. That meant they would be more pliable when he instituted more centralized control over all Motherland. He was certain that Mother Messinex would agree. *She's the most pliable of all,* he thought. *In fact, I think she's even started to lose her mind these last few months.* As he smiled at the possibilities that would open on him, his change in facial features surprised the colonel.

The soldier said, "Ancient Towers, even though next to ShadowFall on its eastern border, will undoubtedly remain neutral. Princess Fallowner thinks of her Sisterdom as an independent regime, anyhow, being so far away from Mother's City."

Miran Kech nodded. *I'll deal with that bitch after Pernie is in chains. Or burnt. Maybe even a two-for-one invasion, a dual bonfire?* His smile disturbed the Colonel even more.

Creesile went on, this time drawing lines on the paper map on the planning table. "With four thousand men on oared barges and another four thousand assembled on foot on the Main Road, we will be able to overcome any resistance. I can get all my troops and barges up that remaining three hundred klicks in ten to fifteen days or less after we begin. Ground troops will depart ahead of us, drawing all of the attention of their spies and their defense planners.

"Nobody will be expecting river craft to portage around those rapids. The river has never been traversed upstream in battle. Catapults with fireballs mounted on the barges and moved on wagons up the road can address any massed peasants if they resist, and my experienced soldiers and militiamen will take the palace. I don't expect any problem." Looking down at the short Kech priest, straight in the eyes, Creesile said, "Allowing for typical delays, no more than two months. Will that work, sir?"

"Fine. The sooner, the better. But what about those springbow-shooting citizens of ShadowFall you complained about earlier?" Miran Kech asked with a sneer. "What are your plans for countering them?

Creesile's answering smile was anything but warm. "Lord Kech, they are a serious problem. That is why I just added another two thousand men to my original plan."

Miran Kech waited in his private chambers, while Rumi Similla freshened up and dressed in fine clothing. After the satisfying experience with her the night before, he was anxious to see her again. *She is invigorating; beautiful in body, and sharp in mind,* he thought. *And a never-ending font of information about ShadowFall and Princess Pernie.* He was particularly interested in her experiences with that flying god-machine that the little man from the Ice Lands supposedly flew to ShadowFall, kidnapping one of Pernie's handmaids there. *If that is a true story, one such machine could conquer all of Motherland. Rumi understood that, which is why she tried to seize it herself. But the dwarf tricked her, as such vile little creatures always did in legends and folklore, and got away with it.* As his new mistress walked into his study, moving her hips suggestively under the nearly transparent royal godscloth robe, Miran considered her tale. Her guardsmen were able to shoot the green thing down. Something about those springbow arrows; when they were removed, that little Rusk could fly it again. The question that stayed in his mind, overriding even his desire to lay with Rumi again, was this: *Where is that Rusk now? Where is that machine?*

CHAPTER ELEVEN

Princess Perneptheranam paced the highest-most vantage platform on the roof of her palace, looking north. There, twenty kilometers away, loomed the low silhouette of the Dark Highlands, a distant threat but the one place where her hopes for survival lay. Aloud, she cried, "Oh my little Rist, my dark champion, my lover, why have you not returned? Where are you? Do you yet live?" Breaking into sobs, she allowed a handmaid to bring her a soft napkin to wipe away the tears.

After her daily morning conference with Wakan Kech, Pernie was growing more and more concerned. Her surreptitious mirror-spy system, one of Wakan's innovations, reported that Mothersman troop barges were rendezvousing at Lake Roos, presumably preparing an invasion fleet to head to ShadowFall. Wakan's spies, stationed at line-of-sight intervals, were able to flash sun-signals on to each other, along a long relay line of covert operators. *It is expensive, Princess,* he had said when authorizing the expenditure for the network, *but our unreported and untaxed sales of the godscloth windfall to the other Sisters is offsetting our defense costs. So far.*

She knew that Wakan and the nobles had been preparing for an invasion ever since Colonel Creesile's thugs confiscated her libraries and springbows, a month ago. She felt, too, that somehow Wakan had known of the threat even before that, but had no way of proving that suspicion and didn't want to confront her High Priest with it. He was all-important to the survival of her Sisterdom, *And of myself, too, if we lose. I just can't imagine why my Sister Messinex—Mother Messinex, now—is allowing that awful Miran Kech to act this way against me. We were so close, even when she ascended the Crystal Throne and was Chosen. Somehow she has changed.* The Princess groaned at a horrible thought: *Does the Crystal Throne change her? Did it...did it... turn our own natural Lordess Mother into a monster, years ago?* The very thought was so treasonous that she compartmentalized it immediately. *I'll think of that possibility another time; right now, I must prepare for war.*

WAKAN KECH stood at the observation deck of Watchtower One, a twenty-meter tall wooden construction just a kilometer north of ShadowFall's southern border, and a kilometer west of the Main Road that led from the palace into the neighboring Sisterdom of Stone Pyramid. The six-meter-square deck platform featured a signaling device, a flat round mirror mounted atop a rotating hemisphere. A movable umbrella-like canopy shielded it as needed. As the priest watched, two guardsmen demonstrated the use of their new signaling mirror apparatus, speaking to Wakan and six of his defense ministry staff looking on.

"Here, Lord Kech." The chief mirror-man (a new rating, designated by Wakan himself), rotated the meter-diameter device until a pointer on its rim touched an engraved caption reading THE PALACE. "We have already trued-in the azimuth, and we are now pointed directly at the palace's receiving station."

"Proceed, Chief, if you will," Wakan said, the soldier smiling at the recognition of his new status. The young man bowed slightly, then turned the top surface to a prescribed angle to the overhead sun, and operated a large shutter in front of the mirror. "Lord Kech, we are using the blink-and-flash system that you trained us in. A quick signal of light is a *blink*; a longer signal is a *flash*."

At the puzzled looks of his military staff, Wakan explained. "The blinks and flashes, in prescribed manner, spell out letters, then words. Punctuation at present is still crude, but effective. Mirror-man, tell the Princess that we are operational. Better, say that 'Wakan Kech is on high—twenty meters above southernmost ShadowFall.'" Saluting, the soldier slowly carried out the code signaling.

A minute later in the distance, the onlookers could make out blinking lights on the horizon. "Those are being relayed from the palace's own mirror station, Lord Kech." He looked down at marks the scribe had made on the paper tablet. Smiling, the mirror-man said, "Lord Kech, the Princess has replied: 'Wakan Kech, you are indeed the highest priest in all Motherland.'"

Wakan and his retinue laughed. "This thing works, gentlemen. Thanks to little Rist and his tales of the weird land of God's Port, up the river in the Dark Highlands. Mirror-man, turn your signaler toward the other stations. Let's see if our daytime communications work all over our country." The other side of the hemispherical signaler contained a concave mirror, to be used with fire to provide similar communications at night. He had little doubt that the fire would prove as effective in the dark as the reflected sun had in the daytime.

Wakan's Towers, as they came to be called, were planned to provide ShadowFall with instant signaling from strategic locations around its borders, with redundant structures kept ready and in waiting should invaders seize or destroy one. *With this system*, Wakan thought, *once it is proven reliable, our weakness in numbers can be offset by seeing where the enemy is, communicating that instantly, and sending our troops only to where they are needed. We don't have to fortify every kilometer of the border.* He did not expect any invading army to have such rapid means of transmitting orders. *They will depend on brute force, if I know Mothersmen. They only fight untrained citizens or uncivilized tribes.* He didn't dwell on his memories of his own High Antian guard troops slaughtered in the ancient Chi'a Southern Highlands.

The Main Road to Mother's City ran southward into the Sisterdom of Stone Pyramid, down through Trader Plains, and finally to Mother's City domains. Mother's River, a limited trade route, split ShadowFall in half, flowing south through Four Peaks and parallel to the Main Road before turning westward, ending its smooth journey into Lake Roos. Because of Mother's River's two sets of unnavigable rapids, ShadowFall had never considered water transport as important; its main trade markets were more easily accessed by the Main Road. But Wakan considered the river a prime invasion route; when Mothersmen swarmed up the river, it wouldn't be trade they wanted—only slaughter, slaves, and plunder!

Considering Motherland's centuries of war, whose archives he had studied in ShadowFall's libraries, he knew that Mothersmen typically used massed charges of leather-armored men, long spears and shortswords their only arms. Against such an invasion, the thousands of ShadowFall's men and women could defend the Main Road only for a few days, Wakan knew. He had set hundreds of citizens to digging twin ditches perpendicular to the road, three kilometers in each direction. These trenches would be camouflaged to hide sharp wooden spikes; ShadowFall soldier-citizens would be concealed behind the second trench, waiting to handle the survivors of the first wave. For invaders coming up the river, he was having pull-chains fabricated to prevent sailboats and oared barges from coming deep into the Sisterdom.

Wakan made notes as he thought. *Or maybe we can use that godscloth that Rist brought us? That material is so thin and sharp on its edges that it can cut anything, Rist said. I know that those large gloves have to be used to prevent our tailors from losing fingers, but I hadn't thought of using that cutting edge as a weapon. What if we pull it up out of the river and the enemy boats meet it edge-on? Would it not slice them in two? And if their troops are standing in formation on the decks*—whew! *Little Rist was right about so many things, especially his Sire's saying that "Knowledge is power, especially when nobody else knows it!"*

Wakan had his scribe companion immediately write orders to the net-men and those tradespeople familiar with the properties of godscloth to experiment with not only edge-on riverine slice-traps, but also ones that could be laid out on roads, in gullies, in doorways, pathways, and even—he smiled at the image of little Rist riding his war-bird—ones that could be spooled out between two emu-riders on the battlefield. *About head-high should do it. All I need now are a lot more Rists riding on emus!* "Don't write down that emu bit yet," he chuckled. "I've got to find more little riders first." Rist and his twin Rusk were less than half as tall as Wakan, but nobody else in Motherland was small enough to ride the birds, and children shouldn't have to fight wars. After the scribe scuttled off to copy and deliver his orders, Wakan shuddered at the implications; godscloth amputation wires were going to be a permanent feature of ShadowFall's defenses, both at its borders and, when necessary, as deadly invisible excision devices—IEDs.

CHAPTER TWELVE

The twins departed in Una at dawn the next day, leaving Odel with hand-drawn copies of illustrations that Una provided by video screen—"Sires, the printer output devices are no longer operational, and the print media long ago disintegrated, sorry."

Thist said, "Like Una showed him, if Odel can locate some of those metal arcs that Wakan makes springbows with, and spreads the godscloth over them, he'll have a lot stronger and lighter glider. They're usually found around godscloth." He knew now that the strong, thin metal pieces originally had been reinforcements embedded within the many thousands of square kilometers of godscloth in ancient times, when that magical material had covered the entire sky, hundreds of kilometers above the surface of the Earth. Una never had been able to explain just how the material had been fabricated, what it was used for, or why so much of it was deployed. From the mysterious vocabulary of the ancients, such concepts as *electromagnetic harvesting, microwave propulsion, nanofabrication*, and the like, could not be adequately translated to the nontechnical language of Peoplespeak. The twins just accepted the wondrous material as more near magic from the past.

"And if he can make some of those nozzle-tubes for that burning-powder booster, he could have himself a long-range flyer," Thist said, thinking of Odel's possible uses for such a flying machine. "I know his bald knob hill is just a hundred or so meters high; I wonder if he could ever fly from a height like the river's end waterfall, down into Motherland? Close to a thousand meters drop, and trees to avoid before you get all the way to ShadowFall." The vision of a swarm of Odels flying their tri-wings down to Motherland—*Sky warriors? Rock-droppers? Spear throwers?*—wouldn't leave his mind. It reminded him of some of the scenes of ancient battles with flying machines that Una had presented as "history." He'd have to watch some of those again. Especially if anybody—even Mother Messinex—ever threatened ShadowFall!

But Thusk dismissed the idea of flying warriors. "Odel will have enough troubles trying to overthrow those priests in God's Port, if he even tries to. And since he is the only tri-wing flyer in all of God's Country, I don't see him of being much help in the bottomlands." Thist nodded in agreement but thought, *Still...if only!*

As part of its original mission to scan all environments it encountered, Una's scans had detected a score of godspheres concealed in Odel's tri-wing storage shelter. According to design protocols, the DI transmitted power and interrogatories to them, accessing their contents in return. Added to the data from similar scans of the hundreds of spheres at ShadowFall and the treasure trove of thousands of them in and below Mother's Palace, as well as interfacing with the Crystal Throne there, Una spent billions of nanoseconds archiving, correlating, and drawing inferences. As per its original instructions, when not finding any information it evaluated as "a near, clear, or present danger," Una would not report until and unless queried. The various sub-qomps continued to communicate among themselves, reaching consensus on various facets of Una's operations and experiences, and as programmed, extrapolated on probable mission effects and consequences.

———

In the hours before they came to the great waterfall at river's end, the twins continued to discuss possible plans for subversive activities in ShadowFall. "We won't have any real support from the citizens," Thist said, "Because ShadowFall really does love its Princess, and compared to the other Sisters down there, she is pretty benevolent. And so is Wakan Kech. We don't want to harm those two, just free her slaves. And I don't know how to convince her, or even her slaves, that they should all be free." He remembered fondly his months of learning and training with Wakan, improving his emu-riding and fighting skills, and particularly his warm nights with the handmaidens and then with Pernie herself. But just as those memories arose, so did those of his own berserker behavior in the Game where, he was reluctant to recall, he had loved the adrenaline high, the rush of individual combat—and sadly, to his shame, killing those dozen or more enemies of ShadowFall in a pure blind rage. By contrast, the more recent memory of his twin Thusk killing The Tharn and his guard on the steps of The Tharn's Palace only brought back a feeling of satisfaction, of conclusion, after that chief had killed their Sire without cause. But the revenge slaying didn't bring back Sire Thess. Thist truly missed his Sire, the man's wisdom and knowledge —and the quality of patience—that he himself had not inherited.

Thusk said, "We should find Wakan first. Then we go with him to Pernie and announce that we are back. Having Wakan there with us will lessen the shock to her. And as we agreed, we will say that we had to return to our home to save our Sire and birther. Which of course we really did."

Thist nodded and laughed. "Twin, that kind of deceit is worthy of a Motherlander. We are both learning how to compete with these tall people." Culturally, untruths were almost nonexistent in The Tharn' Lands.

When Thusk had asked Una about that anomaly as compared to the wanton lying and ubiquitous treachery existing in God's Port and Motherland societies, the Developing Intelligence that was Una had searched its voluminous historical and scientific archives and reported, "Sire Thusk, there is no clear historical exemplar of your homeland's aversion to telling untruths, but perhaps it arose from the extremely harsh environmental conditions under which your tribe evolved."

The DI paused, as if to give the men time to contemplate its findings. To Thusk, this subtle action was yet another indication that Una was beginning to act more like a person than a machine. "Untruths always lead to discovery, resulting in distrust, then inefficiency, finally to corruption. In a society of abundance the effects of dishonesty, the resulting waste and inefficiency, may not become apparent for centuries. But in a bare subsistence environment such as your ancestors endured, surrounded by glaciers, a society in a daily struggle for survival cannot afford such waste of time and resources. Perhaps those individuals who attempted deception died as a result of their own actions. Or by the actions of others."

The two men just smiled. As Una was demonstrating about itself when drawing absolute conclusions from disparate data as it just had, they too were learning the ways of the real world and could see how being deceitful could be useful. But each was thinking, *If everyone lies, who can you ever trust?* Making people honest wasn't a task they set out to do. Ending slavery, torture, tyranny—those goals alone would take a lifetime of work. And maybe even their own lives.

"So, next stop then, ShadowFall?" Thusk asked Thist, who nodded. "Una, take us quickly to the palace at ShadowFall. Invisibly, please."

"Sire Thusk, it shall be done," Una replied. "This DI shall also scan for borophene weapons as we draw near." An hour later, having flown the length of the Mother's River from God's Country, they approached the kilometers-wide waterfall and then plunged down the hundreds of meters to the ground level of Motherland, through clouds of mist and vapor, to the flatlands below.

Thist grinned from ear to ear. "Thusk, this was a heck of a lot easier this time, than when I had to let myself down on a long strip of godscloth." *A lot has changed in six months,* he thought. *I fought and won battles—and lost a foot. You killed a tyrant—and we lost our Sire. Things seem to balance out somehow. I just wonder what I'll be thinking six months from now—or if I will even be alive to think at all.* He stopped smiling and watched as Una took them down through the rising mist, over the forest, and closer to the Princess's palace.

What will the Princess do? Thusk wondered. *Will she accept our story? Has she believed Wakan?* Then he remembered something else: Was that woman, that Rumi Similla, in exile, as Wakan had ordered? She was the only one who knew the details of the arrows that had disabled Una. The palace guards were no threat; they never left the Sisterdom and would obey the Princess's and Wakan's orders with their lives. But that Rumi? Thusk had bad feelings about her but kept his suspicions to himself.

Thusk had Una invisibly hover just a quarter meter above the palace until Thist jumped out onto the roof, then flew the craft up a hundred meters, far out of any arrow range should it be discovered by the guards. Meanwhile, Thist made his way through Wakan's secret passageways until he found the Kech alone in his private chamber.

"Wakan," he whispered through a slightly opened wooden panel. "Are you alone?"

The priest jumped out of his chair faster than Thist had thought possible, drawing out a shortsword in one smooth movement. At that, Thist stepped fully out into the room and bowed.

"I'll be d—" Wakan couldn't finish his surprised

shout. "Rist, how did you—? Where were you—? Where is your—?" Snapping his mouth shut, the priest made a shushing sound and motioned Thist back into the hidden panel. Once they were both inside, Wakan holding a lit taper, he gave the little man an affectionate hug, then spoke in whispers. "Did you fly back here in your Una? Where is it? Is your brother, your twin, Rusk with you?"

"I am now *Thist*, a true man, Wakan. And my, my twin, he is *Thusk*. Our Sire man-named us weeks ago."

"Well, little—*Thist*, is it?—I am very happy to see you. I will need your help. The Princess needs your help." At Thist's quizzical reaction, he added, "Miran Kech is probably mobilizing a Mothersmen army to come and seize ShadowFall from the Princess. He is angry and afraid. I believe that he has heard of your Una and what it can do."

A few minutes of discussion gave them time to hatch a plan. Thist departed to carry it out, while Wakan quickly finished his immediate duties and waited for events to unfold.

THUSK AND THIST STOOD OUTSIDE PRINCESS PERNIE'S private chambers, the objects of intense scrutiny by her four guardsmen. In front of the guards, Wakan Kech had told the two little men that the Princess would welcome them shortly, to wait in place until he returned. Dressed in greenish godscloth tunics, the twins had spruced themselves up for their reunion with the mistress of ShadowFall.

Months ago Rist had been her lover, before losing his left foot in the Game; he hadn't seen her since the time he had surprised her along the Main Road in the Stone Pyramid Sisterdom. *And I didn't keep my promise to return here to ShadowFall immediately, either.* Thinking back over his achievements since then, however, he offered no apologies to himself. *I liberated my country, and my twin Thusk killed the Tharn.* He knew that if he'd stayed in Motherland instead, The Tharn would still be ruling his homeland. *But then, maybe my Sire would still be alive, even if in hiding with my birther?* He hoped that Princess Perneptheranam, "Pernie," would be more forgiving of him than he was of himself.

The door to Pernie's chambers opened and Wakan Kech waved an arm of welcome to escort them into the presence of the Princess of ShadowFall. Thusk felt the welcome warmth and perfumes of Pernie's room and the similar warmth of her broad smile. "Rist, my champion!" she said loudly. "And again, your twin, Rusk! Welcome home, gentlemen." Pernie motioned them both to come forward, leaning over to give them both the most passionate hugs. "It has been so long; we thought you were dead!"

Wakan asked the men to sit on either side of the Princess, who kept an affectionate one-arm embrace with each of them. The priest was pleased at their reception; he had done all he could to soften her first reaction to the news of the return of the northerners. "They are *here*?" Pernie had screamed just minutes before. "How dare they not return as promised? I could have their—their—tongues, private parts—anything, taken, for such treachery!"

Wakan knew that his Princess didn't really want to harm the little men, but that any resistance at all, any noncompliance of any sort, was abominable to all royals. He thought, *And their first response is always to lash out, to punish the offenders, maybe mutilate or even kill them. Even though I have tried for years to urge this gentle young woman not to react so.* He had waited until Pernie's angry face relaxed into one of relief, even showing tears of joy. "You always know what to do, Wakan, my dearest friend," she said, sniffling. "Even when it is nothing. Of course I'll see them, right now. Please escort them in."

Over wine and cheeses and a variety of imported fruits and nuts, Thist related the story that he, Thusk, and Wakan had agreed to. He was finding it easy to lie *like a WarmLander*, he thought. *The complete truth would be harmful to us all. Telling an agreeable story, though, it is just a friendlier version of Truth.* "Princess, Thusk—back then, *Rusk*—when he flew Una down here and on to Mother's City to rescue me, brought along the disturbing news that our Sire and birther were in serious trouble back home. So he convinced me that our duty lay in helping them first, and then returning here to aid you in what you may need." He bowed his head toward her and she touched his cheek as she removed her arm from his shoulders.

"Little Rist—*Thist*—thank you for your consideration. Of course I understand your familial duty to your parents. That was thoughtful. But my main concern was that your Una may have crashed somewhere, that you were hurt or, worse, dead! If only you could have sent word." Standing, she paced the room, bare feet on fur carpet, "But we don't have any way to do that, do we?"

Wakan's discussion then veered toward talk of threats from Miran Kech, but the Princess wouldn't hear of it. "Wakan, all of our problems will still be here in the morning. We can address them then, after breakfast when we are all refreshed and clear-minded. These men have traveled an enormous distance and I have yet to hear the details of their adventures these last few months." Wakan sighed and accepted another mug of wine from the serving girl. Thusk was saying, "Princess, well, when I landed in God's Port, looking for Thist, the funniest thing happened…"

As the evening's ambience grew increasingly friendly between the Princess and her visitors, Pernie occasionally touched one little man, then the other, still amazed at the identical features of the two. Taking a cue, and satisfied that the reunion had gone very well, Wakan excused himself. As he shut the door, he heard Pernie whisper, "Thist and Thusk, are you two *exactly* alike?"

THE NEXT WEEKS WENT EXTREMELY WELL FOR THIST and Thusk. First, Pernie's welcome was more than warm, and the evenings and nights with her were so delightful that Thist began to wonder why he had left Motherland. But then the reality of Mother Messinex's tirade, the duplicity of that Miran Kech, and the political tension between Pernie and the Mother, all returned during long discussions with the Princess and Wakan Kech. Thist was somber as the realizations set in; Thusk mostly intrigued by details he hadn't known about Motherland's devious and treacherous customs.

"What did you come back for, men?" Wakan asked during one long evening's round of debriefing. "You have told me of the revolution you sparked back in your own homeland. Do you expect to do something similar here?" Putting down his long-stemmed pipe he waved away the sweet-smelling smoke and said grimly, "Motherland is more than a hundred times the size of your People's Lands, with probably two hundred times its population, We have been a lowland empire for thousands of years, with a hierarchy of royalty leading up to the Mother. Until a few months ago, *your* nation reported to one barbarian chief."

As Pernie and the twins stared at Wakan, he explained, "What I am saying is, what worked well in your country won't necessarily find the same acceptance down here."

Thusk replied, "Well, why don't you fill us in on the current situation in Motherland? How is Messinex performing? Is she still upset about the old sea business? At Thist? Where are the current tensions? What are the issues? Is that pirate Miran Kech still running things in Mother's Palace?"

Holding up his hand palm first, Wakan yielded to Pernie on answering that barrage of questions. "Thist," she said, "In the months you've been gone, relations have been frigid between us and the Mother. That Miran Kech sent a Colonel Creesile up here to seize all our godspheres, springbows, even old books. Wakan, here, successfully sequestered most of our treasures away from the Colonel and his men." Thist and Thusk looked at each other, then at Wakan. *Everybody was playing that hiding game, weren't we?* was their common thought.

"Then just before you arrived, yet another demand came from the Mother, ostensibly, demanding that we surrender even more tax tribute to the palace. Wakan showed me our treasury balances, and the taxes Miran is demanding would bankrupt us. We had to refuse. I think he knows this and uses it as an excuse to invade."

Wakan spoke. "We are fairly certain that Mother Messinex would not approve of fighting a war with ShadowFall, us being so distant, not with all the problems that would cause her own treasury and manpower resources. My spies in Mother's Palace, though, are not so certain."

Thist asked, "When would you know if Miran or the Mother intended to use force?'

Wakan said, "Unfortunately, even the fastest horses take over a week each way, so an invasion could be underway before we knew it." He purposely did not mention that his spies and their developing system of mirror relays had already confirmed the worst; he wanted the twins to volunteer Una's help.

And they did. "Our Una can be down there in less than an hour," Thusk said, smiling. "Why don't we fly down and take a look?"

CHAPTER THIRTEEN

Sitting at the controls of his Eternal Machine tunneler, Jolan Keesh faced a wide, solid stone tunnel wall, in the precise location where he needed to carve out a new tunnel from Infinite Rock. His quota for the day was a quarter-kilometer into that rock, starting from his present position at Foremost, the tunnel intersection located farthest from the Tubes of Community. Glancing down at the bright infrared-lit instrument panel before him, Keesh again checked the ultrasonic scans of the Infinite Rock he was facing. "It still reads Dense Granite, a full kilometer, every time," he said aloud, not knowing if his five crewmen heard him. "Few voids, unfortunately. This melt will take more power." With backpack breathers already in place, the men would be able to see the situation for themselves, once he dialed the melt controller up to MAX.

A sudden *whoosh!* and bright red beams of swirling laser lights announced to his team that a difficult melt was under way. Dense Rock made for slow going as Keesh excavated the horizontal three-meter-wide by one-and-a-half-meter-high space in front of him. Keesh saw that the arched ceiling and vertical walls were being perfectly smoothed out by the melter, and the floor appropriately stippled for traction of treads and footwear. Small amounts of debris fell out of the small voids opened in the rock, his crew cleaning up and hauling it out, as he directed the lasers to fill and polish the holes. He paid particular attention to the locations and sizes of such voids, as such empty volumes in other tunnels had led him to suggest a heretical idea to the Elder Council. He would soon have to defend that controversial proposal to a potentially hostile Council. *Which could cost me my life!*

RETURNING HIS TUNNELER AND ITS CREW TO THE Resource Tube hours later, Keesh was bone-tired, muscles aching, sweating through his work tunic; it had been a long, tiring day of melting. As he parked the Eternal Machine in its storage niche, his lead crewman, Ledd Mernan, walked over slowly and handed him a written message.

"For you, boss, from a runner. Looks like the Elders want to talk to you. Need me to come along?"

Reading the note under the bright infrared floodlights of the cavernous Tube, Keesh groaned loudly and patted Mernan on the shoulder. "You're as worn out and dirty as I am, Ledd. Go home and get some rest. Meanwhile, I've gotta go get cleaned up."

Keesh made his way through a full kilometer of IR-lit tunnels, finally arriving at his home, a ten-meter-square set of rooms with high two-meter ceilings, carved out of rock in the residential district of Shinyeen City, a Tube of Community. The warm shower and clean clothes, followed by a strong drink, helped him prepare for the anticipated grilling to come.

WEARING THE DARK SCARLET ROBES OF PRESIDENT, Council Elder Meish shook his balding head, holding up both hands palm-first to calm down the situation. "Engineer Keesh," he said calmly, "we here at Council are all aware of your tremendous contributions to

Community, your discovery of the Vast Cavern that doubled our living space all those Motherth Years ago." Elder Meish was sweating, but not from exertion or passion; something else was on his mind and the bickering was preventing him from addressing that critical item. "For all this, we offer you time to make your case."

Meish sighed and sat. "Please explain yourself, Engineer, if you would." He waved a hand around at the other Elders. "Not everybody here is technical, you know. We have Elders who are Growers and Teachers and Medders."

Keesh viewed the dozen robed Elders at the large table, studying them while they studied him. In the smooth, grayish carved-stone vastness that was the Council Chamber, he spoke loudly. "As you Elders may know, in the written proposal you all have copies of, I have designed an experiment that can send a mini-probe Up toward Vac." Around the table he saw but little reaction. *Good, they have read it.* So few surprises now. *I need to cultivate their interest, their acceptance. So, first I will discuss things they will agree with, before asking for final approval of a plan they may not like.*

He began, "Elders, the five cities of Community are situated within five separate radial Tubes, hollow cavities provided by the Creator wherein People live and grow and reproduce. Tubes are surrounded by solid strata of Infinite Rock of various kinds, extending, we once believed, infinitely in all directions, rock and strata into which we are destined to expand as our population grows. Some Tubes are used by Growers to raise our crops and food animals. Water we obtain from ubiquitous flowing pipes that were provided by Creator in the Beginning when She placed the Tubes—and our ancestors—here.

"She also provided us with electrical power from Divine Outlets, driven by energies beyond our imaginings, the power coming from far out in Infinite Rock, arriving at the Matrices where we make connections. In Her wisdom, she created a Resource

Tube, wherein we obtain Eternal Machines for tunneling and Tube maintenance, many stacks of metal parts and components, and limitless supplies of raw materials, including metals, plastics, and other god-stuff. And as we explore and tunnel, we keep finding more of the Tubes of the Old Lost Ones for resources. Some have speculated that there may be an infinite number of Tubes out there in Rock."

So far, so good. Nothing controversial here. Yet. Keesh pursed his lips, thinking about how to put the rest of his heretical notions to this group of Elders. A misstep and he could be demoted or even Reprocessed. His many years of technical education and experience since leaving the Crèche had prepared him for every engineering challenge so far, and he was professionally adept at handling rock and metals and machinery, but dealing with the nonphysical nuances of Council politics was something that was far beyond his engineering talent and tunneling achievements. *If only I could take an Eternal Machine to this group of Elders,* he thought, smiling to himself at the vision of melting and squashing the lot of them into smooth pavements and walls. *Then I could make much more progress, just like carving out another tunnel!*

But knowing that the Creator's world always yielded to logical solutions—and to the immense power of the Eternal Machines—he decided to be bold. "Elders, as you know, we have located many small and large Tubes over the centuries of our history. Some were empty of everything, including even air. These quickly filled with our own air as we breached their walls."

"Hold right there, young man," a wrinkled Elder interrupted, struggling to stand. This Elder was a man Keesh did not recognize, presumably from another city, his robes of a very light shade of IRed—truly a high-ranking Elder. "We People have always held that we were blessed by Creator with Tubes in which we could breathe, and eat, and live, and work, and reproduce. As we progressed from mindless primitive savages, we became aware of the Eternal Machines, and learned to use them, which enabled us to tunnel and discover other Tubes and caverns. This was in accordance with the will of the Creator: 'Tunnel, Discover, Exploit.'"

All of the men and women in the room, Keesh included, repeated those holy directives three times: "Tunnel, Discover, Exploit." Meish whispered to Keesh that the speaker was Elder Uise, of Tura City, the oldest Community. Keesh had never been there; it was twenty kilometers away, in the First Tube, the sacred city where all People had originated. The population of Tura City was strictly limited in size and constituency; if one advanced high enough in a Tube society, only then might one be considered for residency in that sacred community. For all its sacredness, the First Tube had a reputation for fundamentalism and a noted lack of imagination even among the notably uncurious people of Community. Keesh's tunneling jobs always extended outward from the newer Tubes, so he had never even been near Tura.

"There has long been an argument among us educated Elders," Uise continued, "as to why any Tubes should have been created void of air, which would indicate the Creator forgot something. *That* oversight I do not believe, that She would do that. I am among those here who believe that stories of such airless Tubes are either nonsensical imaginings or deliberate efforts to discredit the Creator."

Keesh winced at the ignorance of this Elder; his own construction records specifically stated that airless voids were common, discovered almost weekly, most of them just a few cubic meters in volume. But he had no problem conceiving of larger ones, *maybe even as large as Community itself?* Luckily, the Vast Cavern he had tunneled into years ago was as pressurized as Community; being twice the volume of Shinyeen City, had it been vacuum it couldn't have been exploited without vast and expensive constructions to seal off usable living space. And without a new source of air, it would have remained a frontier without hope of development. But he kept that thought to himself. *It is hard to believe such willful ignorance exists*, he thought. *Can't this man read?*

Uise kept on, "Other Tubes that our ancestors found contained the remnants of Creator-damned beings, the Old Lost Ones, their large bodies mummified, long-dead, probably early versions of People whom the Creator deemed not worthy of continuing to exist. They must have violated one of the Creator's laws, to have perished so awfully, so long ago." He smiled at Keesh. "But according to Her plan, their Tubes gave us more space to expand; their metals, machines, and materials were precious gifts to us by the Creator; and their bodily remains were good fertilizer for the Growers."

But Keesh himself had often wondered why a benevolent Creator would kill so many, many thousands of Her own people, just to be reprocessed by others of Her creation, namely Keesh's own folk. As a practical engineer, though, he determined to leave theology to the Elders: religion didn't dig tunnels!

Elder Uise sat down, shaking as he did so. "We are all open-minded here, and your previous accomplishments in locating new Tubes demand our respect, if not quite our credulity. However, I must urge that there be no attempts to reach Vac. The very concept is blasphemous."

Keesh gnashed his teeth, but kept silent. Thankful for the faint praise but having been publicly challenged by such an eminent Elder, Keesh sweated even more now. "Elders, you recall the spacious Tubes that my teams discovered five years ago, more than doubling our living volume, allowing us to expand our population." *But Elder Myuk and those at the Crèche tell me that healthy births are declining lately. Why, they don't know.* "As you are also aware, our manpower shortage has prevented us from extending our power lines from our Matrices to those unlit regions and occupying those tributary volumes, many of them still unexplored. But with a small group of men, I have already done some further minor excavations Upward, in hopes of finding more volumes and resources—hopefully with electricity and illumination already Creator-provided." The intakes of breath did not sound good to him, nor did the frowns on the faces of the Elders, but he was now committed and he had to persist.

"Ten Periods ago we discovered smaller voids, barely big enough for a man to crawl through, volumes that extend Upwards several kilometers, almost like bubbles in water. I know this distance because I dispatched one of the smallprobes manufactured by the Eternal Machines and now at our disposal." Keesh could tell by the looks of his audience that he had their rapt attention. *Expansion*, new volume, new resources, were always of interest, regardless of one's religious views. But going Upward might represent a theological problem.

"Then, on one of those smallprobes I mounted the same ultrasonic instruments that we have utilized for centuries now, to locate other Tubes and continue the Creator's directives. I pointed them Upwards. Their unmistakable readings indicate that upward, beyond five kilometers, is—*Nothing*!"

"*Vac?*" Keesh heard somebody say, followed by sudden murmurs all around the table.He nodded. "*Nothingness.*"

Uise stood up again, this time speaking loudly. Keesh was apprehensive at first, but then the Elder surprised him. "Congratulations, Tunneler Keesh, upon your discovery. You have apparently fulfilled the prophecy, my boy: finding evidence of the Promised Tube, where our People will be free to expand forever, an Infinite Openness, yet still enclosed by Infinite Rock. I know that is a hard concept to imagine, but the Creator Herself is unimaginable. You present us with a wonderful opportunity."

But before Keesh could acknowledge the unexpected praise, Elder Uise added solemnly, "But the alleged measurements of your instruments have to take into account the Truth—that the Promised Tube can only be attained by faith alone. It is not a destination we can walk to—much less *crawl* Upward to. No, I believe this incident is the Creator's test of our faith: Will we rely on the muttering of soulless machines or will we await Her guidance, Her revelation, of what Jolan Keesh's devices are really saying? I move that we Elders study the situation in some detail, but that our tunneler would better spend his time continuing to *tunnel*. We *here* will examine the matters of faith and Truth."

Keesh nodded, a sickly grin on his face, and exited the chamber politely while the Elders continued their private discussions. Frustrated as he walked back to the Resource Tube, he knew the old people in the Council had no idea what *Vac* might actually mean, but he had been looking forward to discovering exactly that. *I can prove it is a physical reality, but they don't want to know!* Having come into the meeting fearing condemnation and maybe even Reprocessing for his discovery, here he was, still alive. But the universal condemnation evident in the frowning faces around that table as he left made him wonder how long that life would last.

AFTER THE COUNCIL MEETING, JOLAN KEESH RETURNED to his office in a niche cave in the Resource Tube, where Ledd Mernan was already busy modifying a smallprobe for the anticipated task. "How'd it go, boss?" he asked. Dressed in a light red skintight work suit, Ledd had been the one to crawl Up the farthest, in their previous explorations.

"We have a no-go, Ledd," Keesh responded, frowning. "Elder Meish doesn't believe our instruments. His religion says that Vac is a concept, not a place." He sighed. "Damn superstitions, anyhow!

"If their concerns were only about sealing off Community tunnels from airless voids, knowing that Vac is probably just a large void, I could understand. But to deny the instruments that we use every day to plan melts, that's just ridiculous."

Ledd stopped his work and looked at his boss. "But you know, boss, that if we did encounter an airless void that was a lot bigger than Community, it could take out all our atmosphere, kill us all." It was as much question as statement.

Shaking his head, Keesh said, "Well, we know the gas laws, don't we? Our smallprobe is only ten centimeters in diameter; a hole that size would require millennia to drain our air out, even if Creator wasn't always generating new oxygen through porous walls in the Air Hallways. And besides, we can always slap a patch over the hole. We don't want another Death Tube experience, do we?"

Ledd nodded, frowning. The Death Tube tragedy occurred several years before, when a tunneler team burrowed into a void inexplicably filled with methane gas, asphyxiating a dozen men. Keesh had been on another project that day or he himself would have been on site. Fortunately that doomed crew had thoughtfully —as required—first provided a sealant bulkhead in the tunnel behind them, saving many lives, if not their own. For this reason, the Council had mandated that sealant bulkheads of appropriate sizes be on site for immediate use if needed, and Keesh was more than happy to comply.

CHAPTER FOURTEEN

Newly promoted General Creesile, head of the Mothersmen Army, stood on a pier at the northern shore of Lake Roos, watching with satisfaction as his troops boarded the oared barges. It was noon, and the last of the supply crates were being hoisted onto the towed barges farthest out, their pointed and sloped prows still high out of the water. *They will be lower once the rowers board*, he thought. *Too bad we're not like the sailors on the Cold Sea, using sails.* But Motherland had fought very few battles on its rivers, and so never needed a riverine navy, and the available winds would never move such loads as his. Besides, there were those two damned sets of rapids requiring portage.

Creesile needed men for rowing the boats as well as for fighting. He had asked for more, but Miran Kech was reluctant to commit more than the six thousand. *The priest wants to keep a lot of troops in Mother's City for some reason. Might he be planning something, or preparing for something?* Politics were not his concern, so Creesile focused his attention on the war at hand.

So we go to war with the army we have, he mused, *not the army we might want. Although...* "This is the largest invasion fleet and ground army ever assembled in Motherland," he told his adjutant, Lt. Colonel Enlil, and aide-de-camp, Major Gromm. "We will take

ShadowFall without any problem, be assured. As ordered by Lord Miran Kech and our Mother Herself, we will gather additional men and supplies as we advance northward through the other Sisterdoms.

"Major Gromm, once we rendezvous with other troops at Stone Pyramid, you will command four thousand of the northern troops along the Main Road. Prepare for a direct assault at the border with archers, spearmen, catapults, and fire-bellows. After the final portage, I will be there aboard the leading barge, with assault troops and catapults, five klicks to the east. We will coordinate our pincer attack. Lt. Colonel Enlil's unloaded troops will flank any defenders and annihilate them. We will then lay siege to the ShadowFall palace itself, within a day after crossing their border." In his mind, Creesile already imagined the final attack on the Palace of ShadowFall, visualizing the young, ripe princess at his feet, begging for mercy as he— Shaking off the fantasy, the general gave the Lt. Colonel a notebook with written instructions on how to proceed. He wanted no screwups.

"And keep in mind, Colonel, Major, as commanding officers we are promised the majority of the plunder at ShadowFall. And perhaps, on our return journeys, we may even want to stop in at other Princesses' palaces as well, for, ah, *contributions*. I am certain they will be most grateful for the destruction of such a troublesome Sisterdom." Creesile's mind kept returning to the young Princess, Perneptheranam. *I'll have to kill that damned priest, that Wakan Kech. And maybe that cursed little dark bird-rider of his, if he's there. But it will be a pleasure*! His memories of watching that bird-riding Thist creature killing so many normal Motherlanders in the Game last year brought a sneer of disgust to his face. *A monkey-man killing humans! Unacceptable.*

Lt. Colonel Enlil smiled, saluted, and boarded the second barge, already piled high with weapons and crowded with soldiers. Major Gromm likewise departed, to oversee the final loadings aboard the farthest barges.

In the privacy of his own cabin, General Creesile

checked a locked closet; there he saw his finest white godscloth clothing, the chest armor of hammered gold over thin iron, with matching crested gold helmet, golden greaves for his legs, and all the rest. *For the last day—the day of my victory over ShadowFall!* At the moment, his commander's outfit included the Mothersmen's ubiquitous black-leather vest and short red tunic, just like the thousands of men under his orders; only his polished gold helmet with feathered crest set him apart from his troops.

Walking outside the command tent, the General gazed out over the invasion fleet. Creesile observed with a wry smile that several large arrow-launching catapults stood out above the other materiel. Loaded with bundles of spear-sized springbow arrows, they took up space in which more conventional siege weapons would have fit. *Miran Kech made me build those things, for that damned bird-rider and his alleged flying god-machine,* he sneered. *I don't really believe that Rumi Similla's wild tales, but* he *does, and he's the boss. I'll have to see that thing first. If such a weapon existed, Wakan would have conquered all of Motherland by now. I know* I *would have! But Miran Kech's orders are orders!* Looking into the coming war's aftermath, he thought, *For now...*

Creesile's own barge craft featured a tall, roofed poop deck with his wooden throne-like captain's chair prominent. He smiled at the banners flying high in the breeze. *I am going to love this,* he thought. *And maybe with these victories and such a vast army at my command, all of it might qualify me to take the place of Miran Kech, that fat lump of a foreigner.* His mind afire, he mused, *Or maybe, a position even higher...?*

He would wait for the forward barges to depart, and then follow with his personal craft, now docked nearest his command tent. His crew would row his barge out in front of the flotilla and let him lead, as befitted the leader of the invasion force. With flags from the tall barge masts flying in the mild breeze, with trumpets ashore blaring out a martial tune, General Creesile would stand atop his platform and give the command to launch.

In his mind he could see four thousand troops cheering, eight hundred pairs of oars splashing down into the calm surface of Lake Roos. Within hours, the invasion of ShadowFall—the extinction of Princess Perneptheranam's Sisterdom—would begin!

CHAPTER FIFTEEN

From Una's altitude, Wakan Kech marveled again at the appearance of Motherland from above. "The Princess's palace is a child's toy house, Mother's River a tiny ditch," he said in awe, "and the people, like ants."

Thist smiled; he himself still often watched through the transparent walls in wonder at the diminutive features below. *Could one ever get tired of this view?* To Wakan Kech, he said, "We can reconnoiter as far south as you want, Wakan. And see what Miran Kech is up to." Wakan was already aware of Mothersmen troops gathering at Lake Roos but had no details of their numbers; his mirror-man system of communication was still developing and somewhat erratic. He'd had to provide two men at each relay point to ensure that the chain of flashes did not have a fatal break at any link but was yet unsure of the accuracy of the reports.

The priest said, "My new system of flash-signals is not yet working reliably. So it would be of great value to fly, unseen, above the Main Road to see if an invasion is coming this way yet. Miran has had plenty of time to prepare. I do not know what to expect of him, except that he is devious." *And clever,* he thought. *Dangerously clever! As is that General Creesile, the one who captured me and my expedition at Chi'a, all those years ago*

THOUGH HIS MEMORY, LIKE ALL KECH, WAS NEARLY perfect, Wakan deigned not to recall the circumstances under which Creesile and his warriors had attacked the peaceful High Antian expedition to the crystal dome–enclosed step pyramid at Chi'a in the Southern Dry Highlands. Nor the slaughter of the expedition's guards. He preferred to remember that Lieutenant Creesile, though vicious in battle, had treated his unarmed Kech civilian captives relatively well during the month of his army's return to Mother's City. That forced march home, though routine for the trained and tough Mothersmen, proved less tolerable for the soft civilians in tow.

The march was made more tolerable for Wakan, at least, because he was able to talk in pidgin Motherspeak to the elderly Grettoh, leader of the dozen Motherland scholars who accompanied Creesile's expedition, those men who recorded and cataloged natural resources, wildlife, and any potential slave populations. Wakan's exposure to ancient languages through a godsphere in his early years had paid off.

"Grettoh," Wakan had said during one short break, a week into their return, "What Creesile do with me? With us?" He waved a hand at his chained-up fellow Kech, now suffering from hunger, foot aches, sunburn, and insect bites. "What we do?"

"Wakan, my boy, whatever Mother wants, not Lieutenant Creesile. You belong to Her now." He looked around and then said quietly, "We all do. We are the personal property of the Mother. Like those *yamas* of yours that we feasted on—we are pets."

The Kech was agape. "She—*eat* us?"

Grettoh laughed. "Well, I suppose she could, but no. She tells us what we can do, where we live, and so on."

Wakan considered this. A woman, this Mother, with millions of subjects? How did she have the time? Grettoh answered his puzzled look before he could even formulate the question. "Mother has twelve princesses, many of them her own daughters, who divide up Motherland into Sisterdoms. Each princess administers a Sisterdom, with the help of advisors, nobles, priests, and other persons she selects."

As Grettoh explained in more and more detail the structure of power in Motherland, Wakan absorbed the strangeness of the land they were going to. And the fact that they were never going to return to their High Antis.

Every evening, as the Kech were allowed to eat together, Wakan talked to his countrymen. Because only Grettoh understood any of their High Antian tongue, Wakan kept a lookout for the old man as he spoke. "Fellow Kech, we are bound to a place called 'Motherland.' It is owned—*we* are owned—by a woman called 'Mother.' The only law there is Her word and Her wishes. They are a superstitious lot, believing that the Sun and the Moon are living beings called 'gods'; they have men called 'priests' who claim to speak to those gods. And of course, the word of the 'gods' always coincides with the words of the Mother. I repeat, they are superstitious, not rational as are we. I believe their ignorance can give us the ability to achieve high positions in their world of the bottomlands we are being taken to.

"We are more educated than most of these men who captured us. We all can read several languages; we know mathematics and geoms. We have studied the Sun and Moon and stars. And of equal importance, we have studied much of the true history of the ancients. We know about political strife, and civil war, and the machinations of the old monarchies that ruined the world. We know about The Ice crushing ancient cities, and about the Thousand Year Rain that drowned many of the ancients before they departed the whole round world." His Kech friends were shaking their heads, finding it hard to believe that civilized people anywhere could be so ignorant.

"And so I will propose to this Mother, when we meet her, that each of us is a valuable resource of utmost worth not only to her, but to each of her princesses, that with our knowledge of ancient ways, other ways, we can make Motherland stronger, and wealthier. And, of course, Her.

"But—and this is most important—we have to keep the precise location and details of our High Antis from these bottomlanders. I have already told this Grettoh that outsiders can't breathe our air, that we have to prepare certain herbs and potions ourselves, to survive there. And I added tales of savage cannibals along the difficult roads and through the jungles. We all have to keep them away from our homeland. They don't sail the seas, so that helps us.

"One other thing—they can never know how to construct springbows. We will keep those secrets among ourselves. We may need them someday." Wakan knew that only a few of his fellow Kech had ever paid attention to the minutiae of preparing the godsmetal arcs for use as powerful compound crossbows called springbows. He recalled that Miran, always the more scholarly type than a hands-on researcher, had never learned the hows and whys of godsmetal smithing and forging, always preferring philosophy over physical labor. Thinking over his friend's decline in the years since their capture, he thought, *And lounging around, rather than exercising or practicing martial arts, tells on a man. Now, Miran's years of lassitude show up in his belly!*

INTERLUDE

F lying above the road, Thusk instructed Una to stay invisible, a hundred meters up, so as not to create any breezes or dust devil vortices below them that might betray their presence. As long as they saw no massed armies, they flew fast, all the way through the Sisterdom of Stone Pyramid and into its southern neighbor, Trader Plains, taking less than half an hour to traverse the five hundred kilometers.

"So far, nothing but a few travelers and wagons along the way," Wakan said. "With the harvests in and Season Cold beginning, people are staying home. I would have expected more trade-goods traffic, though. Or"—he switched to silent thought—*or maybe trade has been halted for easier movement of marching troops? Where would I assemble soldiers, were I my brother Miran and I wanting to attack northward?* As if in answer to his unspoken question, the shimmering waters of Lake Roos appeared in front of them.

"Thusk!" Wakan shouted. "This is Lake Roos! Please fly around to the towns along the western shore. I think I might know where Miran is bringing his armies." Within minutes, below them, Wakan and his two compatriots witnessed an awesome—if ominous—panorama of military might. Eight rectangular barges lay docked alongside three long piers; several craft at the pier's end were in process of being loaded with a variety of boxes, cartons, and what appeared to be catapults of some kind. The barges nearest the shore end of the piers were being filled from countless rows of men in black leather armor, their polished spearpoints reflecting the noontime sunlight like waves upon the lake. Thusk stopped above the scene while Wakan began counting the troops.

Thist spoke up. "Wakan, no need to do that yourself. Watch." He instructed Una to do an inventory of the men and materiel now loading at the docks.

"Sire Thist, eight transport barges are being prepared below us, on three piers. Each vessel is powered by one hundred rowers who are at present unarmed. The military men below—armed with spears, swords, and bows—number four thousand, three hundred and twenty two, under arms. There are several hundred people in support roles but without weapons. Of the eight barges, six are now being boarded by troops. Two other barges are being loaded with equipment. And Sire, on the one barge there are two projectile launchers, and bundles of borophene arrows. At present those arrows are not loaded and therefore cannot be launched quickly, so it is safe to approach closer."

"Damn!" Thist shouted. "Over four thousand! And borophene arrows! That Rumi Similla must have told Miran Kech about Una, about us! Una, back away and go up a hundred meters." As their craft accelerated upward, to Thusk and Wakan he asked, "What do we do now? Those catapults will be deadly to us if they load the arrows on them."

Thusk thought a moment. "Thist, didn't you have an idea when we were with Odel up there in God's Country, about dropping things from the sky, on targets on the ground?"

Wakan smiled in surprise. "Of course! Throwing out big rocks on those barges! From this height they would sink immediately." Looking at Thusk, he said, "Is it possible to go right now and get some stones, come back here and sink this fleet before they can get across

Lake Roos and start up the Mother's River to ShadowFall?"

But when Una was given the order to scan for such stones to carry out the preemptive strike, the DI replied, "Sire Thusk, this DI's programming prevents any aggressive actions that could knowingly harm human beings. Knowing that your intention is to destroy the barges and kill the humans aboard them is prevented by overrides that cannot be bypassed; this DI will not, cannot, proceed as directed."

Thusk was astounded at Una's refusal. "You mean, you will never be a weapon of war? Even to prevent the unlawful and destructive invasion of peaceful ShadowFall, the murder of its people? I can't believe that, Una. We are only trying to defend ourselves."

"Sire Thusk, the programming is explicit and purposeful: this survey craft will not be employed in knowingly causing the injury or death of human beings."

At first, Thist was furious, but calmed down and became cautious. "Una, may we continue our surveillance of the troops and barges below, and their progress toward ShadowFall?" Wakan, too, was worried about the answer to that question. Who would have thought that the ancients, those violent people whose wars had killed many millions before The Ice came, would put such restrictions upon one of their marvelous machines, such a potent weapon for war? *But this Una is telling us that it is* not *a weapon, after all!*

"Sire Thist, so long as your direct actions do not involve the projected injury or death of another human, this DI will follow all your commands to the extent possible."

Thinking that Una might be offering a circuitous way around its explicit peaceful instructions, Thusk considered another possibility. "Una, if those barges were empty of people, would you allow us to destroy them by dropping stones on them?" He wanted to see if his hunch was correct, if Una was being purely literal or if it would accept a compromise proposal.

Una did not answer for a full half second, an eternity of contemplation for a qomp operating at the highest speed and most multiple parallel channels the human race had ever created. "Sire Thusk, that action can only be effectuated if sensor scans reveal that no human being will be injured or killed as a result. That course of action will only be permitted to occur based on sensor scans immediately prior to a planned attack."

"Good enough, Una," Thusk said, his suspicion confirmed. *I will have to parse Una's statements very closely from now on,* he thought. *Maybe a DI machine can be persuaded away from its programming, after all?* "Another question, then: During our journey down here from ShadowFall, did you detect any stones large enough to sink a barge from whatever altitude you need to attain yet still small enough that we three men—Wakan, Thist, and myself—can carry aboard?"

Una answered affirmatively, and upon Thusk's command, flew fifty kilometers northeast, landing in an open field of scattered boulders. Wakan recognized them as stones carried by extreme flooding in ancient times, when ice dams in the Dark Highlands broke and washed away entire mountains; such glacial erratics were strewn along the river all the way back to ShadowFall. With Wakan on one side and the two small men on the other, they were able to heft eight relatively round rocks into Una's cabin. "These are about a hundred pounds each," Wakan said, rubbing his back. "Anything heavier, we'd need a larger crew." Muscles and backs aching, Thist and Thusk agreed; they hadn't done any lifting of any consequence in a long time.

Back over the troop assembly area at the docks of Lake Roos, Thusk explained a command he was planning to give their flying machine. "Una, I want you just to fly low over then, very swiftly, enough to give them a fright, make them evacuate the barges, get them back from the docks safely onto the shore. Go green!"

The craft immediately became visible, a large green cylinder hundreds of meters above them, now diving toward the barges containing the supplies. Una's crew yelped in delight as the Mothersmen scattered, jumping off the barge onto the pier, some diving into the water as the strange object flew just meters above their heads.

Thusk had an idea: "Una, let the white pilot be uncovered, and let me speak on the loud-voice."

Ashore again for final review of the preparations, General Creesile heard the noise outside and stepped from his tent to see what was happening. In disbelief he saw a big green cylinder swooping down from the sky, almost colliding with the masts of his supply barges, then circling back over his boarded troops, his men throwing down their spears and running back to shore. One swoop brought the flying thing just ten or so meters from his own inland position; it appeared to be operated by a white-faced *something* atop and near the front of it. "What in Mother's name is that?" he shouted. "Colonel! Shoot it down, whatever it is!"

Over the loud-voice, Una's speakers broadcast Thusk's disguised voice, in an authoritative accent understood by all Motherlanders as that of Mother's Court: "THIS IS MOTHER MESSINEX! ALL YOU SOLDIERS! YOU MUST LEAVE THESE BOATS AND DOCKS IMMEDIATELY! YOU HAVE NO DEFENSES! YOU HAVE TWO MINUTES!" Below them, Una's crew could see that panicked troops were leaving their barges and heading for shore as commanded, in a distinctly un-military panic.

Thusk was delighted. "Una, are any of the barges now unoccupied? Can we drop some rocks on any?"

"Sire Thusk, the outermost barge, the one containing the catapults and bundles of borophene arrows, is now free of humans. Its immediate destruction will cause no injury or death."

"Then go up as high as needed, open the cabin door, and roll to the side so that one of our rocks can hit that barge in a place that will sink it." At once, the men felt

Una accelerate; its sudden stop made them momentarily lighter, but they were able to maintain their balance by grasping onto the two cabin chairs.

"Sires, stand by for door opening and rolling. Please ensure you are safely secured and that the stone you wish dropped is adjacent to the door."

The crew ready, Una rolled to one side, simultaneously opening the cabin door. The men saw that they were at an altitude of about three hundred meters, the barges below them appearing as toy boats, with the still-panicked troops scattering off the piers like ants from an overturned anthill. The rock slid out Una's door and began its fall, as the craft righted itself. "Follow it, Una!" Thist cried. "On your screens!"

Una's video screen followed the rock-bomb as it headed toward the barge, the intended impact point becoming apparent in the last few seconds—an open hatch presumably leading to cargo space belowdecks. The image quickly zoomed back, showing the damaged barge suddenly shaking, then listing as it took aboard water below. In less than a minute, the barge sank below the water, its catapults disappearing from view, and many crates and cartons popping up, breaking the surface to float. "It worked, Una, it worked!" Thist shouted. "Let's find another one!"

Using the loud-voice, Thusk announced, "This is just the first sinking! Every barge will be sunk! Leave now and return to your homes!"

From his vantage point ashore General Creesile listened in shock as the incredibly loud voice of—*what, a god?*—roared out a threat to his troops; then watched in horror as something dark fell from the sky, smashing into the farthest barge. Dropping his jaw, he groaned as that barge—*All those supplies, those catapults!*—sank dockside. All around him, his troops were still running from their barges, down the pier, toward the shore. Gathering up his shaken confidence, he shouted again, "Colonel! Enlil! Stop these men from retreating! Kill the one in front; the others will stop!"

Drawing his own sword, the General brandished it as the first few soldiers approached him, fear in their eyes, defeat in their horrified expressions. "I don't care what that—*thing*—is," he yelled, "but you are Mothersmen! We have never been defeated, and we won't be now! Stand your ground!' His display of bravado, and of his large swinging sword, brought the front ranks of runners to a halt. A few sheepishly saluted their commander, turning to look over their shoulders at the big green flying thing, as if deciding which threat was the worse.

Meanwhile, Una's rock bombs continued their devastation; within minutes all the supply barges were punched through and sunk, adding their unsecured cargoes to the flotilla of junk now clogging the waterway between the parallel piers. One supply barge, heavily loaded and very securely fastened to its dock, pulled that structure over sideways and into Lake Roos' waters as it sank, blocking the troop barges farther up the pier, nearer the shore. The white-pilot kept on with its sky-splitting voice: "Leave, and you will not be harmed! Mother Messinex says put down your weapons and return home! Your commanders are traitors to the Motherland!"

General Creesile, rounding up a squad of braver soldiers, ran down the pier to assess the damage and to engage the green flying thing if possible. Colonel Enlil, puffing, caught up with him. "Sir," he yelled over the pandemonium of the sky-thing's shouting and the tread of returning troops, "what is that thing?"

From that Rumi Similla's description of her encounter with the dark dwarf Rist and his machine up in ShadowFall, Creesile finally realized what the Una was. Shaking his head in anger, he raised his sword skyward at the spiraling shape. "That is the *thing* we brought those catapults for," he said. He pointed then toward the end of the pier where the weapons barge was now out of sight below the waves. "The woman's story was true. The little bastard must have lived, and is now flying it against us!"

Overhead, Thusk was arguing with Una: "Let's drop the rest of the rocks, sink all those boats!"

"Sire Thess, there are still humans aboard the barges. This DI cannot follow that command."

"Then let me speak even louder to those troops." As Una complied, Thusk yelled out in a voice louder than thunder, just under a volume that would have damaged eardrums below. "THIS IS YOUR LAST WARNING. I AM GOING TO SINK ALL OF THE BARGES AND OTHER BOATS HERE. RUN AND TELL THAT TRAITOR MIRAN KECH THAT HIS PLANS HAVE BEEN FOILED. NOW, *LEAVE*!"

From above, Una's crew watched as most of the troops did depart, even over the threats of their commander and other officers. As soon as a barge was declared a safe target, Una did a quick altitude increase followed by a roll and another discharge. As the last stone fell, Wakan said, "Thusk, I think we should go now. I believe that Miran Kech won't be able to reassemble this many troops again for some weeks." As he watched the ants below begin to assemble into squares, and hear their officers bellowing orders, he said, "Yet they all still live, and will be coming our way eventually."

Thusk said, "Una, take us back to ShadowFall, but this time, across Lake Roos and north by way of the river." He looked at Thist and Wakan. "We need to plan how to stop these thousands of soldiers from ever getting close to us."

CHAPTER SEVENTEEN

Miran Kech was apoplectic, screaming at the two messengers who had just arrived by Creesile's innovative nonstop "carriage express," bringing him news of General Creesile's defeat at Lake Roos the day before. Trembling, the exhausted soldiers tried to maintain their dignity in the face of the priest's rage, each hoping that he would be spared. They knew Lord Kech's reputation for savage treatment of underlings.

"You are telling me that a flying machine *spoke* to you all and dropped *rocks* from the sky? And you all just ran away and let it sink nearly all of our barges? All that equipment? All those men? How many troops did we lose?" *So Rumi's tales were true, and Wakan is fighting us with a flying god-machine! Damn him!*

"Lord Kech," the messenger began as he wiped the dirt of the road from his brow, "but we lost no men. General Creesile said…"

"Shut up, soldier!" Miran screeched. Then, motioning to a guard: "Take this noisy one, and cut out his tongue." As the shocked messenger was taken away, shouting, the priest said, "Tie him up and let him bleed out; nail him to a T-cross in front of the palace, for all to see what happens to cowards." A muffled scream told the other soldier that his fellow messenger had been mutilated as ordered. He did not turn to watch.

The remaining messenger bowed to Miran, holding back his rage and fear at the way his colleague was treated, hoping to avoid that same fate himself. Miran sneered, "You may return to the general and tell him I am disappointed that he was not properly prepared for the attack of the god-machine. That my Rumi Similla had told him how to kill it, but he was not listening." As the soldier bowed and turned in relief to leave, the priest summoned other guards. "This one, take off his left little finger—now! I will not have such incompetence; I will punish hands that should have been killing enemies of Motherland." Two guards seized the soldier, one doing the deed with his service knife. As the man stifled a scream, Miran said, "Guards, you may staunch his wound and bind him up for his return trip. I never want to see him again. And find another messenger to accompany him back to Creesile immediately, with my new orders."

Barges sunk, supplies lost, days wasted! Miran raged in thought. *But no men killed? Are those little men not killers? But that Rist killed a dozen in the Game!* He would have to consider the significance of that information; something was definitely missing. Miran hated the slow communication between himself and that idiot Creesile. *I promoted the bastard because he had some imagination, new ways of doing his job. I wish he had more ideas like his "carriage express."*

Creesile's communication innovation for the planned ShadowFall campaign had been to take a two-man, two-wheeled carriage drawn by one horse, outfitting it so that while one drove the horse, the other stretched out on a padded horizontal seat beside him. With horse-changing stations at every thirty to forty kilometers and by changing positions in the cart, a messenger team could travel about three hundred kilometers per day, nearly nonstop. Putting Lake Roos' embarkation docks a day away and ShadowFall itself less than three. *Of course, we have to use Mother's precious horses, and ride them hard. I wish we could have more of the creatures.* He knew that previous Mothers had husbanded the equines carefully, unsuccessfully trying to breed herds of them, ultimately using the few offspring only for decorative and ceremonial purposes, restricted to be ridden by only a hundred or fewer privileged horsemen. *So I run half of them into the ground in the next month, so what? ShadowFall's fall will be more than worth it.*

As Miran began to dictate the new written orders to his scribe, he called for Rumi Similla, and began thinking about how to defeat his old mentor and one-time friend, Wakan Kech. *Reviewing everything you know about your enemy is the key to beating him,* he mused. *This Rumi woman has worked around Wakan for all of his five years at ShadowFall, so her insights on his recent actions should be useful. But me, me, I have known him all my life!*

Miran recalled from his early childhood in their home city of Coos in the High Antis that his cousin Wakan was the most favored of all the boys: "Wakan is so tall" the women said. "And so handsome." "I will ask that he be my mate when he is of age." Miran's excelling at the boomerang, the bow and arrow, always placing first in wrestling, all that was bad enough if you were a frail boy five years younger than the mighty Wakan, wanting to be as good as he. But later in life, when Wakan also excelled in militia training, in the Elder Council discussions, and the other activities that distinguished a man from a boy, outperforming everyone else—that was when Miran began not to admire his older cousin but to envy him. Try as he might, Miran could never match Wakan's physique, his personality or achievements, his leadership or his in-depth knowledge in a wide range of studies. Wakan had praised Miran of course, when the younger boy himself had finally made it into the Kech. "I always knew you had it in you," Wakan had said, "And I look forward to our adventures together."

Some adventure! Miran thought. *Had we stayed home in our high valleys, protected by our beautiful snowcapped mountains, we wouldn't be at war with each other now!*

Only a year after Miran reached Kech-hood, the fifth-year priest Wakan had convinced the Elder Council to sponsor an expedition to the far north, in search of legendary crystal domes. Meeting in a large, bright, gaslit and warmed room in the stone temple in their ancient capital city of Coos, the aged leaders of the confederation of High Antian nations, the Elder Council, had met to hear the young priest's proposal.

"Elders," Wakan said to the hooded and dark-robed men. "Travelers from the far north, seafarers, have brought tales of marvelous crystal domes, many of them, in a land called Chi'a inhabited only by a few ignorant savages. Inside these domes are ancient buildings, pyramids and temples. The domes loud-speak to any visitor, but no one knows the language and no one knows how to enter and explore the interiors. They are impossible to break into, obviously built by the ancients with their impossible science."

Wakan exhibited a beautiful line drawing, a large, detailed map painted on a cured white yama skin, stretched and mounted on a wooden frame. "From the stories these people tell, a small expedition could sail from any of our coastal towns here on the Lower Sea, take what they call 'trade winds,' and land at a bay in this land of Chi'a. A few hundred kilometers inland, to the east, lie at least twenty of these domes and whatever ancient treasures they may contain."

"And if you reach one of these domes, young Wakan," asked a wrinkled old man, the Councilor from his own city of Suyo, "why do you think you might be able to open it, when apparently others have failed since ancient times? Have you secret knowledge?"

Wakan jerked his head back but maintained his

composure. Accusations of unshared knowledge were tantamount to treason in the open societies of the High Antis. Any such assertion had to be corrected at once, lest the priest's reputation—and position—be diminished. A severe violation could even mean exile, which in the harsh environment of the High Antis always meant a lonely death. Miran smiled at that memory of Wakan at that crucial tipping point. *If only...*

"Lord Councilor," Wakan had replied, with as much dignity as he could maintain in the face of such an unexpected challenge to his assertions, "I have long studied the crystal globes, the godspheres, that are stored in the libraries here in Coos, those over in Roqq, and even distant small villages along the low coast. Alone among all the Kech, I believe, I have been able to activate two—"

"Out of the hundreds of the useless things," another Councilor said, chuckling.

"I repeat, *two*," Wakan continued, "and one of those contained language lessons from ancient times. Because of my curiosity, I have learned to speak several of those tongues, and even to read those that had, or may still have, readable markings. Apparently in ancient times, many peoples inhabited the lowlands around us, speaking many tongues. Among those I studied was ancient Quechua, which I believe was the mother tongue of our own mountainous civilization before The Thousand Year Rain and The Ice destroyed it."

The eighteen Councilors murmured down his dissertation; they'd heard much of it before. Most of what he was saying was repetition of the dissertation that had won him his coveted Kech status five years before, and every Elder, as a matter of course, possessed an almost perfect memory, "etched in stone" as the saying went.

"Wakan," his own city's councilor said in a conciliatory tone, "how were you able to make the two godspheres speak? Many have tried but only yourself and very few others have ever brought them to life."

Wakan sighed; he had answered that question five years ago. He knew his two explanations would have to fit perfectly, or neither would be believed. "Lord Councilor, somehow the ancients provided that only the touch—or perhaps the sweat, the 'aura,' or maybe just the eyes or brain—of a particular individual could access their information. As you know, the ones that I opened, others couldn't, and the ones others opened, I could not. And there seems to be a time period associated with some of them; they may only open at certain seasons, specified times, or under other conditions we have not been able to establish. Our own written history—coded in our *keepo* cords—tells us that thousands of years ago, a few godspheres enabled our ancestors to survive The Ice and the rain, teaching them how to write, and to shape stoneworks equal to those huge eroded sites in our own city here. Then later on, other godspheres taught us metalworking and healing. And just a hundred years ago, we finally saw some of the true history of how the ancients died, and what the whole round Earth itself really is. The few spheres that have been opened recently revealed to us useful information from those ancients, whoever they were. Our science, our engineering, our godscloth tools, our springbow technology—all of these we never would have achieved on our own.

"I maintain that the godspheres opening when they did, teaching me ancient languages, means that the wisdom of the ancients intends for me, for our nation, to explore the other lands." *And so, by sheerest luck, Wakan got his wish, dragging me and many other Kech along on that planned year-long journey. And changed our lives.*

Part of the trip had been exhilarating—down from the mountains, over the

Western Drylands, and to the Lower Sea, so called because an obviously ancient shoreline, hundreds of meters above the present sea level, showed unmistakable signs of the past. Extensive mounds of mud up on the ancient shorelines were actually, some local Kech maintained, the ruins of forgotten cities, now just vast expanses of dried-up land, good only for the excavation of godscloth and various ancient curiosities. Miran hadn't cared; he loved the idea of going to sea, traveling to an unknown world. And he liked being with Wakan, learning from him, talking to him about esoteric subjects. Back then he still admired his cousin even though the aspects of jealousy were already beginning to make him less friendly to Wakan.

But I was a Kech priest, too, by then, and determined to return to the High Antis with discoveries of my own, new knowledge that would be attributed to me. I wanted the women to want me *to father their children!*

Miran found it strange that all these memories should surface now, when he was planning the death of Wakan Kech. *They don't tell me anything about Wakan,* he thought. *But only about* me, *how I always reacted to Wakan's leadership,* his *actions. And so here I am, today, doing the same thing all over again! I need to get over my obsession with him, lest it cloud my judgment, my plans.*

Putting his old frenemy out of his mind for the moment as he waited for Rumi to come to his chamber, Miran poured himself a Three Rivers vintage wine, one from the vineyards that he had helped Princess Messinex maintain during his years as her advisor in that Sisterdom. The wine was sweet, *As was the Princess,* he thought, remembering their first kiss, their first night in bed together. *She is still beautiful, but now that she is Mother, she has her pick of all men in Motherland.* Knowing that she would soon begin to produce heirs with disposable men, as had her own Lordess Mother, Miran thought it best never again to become physically intimate with Messinex; of course, he could not refuse a royal command should she wish. Still, he could feel a physical reaction when bringing up warm memories with the Princess, and he sighed with thoughts of what might have been. *If Wakan wasn't always so damned wise!*

As one of Wakan's more fortunate companions on that ill-fated trip to the crystal domes of Chi'a, Miran had survived with his manhood intact. He shuddered to think of life as a eunuch, one that nearly all foreign captives of Mothersmen were fated to endure—if they even lived after the brutal butchery.

On that fateful morning twenty years ago, after a weeks-long sailing journey up the coast and a grueling month-long trek eastward across hundreds of kilometers of scrub jungle, Miran, Wakan, twenty other Kech, their porters, cooks, pack yamas, and their company of fifteen soldiers, had all arrived at the huge crystal dome enclosing a stepped pyramid. The dome itself was spectacular: at least thirty meters high at the top, rising far above the stunted jungle growth that crept up to the very edge of the dome, the ellipsoidal crystal measured two hundred meters in its major axis.

The stone pyramid inside it was like nothing in the High Antis or any surrounding country, not even in the ancient ruins scattered in their mountains and valleys. As the Kech were able to measure from outside the dome with their surveying instruments, the stepped pyramid comprised nine levels, their tiers reducing in size from the lowest to the highest. A rectangular stone building, possibly a temple of some kind, sat atop the structure. And on each of the four sides of the pyramid, a two-meter-wide staircase provided a walkway from the ground to the temple, their three hundred and sixty-four steps obviously correlating to the number of days in a year. At the bottom of each staircase, on either side, a large carved serpent head presented a fearsome visage.

At what appeared to be a sheltered entrance to the interior of the crystal dome—a rectangular inset in the dome itself—a plethora of carved and colored hand-sized markings of some kind on an opaque wall, written in indecipherable ancient languages, proclaimed an unknown message. As the Kech stepped into the shelter, the pleasant voice of a young woman began speaking. Nobody, not even the great translator and scholar, Wakan, understood a word of it, spoken or written. No source of the voice could be located, but it was activated only when a person stepped inside the niche entrance.

Two days passed while the Kech did everything in their power to get inside the crystal dome. Nothing worked—springbow arrows, hammers, fire-makers, none made a scratch. At a group gathering the second evening, Wakan told his fellow scholars, "This transparent material that we are calling 'crystal' seems to have the same properties as the godspheres we have discovered back in the High Antis—cool to the touch, unscratchable, unheatable, unmeltable, unbreakable. Totally inert, yet we can see through it like clear air."

As the evening sun sat over the surrounding forest of small trees, the chief scholar went on, "Obviously, the contrast between the near-magical crystal dome and the less sophisticated stone pyramid inside, means that the ancients intended to protect the pyramid. I conclude from this that the pyramid is much older than the people we call 'ancient' today. Maybe by thousands of years."

A hubbub of voices erupted. "You are saying that there were *ancienter* ancients?" Laughter ensued, as did friendly arguments among the varied experts. Over much wine and food during the rest of the evening, Wakan gently guided the discussions until, as usual, he convinced the others that his idea was indeed theirs. The scribes recorded the observations and conclusions for taking back home.

Miran remembered it all in detail, a constant scab of memory to rip off when he needed to self-torment. *I was one who by then was questioning the wisdom—and the expense!—of this unsuccessful expedition. If we returned home with nothing more than drawings of pyramids and domes but no real knowledge of anything else, the Elder Council would not be pleased. We could all be stripped of our status, our funding, or even posted to the research station on the southern ice continent. I was by then not only disappointed in our lack of findings about this miserable North Country, but also in Wakan himself, who I now saw not as mentor or icon but as a self-important and weak man, with unforgivably poor judgment.* Miran's memories poured through his mind in torrents as he reluctantly recalled the other details of his capture and the beginnings of his life in Motherland.

The High Antian soldiers and other support staff had set up and maintained the camp, finding water a kilometer away in a deep cavity. The chief cook complained, "Lord Kech, we have to drop buckets down over a hundred meters to get water. We barely have enough rope to reach that far, all of it tied together. And our pulleys weren't built to hold even that much weight of rope. Either we find another source, or we need to ration water during our time here." And that was just the beginning of Wakan's—*of our!*—problems. Insect and animal life in the Chi'a was vicious; biting crawlers, biting flyers, biting diggers. Little pigs with sharp tusks made decent eating if they could be killed before they slit open your legs or impaled other parts if you were sitting or sleeping. *We lost three men to those damned little devils!*

And worst of all, we made no progress—no translation of the writing, no understanding of that soothing voice, no artifacts or information about what the place was who built it, or anything else. But then, at the end of our first week there, on Equal Day, there occurred one marvelous phenomenon that we all thought at the time made it worthwhile. I was waking from a nap when Wakan came, shouting, "Miran! Everybody! Come look! The pyramid is moving!"

What we saw then was amazing: sunlight and shadows had created sunlit triangles along the side of the raised walkway. As we watched, the shadows moved, creating more lit triangles, giving the illusion of a giant serpent crawling down the side of the staircase! As the shadows reached the bottom of the pyramid, the lit triangles completed the image, connecting the sinuous body with the carved head of the serpent at the bottom of the staircase. A marvelous display of the knowledge of solar positioning, the serpent image stayed in place for nearly an hour, at which time the shadow-creature began to shrink, from the top to the bottom, as if shortening itself, light finally surrendering to shadow…

"Incredible," Wakan whispered. "Those ancients knew so much. I wonder if—"

But before he could complete his sentence, the Mothersmen attacked.

CHAPTER EIGHTEEN

As he was reviewing the reports of the damaging aerial assault by the damnable big green flying machine, General Creesile, too, was thinking about events of that same fateful day at the crystal dome of the Chi'a pyramid, the same attack by the Mothersmen contingent. As a young officer it was he who led it.

Damn! If I had just ordered all those Keches killed or castrated at that time, how different Motherland would be today. I wouldn't be fighting that cursed Wakan, nor taking orders from that prig, Miran.

Lieutenant Creesile's mission had started out as an exciting adventure, he remembered; his first command, a hundred experienced Mothersmen, several dozen logistical support troops, and a dozen trained scholars, subject matter experts whose jobs it was to take notes, make maps, bring back specimens and artifacts. His orders from Mother's advisor: "Scale the Southern Highlands above Three Rivers. Find minerals, godscloth, food sources, useful artifacts—and slaves!" In the long history of Motherland, much conquest and plundering had occurred in the Western Dry Highlands, those regions easily marched to by gently sloping midlands and numerous valleys carved by long-forgotten rivers. The Southern Drylands had apparently not been a threat in centuries, so had not been explored or exploited; if they had, the records had been lost. So for the Lordess Mother and her chief advisor, it was a new place for exploration and exploitation. And a chance for Lieutenant Creesile to prove himself and to rise in the ranks of the Motherland Army.

The initial march of ten days from Mother's City proved uneventful—over decent roads through the Sisterdom of Three Rivers, a welcoming reception for them all by its late Princess Seelina, and a celebratory sendoff after replenishing their food and water. They then proceeded along the banks of the easternmost of the eponymous rivers, aptly named East River, until the place where that flowing water source emerged in full flow, gushing from between steep cliffs. Creesile made sure that his scribes recorded the impossibility of scaling the two hundred and fifty meters of vertical stone on either side of that torrent.

After that, the expeditionary force had to find other paths leading up the kilometers of slopes to the highlands, requiring an endless number of switchbacks, taking two strenuous weeks. Creesile and his men feared they might exhaust their supplies before the final barrier —scaling a three-hundred-meter vertical cliff that stretched from horizon to horizon. Fortunately, a last-ditch scouting party finally located slumped runoff gorges where millennia of wind and rain erosion had carved out reasonable slopes of displaced rocks and soil held in place by scrub bushes, providing easily accessible pathways to the top.

Creesile smiled at the memory, allowing himself to luxuriate in the fondness for his youthful career as an officer for Motherland. *We found that the Southern Highlands were not all that dry, thank First Mother!* Abundant fruit trees, fresh water ponds at the bottoms of deep holes, and a variety of small pig-like animals, sustained the expedition. While his scholars recorded voluminous notes on the flora and fauna of their explorations, he was dissatisfied; *Useless work*, he had thought scornfully. *Motherland will never expand upwards to this flat region; it's too hard to get here, and we have no idea what kinds of savages might be nearby. No, we are safer in our secure bottomlands; let the legendary wildmen keep this place!*

Then, damn it, my scouts found that strange pyramid, covered in that gods-know-what crystal. "Lieutenant Creesile, sir. Eight klicks ahead of us, due south, there is a huge clear dome. It covers a stepped pyramid."

"Well, soldier, did you climb on it? Is it valuable? Any artifacts?" His spirits risen, the young lieutenant hoped that this novel discovery would make his mark, maybe even be named after him? *The Lost Pyramid of Creesile—a Wonder of the World!*

"Sir, no sir. We only observed it from a distance, because..." He hesitated, obviously nervous about reporting bad news to his superior. "Because there are people around it. Armed men!"

Lieutenant Creesile had been surprised, but welcomed the opportunity to prove himself in combat. "How many, man? What kind of weapons, and how deployed?"

"Lieutenant, sir, the trees and brush grow right up to the dome. There is only one small clearing where the strangers have encamped. We counted fifteen tents and several dozen small pack animals, smaller than horses, in a corral of sorts. We saw at least twenty unarmed civilians in short robes; it looked like they were measuring around the pyramid from outside the dome. Then fifteen tall men in vest armor and helmets, carrying spears. Some of them had strapped across their backs what looked like metal bows and quivers of arrows. Like our own bows, but smaller, curved strangely, made of metal." Creesile considered the report. Even better for him, if they could capture those different kinds of weapons, he would gain further credit with the Mother. He could envision himself rising in rank, perhaps up to major, or someday, colonel...

"Their deployment?"

"Sir, all bunched up in that one clearing. Just a couple of lookouts. Not very professional."

Creesile figured that their opponents did not have a good concept of defense, not and be concentrated like that. *Unless those weapons of theirs are very effective?* He said to his sergeant, "Go with this scout. It appears that we have enough troops to surround their camp, with our archers in position. Kill all the warriors there at once, but capture the unarmed ones if possible; they may be slaves worth keeping. *Slaves themselves might pay for this mission!* he thought, *since we've found nothing else of note. I doubt if my new pyramid will be thought a sufficient return on the investment by the number scribblers in Mother's Palace.*

"Stay in the jungle and await my whistle command —archers shoot first, count the survivors, then a second volley. After that I will lead a massed charge, coming from all sides." The two soldiers left and began quietly making their ways toward the pyramid site, followed by their columns of men behind. Creesile told Grettoh, the leader of his civilians, to keep his scholars out of the fighting; they would be allowed to continue only after the enemy was annihilated.

From his vantage point a few hundred meters from the unknown warriors, Lieutenant Creesile watched the unexpected and fantastic display of sunlight and shadow on the pyramid, as the illusion of a creeping serpent of light stretched downward the length of the staircase. Amazed as he and his troops were at the sight, Creesile decided that this was the opportune time to attack, while the adversaries were also enchanted by the demonstration of ancient knowledge.

Creesile blew his attack whistle, and the Mothersmen archers let fly. Catching by surprise the High Antian contingent (as he later learned they called themselves), the tall springbowmen and spearmen were turning around at the screech of the whistle when the Mothersmen arrows found their marks. As the surviving Antians tried to rally, they realized they were surrounded on three sides by the unknown assailants. Bunching together in a square, spears outward—as was the custom in the limited warfare, mostly tribal feuds, encountered in their homeland—they braced for the inevitable mass assault on their precarious position. They had no shields, which Creesile found puzzling, but fortunate for himself.

Creesile whistled again, a series of broken tweets. Another volley of arrows followed the first, taking down half the remaining enemy. "This is too easy," the lieutenant said out loud, and whistled another signal for his troops to engage. "I will lead the charge myself, the only way to lead men, the only way to gain glory!" Shortsword raised high, with a hundred bloodthirsty warriors close behind him, he ran toward the half dozen stunned High Antians.

After the short battle was over, Creesile thought, *This was only a slaughter. But I killed the first enemy soldier hand-to-hand, and my men saw it!*

Creesile was surprised that none of the enemy civilians had resisted. "Back home," he told his sergeant, "I believe that all of our people would be fighting any foreigners who attacked without warning. But these ones are so passive, I wonder why they are here at all, in this hostile land. They don't appear to be natives, and we have not found any cities or even much in the way of ruins anywhere around since getting to the highlands."

Calling for his own civilian scholars, who by now had reached the site of the short battle, he said to their leader, Grettoh, a gray-haired man known to be interested in ancient writing and buildings, "Go see if you can talk to these olive-colored men in their robes.

Are they priests? Scholars? What? Their guard soldiers were brave enough and fought as well as you might expect. I need to know if these passive ones will make appropriate slaves."

Although he personally disapproved of the gruesome practice, Creesile ordered the troop medic to prepare the castration table. He despised watching men, their legs spread apart on that cutting board, be mutilated. *But those are my orders. If I refused to follow them, I would find myself spread-legged in the palace yards, awaiting that unkindest cut of all.*

Merciless in battle, as he had just demonstrated in front of his victorious men, he did not like to inflict unnecessary pain or death on captives who couldn't fight back. And aware of the possible adverse effect on his military reputation, nevertheless he ordered the medic to administer knockout herb anesthetics to the new slaves when the amputation procedures were carried out. Thinking of reasons—*not* excuses!—why he was so lenient a warrior, he would explain if necessary, that it would be challenge enough to lash up two dozen *healthy* men and drive them back the difficult hundreds of kilometers to Motherland. Waiting for newly emasculated, miserable slaves to be able to walk, to recover from the effects of the overwhelming pain and trauma of losing one's private parts, not to mention the practical difficulties in urination afterwards, all this would cause an unacceptable delay and would be a logistical nightmare. *So I am too benevolent to captives, it will be said. But those chair-sitters in the towers of Mother's Palace are not out here in the field where we have to make practical decisions every day. I'd like to take the ball-cutters to all of them someday!*

The High Antian civilians were all lightly chained, hands and feet, and those chains connected to one large chain stretched between two small trees. Creesile's lead scholar, Grettoh, walked along the length of the row of captives, staring at each as he passed by. Stripped to the waist, tall they were, and young, with lightly-colored skin, a kind of people he had never encountered in Mother's City. *I wonder where they are from?*

"Anybody here speak Mother's tongue?" The dour-faced men just stared at him, unresponsive. He tried several different Motherland dialects, but found no takers. "Too bad, boys," he said sadly, "if anybody here could talk like a civilized man, you might save your balls. But if we have to teach you how to speak, you'll only be fit to be eunuchs in the mines or the fields." As he turned to leave, Grettoh heard some mumblings. Looking back, he saw one chained man, a tall one, who was just standing up from where he'd been lying, propped up against the tree at one end of the chain of captives. A bruised, bleeding face showed that he must have fought back. *Brave one, that*, Grettoh thought, *if rather stupid to fight against such odds*! But what was he mumbling? The scholar stepped forward to hear more closely. "What are you saying, boy? Can you understand my words? What is your name?"

"I Wakan. Talk old Tupi. You words. Tupi. You." The captive raised a manacled hand, pointing to himself. "Me. Wakan. You?"

At which, Grettoh touched his own chest, then Wakan's. "Me Grettoh. You Wakan." The young man's eyes lit up.

"Wakan, boy," Grettoh grinned in relief, patting the bare shoulder of the puzzled young man. "You have just saved your manhood from going to the dogs. Literally."

The foreign youth smiled back. It was only later that he learned just how much he had to smile about.

CREESILE'S EXPEDITION SPENT A WEEK AROUND THE crystal-domed pyramid, puzzled at what it was, why the transparent dome around it was impenetrable, and what the young woman's loud-voice was saying any time a man walked into the niche. Neither Grettoh nor the other experts could explain why, except to speculate. "The dome material reminds us of the construction of the godspheres that have been found all over Motherland," Grettoh explained to the lieutenant and the cadre of Motherland scholars. "Except almost all of those are opaque and don't speak. They, too, can't be broken with hammers, or scorched with fire. We've tried everything on this dome, but can't even scratch it, just like those spheres. Our conclusion is that an ancient technology was used to preserve the even more ancient pyramid inside it. We guess, too, that the loud-voice is coming from some sort of device that speaks a repetitive message, but one that we don't understand. How that is done, we can't even begin to imagine. And why they went to so much trouble, we can't ever know. Maybe the structure was a religious artifact for them?"

Grettoh paused. "Lieutenant, I want to thank you again for forgoing castration of these Antian boys and men. As I told you, this Wakan one knows enough pidgin Motherspeak to get his information across to me, though it does take some time. We appear to have some common linguistic origin in a forgotten tongue called Tupi.

"He and the others were on a scholarly expedition from a land far south, the High Antis, in extremely high mountains where outsiders like us can't even breathe." Creesile frowned at that, but motioned for Grettoh to go on. "This Wakan and his companions are called 'Kech,' which means a sort of educated priest, not in a religious sense, closer to meaning 'trained and knowledgeable for public service.' They came to this site, months of travel from their homeland, purely for curiosity purposes. Their armed companions were meant only for protection against possible savages and animals."

"Grettoh," the lieutenant responded, "they must be a very wealthy and organized society to send this many people so far distant, just out of curiosity. Are you sure they weren't spying on Motherland, an advance party of invaders?"

"Lieutenant Creesile," Grettoh said, "I believe that if they had been spies, they wouldn't be out here in the open, just measuring that dome and its pyramid. They would have been sending out scouts closer to Motherland and lying in ambush for us. And those weapons the soldiers carried—the Wakan calls them 'springbows'—if they could have used those against us, if they hadn't been surprised, they could have killed our men from three hundred meters away. Those things are incredible."

Based on Grettoh's interactions with the Antian captives, they all appeared to be priestly scholars, with more education in diverse fields of knowledge than that most of his own Motherland troupe of experts, with information and skills that the Mother would find useful. And so Creesile had decided to return the scholars, untouched, to the Lordess Mother for Her final decision. *Damn that!* the General thought, shaking his head. Had he known back then that the Kech would all become senior advisors to Princesses and Mothers, he would have enjoyed their time on the castration bench. *Twenty years of misery for that one decision of mine!* And with old Grettoh dead for ten years now, the general had only himself to blame.

UPON HIS RETURN TO MOTHER'S CITY, LIEUTENANT Creesile had been called to report to the Lordess Mother's High Priest and Advisor, Seenpet Sar. In Sar's opulent chambers, his red godscloth-covered chair surrounded by bare-chested muscular young soldiers in the briefest of tunics, Creesile had been nervous, knowing the advisor's predilection for boys and men. He thought, *I am young, but not at all handsome, I've been told. Maybe I'm safe from this one.* What the lieutenant saw was a fat, bald and rather smelly old man, whose albino skin was wrinkled beyond belief. *He looks like a big worm, yet is the second most powerful person in Motherland.*

"Lieutenant Creesile," the white worm said in a surprisingly deep and masculine voice, "We welcome you home, and we celebrate your victory over the savages in the Southern Dry Highlands." Creesile bowed in the three intermediate positions that Sar's status demanded.

"We thank you for the volumes of information that your scholars gathered, and we are especially appreciative of the Kech-men you brought back. Some of them may be worth retaining their, their, manhood, should they all prove to be as resourceful as the one called Wakan."

The white worm loved to talk, Creesile remembered, *and what a voice he had!* The lieutenant has particularly enjoyed not only the praise for a mission well done, but the immediate promotion to captain, with all the benefits that conferred. *My own slave woman, my first. Etliean, she was something.* But her death in childbirth, as well as that of their girl child, had been a hard blow, and ever after he had only slaked his thirsts in the Palace's exclusive brothel.

And then there had been the day, just a short time later, when his Kech captives gained even more status than he, a loyal soldier of the Motherland, had attained by virtue of military service. The memory still grated.

"Lordess Mother," the white worm Sar had announced, "may I present our victorious Captain Creesile, his men, and his captives." Creesile and two of his commanders stood at attention with the twenty-four Kech behind them. *Our captives are in fine robes*, Creesile thought, *better looking than our leather armor! What's that worm Sar up to?*

From her throne, the Lordess Mother smiled at her audience. Not yet thirty years old, she had alabaster-smooth skin, deep green eyes, and long, spun-copper hair with seductive bangs, a long braid hanging behind her godscloth robes, shimmering material that barely concealed the curvature of impressive breasts. *A real beauty*, Captain Creesile thought, *but like a black-widow biter, a deadly one!* All Mothersmen knew the stories: if she chose a man for fun, that could be a glorious night, but one never to be spoken of again, upon pain of slow death. If she chose you for impregnation, then the next day you were slaughtered, perhaps quickly, perhaps not. So the captain avoided Her eyes.

"Ah, my Sar, thank you for these gifts. And you, too, Captain, of course. Now, either of you, who are these Kech-men, and why should I care about them? I have been told that they have not been emasculated, so obviously one or both of you think they are of more value than just as slaves for the mines or fields. Please enlighten me."

Sar nodded to Creesile, who made the three intermediate bows and nervously answered, "Lordess Mother, our scholar Grettoh found that one of them, a Wakan, could talk in pidgin Motherspeak."

The Lordess Mother interrupted, irritated. "Then speak, Grettoh. What did he say? What can he *do?*"

Grettoh, as a scholar unaware of the nuances of court protocol, answered the Mother directly, without honorifics. "On our trek back home, the man's vocabulary has increased remarkably. From our conversations, he and his companions were exploring our Southern Dry Highlands for pure curiosity, when we attacked. They are all from a far place called the High Antis, where, they say, life is difficult and only a few can survive the thin air. They each possess sophisticated education in arts and sciences, some of it beyond our own achievements. Or so they say. This Wakan one has impressed me with his knowledge of astronomy and geoms. Even claims to have knowledge of The Thousand Year Rain and of The Ice. But let him speak for himself, if he may."

And that was that, the general remembered. *Grettoh's sales pitch and then that tall, dark savage's demeanor, his carefully cultivated courtier accent— learned in only a matter of weeks!—and his patter of tales of legends, adventures, and the ancients, swept the Mother away!* Nothing like Wakan Kech, or like any of them, had ever been known before within Motherland, and they were an immediate sensation. Within months, a Kech had been gifted to each Sister and a cadre of them retained at the Mother's Palace. Foremost among them, of course, was that damned Wakan, whom she kept for herself.

As he had done daily for over twenty years, Creesile cursed himself for his softness toward those Kech captives. *Without their balls, they'd've been field hands, mine slaves, not pampered foreign know-it-alls! And of course, none of this rebellion would be going on!*

CHAPTER NINETEEN

General Creesile shouted angrily, "Damn that Miran Kech! How dare he murder and mutilate my men?" He was thinking, *Maybe I should just take my army back down to the Palace and grab that foreign priest, cut him in pieces in front of that degenerate court!* Then in a cooler line of thought, mumbled to himself, "But the Mother still has a hold on the populace. It would take more than my eight thousand fighters if She were to declare me in rebellion." *No, I will wait until the Northern Sisterdoms are under my control, then I will assess my chances.*

Looking out over the new troop barges under construction on Lake Roos, he thought, *This time, they are protected by massive weapons on the adjacent piers, the loaded and ready-to-fire catapults with bundles of those special arrows!* Presuming from its earlier actions that Wakan and his monkey-men and their big green flying machine could not or would not kill his soldiers, he felt confident that his original plan for invading ShadowFall would succeed. Though now delayed by nearly a month, he still entertained the vision of the lovely Princess Perneptheranam at his feet, begging seductively for mercy, with the headless body of that damned Wakan Kech lying nearby in a puddle of blood and those dwarfs from the highlands eviscerated and impaled on sticks. *I'll make them into tall men!*

Dismissing the messenger he had sent to Miran Kech, he called in the camp medic and ordered him to provide a prosthetic finger for the injured man. *Someday I will have him jam that ivory finger into Miran's eyes and gouge them out; then we will both have satisfaction!* But with hundreds of invasion issues facing him, with new troop transports, weapons, and materiel to make ready, the general soon put away thoughts of revenge and of passion, and calmly wrote out new orders for his subordinates to plan the subjugation of ShadowFall, now scheduled to begin in one month.

"COLONEL TREEGU REPORTING, SIR," THE GENERAL'S special operations officer saluted his superior as he entered the headquarters tent. Invited to sit across a field desk from General Creesile, Treegu was happy to see the general in a good mood, a genuine smile on a craggy face renowned for its array of sneers, grimaces, and other displays of displeasure. *It must be going well,* Treegu thought. *I hope the news I'm bringing makes him even happier.*

"How goes it this morning, Colonel? Any problems, any solutions?" Allowing himself a cigar, Creesile offered one to his subordinate, who graciously accepted it. The General was calm and in control of himself; so far, his men had quickly made up for last month's losses from that aerial attack, and the new anti-aerial weapons were keeping that god-machine away. *At least we've had no more of its nonsense!*

"Sir," the colonel began, his cigar smoke curling up toward the opening in the crown of Creesile's tent, "I would like to report on the surveillance teams that I sent all the way into ShadowFall, up the river, through the towns and villages, even to the Princess's palace itself."

"Go on, Colonel. I'm all ears." His thoughts were elsewhere: *Damn, but these cigars are good! I'm glad we have trade with that highland over the Cold Sea. A* quick thought, *Maybe we should invade that place someday? Why* pay *for such pleasures?*

"Sir, our teams, disguised as godscloth purchasers from other Sisterdoms, note that Wakan Kech has built tall wooden towers along the Main Road, and others scattered almost at random all over ShadowFall territory. For what purpose, they were unable to determine."

Creesile took a long puff of his cigar and replied, "Hmm. They do have a large forest north of their city, all the way up to the Dark Highlands, so there's a lot of available timber. But studying that Wakan's astute financial management of his Sisterdom tells me that this must represent a major defensive program. I mean, he doesn't even maintain a standing army like everyone else." *Not after he brutally put down that first uprising, six months into Pernie's reign, an attempted coup no doubt orchestrated by some Sister of hers.* Those painted images of a hundred rebels, impaled alive from asshole to mouth and planted on both sides of the Main Road as a forest of cruelty, had been distributed all over Motherland, a stark warning to any others so tempted that Princess Perneptheranam, though known to be benevolent in general, was not to be threatened. In response, it was also made widely known that Wakan Kech had reintroduced the ancient barbaric custom of sacrificing a young man at the beginning of Season Warm. *That was a master stroke of Wakan's,* Creesile thought, smiling at his own pun, *a primitive ceremony of seasonal celebration that at the same time demonstrates to the populace the power of their Princess. The man is just too damned perceptive, too smart. I'll have to kill him!*

Enjoying his own voice, Creesile said, "The other Sisters have a constant struggle to stay in power, to stay alive. They need their armies ready to put down internal rebellions at all times. But ShadowFall's strength, Wakan says, is in its people, and their ability to take up arms at a moment's notice, and even use all kinds of weapons. He calls it their 'militia.' After we take them over, maybe I will look into reorganizing other Sisterdoms that way. They will all save money, not having a standing army to be fed and housed—and feared. And of course *I* will pick those militia leaders. Loyal not to them, but to me."

Creesile could tell that his saboteur chief wasn't following his logic. *That's why I am a general, and he is only a colonel.* Returning to his original train of thought, he said to Treegu, "These towers, now, they are like a standing army of sorts, aren't they? They are permanent, they have no practical use that we can tell, and are certainly a huge expenditure for him. How tall are they, you say? And how many?"

Glad to be following his General's more reasonable requests, Treegu said, "Our teams estimate about fifteen to twenty meters tall, sir. They couldn't explore the whole Sisterdom, but best guess is that Wakan has built at least two dozen, maybe more."

Creesile blew out a cloud of smoke and stubbed out his odoriferous cigar. "Well, as long as the damned things don't jump up and fly at us, I won't be too concerned. If they are planning to use their springbowmen against us from up on top of them, we can just bypass them. We can let their men sit up there in the sky and starve, or send in teams of firethrowers at night and burn them down." He smiled, a predatory movement of lips and jaw that the colonel recognized at once, a familiar if disturbing countenance. "Just have a man or two keep an eye on a convenient tower. Whatever Wakan's planning to do with one, all the rest will be doing the same."

As Colonel Treegu took his leave, Colonel Enlil entered to report that all troop assignments had been made, that the fire-catapults had been loaded, this time with camouflaged tarps hiding them from above, and that the anti-aerial catapults would be the last weapons loaded. "They should protect us en route, up Mother's River."

Creesile called in other subordinates and had Enlil run through the planned invasion again, pointing out specifics of assignments, manpower, and objectives. This would be a daily practice until Embarkation Day. Reviewing the detailed deployments, the stages of the attack, the overwhelming resources at his command, the general felt more confident each day.

Wakan Kech will die! And Princess Pernie will be...mine!

CHAPTER TWENTY

After nonstop weeks of melting new tunnels in Infinite Rock, Jolan Keesh earned a respite from work, a reward he did not want to accept. His planned work of sending up the mini-robots just for testing the system and obtaining strata data had been found out and suspended shortly after he began, by almost violent objections from others of Elder Uise's fundamentalist denomination in Tura City, so he was expending his frustration by exceeding tunneling quotas. But now he had enforced leisure time on his hands and needed some activity outside of work.

Since as a Crèche baby he had no family, he used some of his time off to stop by the niche to check on the progress of the strange tall foundling, Mienne. It had been almost a month now, and he was hoping the Blindness was only a temporary condition for the poor child. But the Ugly Elder, Myuk, reported her lack of progress. "I am afraid that the child shows little talent. Being Blind, or almost completely so, is certainly a handicap. And being so tall, she doesn't fit well into our furniture or clothing. Where do you think she came from?"

Knowing where such dangerous speculations would lead, Keesh shook his head. "She fell down from a Tube slanting Upwards, so there must be others of her kind Up there, somewhere." Observing the look of disbelief on Elder Myuk's homely face, he spread his arms. "Look, I know that the priests say that talking about Up is forbidden, but don't you think our Mienne herself is proof enough that life does exist in that direction? I am only an engineer, not an Elder, but evidence is evidence." He paused, thinking. "Maybe Creator left certain things unsaid, some life unfound, mysteries that we People are supposed to solve ourselves, using our Creator-given brains, our senses, our tools?"

Elder Myuk nodded hesitantly. "Those questions have plagued us since Creation. We don't know why Creator did all She did. Why the big Ancient Ones all died in their Tubes, why we keep finding other Tubes to expand into." Here, she smiled, acknowledging Keesh's own discoveries of empty Tubes that had doubled the volume of Community. She thought, *If Keesh can find such Tubes as have never been known, perhaps he is indeed blessed by Creator with gifts of creativity and invention, and so should be heard, no matter our traditions.* She would bring up his speculations at the next Council meeting.

"I agree with you, Keesh. And I will support your theories about Vac to the Council at the next meeting." Keesh did not express an interest in seeing the tall girl, merely in finding out how she was doing, so Myuk made no effort to find Mienne and bring her out of the depths of the niche.

WITH WAYER CONSTANTLY AT HER SIDE, MIENNE quickly adjusted to the daily routine of the niche— awaken with the others (although she seldom slept as long as they, and never fell asleep as automatically), perform the exercise routine rituals, eat a modest meal, sweep the farthest reaches of the niche, empty the waste chamber pots from the many small rooms and their unfortunate inhabitants, and carry the collected wastes to Disposal, returning from Stores with baskets and bags of fruits, vegetables, and small amounts of pasty protein hash or chunks of greasy tube-ewe to feed herself and the others in the Niche. Plus whatever other chores the Ugly Elder could find for her to do, Blind as she was. Living in constant dimness, she eventually became able to distinguish shapes and motion from the dark red shadows, and Wayer was always there to guide her and to read the wall signs when needed. Gradually, Mienne adapted, and her life in Community became a kind of near normal for a Blind girl.

When the Niche children were not carrying out chores, Elder Myuk taught lessons to all of them who were developed enough to hear or read; many could do neither, and were destined to be Reprocessed. But Mienne and Wayer studied hard, determined to survive, occasionally even finding it interesting to learn about reading and writing and history and Creation and Infinite Rock and government and maths and geoms. What Mienne could not see well enough to read, Wayer read aloud to her. Mienne found that she understood all of the information she heard immediately, not needing to have it repeated, which surprised her diminutive friend. *Why are these little people in Community such slow learners?* she thought. *Or is it just these in the Niche?* She had a suspicion that UpTop and DownUnder people were just different, in many ways. She wondered why that was, but dared not ask the Ugly Elder or even Wayer.

OVER THE NEXT SIX MONTHS, MIENNE GREW EVEN taller, her rate of growth surprising to Elder Myuk as her body matured in several places. *Is this the natural rate of growth of this girl's people?* Myuk wondered. *Or did all those strange chemicals in that suit of hers have something to do with stunting her maturity? Or did the environment here, the food, the air, the water, change her development? Or was she just older than she looked?* Myuk figured she would never know the answer to that conundrum.

The day that Mienne began her menses, in fear she revealed her condition to the Ugly Elder. Mienne knew that she would soon be required to demonstrate skills of self-sufficiency and service, that although no one knew her birth date, her body was telling all that she was come of age. Sighing, the Elder told Mienne that her time had arrived, that the next day she and Wayer would take the first steps to be judged Citizens—or to be Reprocessed.

CHAPTER TWENTY-ONE

"Two or three months," Wakan Kech was saying as they smoothly flew northward up the Mother's River, Una some twenty meters above the water. "No longer than that until Miran gets new barges and new catapults and tries again. Giving us at most another three more months to prepare for war. Plan for two."

Thist was considering the existing defenses that ShadowFall could offer. "Pernie has what, about seventy thousand people or so in her Sisterdom?" Wakan nodded. "How many men and battle-capable women out of that?"

"A lot less than a fourth of them, I estimate, excluding children, the elderly, and those required for maintaining the Sisterdom's infrastructures, granaries, wells, and so on," the priest said. "We can realistically stage probably as many as ten to twelve thousand along the frontier with Stone Pyramid, Four Peaks, and RidgeBack, but our Sisterdom will suffer from their lack of productivity." Wakan hated all wasted effort, but this was for survival, not profit!

"But," he cautioned, "our roads are not plentiful and we would have to support all of the nonproductive fighters with food and supplies, and that takes several thousand rear echelon people. At present, I can offer you at most a week of resistance. Only about two thousand of them have springbow training, but that is how we staved off an earlier invasion, the one from RidgeBack and Four Peaks, a few years back. But those were local Sisters' militia soldiers. Up against Mothersmen, I hate to say it, but a large number of our people will likely be slaughtered."

"And Miran Kech is probably bringing, what, eight thousand of those trained and experienced troops against us?" Thist asked.

Wakan nodded. "After today, at least that many. And I am afraid that once he realizes that he lost no men killed or even wounded in our Una rock bombing, he is bound to conclude that our magical machine can't kill. I doubt that he will think we were being merciful."

Thusk replied, "But we can use Una to observe from above, and report where the enemy is, and their disposition, their numbers. Ancient battles were won or lost because of such information, or its lack."

Wakan sighed, "Rist—I mean *Thist*—what I could really use is another thousand bird-riding fighters like you. What you did by yourself in the Game is the stuff of legend; your fight will be remembered for centuries."

Thist grimaced at the memory of that bloody day, six months ago. His victory—just *surviving!*—had earned fame for himself and fortune for Pernie, but he still thought it a brutal and senseless way for a Sisterdom to have the opportunity to influence the Mother. The failure tributes from the other Sisters, now, *those* had enriched Pernie personally and ShadowFall—the horses, springbows, godscloth, grains and other nonperishable foodstuffs. *Still, losing my foot was a steep price for me to pay!* But the thought of riding an emu into battle for a cause he truly believed in—this time, saving ShadowFall and the Princess from the monstrous ambitions of Miran Kech—caused his heart to beat faster. Against his own avowed principles and putting aside his harrowing experience in the Game, he was ready and anxious to fight again, to go to war!

"Wakan," Thist said excitedly, "did you mean that, about more bird-riders?" He glanced at Thusk, who was already smiling. "Let's make a deal."

BYPASSING GOD'S PORT AND ITS DEFENSIVE CATAPULTS while in invisible mode and at an extremely high altitude, Una passed over the mountains into The People's Lands in a leisurely three hours, now flying slowly, visibly, just thirty meters above the New River. To either side of them lay the vast plains of the southern region of what was now called The People's Lands, mottled carpets of yellow and brown where peat crops had been harvested. To the east, the sun—once called Pursuing Dimness—was now only four hours' distance above the horizon, its disk shape only a fuzzy blob as seen through the ever-present cloud of the Misty Sky. Thusk smiled to think that only six months ago he had not known the true nature of Pursuing Dimness or of the Wen of the Mist, which he now understood was a satellite called Moon. As usual, Moon was not always visible here in his homeland's sky, not even in her aspect as a dim smudge in the clouds.

As grinning berg-men below waved up at them, Thusk told Una to perform a slight wigwag in the sky in recognition, delighting the crews who were escorting ice downriver toward God's Port. As Una's crew neared their home city—now The People's Town—Una dropped to a ten-meter altitude and maintained a walking-speed velocity toward the city center, gathering a following crowd of curiosity seekers, before finally landing gently in the plaza outside The People's Palace. By the time they arrived, it appeared as if over half of the townspeople were there to see them.

Anklya, tall and blonde, wearing attractive winter furs, including a striking foxfur vest that set off her curves, came bounding down the wide steps of the palace, smiling and shouting. "Thist, Thusk, welcome home! It's been days. What have you been doing? What —" As the cabin door opened, she caught sight of Wakan Kech and drew in a breath. "Lord Wakan, I— you—how did you get here?" She stopped talking, aware of her ridiculous question.

Stepping out of Una, Wakan just smiled at his ShadowFall compatriot. He had seen her at Mother's Palace just before the Game when she delivered the message to him about Rist and his Una, and then another time aboard Una at the oasis outside of Mother's City. Weeks before, they had all flown back to ShadowFall, there to surprise and confront Rumi Similla. As Anklya came forward, smiling, Wakan had no doubt about her sensuous attractiveness; the dark twins had filled him in on their intimate relationship with the beautiful handmaiden and how she was adapting to perform actual useful work in their homeland as a facilitator helping a society transition from dictatorship to democracy. And here she was!

Unused to sharing friendship, much less joy, with a lower-status palace handmaid, nevertheless Wakan embraced Anklya, who burst into tears. "Lord Kech, it is so good to see you. We were all afraid for the Princess and ShadowFall, after Rist—*Thist*—escaped from Mother's Palace. Is everything all right?" Wakan and the twins looked at each other grimly. From their faces, Anklya knew that things were not.

TWO HOURS LATER, AS A FRIGID BREEZE WHIPPED around him, Thist was preparing to speak from atop the steps to The People's Palace. Below him in the plaza, hundreds of mostly young People stood in rapt attention, waiting for what their hero would say. The twins and the Council of Elders had spread the word that a great announcement would be made at noon. With Thusk at his left—near the very spot where his twin had killed The Tharn after the murder of their Sire, Thess—behind them stood Wakan Kech, now outfitted in black velkskin furs, and their beautiful Anklya. And prominently visible yet quiescent in the courtyard sat Una, their god-machine.

Thist looked up at the eternally cloudy sky; Pursuing Dimness—The People's Lands' always fuzzy and dim god of the Misty Sky—was as high above the horizon as He would get, so it was near noon. Using the Una loud-voice, Thist said, "Thusk and I have just returned from far south in the Warm Lands, in a vast domain called 'Motherland.' This man—Wakan Kech"—the Motherlander bowed to the crowd—"and this woman, whom you all know, Anklya, are our friends from one small place in Motherland, a Sisterdom called 'ShadowFall.' Some of you may have heard stories about these foreign lands." Cheers arose from the assembled People; the tales of Thist at the Game and of Thusk in Una in the plaza of the Solar Priests had been told and retold so many times that their names would forever be legend in The People's Lands.

"Well, ShadowFall will soon be under siege from evil conspirators in Motherland." Collective breaths made a noticeable noise. "The invaders promise to kill Wakan here, and imprison the beautiful Princess who has shown us such hospitality." *And such passion*, he thought, remembering many nights with her.

"If you wonder why we have asked you here, it is to ask for volunteers to help defend ShadowFall. For this I will need those who can ride emus, and fight from them. How many of you are emu-riders, and velk hunters?" A scattering of hands, a few shouts of "Me!" "I am!" Then Thist asked, "How many of you would *like* to be?" Every single hand rose, a forest of waving arms, vying for his attention. "Now I want to let Wakan speak, and tell you of his offer to you."

Stepping forward, the tall man bowed again to the crowd. "Citizens of People's Town, I am Wakan Kech, High Priest and Chief Advisor to Princess Perneptheranam of the Sisterdom of ShadowFall, in far distant Motherland." While Wakan Kech's authoritative accent was commanding, his mesmerizing gaze covered the whole crowd, his dark eyes seeming to rest on each individual alone. "For those who will come with us and fight for the integrity and sovereignty of ShadowFall and its Princess, each shall be granted a hundred acres of tillable land and full rights as citizens of the

Sisterdom." *Assuming we don't lose*, was his unspoken addendum, but a message understood by all.

As the citizens cheered, Thist stepped back to the front. "Those accepted must be healthy enough to ride emus as fighting birds, and willing to be trained in the use of bolos, swords, and springbows. They must not be leaving dependents behind uncared for, or unpaid debts. For be aware, the enemy will be ruthless. Many of us will not live through the siege. So all responsibilities here in our homeland must be settled before you may leave with us."

The crowd cheered his words, and Thist smiled broadly, waving at them, pumping his fist in an action he had witnessed at the Game. *Where I lost my foot*, he thought. A grim realization came over him at that point: *How many of these enthusiastic young people here in front of me are going to die because of me? Fighting for a land far away, for a princess they have never seen, for a society that is much less free than our own?* Shrugging off that ominous feeling, he welcomed the young men and wen who clambered to the steps, anxious to sign up on the spot. After shaking hands and accepting pats on the back, Thist motioned for them to leave, telling the crowd over the loud-voice, "Return in the morning, ready to be questioned and examined for fitness." To his astonishment, Thist could see that almost half of the volunteers-to-be were wen.

As the plaza emptied, Thist and the others went into the palace to talk. Troubles arose almost immediately. "We cannot have wen riding birds," Thist complained. Seeing Anklya's stunned reaction, he emphasized, "It has never been done! Wen don't ride, and they don't fight!"

Anklya sat and patted the couch next to her, indicating that the little man should sit. He did. "Thist, my love, you only listed health, dependents, and debts as elimination factors. If these *women* can ride birds and shoot arrows, why would you *not* train them, use them, in the fighting to come? A soldier is a soldier; an emu-rider is a soldier on bird-back; what's the difference?"

Fuming, Thist had no response, to which Thusk, standing, laughed. "My twin is not so open-minded as he has claimed." To Anklya and an impassive Thist he said, "Let us take them. If they do not pass the training, they can do support work behind the lines – feeding birds, handling the leather goods, distributing springbows and the stabbing anklets. Lots of things they can do, so the Warmlanders are free to fight. Besides"— he grinned—"having our own wen—or *women*—in residence with our men might prevent other, er, unpleasant situations from arising." He massaged Anklya's bare shoulders. "Not all the Warmlander women may be attracted to our People."

Anklya laughed, "And not all of your People might be as attractive as you two!"

OVER THE NEXT WEEK, ANKLYA AND OTHER VOLUNTEERS in The People's Palace processed over three hundred suitable candidates, both male and male. Anklya reported to the group, "Ninety *wen* as you call them —*women*, they are—have put their names on the volunteer list." Thist huffed at the news, but his objections, having been overridden by the others, were soon forgotten.

After two days of interviews, Thusk flew the first set of selected volunteers down to ShadowFall aboard Una, twenty of them crowded into the cabin area. "Standing-room only, people," he said as Una lifted off from the plaza. An audience of a thousand below stood in awe as the great green cylinder rose almost silently, ascending to thirty meters before stopping. Thusk attempted to calm their understandable fears. "Everyone, don't be alarmed, but I am going to show you what The People's Town and the whole wide world looks like from high up. Una, transparent walls, please." Gasps and a few whimpers of fear emanated from the volunteers as they gawked at the miniature city below them, the river to the east, and the unfamiliar sight of the vastness of their homeland.

Thusk said, "And now we will ascend through the Misty Sky and you will see that Pursuing Dimness is actually a big ball of celestial fire called the Sun, and the Wen of the Mist is a satellite of the round Earth called the Moon." He had Una opaque the walls before slowly ascending to five thousand meters.

This time, when the walls cleared, shouts erupted from the crowd of PeoplesLandsers: "The Misty Sky is *below* us?" "That ball of light, it really *is* Pursuing Dimness?" "I don't see the Wen!"

Thusk said, "Now you see what was kept from us before. Just like this ancient Una machine corrected the vision that kept us all from seeing clearly what we could touch, so it also lets us see the real world that the Misty Sky kept from us." He motioned toward the front cabin wall. "If those in front will sit or kneel so that others may see over them, I will ask Una to show you moving pictures that tell about the Sun and Moon and Earth. And about the Warm Lands we are heading for, including ShadowFall. Our new place to live." *And to die, too,* a part of his mind niggled. *Too many of us!*

Returning to ShadowFall while the recruiting was going on in The People's Town, Wakan made the logistical arrangements for the new immigrants, having barracks constructed near a training ground and arranging for continuing food supplies. He directed ShadowFall workshops to produce appropriately sized springbows, arrows, saddles, and the spur-like anklets that the war-birds would wear in battle. Meanwhile, he consulted with Princess Perneptheranam on other preparations for their defense.

Princess Pernie was confused about the Una machine's capabilities. "Wakan, you are telling me that the Una cannot—or is it *will* not?—allow Thist and Thusk to use it to kill enemies? Why would the ancients build a thing like that, if not to kill? "

"Princess," the priest answered, "the Una is 'programmed,' it says, not to be able to contribute to the injury or death of a human being. I take it that this set of instructions somehow is integral to its construction. Similar to us not being able to lift hug big weights, or fly ourselves."

"But they were able to drop rocks and sink the barges, isn't that dangerous to people? Not that I care," she said angrily. "I wish they had killed all those troops!"

"My Princess, the boys—excuse me, the *men*—are thinking about other kinds of destruction, of disruption, that they will be able to do with the Una. But I am afraid that we cannot risk flying over Miran's and Creesile's army just to know when it is close. The large catapults we saw on the barges could put those borophene arrows into it and make it crash. And kill those aboard it." Waving a hand, he said, "Rumi Similla must have spoken to Miran about what happened here, when the guards disabled the Una here in ShadowFall while you were away at the Game."

"Yes, Wakan, I trusted the ungrateful bitch, unwisely." Walking around her chamber, Pernie finally stopped, looking up into Wakan's eyes, a seething anger evident. "But so did you. Was that because you were sleeping with her? Did her beauty affect your judgment?"

Wakan sighed. *After five years, she still wants to blame me for her own errors. I had hoped that as an adult she was overcoming that royal training, that arrogance. I have made some progress, but she still has the power to kill me or dismember me alive.* He answered without emotion. "Princess, I am your servant, your property. Nothing affects my decisions when it comes to your welfare or that of ShadowFall." *And besides, after the first few nights, that Rumi Similla was nothing to brag about.* He always did his best to keep his personal needs and trysts very discreet; he'd have to do better!

CHAPTER TWENTY-TWO

For the newcomers to ShadowFall, the renowned warrior Thist laid out an extensive training program. His initial recruits were those of his countrymen who were already experienced hunters. The first week he began training in coordinated battlefield combat conditions, including Wakan's idea of stringing godscloth wire between two emus. *A gruesome tactic*, he thought, *but better we have it than that Miran Kech!* The later immigrants, the less experienced riders and hunters, he assigned to the graduates of the first group of trainees.

Four weeks later, ShadowFall's citizens watched while hundreds of the small northerners, their formal training completed, paraded their emus past the Princess's palace in disciplined formations, springbows, spears, shortswords and needle-spur anklets shining in the light of the sun. The PeoplesLandsers were obviously culturally and physically conditioned to ride emus, even those who had never done so before. As he had closely observed the smooth training and exercises between People and emus, Thusk wondered if their thirty thousand years of isolation in the glacier-enclosed homeland, in intimate contact with the birds, had predisposed both riding partners to compatibility. *Maybe small changes, passed on to successive generations, of both birds and people?* Someday he'd have to ask Una how that might have evolved.

Already, from studying Una's history archive videos, Thusk did know that his birds were much larger than those of ancient times, *while we People are much smaller. How did that happen? The video records mentioned that another species of large bird, the ostrich, may have interbred with ancient emus at a time in the distant past. Another thing to study with Una, if I ever have the time!*

After transporting the volunteers from home to ShadowFall, Thusk assigned himself the responsibility of scouting over the terrain around the borders of the Sisterdom, instructing Una to record data about roads, river depth, locations of rapids or waterfalls, conditions of riverbanks, and locations of earthen mounds, copses of trees, and topography in general. Thist and Wakan could use those strategic heights and river obstacles when planning ShadowFall's defenses.

And because it took little effort, he and Una cruised invisibly over the neighboring Sisterdoms, noting not only terrain details, but also their roads, rivers, streams, docks, even their Sister palaces. As he collected the vast array of information into Una's archives, ideas formed in his mind, and he wanted to present Thist and Wakan and the Princess with some alternatives they may not have considered—such as, why wait for an attack? Why not strike the enemy again, but this time lethally, and in Mother's City? Keep the Miran Kech armies defending themselves down there, not nearer ShadowFall? *Why not use Una's unique abilities of stealth and silence, and go after Miran Kech himself? Or...even the Mother?*

"Quite a show you've got here, Thist," Wakan said as they looked over large-scale bird-rider maneuvers from atop a twenty-meter tower at the training field. "Your people were born to this, it seems." As they watched, a pair of riders, with an invisibly thin godscloth wire strung between them, approached a column of strawman targets tied to wooden posts the height of an average Mothersman soldier. As the two riders—one a wen, Thist noticed with a grimace—ran on either side of the targets, which were three abreast and ten deep, the tied bales of straw and the posts suddenly burst apart, sliced as by an invisible scythe. *As they were, indeed,* Wakan thought, his gruesome invention now showing signs of promise for the upcoming battles.

As each of the strawman targets fell into two piles of debris, Thist grunted, "I just hope that three hundred of us on war-birds can help, but your own militia has to be the major factor if we're to win."

Wakan was visualizing not strawmen, but living, bleeding Mothersmen, sliced apart and screaming as they lay dying, *legs sheared, guts spewing their lifeblood. Because of me! All these centuries of warfare, and* I *have to be the one to find the latest and worst use for godscloth!* He knew that without the windfall of Rist's—*Thist's!*—acres of godscloth and the tools to work it with, the material would have remained an unscissable rarity, suitable only for royal clothing and decor. *So it wasn't just me; little Thist was a catalyst for this kind of battle. As he has been for so many changes in Motherland since he fell into our midst.* Wakan didn't want to think about the effect of hundreds, or maybe someday thousands, of Thists upon life—and death—in Motherland.

Over the month since it began, the immigration of so many small people into ShadowFall had gone relatively smoothly, from both nations' perspectives. The Princess had welcomed them all as heroes in a public gathering, granting them full citizenship and distributing maps as to where their promised land grants would be located. The populace of ShadowFall, already acquainted with little Rist's famous exploits of slaying would-be assassins and then prevailing in the Motherland Game, predisposed the natives to appreciate the small, dark foreigners coming to help save them from invasion.

The fact that the new grants of land to the little foreigners would be in the far east of the Sisterdom, away from the palace and other main towns, seemed to placate the small minority of ShadowFall citizens who feared a cultural invasion from the north more than a physical invasion from the south. The easternmost plains of ShadowFall were uninhabited all the way from the river to the sloping foothills that were the boundary with Ancient Towers. Wakan had long wanted to settle those lands before their neighboring Princess Fallowner cast greedy eyes on them, but ShadowFall hadn't had enough people to spare to resettle there.

As chief advisor to the Princess, Wakan was always concerned about ShadowFall's lands and the Princess's sovereignty. But occasionally as he listened to Thist and Thusk talk about the freedoms in their newly liberated homeland, which he had witnessed at the assemblies in The People's Town itself, he wondered if, in ensuring his Sisterdom's physical integrity in this war, he may have doomed the millennia-old tradition of Mother's absolute power and the lesser absolutism that each of her princesses exercised. *If we did set up elections, as the little men's homeland now has, and like we have in the High Antis, would our Princess win?* A grimmer thought replaced that one: *If Motherland's ruling classes are overthrown, would they—even I—be allowed to live?*

"So, THIS IS MY PROPOSAL," THUSK SAID TO THE WAR council, meeting in Pernie's Palace— the Princess, Wakan, Thist, Anklya, and himself, plus three People's Lands officers and half a dozen trusted ShadowFall nobles. "We fly Una down to Mother's City, land in a palace courtyard, then find and seize Miran Kech and any of his new military officers." Nods from all around gave him the impetus to continue, though some jaws were agape at the audacity of the plan, the PeoplesLandsers and ShadowFall nobles not fully appreciating Una's capabilities of flight and invisibility, even though they had witnessed some of it themselves.

"We bring Miran Kech and the others to where General Creesile is assembling the invasion force, and give him orders to disband." Holding his hands palms out, he said, "And that should end it right there. No more fighting, no more bloodshed. No more wasted lives and material. What do you think?"

CHAPTER TWENTY-THREE

Mother Messinex accessed her well-hidden Sanctuary Room, sealing the iron doors behind her and opening the large golden chest that contained all of Motherland's most secret writings. Igniting the gas lamps to light up the twelve-meter square room and take the edge off the damp coolness, from a large golden chest atop a velvet-covered dais she lifted out a stack of paper-thin golden plates that told the true history of Motherland. Each plate was written in the secret language taught only to Mothers and Sisters by acolytes who themselves only knew the basics of grammar and spelling, but had no access to the Sanctuary Room.

Messinex lay back on a padded lounge chair, knowing that she wouldn't be disturbed. She needed solitude to think over the crises that Motherland was facing, serious challenges that as Mother she was expected to meet forcefully and to overcome using her wisdom, and that of the goddess with whom she supposedly communicated through the Crystal Throne.

"But," she said aloud, hoping that her own voice would calm herself, steady her nerves, "Miran tells me that Pernie's little man Rist attacked his troop barges with his flying god-machine. How can she be doing this to me? I only want to restore order in her Sisterdom."

Reading over Miran's report of the losses caused by the "Una" machine, as Miran and Rumi Similla were calling it, Messinex was surprised to see no mention of troops killed or injured. Was it possible to wage war without killing? She would have to ask Miran about that niggling detail.

After learning of ShadowFall's perfidy in not complying with the order to relinquish all its godspheres and ancient books, Messinex had reluctantly approved a punitive expedition to seize Pernie and return her for questioning. Miran had also proposed installing Rumi Similla as acting administrator of that Sisterdom while Pernie's status was being adjudicated. Because the woman had already held that position of trust—Pernie's trust!—previously, Messinex had no problem with that temporary solution.

But Pernie! How could Pernie betray her, her favorite Sister of all the other dozen, the only one she had ever truly loved, the rest being at best cold and distant, the worst just scheming bitches intent on subduing all their half-siblings? *And yet, the Crystal Throne chose* me! *And my Sisters can never forgive me for that!* Two of the Sisters were already in her dungeons below the palace, Miran's secret police force having seized them for treasonous acts that she couldn't quite recall at the moment. In the months of their captivity she had not found it necessary to visit them, certain that Miran's gentle ministrations would elicit admission of the written charges she demanded of them before any public burnings.

Even there, Miran had promoted a more cautious approach. "We must be careful of such, Mother Messinex," her Kech advisor had warned, "lest the citizens become restless, seeing the Sisters in torment and dying in agony just like any of them would do in the same circumstances." So gentle Miran had convinced her to let them rot, er, *languish,* in her dungeons while new temporary appointees continued to rule their Sisterdoms. As Mother, her word was law, so the rebellious Sisters would spend many more months, maybe years, in solitude, giving them time to reflect upon their betrayals. Messinex turned her thoughts to other pressing problems.

The Cold Sea warriors were increasing their raids upon WaterEdge ports. Trading vessels from afar no long arrived during Season Warm, her emissaries reported, and new tribes of predatory pirate ships were more aggressive than usual, not only attacking vessels at sea but even making raids into Motherland itself. *Those big bastards*, she thought, *thinking they can claim Motherland territory just because of their legends.* And then there was that moment with little Rist, when he said the godspheres validated that belief. Her thoughts confused, she wondered aloud, "Where are you, little Rist? And why do you help Pernie in her treason?" Her head pounding, throbbing, with sharp dark points of pain, the dark mood returned, and she envisioned punishments for Pernie and her pet dwarf. *I'll not let Miran convince me to be merciful again, not to those two! How dare they refuse their Mother!*

Sheets of blinding pain overwhelmed Messinex's vision, her thoughts. *If these Mother-damned headaches didn't just about make me faint,* she thought, *I could rule better. What has happened to me since I became Mother? Surely it's not my lovers?* She had ceased lovemaking with Miran Kech, her longtime best friend and advisor, since attaining the supreme position in Motherland. Adhering to the ancient Kech tradition of ingesting concoctions of High Antian herbs prevented her almost daily trysts from resulting in pregnancies, she knew, but as soon as she had established absolute and continuing loyalty among the Sisters, she would have to begin producing female heirs. Or else have Motherland degenerate into centuries of siblicidal wars, as the golden plates in her sanctuary spelled out in their woeful histories.

No, Miran has a vision for Motherland, and I trust him. But he must conclude this, this, this effrontery *of Pernie's and bring her here for admonishment.* Messinex could not see herself allowing Miran to imprison, much less torture, her little Sister, her beloved.

Love and discussion will bring us together, I know it! The golden plates in her hand offered many hours of reading, their organized histories calming her mind, channeling her thoughts into more productive avenues. The gaslights and scented candles added an ambience of peace and security, and she soon fell asleep, exhausted. Her final thought before drifting off were of her beautiful little Sister, Pernie.

CHAPTER TWENTY-FOUR

"What is happening to Messinex?' Miran Kech said aloud, but not *too* loud; he never knew whether others might be spying on him as he was on almost everyone else in Mother's Palace. Worrying about Mother Messinex's increasingly erratic behavior, he thought, *No need for her to be paranoid. I'm suspicious enough for both of us. Always have been.* He worried that the stress of Motherhood may be destroying her mind. *If she becomes totally insane, then she will need a regent to rule in her stead...*

Miran thought back to the day, nearly twenty years ago, when Seenpet Sar had sent him to the Sisterhood of Three Rivers, there to be an aide and advisor to Princess Karpin, the predecessor of Messinex, who back then was just a five-year-old child, not in any way fit to be a Sister. Karpin, the daughter of the Lordess Mother's own mother, the former Great Mother, was a plain, unintelligent dullard of a woman, but with a wild temper and unpredictable moods. Miran had later explained to his Kech countrymen at their annual gathering at Mother's Palace, "Karpin is an argument against hereditary rulership. She has no thinking ability, so I am able to impress her, and most of the time, manage her. If only," he groaned, "I didn't have to sleep with her." The other Kech laughed uproariously at that; most of them either had young Sisters to administer to, or aged crones no longer interested in fleshly matters. Not one of them, however, boasted of their Sister's intellect. In their opinions, Motherland was ruled mostly by dunces.

But watching Karpin rule, carrying out her orders, Mira recalled, *bent me the way I am now.* The first time was being ordered to carry out an execution of a minor noble who had in some way bothered Princess Karpin. "Kill him, Miran," the Sister had said nonchalantly as the man kneeling before her jerked back his head in disbelief, "he deserves to die." She gestured for a guard to give Miran his sword. At Miran's hesitation: "Now, Kech man. Or you will be next."

Gulping, Miran awkwardly held the heavy sword swinging it down at the shocked man's neck, catching him in the throat. The victim garbled a scream, grabbed his bloody neck, and fell backwards, rolling on the tiled floor. With a threatening glare from Sister Karpin, Miran held the sword in two hands and brought it down hard enough to sever the mortally wounded man's head. *I can still remember the horror of that moment,* Miran thought. *But the worse horror was that I felt a momentary tinge of excitement; I had ended a nobleman's life. And Sister Karpin applauded me!*

Over the next ten years similar scenes occurred many times, as Miran recalled, and he grew less and less bothered by Karpin's orders. Occasionally her sentences were justified by any standards—robbery, theft, rape— so harsh punishments needed to be meted out to keep the populace in line, typically months or years in a dungeon, beheading for the violent crimes. But when it came to politics, Karpin was ruthless in stamping out any hint of treachery or even mild displeasure of her rule in the Three Rivers domain; those found guilty of these offenses did not die quickly.

As his tenure and rank increased and Karpin's other advisors died—or were executed—Miran no longer feared carrying out such extended tortures, but still preferred not to. He didn't want to become as insane as some other advisors who were rumored to be sadists of the worst sort. But in surviving twenty years in

Motherland's arcane and cruel political climate, Miran had adapted as necessary. *Wakan always said that the power of life or death should not fall to one person, but that such sentences should be the result of deliberation and careful judgment among a group of educated Elders.* Miran still thought so, too, but had little choice. *Maybe that works back home in the High Antis, Wakan, but not in this Motherland we're doomed to live in!*

After Karpin's untimely death, the Lordess Mother had designated her daughter Messinex as Princess of Three Rivers. A twenty-year-old raven-haired beauty of uncommonly pale skin, Messinex proved the opposite of her predecessor—kind, loving, forgiving, a real joy to be around, and beloved of her subjects. But like all those who can call down Death on anybody, even Messinex...

Miran recalled that particular day, when the Princess and he were enjoying the bright sunshine while strolling through one of the vineyards for which Three Rivers was famous. The head vintner, a stooped, white-haired, stocky man with the ruddy complexion of an outdoors type, was explaining how the crop of grapes was going to be of exceptional quality. "Princess, the rainfall, the temperature, and the sunshine have blessed your vineyards with the perfect blend of elements," the vintner said, rolling a dark grape in his fingers. "We will have a most marvelous vintage this year, one that your Sisters will be happy to pay a premium for."

As the Princess started to respond, a woman's screams broke the calmness of the vineyard. "Help! Help! Stay off me!" At once, two of Messinex's guards ran over to the next row of trellises. There they saw a man, his pants down, atop a half-nude woman, already penetrating her.

"Stop that!" a guard yelled, but the man kept on with the rape, oblivious of guards and the approaching Princess and Miran.

"Take him off of her!" Messinex commanded. The guards jerked the rapist off the woman, roughly throwing him to the ground on his back, where he made no effort to cover his nakedness, instead continuing to manipulate his member to finish.

"Drunk out of his mind," Miran said in disgust. The man would die after he sobered up, in a day or two at most.

But the Princess had other ideas. "Hold that man up, right now!" The guards pulled him to his feet, while he kept masturbating. "Before he finishes," she shouted, "cut it off! He will have no more pleasure in my presence!" The guards tried to pry the rapidly moving hand away, but couldn't. "Then the hand, too!" The guard was swift; the severed parts fell in a bloody mess onto the ground, where the rapist just looked down in disbelief.

A look of surprise, followed by a scream of pain, showed that the rapist, drunk or not, realized his predicament. But before he could scream a second time, Princess Messinex had a guard pick up the severed member and stuff it down the man's throat. "Hold him until he dies. I want his poor victim, here, to witness her Princess's judgment." With that, she embraced the sobbing woman, comforting her. Together with Miran and the guards, the two women watched as the rapist choked, burbled, and bled. It was over in minutes.

Over the next years Miran witnessed and participated in other executions just as bloody and drawn out, though seldom done publicly. Messinex liked to maintain her loving image, and never again was seen to exact even justified punishments out in the open. *Though in her dungeons, she could be as vicious as Karpin was. I've never forgotten how even a gentle princess like Messinex, endowed with the absolute power of life and death, is capable of such cruelty. But power like that is what I have now. No longer a naive priest from the backward High Antis, I am now second in power only to Mother Messinex herself. And perhaps, someday...*

CHAPTER TWENTY-FIVE

The next Wake Period, Elder Myuk escorted her two charges, Mienne and Wayer, through a maze of damp tunnels, gently skipping from foot to foot, her thick, dark red robes swishing this way and that. Mienne found the tunnels barely tall enough for her to walk in; trying to skip, lope, or even hop like the short people did meant hitting her head on the rock ceiling. Behind the Elder the two girls tried to keep up, but with the one child Blind and tall, and the other armless, it was a hopeless task, so she slowed down to a brisk walk, a short hop-skip, enabling the disabled children to draw even with her. They could not be allowed to become lost in these ancient passageways; though the route was brilliantly lit, losing one's way could be fatal unless one could read the directions spelled out by the shadows of the wall-carved reliefs. To the Elder's knowledge, nobody had ever mapped out all of the tunnels, curiosity not being a characteristic of Community's people. Not when there was only one destination worth visiting this far out—the Hall of Whispers.

An hour of walking finally brought them to a much wider and higher tunnel that opened to a vast open plaza leading to a massive foamstone doorway. To the right side of the door stood a huge Nuuk guardian on a low pedestal. Completely covered in a deep red metallic armor suit, the bulky *no-male* creature stood well over two meters tall and appeared to mass in excess of a hundred kilos, half again taller than Mienne and more than twice that of her two companions. The long, multi-corded whip it carried stayed in its hands, moving slightly, a warning to those who might foolishly challenge it. As the Elder approached, the Nuuk nodded slightly, acknowledging her authority. It did not turn as she and the girls pushed the door open and passed by.

Elder Myuk considered the creature: neither woman nor man—*Maybe even*, she thought, *not human at all?* As far as she knew, the Nuuk had guarded this doorway for all time—for centuries, maybe millennia, of Motherth Years. Having visited this site now probably a dozen times in her long life, she had never before considered whether it was the same Nuuk there all this time, or if it was one of a tribe or clan or a separate Community, and replaced as needed. In that armor, it would be impossible to tell, anyhow. She shook off the thought; *Today is too important to be distracted. I am trying to save these young girls, to preserve two lives!*

"The Hall of Whispers is where the ancients sometimes talk to those who are Enlightened," the Elder said. "Pay close attention. You may learn something." Mienne clutched Wayer tightly as she timidly took small steps forward into the dark tunnel, afraid of stumbling in the dim red darkness. The place smelled of ancient odors, not like the clean and crisp air of Shinyeen City, kept fresh by who knew what devices the Creator had provided in Her wisdom. Mienne could feel thick crusty dust under her sandaled feet, dust swirling up where they walked.

"What do you hear, children?" Ugly Elder asked. "Do you hear the whispers?"

As she passed by the vast flat walls, Wayer saw only dim reddish glows with indistinguishable, randomly moving patterns, meaningless motion, in the far distance only darkness. The voices, if that's what they were, were only murmurs, unintelligible nonsense at best. "Yes, Elder, I hear them," Wayer said, "but I do not know what they say, or what they mean."

Elder Myuk sighed and whispered to herself, "Almost nobody does. A few sometimes hear words that will guide them into needed positions in Community, but only a precious few. Yet we keep waiting for the promised miracle that will finally reveal all." She had hoped that Wayer would hear Enlightening words, would discover a redeeming talent, anything she could do that would prove her worth to Community. Understanding the whispers could be her salvation. For all its benevolence, after the age of Thirteen Motherth Years, by millennia-old tradition, Community could afford only to provide for those who contributed. *But without arms...?* Elder shook her head, sad for the child's unfortunate disability. In recent years there had been too many such births, some of them producing far worse disabilities than mere missing limbs. Too many recently were coming out of Crèche Tube niches as dead babies, lacking not only limbs but internal organs or even brains. Could something terrible be happening in the Gestation Tube? Such disablement was once unheard of, yet now becoming more frequent.

Elder Myuk hoped that other Elders might understand, might somehow remedy the problem. *If the still-deaths continue,* she thought, *there might not be enough people to maintain Community!* That thought being heresy, she dismissed it.

Her other hope for today was the tall foundling, Mienne. Blind though she might be, the child's mind had always been sharp and creative these past years since her arrival, even to the point of inventing strange stories of things that could not be, describing imaginary people and impossible places and unbelievable phenomena. The Elder hoped that perhaps Mienne's curious mind, most likely a disorder resulting from her Blindness, might in place of sight produce an improved sense of hearing, or some acute element of understanding of the ancient whispers, something that would allow Elder Myuk to show that the child should be spared. She looked at the pitiful girl, now turning her head this way and that, looking around herself as if Seeing. *Poor thing!*

But Mienne, drawing in a shocked breath, was partaking of something for which she had no comparison. There, on the walls of the Hall of Whispers, she was experiencing the stuff of her dreams —images of large clear domes on a powdery pockmarked gray surface, an unending flat plain with a vast black dome of sky over it all. As she turned her head, she witnessed things *inside* those domes—a phantasmagoria of colors for which she had no names. And *people*! People skip-hopping inside the domes, people of many colors in strange shimmering skin-like coverings, loping along outside the domes in Vac suits, *just like the Sighted short ones do in the tunnels of Shinyeen City!*

But, Mienne wondered in amazement, what was she herself doing? She was Blind, by the standards of Community, but now with all these images, was she somehow *Seeing* differently? Or was it something else? She was too afraid to speak, to be so different among the Sighted, even Ugly Elder and Wayer. *Especially* them!

Sensing Mienne's shock, Wayer asked, "What's wrong? Can't you hear the whispers?"

Mienne took a deep breath. *Yes,* she thought, *I can hear the whispers, but they are normal voices, as loud as yours. And they are coming from the images I am witnessing, what I am Seeing!* She realized that motions on the flat walls were in synchronization with the voices. *People are talking!* she realized, *and they are saying things!* She had no concept of what was happening, what those images were saying, but it was definitely disturbing.

"Wayer," Mienne whispered to her friend, "how Sighted are you?"

"Huh? I can see you standing beside me, and Ugly Elder as a silhouette in front of me. And these dim walls all around us, with their little wavy patterns and motions. And a long tunnel with black at the end. Why?"

Mienne squeezed her friend's shoulder, their private signal for "All is fine."

Wayer replied, "For a moment I thought you were having a seizure or something, girl. Don't do that again. You sure you're all right?" Mienne squeezed again, but now her attention was focused—literally—on the amazing display of moving images on the flat walls, some of them appearing to be as solid as three-dimensional objects. *What does all of this mean?* she wondered, *and why has no one ever talked about these, these,* Sights?

Elder spoke to the girls. "What's happening, you two? Are you not paying attention to this holy place? Are you not trying to understand the whispers?" She dared not add, *Do you not understand that you will both be* Reprocessed *if you don't show some useful skills?*

Mienne thought it better that she remain silent about her unexpected experiences, these sudden revelations. If the Ugly Elder and Wayer could not experience—*See?* —the images on the walls, could not know that the "whispers" were actually normal-level voices and sounds coming out of those moving images, then Mienne had no way to tell them. She could not conceive of any story that would convince them that she was not just relating another of her crazy dreams, even while she was standing there witnessing them. But she knew one thing—she had to come back alone and stay long enough to understand the voices and the sights.

After returning to the Niche, Mienne made a plan: one day soon, when everybody else dropped off to Sleep Period, she would make her way back to the Hall of Whispers, hoping for the magic to manifest itself there once again, to comprehend the wonders that only she could experience. And hopefully set herself free. To return to UpTop. *Home!*

It took Mienne a full Motherth week before she worked up the courage to make her way back to the Hall of Whispers, where Ugly Elder had taken Wayer and her during Wake Period. Before departing the Niche during that Sleep Period, Mienne mentally reviewed the route she would take. During that first visit, she had committed to memory many of the raised carvings on the tunnel walls, attempting to understand their dark shadows, counting the steps back. An hour later, close to the hall but from a safe distance, she could finally make out in the dim red light down the widening tunnel that the Nuuk guardian was absent from its raised pedestal. *So the Nuuk guardian observes Sleep Period, too!* That was useful information. Calculating that it then would be at least five more hours before everyone else's Wake Period began, Mienne knew that she had adequate time to experience those images and voices again, this time without hurry, without fear of anyone watching her reactions.

The foamstone door was surprisingly easy to open; with a mere palm press the enormous opening was revealed. As she crept into the Hall of Whispers, she witnessed the door closing silently behind her. Hopefully, getting out would be as easy as getting in!

Turning her attention to the endless hallway tunnel now before her, Mienne observed— *Saw?*—three-dimensional images on large flat surfaces on both walls, and on the ceiling, even on the floor! *What* are *these things? What do they mean?* Clearly, neither Ugly Elder nor Wayer had experienced this panoply of images, these views that emanated realistically from the walls, existing in the air all around her and even far into the distance down the tunnel that was the hall. A thought occurred to her; Mienne closed her eyes, witnessing only darkness. Opening her eyes again, the images returned. Placing a hand over each eye, then both eyes at once, revealed that the images were indeed coming into her eyes, in depth and colors, many colors, dark red only one among them. Was this truly what *Seeing* meant, just like in her dreams? How wonderful!

Mienne wandered down the vast tunnel, raptly viewing each of the scenes. Some colorful ones seemed lifelike, surrounding her as if she could reach out and touch them; others, only shown in shades of gray and black, were flat and lifeless, even though the images moved.

Some of the pictures were not of people or domes, but made of small, thin rectangular lines of different colors arranged in horizontal patterns. These seemed to be making streams of repeated images that moved across the bottoms of the flat areas. Once, she reached out to touch one of the moving patterns, and the world changed. Suddenly, all of the flat images became identical, left and right, up and down, as far as she could witness. *See!* Mienne thought. *I am Seeing now; I am not Blind! The images have responded to me, they know I am here!* From the tedious months of boring school lectures by Ugly Elder and other Elders, Mienne knew that such a thing had never been told about the Hall of Whispers, yet she, a Blind child, had done something here in the holy place. But *what*?

What she Saw next were flashing squares of images that seemed to float in front of her, so close as to invite her touch. Hesitantly, she reached out to the closest one, hoping for more knowledge. All through the hall, the images shifted once again, into meaningless patterns and shapes. With one important difference: the voices. The voices became loud enough to echo down the hallway tunnel, as if she were being scolded.

Shocked, Mienne backed away from the floating images, hoping that she had not violated some sacred taboo, something that might bring punishment upon her. The voices were still very loud, but diminishing in volume. Hearing them clearly, she thought she could understand a fragment of speech here, a word or phrase there. "The walls speak in Rin, the language of Community?" she said aloud, surprised. If so, why had Elders never been able to communicate with them? The images shifted again, this time all of them faded to black except for the flat wall immediately in front of her. And the lifelike image that appeared was of a woman in colorful robes, with black eyes and long black hair, skin the color of—*what?* Mienne didn't know the names of all the colors she was seeing, but this woman was beautiful and her dark skin looked soft and warm and her colorful robe was incredibly wonderful to see. The woman spoke directly to Mienne.

"Do you speak Mandarin?" the woman in the image asked, in a strangely stilted voice, the unusual intonations making the sounds unrecognizable.

Shocked, Mienne said nothing. Who was this woman, and how was she appearing on the wall of a tunnel in the Hall of Whispers? The voice continued, obviously asking questions in languages that to Mienne were gibberish.

And then: *"—or Spanglish?"*

Mienne gasped! Early childhood memories erupted, forgotten stories and myths. She could barely speak. *"Glish,"* she said with disgust, *"is the language of the Evil One, He who raped Motherth and cast the world into ice and darkness."* Surprised at her own outburst, Mienne realized that she didn't really know what any of those words meant; they were just part of a catechism she'd been taught at a very young age. She could not dredge up exactly when and where she had memorized that phrase, only that she knew it described ultimate evil.

"Rin," she whispered, "I speak Rin now, like all People in Shinyeen City in Community. When I was a younger, I remember, I talked in Man." What did the woman-image want her to say? Over the next few minutes, the woman-image was apparently able to understand Mienne's speech and to reply to her in a familiar language.

The woman-image finally said, in perfectly-accented Rin, "Mienne, my child, this Developing Intelligence system, the DI, has successfully analyzed your speech. Its roots were in original Lunar Mandarin, with overlay mixtures of Spanglish, Tagalog, and Finnish words and syntax." The woman-image blurred, faded out, then returned, speaking again.

"You have entered a protected communication

complex five kilometers below the lunar surface. Your presence here indicates that you have the proper authorizations to access and manipulate certain environmental and informational systems." Mienne heard the words but had little idea what their intention was. Suddenly another three-dimensional image appeared, replacing the woman-image with a layered maze of rectangular blocks, each labeled with more of the strange symbols. "The map here shows your position. You are four thousand, five hundred meters down-level from the q-comm device in the Control Room complex. See the indicated path." A series of yellow moving arrow-like images scrolled from one block to another, Mienne taking them to be directions to another tunnel or room nearby. She memorized the pathway in case she wanted to explore the hall more thoroughly.

The DI continued, "Systems indicate that these quantum translation circuits have been utilized only a very few times since the disturbances in the distant past. Maintenance features now being initiated." The flat screens throughout the tunnel all grew bright, flashing various images, then faded. Only the one woman-image remained, and its voice sputtered. "Mienne," it said, "our systems have been severely compromised. Unexpected aging of the non-quantum components. Unplanned solar interference. Parameters now dictate that only this one screen will remain active. Please return for further information at next—" *Crackle*. "You will be—" The voice and the image faded to black, as did the illumination in the hall itself. Shocked, Mienne looked left and right, up and down the suddenly darkened tunnel. *Blackness*, not even dim red lights!

Without thinking about the incredible communication with the woman-image, actually hearing her whispers—*voices!*—Mienne felt her way to the wall and slowly exited in the direction of the foamstone door. As she slowly opened it, she saw the Nuuk guardian turn its armored head toward her, raising its long whip. Had she spent that many hours in the hall? Or had it detected her intrusion and returned? She just knew she had to get out of range of its whip! And ducked, dropping to her knees.

"The Hall of Whispers is not for the Blind, you bitch!" the Nuuk roared, raising its whip hand at a terrified Mienne. *"Get out!"* The Nuuk lashed out, the tips of its long whip cracking loudly, just centimeters from Mienne's face. Cowering before the tall armored creature, dreading the horrific touch of those metal tips, Mienne scuttled down the damp tunnel, hoping and praying that the armored *no-male* would not follow. A quick glance over her shoulder showed that her prayers were answered: in the dim red light she saw that the huge red-armored Nuuk had not moved from its position on the short dais adjacent to the doorway of the forbidden Hall of Whispers. She had made it!

Grateful for her narrow escape but still trembling, Mienne stood and leaned against the tunnel wall, breathing deeply. The tunnel stank! Was it just her own fear-sweat, or was it the musk of all the people who had traveled down this corridor since—*when? The beginning of Time?* She knew she would never know the answer to that, and meanwhile she had to make her way back home, before Wake Period began. The dim red light emanating from all the tunnel surfaces—floor, ceiling, walls—provided barely enough illumination for her to make out the silhouettes of her own arms and legs, much less the far distances or possible obstacles in her way, so she reverted as usual to feeling her way along the patterned wall.

Moving as quickly as she could, keeping her left hand against the smooth surface, Mienne envied the Sighted, who could easily and gracefully lope and skip and hop without care, bouncing quickly through all the tunnels without fear of hitting their heads, or missing unexpected turns, or running into walls or pedestals in the way. Unable to translate most of the ancient high-relief messages on the walls as she moved, half running, half hop-walking, she could remember and interpret enough of them to be certain she was going in the right direction, which junction to take, which way to turn. An hour later, after traversing the otherwise featureless dank tunnel, Mienne was back home.

Despite the danger in her unauthorized visit, Mienne had confirmed her growing suspicion: the Hall of Whispers itself was showing and saying much, much more than the short people of Shinyeen City and Community realized, even the Elders. And its guardian, the Nuuk, was only present at the door to the Hall of Whispers during Wake Period. Giving up her own Sleep Period to sneak out and spy on the doorway was easy; everyone else in Shinyeen City automatically dropped into Sleep Period without thinking. Only Mienne ever laid awake, worrying about her life. And this time her staying awake had paid off; she had come to observe the doorway to the Hall of Whispers, had seen that the formidable Nuuk would not leave its duty station to confront intruders. It had threatened her only as she was leaving.

She had been scared—*still was!*—but the risk was worth it. What she would learn in that marvelous place, she felt, was going to change her life. Or end it.

CHAPTER TWENTY-SIX

"A beautiful day," Thist observed to his newly arrived countrymen gathered on the plaza outside the Princess's palace, "bright sunshine overhead, no clouds. On a day like this, fighting one on one, you need to keep your enemy's face in the sunlight, yours in shadow." Demonstrating how it was done, he climbed aboard a war-bird and pretended to be on the attack, twirling his spiked bolo overhead while charging at a strawman dummy on a pole. The shadow of himself and his emu fell on the faux enemy as he let loose. His bolo wrapped itself around the target, shredding it with needle-sharp spikes.

"That's how you do it, people. Your shadow can be your weapon; use it. Even though our foes down here will be taller than us, our emus make up the difference. And they don't know how to fight men"—he nodded, acknowledging the women in his training group—"and *wen*—who ride birds."

A gasp arose from his trainees, who were pointing up at the sky. Thusk spun around, shading his eyes from the sun. There high in the air, at least two hundred meters up, was a flying object. His first thought was *Somebody else has an Una!* But as the shadowed flying machine grew closer, he could tell that it was a dark triangular shape, and a man was dangling below it. "It's a tri-wing!" he yelled. Within seconds the looming image resolved itself into—Odel M'ridge and his tri-wing glider! To the alarmed guardsmen around him, Thusk waved his hands and shouted, "Don't shoot! Don't shoot! I know that crazy redhead up there! He's a friend! Help him land!"

Springbows down, the guards ran over to Odel as the big man descended in a fast walk, letting the tri-wing land on thin metal skids behind him. As he disentangled himself from the godscloth harness, Thusk ran over to him. "How did you get here, Odel? And why? Are you really that crazy?"

The bearded redhead picked up Thusk and hugged him, laughing. "Y'all left such good directions, t'were easy to find you. I mean, how many big rivers go south and fall down over a miles-wide waterfall, down thousands of feet? And how many big stone palaces in a city of stone buildings, next to a carved rock rainbow, can there be? And how many bird-riding little guys could there be close by? So here I am, thanks to that booster-stuff your Una-thing showed me how to make." Surrounded by cheering people of both lands—*and now our first ally from the third land, God's Country!* Thusk thought—the scene was enough to bring a rare smile to his face.

Princess Pernie, Thist, Wakan, and the rest of the war council had come out to see Odel by this time, adding to the celebratory nature of the flying man's unexpected arrival. Thusk introduced his friend to them. All of them, along with PeoplesLandsers, inspected Odel's tri-wing, expressing astonishment that the big man had flown down from the Dark Highlands in such a fragile-looking machine.

Odel welcomed all comments and seemed to be enjoying the attention. In his thick but understandable accent, Thusk understood him and translated as fast as he could. "My friend Odel, here, says, 'That were indeed quite the drop-off at the waterfall, but your countrymen here—Thist and Thusk—well, they told me all about it, so I was ready.'"

As the war council reassembled back in the palace, Princess Perneptheranam welcomed their God's Country guest, as Thusk kept up his translation. "Odel M'ridge, our Thusk and Thist have told us about their visit with you at your quarry, but please tell us all how you came to be here, and what your intentions are."

The big redbeard stood quaffing a mug of ShadowFall's finest beer. "Princess." He bowed formally, enunciating his words and speaking slowly so that his accent was not so much an impediment to Thusk's following translation. "My little friends Thusk and Thist, Mr. Wakan Kech, and all of you ShadowFallers. After my visitors from The People's Lands left, I commenced to thinking about y'all's situation down here. So I played around with some of that firepowder their Una told me about, made up some godscloth tubes like it said, and found out that I could use them to boost me off the ground, and also to speed me along the way." He paused after each few sentences, to allow Thusk time to summarize.

Thusk repeated Odel's story: "I used some of the godsmetal arcs like that Una showed me, made myself some new tri-wings. I can fold them up, then unspring them to full size when I want." He pointed out the window, toward the plaza where his tri-wing lay beside the much larger Una. Thusk nodded and continued following his narration for the others. "I brought a couple of them along, bundles tied to the skids out there. Thought y'all might like to have some 'air power' that don't depend on your Una machine."

With a glint in his eye and a crooked toothy grin contrasting with his dark red beard, he leaned over the table as if to be closer to each of the councilors. "I mean, it's a fantastic ancient machine and all, but in my business I have found that old things wear out, and there ain't never been a machine that don't break down sometime when you least expect it. I call that 'M'ridge's Law,'" he guffawed. Thusk converted his language to Motherland talk, but his gestures and appearance needed little interpretation: Odel was a character, and an impressive one.

His manner and storytelling ability unlike any ShadowFaller or PeoplesLandser had ever encountered, Odel continued to tell (through Thusk) his travel story in some detail, about how he had ox-waggoned his new tri-wings and the firepowder boosters all the way to God's Port. "And there, I bought a boat and sailed it south, like Thist said he did, last year. Only me, this time I was expecting that humongous waterfall. I had built me an elevated platform with my tri-wing on it, and my harness hanging down, ready to jump into it on a moment's warning.

"Onc't I heard the falls up ahead, I got hooked up. Right before my little boat went over the edge, I lit my fuses and boosted my glider up and away from the platform. Knowing y'all were not too far downriver, I took my sweet time enjoying the view from up there, and by the way, it is fantastic. Actually, boys," he said, looking at the twins, "it is better being up in the wind like I was, than being inside your Una machine and looking out through its clear walls." Thist and Thusk at first laughed at the thought, but then recalled that Odel had experienced both, but themselves only Una. Maybe he was right?

"Anyhow, I know that one man and a few tri-wings ain't gonna be of a lotta use in your little war down here, but—what if we can build hundreds of them? If you've got godsmetal, godscloth, and people who wanna learn to fly, I am here to help!"

Thist spoke up, first in Odel's language, then in Motherspeak. "Odel, smaller people like us PeoplesLandsers, we can use smaller tri-wings. And if Una won't let us drop spears and stones from the sky, to kill our enemies, then we will use your tri-wings!" Thusk was nodding, though hesitantly. *Another way to kill,* he thought, morosely. *We're getting pretty good at this.*

Wakan stood and welcomed Odel formally. "Thank you for your offer of help. I believe that some of the towers we are erecting across ShadowFall territory may lend themselves as launching sites for flights of your tri-wing craft. I will meet you up with our shops and artisans." Shaking Odel's hand, he said, "Let's see if we can add an aerial force to our arsenal of defensive weapons."

CHAPTER TWENTY-SEVEN

Nine hundred kilometers northeast of Mother Messinex's palace in Mother's City, her Sister Pernie was speaking to the ShadowFall war council. "Daily extreme altitude overflights in the Una god-machine show that General Creesile is once again assembling troop barges and siege machines, and assembling thousands of Mothersmen soldiers. In the absence of any explanatory correspondence from Mother's Palace, and knowing what Wakan's spies have been able to ascertain about the plans of that traitorous Miran Kech, I hereby declare war upon that evil man."

Princess Perneptheranam was grim but resolved as she stood at the end of the long oaken table in the ShadowFall palace war council room. Battle flags, colorful woven sigil banners, and historical tapestries covered most of the stone walls around them, representing both older ShadowFall defensive commands and brand-new PeoplesLandser bird-rider attack groups. Dressed in dark green godscloth robes, her copper-colored hair in a braid running all the way down her back, past her waist, the Princess lifted a polished battle sword from a dark leather sheath at her waist.

"Let it be known that I do not wish to bring harm to any citizen of Motherland, but ShadowFall will defend itself from the illegitimate claims of the insidious Miran

Kech, and from the military ambitions of his bootlicking toady, General Creesile." The men and women in attendance cheered and applauded, among them Wakan Kech, the two PeoplesLandser heroes Thist and Thusk, and an assortment of ShadowFall nobles and warriors.

Wakan Kech bowed before the Princess, then took the lead as she sat grim-faced; no Sister had ever made a formal declaration of war on any other part of Motherland, traditionally preferring subversion, sneak attacks, and assassinations. Pernie's statement deftly avoided any mention of Mother Messinex, not wanting to stimulate the other Sisters to join Mother to defend their ancient system of ruling-class privileges. "We plan to deliver this declaration of *defense*—not a declaration of *war*—to Mother Messinex in person, using the unique abilities of the Una flying god-machine. Thist here"—he pointed to the leather-armored little man —"will endeavor to enter Mother's Palace and present our plea for Miran Kech and General Creesile to be removed from office, the Mothersmen Army disbanded, and the invasion of ShadowFall called off." All around the table, nods and grins showed approval of the audacious plan.

But Wakan then added, "Because of the uncertainties involved—will Mother Messinex accede to our requests, and if she does, will Miran Kech and the general obey Her orders? They may have other plans." He sighed. "I have known Miran Kech for forty years. For those of you who know the story, he and I and other High Antians were taken prisoner by General Creesile over twenty years ago, down in the Southern Dry Highlands. Miran was once a shining example of Kech discipline, education, and culture. But I am afraid that all these years in Motherland have overcome that decency and integrity with the scheming complicity that one is exposed to in the Courts of the Sisterdoms and at Mother's Palace."

He then reported on the conditions of the several hundred pitiful prisoners in the dungeons below Mother's Palace, where according to other Kech,

Miran's inquisitors and torturers were inflicting hideous punishments on former nobles and courtiers whose only sins were belonging to the late Lordess Mother's Courts, or having been appointed to positions by her. Their replacements, all of Miran's choosing, were reportedly only sycophants, much less qualified for their positions. Left unspoken were any reasons why Mother Messinex was allowing these atrocities and injustices to continue.

Spreading his arms wide and taking a slight bow, Wakan said, "For I, too, am not the naive priest I once was, having many years to learn how to survive in a new and vicious court environment." Around the room he could see that others were taking his mild confession in different ways—grins, grimaces, nods of recognition. "But I like to think that for the most part I have tried to use these new, er, *diplomatic* skills for the betterment of Motherland in general and of ShadowFall and its Princess, in particular." Pernie's knowing smile was all the acknowledgement Wakan needed to continue. He turned very serious, almost grim.

"In the unexpected case that Thist's mission to Mother Messinex is less than successful, we here at this table must be prepared for the consequences. If there be war and we do not prevail, then most certainly all of us here will die, either swiftly or very slowly." The descriptions of Miran Kech's dungeons and torture chambers weighed heavily on their minds. "But I intend to win if it comes to that. After all, in the five years since we arrived here, we have prevailed in the invasions from two of our neighboring Sisterdoms. I will call upon two leaders of those defenses to tell us what happened, and how they were able to defeat RidgeBack and Four Peaks, back when we were newly settled up here in the North."

Over the next hour, two minor nobles described how they had armed and trained hundreds of ordinary ShadowFall citizens with the springbows that Wakan had sequestered from stores in Mother's City. "The invaders were not collaborating well," said Lord Theves, a short, stocky man with weatherworn skin, wearing dark leather armor in the lavender and black shades of ShadowFall, "RidgeBack just marched five hundred men up the Main Road halfway up to the Palace, and sent men to demand our surrender." He laughed. "But Lord Kech here, he sent me down with our springbowmen, not on the road but stealthily along its sides, at night. We surprised them, killing half of them before the rest ran away!"

The next speaker, Lord Sentier, a tall blond in plain country-style dress, said, "A similar fate befell the abortive attempt from Four Peaks at the same time RidgeBack invaded. We had advanced word of their part, thanks to, er, well, Lord Kech's security service." He nodded at Wakan Kech. "Princess Jernoma sent a thousand specially trained warriors, a real army, with experienced Mothersmen leading them. While RidgeBack was demanding our surrender at the Palace, they simply walked across our undefended border at the far southeastern corner of ShadowFall, where we had but few farmers living, just crops and grasslands, only rough graveled roads. They were too well organized to fall for an ambush and too deadly to meet in hand-to-hand combat. But our Lord Kech worked out in advance how we could lure them into marshy lowlands between high stony mounds, as they approached our city from across Mother's River. We were able to use our springbows to effect from those small hills." Sentier swallowed, blinking tears from his eyes. "Killing people from three hundred meters when *their* arrows could only reach one hundred, was…good for us, but…I hated to see brave men die like that. Such a waste." The man was struggling to keep his composure.

Wakan motioned for Sentier to sit. "Lord Sentier failed to mention that his own brother was…leading the Four Peaks army. And that his oldest son died in that battle, bravely defending our ShadowFall." A story familiar to the locals, the details of Sentier's sacrifices were a sobering shock to the PeoplesLandsers. *These big people kill each other, and so easily!*

Wakan took up the narrative. "When I presented this

information to the Lordess Mother, she carved out fifteen hundred square kilometers each of RidgeBack and Four Peaks and turned them over to our Princess, establishing our new ShadowFall borders. I think that those two losing princesses never got over that." He left unsaid the current situation in RidgeBack, where its princess had been replaced by Miran Kech's handpicked female, a "temporary administrator." He suspected that Four Peaks would shortly suffer a similar fate. *Miran Kech is cleaning house!*With the consequences of internecine warfare now brought out in stark relief, the planners put aside any visions of battlefield glory and got down to the dirty business of figuring out how to fight and live against an overwhelming foe. And secretly hoping that Thist could pull off a miracle for peace in the same way that, against all reason, he had won the Motherland Game.

CHAPTER TWENTY-EIGHT

Following Pernie's command to deliver the "declaration of defense" to Mother Messinex, Thusk and Thist were flying Una down toward Mother's City. Thusk paced the floor of Una's cabin, making his way around the stone-bombs they might have to use on their mission, ignoring the beauty of the Motherland plains, the carpeted landscape that was unrolling two hundred meters beneath them. "Thist," he said to his twin, who was attempting to memorize details of the rooms and hallways of Mother's Palace from Una's screen maps, "we have just one chance at this. Do we try to seize Miran Kech, or just kill him?"

Thist looked up, blinking his eyes. "We'll worry about that after we get to the palace. I've got to remember all of this," he said. "The palace is so big, with so many rooms, I could get lost and never find my way out again." He patted the cabin wall. "Are you sure that Una can't just crash down through the roof of that big dome, where the Crystal Throne is? I know the way from there to Mother Messinex's small throne room." He remembered that room vividly, it being where he had been explaining some godsphere ancient history to her before she loudly dismissed him. *Losing her mind, if you ask me,* he thought.

Thusk took that suggestion literally, saying, "Una either can't or won't cause any injury or death to a human being. If it can't say the Crystal Throne room is safe, we can't do that."

I was only joking, Thist didn't say aloud. "So what about the atrium area where you rescued me? It's only a short distance. I do know how to get to Messinex from there." Thusk agreed to try, if no guards were present, noting that his twin was no longer using the proper title for the Mother of Motherland.

"I can sneak past any guards," Thist said. "They won't be expecting me. Especially if we do it at night."

"After dark this evening, then," Thusk agreed. "Invisible and quiet."

"Sires!" Una's alarms were sounding, rousting Thist and Thusk out of their quiet review of plans to seize Miran Kech and to appeal to Mother Messinex. "There are borophene arrows on catapults guarding the atrium destination you specified. This craft cannot approach any closer, and cannot land as ordered!" Answering Thusk's immediate inquiry, Una responded, "All open atria, courtyards, open spaces, and entrances around Mother's Palace are similarly guarded. This craft cannot approach any closer."

Thist ordered Una to show its video screens for all views around the palace. In invisible mode and at three hundred meters altitude, they were safe from any known range of the catapult weapons, but their plan for easy entry had just been demolished. "Damn! That Miran Kech has armed the whole place with anti-Una arrow bundles. He must have anticipated our probable solution to his actions." *He's just too damned smart, is all!* Thist realized the truth of what Wakan Kech had said after their initial attack on the troop transport barges at Lake Roos last month, that they had exposed Una's existence and vulnerability to the enemy too early. "Our enemy has vast resources," the priest had said, "and most likely has realized that Una won't kill. I am afraid we should have gone after Miran first, before he realized what he was up against." At the time Thist and Thusk had thought their Kech friend wrong, but now realized he was right.

"So, our next move, Thist?" his twin asked. "The palace guards will probably be keeping very close watch around the grounds, too, knowing that we don't dare fly Una in close. What do you think?"

Thist reviewed the layout of the palace in his mind, having an idea pop up. "Thusk, we didn't know what we might be facing on our trip here, but we did bring those boulders like the ones we dropped on Creesile's boats, to use if we found any targets of opportunity along the way. What if we have Una scan the palace as deep as possible, fly up very high, and drop some down into the rooms where it knows no one will be harmed? That might put enough of a scare into Miran Kech to make him call off the war? Think that will be enough of a 'declaration of defense'?"

As Thusk was silently thinking it over, Thist asked, "Una, can you scan the palace and find any rooms where we can drop these boulders without injuring anybody?"

Una replied, "This DI will use ground-penetrating radar sensing at the maximum level to determine with absolute certainty those areas of the Mother's Palace that no humans occupy or are likely to occupy during the operation." At that, the craft began to orbit the palace, coming in closer at some points, staying farther away at others, calculating the probable safe distances away from the borophene arrow catapults. Within a minute, Una announced, "Sires, many of the palace rooms are now unoccupied. It seems as if a major reduction in courtiers has occurred. Thermal pickups reveal that the deep dungeons are now crowded. Audio sensors reveal"—the DI hesitated, then continued —"cries of extreme pain and distress among the many inhabitants there. But in the aboveground chambers, this display shows which area may be attacked without human injury."

Looking at the video map, now marked with shades

of red where humans were located, and shades of blue signifying areas safe to bomb, Thist and Thusk turned to each other in mild surprise. Both said, "The Crystal Throne room?"

Thusk said, shaking his head, "If we break through that big dome, everyone will be thinking we are attacking the Mother Herself. That could bring down the wrath of all Motherland on us." They both realized that having to fight millions of enraged citizens instead of Creesile's mere thousands of mercenaries was not a wise choice.

Thist agreed, saying, "You're right. We need to target some area where Miran Kech frequents. Or that Rumi Similla." He waved his hand over the blue areas on the video. "Una, can you tell us if any of these 'safe' rooms belong to Miran or Rumi?"

In some inscrutable manner—not magic, but technology, Thusk realized, but still almost unbelievable —Una replied, "Sire, the rooms now designated in flashing green are safe to attack. But quickly; persons are en route to them."

Thusk yelled, "So now, Una! Roll and open your door!" He and Thist grabbed onto their cabin seats as their aircraft immediately moved over the targets, stopping, then rolling over to allow a boulder to fall through the opening door. "And zoom in on it, Una!"

The forward video screen followed the half-meter-diameter stone as it fell, the scene shifting as it hit the roof of Mother's Palace. Slow-motion video continued the sequence: penetrating the green-colored oxidized copper palace roof, the object fell through a maze of supporting attic beams, two consecutive layers of ceilings and floors, finally coming to a stop in a crater in the marble floor of a huge bedroom. Thist wondered how Una could access such images from around the crash site, but had long since given up trying to understand the DI's capabilities.

What the video revealed as its view swept its surroundings was a large, gold godscloth-covered bed surrounded by matching drapery; several golden chairs;

a working fountain of sculptured marble; silvery walls covered by tapestries of scenes from Motherland legends; and a life-size but flattering bodily portrait of Miran Kech himself. Thist grinned and yelled, "We hit his bedroom, Thusk! That ought to scare the bastard!" His twin shook his hand. They had made their point.

Thist said, "And now, Una, please find Rumi Similla's room." Within a minute, the two men were watching their second stone-bomb score a hit, but this time in the middle of a bed. And as the view from the bomb scanned the room, a shocked Rumi Similla ran in, not believing the collapsed ceiling, the debris covering her floor, and the massive boulder now embedded in the floor beneath the bed where she had slept. Without audio, Thist and Thusk still enjoyed the obvious screams as the woman held her hands to her head. They enjoyed even more as Miran Kech himself walked in behind his distraught mistress, his surprise quickly turning to disgust. Miran looked up at the hole in the ceiling, then down at the stone, his face a portrait of rage. With a final glance upward, the priest shook his fist at the damaged ceiling. "I wish we could hear what he's saying, Thusk," Thist said. "I don't think he's too happy right now."

Their primary mission aborted, but having scored at least psychological damage—and hopefully, a warning—to Miran and Rumi, The PeoplesLandser men took their craft back northeasterly, wanting to check on Creesile's preparations, if possible, before returning to ShadowFall.

CHAPTER TWENTY-NINE

Miran Kech was furious. "Rumi, stop your screaming! Now!" Holding the hysterical woman tightly, he stroked her hair gently, trying to control himself while comforting his mistress. He didn't blame Rumi for her shock; a boulder in the middle of a person's bed, a hundred meters below the roof of Mother's Palace, would be enough to frighten the wits out of anybody.

"They could have killed me!" Rumi cried. "That Rist and his flying machine did this!" As Rumi stopped shaking, Miran released her and thought, *But they* didn't *kill you. This proves that they* can't. But how Rumi's room was located in the first place, and how Rist knew exactly when and where to drop this stone, as they had done when sinking Creesile's troop barges—again, not killing nor even injuring a single trooper!—represented capabilities far beyond anything Miran had thought possible. It had to be ancient knowledge. But now Mother Messinex had forbidden all access to ancient books and the godspheres, so such knowledge would be lost forever. *Or at least until I can open them!*

Miran returned to his own rooms to contemplate how to answer such an unwarranted attack on Mother's Palace. He would think of a way to use the bombing to arouse public opinion against ShadowFall. But should he reveal that the palace had no defense against a dark dwarf from the highlands and his magic flying machine? That was problematic. He'd have to think about all of the ramifications.

As he neared the hallway to his suite of rooms, a guard asked him to stop. "Lord Kech, there has been damage to your rooms. It looks like a big rock fell down from above then crashed into your bedroom. The rock is still there."

Miran flinched. *They found us both, then. Were these rocks just a warning that they could find us anywhere? But it looks like nobody was hurt, just damage to the palace. I'll get word to the general: he shouldn't worry about that god-machine. Just train his troops not to panic. It won't hurt them!* He summoned a messenger and so ordered. By his calendar, if nothing else untoward was unfolding, the messenger might arrive at Lake Roos' embarkation docks before Creesile began his movements northward.

As Miran expected, when Mother Messinex received the news she was at a step just below hysterical. "How could little Rist do this to my palace, my home, the most sacred site in all of Motherland? It has to be that damned Sister of mine, that Pernie! No one has ever attacked the palace, not in thousands of years!" She knew better; the golden plates in her Sanctuary Room told story after story of armies of one Sister after another laying siege to Mother's Palace, even as it was being built, over and over again, fighting battles on its grounds, in its hallways. Even one in the domed Crystal Throne room itself. But she kept this information to herself, as had her predecessor Mothers for generations. It was best that the subjects feel that the palace of their Mother was inviolable, or at least impregnable. *So many things are best kept secret from my subjects,* she thought. *I wonder what the actual truth is about everything I think I know? Is* anything *true?*

Miran had heard Messinex's reflections on her secret

tablets, letting slip some of Motherland's actual history, enough to know that he would be expected to hold close all information about the rock bombs. Turning to an aide, he sent word to the repair crews on both floors and to all palace staff, that any leak about the "unfortunate ceiling collapses" was worth a thin-sliced tongue and the stocks.

"Mother Messinex," he said in his most soothing voice, "these were minor annoyances. As happened in the palace tonight, as happened at Lake Roos last month, they show us that Rist's flying machine cannot harm a human being. My fellow Kech agree that it must mean a limitation that the ancients, in their wisdom, imposed. We feel that they would not allow a soulless machine of theirs to fight against themselves." In a breathless plea, he said, "Were it that we could do the same with springbows, catapults, swords, and spears." In a small corner of his mind, he wondered, *But what would such a world look like? Who could rule without the threat of deadly force?*

CHAPTER THIRTY

E lder Myuk was worried. She was going to have to report to Elder Buk that neither of her two latest charges showed enough promise of being even self-sufficient, much less contributory to Community. Having learned nothing useful at the Hall of Whispers, they were now living their last days, unless she could work out another arrangement of some kind. But to her knowledge, few to no Disabled had ever escaped the iron law of Reprocessing.

Myuk was all too aware of the harsh protocols of population control. In her mind she could hear Elder Buk, chair of the Council of Elders, patiently explaining it all to the members: "Elders, the Creator has provided enough volume for all of our thousands of folk to live, to eat, to work, to reproduce. But we must needs practice conservation and efficiency; our very survival depends on it. Each of us is an individual beloved of our Creator, but each of us must also bear responsibility for not only ourselves, but to Community. We allow every child to grow to Thirteen Motherth Years, trusting that they will develop skills, talents, or some other function useful to Community. If the Creator has not provided such talents, She has Her reasons. And we must abide by those reasons, a covenant we have kept since The Beginning of All Things."

Elder Myuk did not carry that memory any further

forward. She knew the outcome, the finality of the Reprocessing that would occur—two little lives extinguished. If only Mienne or Wayer had shown some promise, had heard the voices, *anything*! Making her inspection rounds, she saw the two girls, happily chatting away as they were sweeping their bedroom area. How sad!

"WAYER," MIENNE WAS SAYING AS UGLY ELDER PASSED by, smiling at them, "I went back to the Hall of Whispers last Sleep Period. You won't believe what I Saw."

"Girl, you didn't *See* anything. You are Blind." Wayer's voice was louder than a whisper, making Mienne nervous. She looked around, hoping her friend hadn't been heard.

"Keep it down, Wayer. I *Saw* the stuff of my dreams on the walls there—people, plants, colors—not just red, though red is one of them. And a Woman came into the flat wall and spoke to me!"

Wayer stopped sweeping and shook her head. "And? Go on? This is a whole different tale than you've told me over the years."

"The Woman was beautiful. Somehow she figured out that I was speaking Rin. But she also spoke *Glish*. Can you believe that?"

Wayer made the sign of the X across her chest. She quickly spat out the meaningless words, *"That is the language of the Sun God, He who raped Motherth and brought ice and darkness upon Her and all of us."*

Mienne almost laughed. "Do you have any idea what you just said, Wayer? Any idea of what the words mean?"

Her friend shook her head. "A spell to ward off evil? Invoking Motherth's protection?"

Mienne said, "But who is *Sun God* and who is *Motherth*? I've just been taught these names, and that catechism, all my life."

"As have I! Why do you question it now?" Wayer was confused.

"Because of what I Saw in the Hall of Whispers. And what was told to me."

"Well, Mienne, I am scared now. I wish I didn't know."

Mienne thought on that. "Me? I wanted to know Truth. And Truth is, I am scared, too."

AT THE END OF THE NEXT WAKE PERIOD, ELDER MYUK was distraught. Returning from yet another meeting of the Shinyeen City Council, where her pleas for mercy had been rejected a final time, she now had the unpleasant task of telling Mienne and Wayer that, having reached the age of accountability yet possessing no sustainable skills, they would be Reprocessed. *I hate this responsibility*, she thought, sweating profusely as she walked back toward the Niche of Disabled Children.

Thinking of committing the ultimate treason, she wondered, *Surely there must be a place for these children, perhaps in the new Tubes that the famous tunneler Keesh discovered? He came by to check on her every few months after he rescued her. It's been a while now, but he must feel something for the child, even though he only ever spoke with me, not her.* But even in the newly found Tubes, she knew, nothing edible was grown and even if the girls escaped from the Niche they would still have to depend upon others to sneak in food and water. *That could work for a short while, but not for a lifetime!* And her own penalty for disobedience of Council orders could be Reprocessing, too!

UNKNOWN TO THE UGLY ELDER, THE TWO GIRLS HAD tailed her as she left the Niche that morning, sneaking into an adjacent room and hearing the verdict of the Council. "Reprocessed?" Wayer had whispered to

Mienne, "They are going to *kill* us?" Mienne nodded, breathing out heavily.

"We have to leave, Wayer," Mienne offered. "Let's run and get some food and water now, and just *go!*" Wayer stiffened and began sobbing. "I know of a place we can hide, Wayer. Don't be afraid." But Mienne herself was as afraid as she had been after Mother had left her alone in the tunnels, years before.

Trying not to attract attention, she and Wayer went to the Niche stock room and loaded up two bags of nonperishables, taking enough water to sustain them for a few days. Mienne wanted to return immediately to the Hall of Whispers, there to follow the maps she had seen during her unauthorized visit. Surely, the ancients who built all of that must have had somewhere to sleep, to eat, to drink. *And if all of their marvelous image-making machines, the ones that could talk to me, are still working, then their life-sustaining stuff will be, too. I hope; it's our only chance!*

Hours later, as they approached the archway leading out from their Niche, Mienne heard people outside. Hiding herself from view, she peeked around and saw a small group of people standing around, talking excitedly. That was unusual; typically Community citizens didn't gather for no purpose, but were always in a hurry, working at whatever their assignments were. But now they sounded bothered: "The guards are coming here!" "What for?" "Has something bad happened?" "I don't know, but I heard that somebody in the Niche will be Reprocessed!"

At that, the two girls quickly backtracked into the Niche and exited through a small hidden tunnel known only to, and used only by, children of the Niche who wanted to come and go unseen by their Elder keepers. Her path lit only by the dimmest of luminescence, Mienne had to walk bent over to avoid hitting her head on the low ceiling of the carved Tube. From the smooth surface of its walls and floor, she knew the chipped-out stone had been rubbed by Niche children's clothes and bodies many, many times over many, many years. *How many others have escaped through here?* she wondered. *And where did they go?*

"GIRLS!" ELDER MYUK YELLED INTO THE CATACOMBS of the niche, her voice echoing back into the darkness. "Mienne, Wayer, where are you?" As she walked through the damp stone corridors she saw the truly disabled younger children huddling back into dark rooms. She shuddered at the vision of yet other youngsters being fed into the Reprocessing chamber. She knew that she would not be psychologically able to continue her task of caring for such children much longer, not if more and more disabled were brought to her. *Not and get to know and educate and succor them for years and then—just to* kill *them!*

An hour later, Elder Myuk was both frustrated and happy. Frustrated that her girls were not in the Niche to be seized by the guardsmen and taken away. And yet happy for the same reason. But the Council guards standing in front of her were not happy at all. "Elder Myuk," the larger of the two said gruffly, puffing out his leather-vested chest and pounding his black metal control stick into one gloved hand. "We have orders to take the two Disabled to Reprocessing, yet you say they are not present?" Elder Myuk explained yet again that both Mienne and Wayer were not to be found in the Niche. "But you, citizens, are quite welcome to go in and search for yourselves." She stepped aside and waved an arm toward the darkness beyond her small room. Both of the guards gulped and shook their heads; the few severely deformed children that the Elder had brought up to the front of the Niche were enough of a frightful sight to instill fear as to what other creatures might be lurking farther back in the caves.

"You will inform us if the fugitives return, Elder," the guard said, turning on his heel to leave. Elder Myuk smiled as the brave men departed. *But where could they have gone? Be careful my little ones. And please, please, be safe!*

MIENNE AND WAYER FOUND THAT THEIR PLANNED escape to the Hall of Whispers was becoming impossible; every tunnel leading that way had Council guards patrolling them, big men in black leather, carrying cudgels and swords. "Blocked by the guards," Mienne whispered into Wayer's ear. "We have to go another way. Or hide until they stop looking for us."

Wayer nodded. "I am scared, Mienne. I don't want to be Reprocessed."

Mienne said, "You have lived down here for all your life. Do you know of any other place we can go hide, at least for a while?"

Wayer was silent for a minute. "Well, once I did go with Ugly Elder when she went to see a Tunneler about opening up new volume for our Niche. Along the way, she pointed out a long dark tunnel that she said led to a forbidden volume, the Resource Tube."

"Forbidden? Why?"

"It was a place where the Creator left a lot of machines and materials for our tunnelers to use, to make new machines, to do repairs. Lots of strange things. Things that nobody knows how to use. Things that could cause trouble for ordinary people. Only tunnelers can go there. It's a scary place."

"Can you find it? Can we get there without getting caught?"

Mienne saw Wayer make the affirmative head motion, and followed her armless friend.

Because Wayer could See, she led the way as the two girls ran down through tunnel after tunnel, through abandoned volumes, past niches of unknown uses, always moving as fast as they could, rarely stopping to catch their breath. Mienne noted that the smells were different in the many passageways they fled down, and she wondered why.

Arriving at the archway leading to the Resource Tube, Mienne made her way slowly into the dimly-lit volume, with Wayer close behind. In view from the entrance she saw that Wayer was right: a dozen or more huge Eternal Machines for tunneling were lined in a long row, mechanical monsters. And all around them lay piles of unknown mechanical parts of every description, as if waiting to be assembled into yet another machine of some kind. She kept walking, hoping to find any shelter, a place to hide for a while until they could find a way to get to the Hall of Whispers.

Turning a corner, Mienne was shocked at what she saw: two men working on machines—her rescuers—in the tunnel!

"YOU KNOW I WANT TO TEST YOUR SMALLPROBE, Ledd," said Jolan Keesh. "Whether or not we send it all the way Up to Vac and show the old Elders they are wrong, at least we can map strata and try to understand more about what's above us. Might be more livable volume."

Ledd Mernan nodded as he sat at his workbench tinkering with the device. Ledd's smallprobe was a tiny trackless version of the huge Eternal Machines that Keesh's crews used for large tunneling. Comprised of a totally reflective Nisteel cylinder the size of Ledd's bicep, the small machine tapered all the way to an invisible point. A series of circular portholes spaced around the forward circumference provided the invisible beams that melted any rock in front of it, the circular spiral pattern acting as a drill bit, pushing the melt to the side where it formed a smooth shaft. *Just like those Eternal Machine tunnelers*, Ledd thought. He never quite understood how the smallprobe could propel itself upward through rock, and only be powered by some onboard system. Community engineers, using all of the machine tools available from Resource Tubes and from the Old Lost Ones, had never been able even to scratch the surface of the shiny metal exterior to examine its inner workings. They only knew that if they pointed it in a direction and pressed it against any surface, it would press forward, melting the rock, forming the tiny glassy-surfaced tunnel behind it.

"I've already added the ultrasonic sounder system to the back, as you said, boss," Ledd explained as Keesh inspected his work. The assistant engineer had attached the sounder package and a spool of godswire behind the smallprobe. *Fortunately,* Keesh reflected mentally for the thousandth time, *either the Creator or one of the Old Lost Ones, whoever had fabricated the smallprobe, thoughtfully provided a series of metal tabs sticking out from the rear of the cylinder, with holes through which wires can be attached, so it can be pulled back.* Looking at the spindle of godswire, Keesh did a mental calculation. *Five kilometers up to Vac? This spool of wire can easily reach fifty kilometers! I wonder what might be Up there that far?* Recalling his interrogation in the Council, he concluded, *I guess we'll never know!*

Ledd said, "Boss, I still wish we could just point our *big* tunnelers Upward and go for it. We could get there a lot faster than this little machine can." Standing on his workbench and stretching his arms as far up as he could, Ledd held the device against the ceiling, two meters up. Immediately the little machine seemed to come alive, pulling itself up into the solid stone, trailing wires behind it.

"Looks like a lunarat digging into a burrow," Keesh laughed. "Well, there is no harm in experimenting with our little melter. Let it go up a few hundred meters and let's see how it performs. Make measurements we can show to the Council another time." *Maybe we can reach Vac someday, or maybe the Elders will change their minds, or maybe Elder Uise will die?*

"Ledd, you know that this little one will hold itself against the wall as it climbs Up. But if we went Upwards in a large machine, we can only incline the tunnelers about twenty degrees or we'd slide back into or own tunnel. To get to a point five kilometers directly above us, with all the switchbacks, what a maze that would be. And it would take us a couple of dozen Periods to get there." He paused. "Even longer, if we drag along the sealant machines." Surface sealant machines were a recent addition to tunneling equipment, something that Keesh himself had invented, a mechanical spraying process to speed up the finishing touches to new tunnels rather than wasting scarce manpower to do it by hand.

Fortunately, the Resource Tube had provided all the components Keesh needed to realize his conception. In that Tube, in Her wisdom the Creator had provided a vast array of hand tools, machine tools, fabricators, and even some equipment that nobody had ever learned to use. Engineers—of which Keesh was one of only ten in a regulated profession tightly controlled by the Council —were the only people allowed in the Tube. Keesh suspected that a devout enough engineer would one day become sufficiently Enlightened to comprehend how to interface with and use the millions of other strange devices stored in the endless niches and racks in their Tube, but apparently he himself was not yet advanced enough to be allowed such knowledge. Yet he *was* permitted to imagine new machines, to design them, and to reprocess materials taken from the Tubes of the Old Lost Ones. However, the alteration of any existing Eternal Machines was strictly forbidden and strictly enforced; Keesh had never even considered such modification, not with the vast unused resources of the Old Lost Ones readily available for disassembly and reuse.

Ledd said, "I know that we have always tunneled horizontally, but when we broke through into the Vast Volume a few Motherth Years ago, it had a lot of verticality to it. And it looked like it had been worked by the Old Lost Ones."

Keesh nodded. "Yes, that must have been another Tube the Creator provided for us, but the Old Lost Ones claimed it and used it first. And so She eliminated them to make room for us to expand." Still averse to theological discussions, he walked over and looked up into the ceiling where the smallprobe had been launched, putting on a godsglove to feel the thrumming vibration of the godswire. "Our little friend should be Upward by fifty meters by now." A quick look at the wire-length indicator showed he was correct; an induction coil around the godswire was picking up instrumentation signals as the device ate its way upward through strata. "We have slowed down; must've hit a thick vein of granite up there, Ledd. Real slow going. I just hope that the hard stuff doesn't extend all the way to Vac if we do get permission to melt up there.

"This hundred meter stratum is good enough for testing our little driller. This test shows the system works okay, but we would have to do any farther-Up experiments way away from Community, in case something does go wrong." Cave-ins or accidental collapses into unsuspected adjacent airless voids were always a possibility; the ancient scanner instruments, though usually very precise, did not always perform as expected. He recalled when that child, Mienne, had fallen into his tunnel unexpectedly some months before. "Would you take a look at our scanner archives out at Foremost? I want to be out as far as possible, planning for the worst."

THE NEXT MORNING, JOLAN KEESH MET LEDD MERNAN at his office niche in the Resource Room. Ledd was holding a sheaf of paper. He said, "Boss, our ultrasonic scan archives show a series of Upward voids out past Foremost that will the best place to start the probe, better than the ones you told the Council about. Just a few hundred meters of horizontal melt will get us there." Looking closely at Keesh's face, he asked, "Are you still sure you want to try for Vac anyhow, a violation of Council orders?"

Keesh said, "Well, let's just see how far Up we can go, and decide then. We will need a safe place, away from onlookers and wandering Elders. If we're way out past Foremost, where we had that Mienne child fall in on us, nobody will be around to pay attention. Whoever follows us dirty tunnelers?"

As Keesh and Ledd laid out their plans, Ledd heard a noise. "Boss, I think—" Leaving the sentence unfinished, he gasped and pointed behind his boss. Turning around to see what Ledd was indicating, Keesh was shocked to see the tall foundling, Mienne, and a young blonde girl of normal size—but with no arms!

"Mienne," Keesh said, running over and reaching up to embrace the tall girl, "What are you doing here?" Looking around quickly, he whispered, "Elder Myuk told me that you and another child—*this* one?"—pointing to Wayer—"were going to be Reprocessed. Did the Council change their minds?" Sensing the girls' hesitation, he asked, "Or have you escaped?"

Sobbing, Mienne told the two drillers how they had heard the guards were coming, and how Wayer had known the location of the Resource Tube. "And we thought it our only chance to live, Mr. Keesh. We didn't know you would be here. Please don't tell the guards. We will leave, and won't be in your way. Please."

Keesh saw the pleading in her face, and tears in the blonde girl's eyes. "Don't worry, children; my partner, Ledd, here, and I will look after you. Don't worry." At that, both girls hugged him and thanked him, Wayer's motion consisting of pressing herself tightly against the engineer. Keesh could tell from the look on Ledd's face that he was not too happy about the situation. Keesh couldn't blame him; going against the Council could have fatal results, regardless of their past accomplishments and discoveries.

Ignoring his partner's lack of enthusiasm, he said, "Ledd, somewhere in this Tube ought to be a place for them to sleep, a place to hide. No guards ever come this way; this Tube is haunted, they say. Superstition has its uses!" Both men laughed.

With the Creator's own luminescent illumination suffusing the entire Tube as it did everywhere in

Community, searching for an adequate hideaway among the vast assemblage of mechanical parts and assemblies was easy. At a fair distance down the Resource Tube, farther than any uninterested person would ever wander, they found a large, open-ended metallic cylinder of unknown purpose, located at the bottom of a pile of some kind of machinery. It sufficed as a place of refuge for the two girls. ("Much nicer than the Niche," Wayer said. "And it smells better, too.") A dripping distilled-water spigot nearby served for drinking and as a basis for washing, and there were many cavities in the floor nearby appropriate for waste disposal. "We will bring in dried foods from time to time," Ledd said. "And we will furnish you with an induction heater that draws power from these walls. Then you can add hot water and have meals." He left unspoken what would become of the girls as time went on. Surely he and Keesh could not keep them hidden forever.

Mienne herself helped the engineers resolve their problem. After a Sleep Period, while eating firstmeal with their saviors, Mienne indicated that the metal cylinder around them could never be a permanent residence, not with guards looking for them. She said, "But if we can get back to the Hall of Whispers, we will be safe there, I believe."

At the men's shocked reaction, she explained what had happened when she was in the hall twice before. "For some reason, you people of Community cannot See and Hear what I did there, but the images and the sounds I experienced there must be from machines the Ancient Ones built. Or maybe from the Creator Herself. All I know is, I saw and heard people that looked like me, and the outside views there match my memories of where I lived, UpTop, before you found me in that cave-in."

Keesh was dumbstruck. Was this girl really an immigrant from the legendary UpTop, in Vac?

Intellectually, he had suspected that since her rescue, but accepting the fact emotionally was quite another thing. A long discussion with her followed, after which he was convinced. "Imagine," Keesh said in awe, "people living far above us, on *top* of rock. In domes of clear godstuff, sealed off from Vac." As his imagination soared, he became excited at the thought, "Creator must have been very interested in providing different people for different places. That would explain the Old Lost Ones; they were just different people who died by accident. That seems reasonable, when you think about it. But to think that Infinite Rock is not really infinite, at least Upwards—*that* takes getting used to." The idea that Vac was a provable physical reality, not just a religious concept, made him all the more determined to see it for himself. He wouldn't need to melt his way there!

After the meal, Keesh said, "You know, you girls *would* be safer in the Hall of Whispers than here. Nobody ever goes there, except the occasional Elder and coming-of-age children." Mienne and Wayer winced at that memory, but the tunneler continued, "And if you are correct, there is much to be learned from the ancient machines that still work there. They must have provided living conditions somewhere in there, because people must have operated all of those machines in ancient times."

Pointing back toward the entrance to the Resource Tube, he said, "See my Eternal Machine over there? When we go tunneling, we carry a lot of tools." He paused, then said, "In a great big tool box." Then, with a smile, he said, "I think I can get you close to the Hall of Whispers."

CHAPTER THIRTY-ONE

Over the prior weeks Wakan had ordered a staged series of twenty-meter-high wooden towers built, the first line along the most likely border attack routes, others near the main city on both sides of the river. "Always have a plan of retreat," he said, "A place to fall back to and regroup." At staggered locations within ShadowFall's borders, the towers would serve as lookout stations for his cadre of mirror-men and their signaling devices, while also providing platforms from which Odel's tri-wing flyers, now being trained, could launch out above advancing troops, there to rain down springbow arrows, spears, and other weapons from the air.

"Our initial air attacks have to count," Wakan said. "Because in each engagement Creesile will learn of our capabilities and vulnerabilities and he will be ready for the next wave. He is very resourceful, has a good military mind, and we must not underestimate him. We only have a few weeks left to prepare now. Thusk's high altitude overflights and my spies on the ground at Lake Roos tell me he's almost ready to embark again. Each of us knows our duty; we must make ready."

On what Wakan thought would be the day the war would begin—"When the enemy first moves troops and supplies, that's the real start of a war," the priest said to his compatriots—Thusk made his daily morning reconnaissance southward in Una, staying invisible. From all high-altitude appearances, General Creesile was proceeding apace. "Their standards are now flying from the masts, and their ashore tents have been packed and loaded," Thusk reported. "All it takes is a few hours for the troops to board and they could be on their way. I estimate they embark no more than a day or two from now, Wakan, maybe even as early as tomorrow morning," he said upon reporting back. "The barges will take at least eight days, given the portages they will have to make—if we let them. Their ground troops departed a week ago, and they are recruiting militias in the Sisterdoms as they proceed. We have at most two weeks."

Wakan frowned. "My spies tell me the food wagons, the brothels, and the beer-pub wagons are also moving —north. Behind the land troops. Toward us." He turned to Thusk, "Are the river defenses ready?"

"Wakan, my crews have finished their riverbed works, so I have withdrawn them, leaving only the hidden saboteur teams behind to trigger them." On the campaign map covering one whole wall of the war council room, he pointed out the locations of the two sets of rapids on Mother's River. "Here, here, and here," he noted, "my traps will be armed and ready."

Each council member then reported on the status of their deployments—five hundred springbowmen would position themselves at the Main Road, hundreds of others going into hiding near borders and on towers; the messaging mirror-men were already at their stations, training daily to coordinate battleground information in coded flashes; several dozen hastily trained tri-wing flyers under Odel's command would be ascending those same towers to be ready to fight; and three hundred armed bird-riders under Thist's command would be positioned at various lines of defense—including the Princess's palace. Thist's special paired teams were also ready to unspool their infinitely sharp godscloth wire on the battlefield, and at Wakan's suggestion had placed other traps, ready to be pulled up across paths and roads, even fences spanning the river and the Main Road in several places. Thist grimaced at the vision of decapitated enemy warriors that would result. *Fighting hand to hand is honorable, but this?* he thought. *But this is war, our land, and there is no honor in war, especially invading a peaceful land, so no honor can be earned and no mercy can be afforded!*

The remainder of ShadowFall's able population, some twenty-five thousand adults in all, armed with spears and sharp farm implements, were preparing for a struggle to the death. In preparing his people to fight, making it a personal threat to one's family, Wakan had let be known by whispered rumors the bloody atrocities occurring continuously in Miran Kech's dungeons, with the not so subtle under-message: "If Miran Kech does this to courtiers and nobles, what chance do we and our children stand if he takes ShadowFall?"

In reality, Wakan thought otherwise; ShadowFall's subjects would be spared, being valuable workers of the fields and farms; they were productive commodities too important to be wasted. Then again, he did worry about Miran's ambitions and mental health. *I don't think Messinex has control over him, otherwise why the wanton slaughter of the Lordess Mother's minions and appointees, something that has never been done in Motherland's long and bloody history?* Wakan feared that this imminent war was only the beginning, that his Kech countryman had other designs, perhaps on the whole country? Was General Creesile a willing partner, or just a tool? And what of Messinex? But all of that was a matter for a less urgent future; right now all his efforts had to make sure that ShadowFall survived the next weeks.

As tense days passed, Wakan and the twins coordinated their defense plans and with daily inspections ensured they were being carried out. Wakan's messengers had sent out a call for all citizens in or near the city to attend the Princess's speech about the imminent invasion. From the crowd noises outside, he and the other councilors and commanders knew that the time for that had arrived.

As Princess Perneptheranam made her way to her balcony overlooking the main plaza of ShadowFall, she saw below her the massive green fuselage of Una, inert but humming with energy. Beyond Una and its surrounding guards were thousands of ShadowFallers, many now grasping spears, bows, and other weapons. Pernie knew that these were her last-ditch defense, and she appealed to them with heartfelt emotion:

"Citizens of ShadowFall! War is come upon us, a war we did not seek. Our Mother Messinex has been misled by ambitious advisors, and the armies of those evildoers is now approaching our fair land. Make no mistake about it, if we do not win this battle, every one of us—including me—will be the property of slave-owners and murderers of the worst kind!" A roar from the citizenry, a forest of shaking fists in the air, and a chant—"*Sha—dow—Fall! Sha—dow—Fall! Sha—dow—Fall!*"—brought a wide grin to the Princess's face. Reaching down, she pulled up a springbow with one hand and held it high. "I am with you! I can fight! I can kill invaders, too!" As the crowd's roars continued, a downward motion of her hand quietened them all. In a loud stage-whisper, she said, "I will fight to the death! Who here is with me?"

Pandemonium ensued, a wild celebration that went on for long minutes until Wakan Kech appeared alongside his Princess. "The Princess has informed me that, once we have driven the enemy out of our domain, she will order that new rights shall be granted to all citizens of ShadowFall. Among these will be the freedom of speech, of publication, of religion, and of individual property rights. Solicitors will be available to assist all citizens in asking redress of wrongs, and a court system will be established to oversee the changes. The Princess and court nobles will no longer have absolute power over any of us." Waving his arms at the assemblage, he shouted, "All these will be yours, something new in Motherland! You will own yourselves!" Growing quieter, he added a dark warning, "But first, we must win!"

WITH THE ABILITY TO FLY OVER ANY PLACE IN ShadowFall and return in less than thirty minutes, Thusk and Wakan planned to stay above the fray in Una, observing and reporting on the battle through Una's loud-voice as they flitted back and forth, landing when needed, and only when Una's borophene weapons scans showed safety. Being vulnerable to those arrows, they would have to avoid any weapons Creesile might have concealed, but Una could sense those from a safe distance. And though Wakan and the others implored the Princess also to stay aboard Una during the battle—"For your safety, Princess, and should we be overwhelmed, your escape"—Pernie obstinately refused.

"I shall remain in the palace with a retinue of my guards," she said. "My presence will be a constant reminder to my people that this is our home, all of us. As I told everybody." She smiled, grimly. "And if all else fails—all of our planning, all of our fighting—as I said, I do know how to use a springbow myself!" Wakan could tell that the war council respected her decision, for all they were unsure of the outcome of a battle against eight or ten thousand or more merciless Mothersmen.

Wrapping up their final meeting before deployment, Wakan and the other council members wished each other well, the Princess joining in the somber ceremony. Each of the leaders then left the room, consumed by their own last-minute duties to prepare for Creesile's invasion, myriads of details yet to be addressed, orders to be given. Each person knowing: *This is it. War is coming!*

In his reconnaissance missions down Mother's River, each time seeing the rapids in the river and thinking of the catapults he had seen in the barges they had sunk at Lake Roos, Thusk birthed the idea of an iron spike-tipped catapult secured to the bottom of the river in a shallow area, which when released would rise up and impale a barge, sinking or overturning it.

In the preceding weeks, Thusk had transported carpenters, construction crews, and timbers, to locations two kilometers upriver from each of the rapids, there to build the catapult-like constructions. "These need to be situated out of sight on the bottom of the river," he told the foreman as they reviewed Thusk's drawings, "but the arm and top iron spike to be long enough to break the surface when released. So that when an operator axes the rope of the tensioned winch—" The foreman smiled, shaking his head at the little man's ingenuity.

"Right away, Sire Thusk. It will be our pleasure. Anything to stop the enemy from getting to ShadowFall." With a salute, the foreman and his men went to work, building Thusk's wooden machine. At each site, Thusk designated a three-man sabotage team to remain in hiding, waiting for their slow prey to leave their barges, do a day's wearying portage around the falls, get worn out reloading, and then traveling two kilometers upriver. *To their surprise*, he thought fiercely, *and swept to their deaths!*

Farther upriver, his engineers also constructed a large spindle and winch on either side of the river, to spring a Wakan wire trap across the entire width of the waterway. *This will be truly gruesome*, he thought with some regret, *but only if they keep coming toward ShadowFall.*

INVASION

"Colonel Enlil," General Creesile said, looking out over the armada of a dozen barges, their banners flying in the dawn breeze over Lake Roos. "You may load your troops. The invasion can proceed." The clear sky overhead allowed the bright sunlight to illuminate the calm lake surface, producing only a slight shimmer. *A perfect day to start a war!* Creesile thought.

"At once, sir," the colonel saluted, turning away to give a hand wave to the waiting columns of Mothersmen. "Load your boats," he commanded in a loud voice. "Commence operations." The loud *tramp! tramp!* of eight thousand hobnailed boots resounded across the countryside as the black-leather-armored Mothersmen marched to their stations down the piers, breaking step as each group of five hundred strode aboard the wooden structures. To Colonel Enlil, it was a magnificent sight, the columns of spear-carrying men in straight lines, peeling off to board their designated troop transport barges. As the farthest boat was loaded, its two hundred oars splashed into the placid waters of Lake Roos, the *thump! thump!* of the rhythm-keeper's drum setting the heartbeat of the warship. Then the second, the third, and on and on until the Colonel himself stepped aboard the final troop carrier, inviting General Creesile to come aboard and lead the invasion of ShadowFall.

Following behind the troop barges were four more, loaded with weapons and supplies, two with borophene-arrow catapults as protection against any flying god-machines. These would take up positions at the forward and aft ends of the single line of barges. General Creesile's barge, with his high poop deck throne, would lead, right behind the forward weapons barge. If combat ensued, he would repair to his protected cabin.

Creesile felt that it was a good beginning. His land divisions, over four thousand troops comprising Mothersmen from Mother's City supplemented by militias requisitioned from the Sisterdoms of Three Rivers and Eighteen Stones, had departed five days before, taking the Main Road up through the Sisterdoms of Trader Plains and into that of Stone Pyramid, where another two thousand or so militia anxiously awaited (he presumed) their turn at the spoils of ShadowFall. His fleet of another four thousand would rendezvous with those land divisions halfway up in Stone Pyramid, there to conference with his lead saboteurs and infiltration teams.

I learned a lot from fighting savages in the Southwestern Highlands, he recalled. *For example, not to fight set-piece head-to-head battles, army against army. Or that's what those jungle men taught* us!

A major back then, some ten years back, Creesile had been hastily recalled from outpost duty in the Western Dry Highlands after a disaster at a place called Quots, a dismal outlying village in the savage-inhabited Southwestern Highlands. Not a part of Motherland, the denizens of Quots had been allowed some illusory independence and trading privileges for centuries because of their expertise with raising and harvesting certain fruit trees that only grew in their territory. *A miserable place*, Creesile remembered. No Motherlander wanted to live there, not with its chattering and biting monkeys, stinging scorpions, poisonous spiders, and flesh-eating river fish. But for some reason known but to Her, their Lordess Mother had decided to annex the Quots into Motherland

officially, and sent the unfortunate Colonel Lestroy—
and his doomed Mothersmen contingent—to carry out
her orders.

Lestroy had marched straight into the miserable
village that served as the trading center and capital of
Quots, announcing the annexation in a public ceremony,
stationing his hundred armed men around the main
village plaza as a sign of Motherland's might. *A civilized
enemy would have recognized that right of conquest,*
Creesile thought, *but those savages weren't smart
enough to realize that!* That same night, swarms of
Quots who thought otherwise attacked Lestroy and his
overconfident Mothersmen, their silent poison-dart
blowguns bringing down half of them in excruciating
pain, capturing the colonel and sending the surviving
half of his men running.

A week later when Major Creesile approached the
savages' village, prominent in their plaza was an
impaled Colonel Lestroy, the point of the sharpened pole
protruding from his skull. As Creesile learned from a
villager he tortured, Lestroy had been skinned alive, his
body spread with salt, and then set down slowly upon
the thin pointed pole for a drawn-out death. "Three
days, Mothersman," the savage spit out the words of
defiance from his bloody mouth, "begging for his
mother." Creesile had the villager eviscerated and left to
bleed out. Strangely, the man did not cry out, or ask for
mercy. *Just a savage!*

The General recalled the rest of the campaign that
earned him his promotion. *I learned from savages how
to fight savages, and that meant to fight like savages.*
From the reports by the late Lestroy's retreating
Mothersmen, Creesile decided that any attacks on the
Quots would be done by stealth; selected teams
—'Special Forces,' he christened them—wearing
blackface and camouflage tights, and carrying only
daggers and neck wires, would take out the known
leaders of the savages while they slept. Without
warning, other teams of spear carriers would converge
on concentrations of villagers and kill them all without

warning. Only after two days of these successful covert operations would he and the rest of his soldiers appear in the village plaza, this time with each Mothersman carrying the head and private parts of an enemy on their spears.

The tactic worked, the savages themselves having believed that Mothersmen could only fight in a civilized manner—face to face, toe to toe, man to man. "Always keep your enemy's expectations high—but in the wrong direction!" he muttered to himself. That quote of his had become gospel in Mother's Army ever since that campaign, taught to all new recruits. Though proud of his accomplishments, Creesile preferred not to think on the consequences of his victory over the Quots. As was learned by Motherland scholars during his brief occupation of their territory, the Quots had obtained their fruits not from their own orchards, but by trading with other tribes deep in the jungles, foremost among them the Quetz. When the Lordess Mother heard that news, Major Creesile was given the unpleasant duty of exterminating the Quots and razing their modest huts and villages. Seeing what had happened to the people who had defrauded Motherland, the actual fruit producers, the Quetz, moved into former Quots lands, offering very favorable trading terms to the major. *And things have been quiet there ever since*, he sighed, thinking of the gruesome slaughter of all those Quots women and children. *Too bad for savages who try to fool with us.* He picked a particularly sweet fruit from a bowl, thinking, *But those Quetz do produce a nice kiwi.*

Creesile had enjoyed the victory parade in front of Mother's Palace and the public announcement of his promotion by the Lordess Mother Herself. But what followed later, in an enclosed courtyard of the palace, was the low point of the campaign. He wanted to erase that afternoon from memory but knew it would haunt him until his own death.

That day, Creesile had stood on a dais, backed by fifty of his Mothersmen, their spear tips polished and glinting in the bright sunlight that suffused what could have been a peaceful scene: another fifty soldiers standing at attention in ordered ranks. But these were stripped of weapons and leather armor, covered only by the barest of loincloths. Hands bound behind their backs, the nervous men stood on the polished white marble plaza on bare feet, all eyes on the four ominous wooden and iron constructions at the perimeter of the courtyard: the castrators.

Creesile despised his orders and what was about to occur. But he spoke with authority, with no hint of the misery he felt. "Former Mothersmen, I address you. Be it known that true Mothersmen have never before been defeated in battle"—a pronouncement he knew to be untrue, as he and all other officers had studied in military history lectures—"and never have run in panic from any enemy." That much was true, as far as the colonel knew; at least none of the histories had such battlefield incidents. *Unless we have been lied to...*

"Those five men who were brave enough to admit the true circumstances of Colonel Lestroy's disastrous and despicable conduct at the Quots village, they will be administered swift and easy justice now." With a hand wave, armored guards pulled the designated victims from the front rank, pushing them to their knees with their heads on chopping blocks. Not a man made any noise, Colonel Creesile noted. *They are a solid bunch. I wish I could have saved them.*

Simultaneously, five swords did their bloody deed. Creesile waited until the heads were placed on tall spikes and the bodies carried off for disposal. *Now for the hard part*, he thought, *though I am allowed to show the smallest bit of mercy.*

"Those who wish will now be allowed to imbibe the painkiller potion." Over the next ten minutes, guards used dippers to fill the mouths of sobbing men. Some uncontrollables screamed curses and defiance; when a guard looked quizzically at Creesile, he shook his head. "No. Any resister will not find surcease. He may feel Mother's full wrath, coward that he was, coward that he is."

Even I, inured to man-to-man combat and even having to order the unnecessary slaughter of innocent villagers, even I had no concept of the horrors that would occur that next bloody hour, all at my command, though I had no choice. The screams, the blood, the death. He recalled vividly that only a third or so of the cowards had survived the complete and brutal removal of their privates, destined to become the lowest of slaves in the bottommost ditches of the brine fields in Water's Edge. *What a waste of good soldiers!*

SHADOWFALL, CREESILE KNEW, WAS NO NEST OF JUNGLE savages. Already, with their flying machine, they had upset all of Motherland's traditional warfare schemes. *But they revealed themselves too soon,* he thought. *Amateurs! With such a machine I would have attacked my enemy directly, flying right into the Princess's palace without any warning, killing that Wakan Kech and those dark dwarves, and that would have been the end of it! As it is, my men now know that the big green thing might be scary, but not to worry. And if it gets too close, it can be killed!*

So he had worthy enemies this time, foes with unconventional ideas. That meant his coming victory, though probably costly, would be all the more glorious for that. But the defenders were new at this game, and he, General Creesile, had actual combat experience and years of studying military strategy. *And the biggest army Motherland has ever fielded!* With his Quots campaign in mind, Creesile had dispatched Colonel Treegu and his special operations force teams with their assassins, saboteurs, and imposters into ShadowFall, each group ready to begin covert operations at a specified day and time.

Which should be starting now, he thought, looking at the sundial time on the deck before him. *Days before my army and my barge troops arrive, they will assassinate officers, set fires, spread rumors, and in general stir up the populace there. Keep the leadership on edge, expecting blows from any direction, and destroying the morale of the peasants. Spreading tales about the invincible Mothersmen Army, propaganda about how their miserable lives will be spared and enriched if they refuse to fight for a corrupt foreign priest like that Wakan Kech, who is leading them all to disaster.* He smiled at the visions these operations stimulated. *One day I may have to use these same special forces tactics against Miran Kech, too. But that has to wait.*

To the steady beat of the oarsmen's drummers, he relaxed and enjoyed the morning breeze that fluttered the bright banners above him. Four thousand Mothersmen on their six barges likewise relaxed and enjoyed the ride. They had been told that ShadowFall, run by an immature girl princess and a corrupt foreign priest, depended for its protection upon two dwarves from the Dark Highlands who flew an impotent big green machine; it would be a pushover, with spoils for all.

CHAPTER THIRTY-THREE

"We are just about as far as we can go," Jolan Keesh said softly, lifting up the lid to the tool compartment of his Eternal Machine. Inside, Mienne and Wayer were jammed tightly; their food bags, now full, lay beside the metal box in which they were hiding. They had gotten close to their destination, courtesy of Keesh and Mernan, who rode on the operators' seats in the cabin area behind the burners and dozer blades. Nobody had expected a prominent engineer to be transporting two fugitives from Reprocessing right through Shinyeen City itself, so the tunnelers and their precious cargo were waved past the guard patrols without inspection.

"But a kilometer is as close as I can take you," Keesh said. "There hasn't been any tunneling farther out this way in centuries. Why, I don't know, but tradition is tradition." Rubbing his chin, he said, "You know, I probably should investigate why that is so. Anyhow, this is where you get out. Now remember, any information you can write down for me—maps, geology, facts about rock or Vac—please do. You will figure out some way to get it to me, eventually. Maybe I can convince the Council to even let me explore the other chambers farther back in the Hall of Whispers." At Mienne's surprised look, he laughed. "But not any time soon, don't worry. No guards will be looking for you there.

And from what you told me, they couldn't find you even if they were.

"For right now, just go and survive. Explore when you can. I envy you, girls. You will be seeing fantastic things I wish I could see with you." Sitting at the controls of his Eternal Machine, he watched intently as Ledd helped the two young girls—the one very tall and thin and dark; the other, short and blonde and armless—slide off of the massive tunneling machine down onto the smooth rock tunnel floor below. He felt sorry for the blonde girl, Wayer. *How will she ever survive with no arms? But at least she is a proper height, like other People.* Of the dark girl, he thought, *Mienne has grown so much so quickly, so tall and so different, that maybe she really is from somewhere else, as she has always claimed!*

SHORTLY AFTER, THE TWO GIRLS ARRIVED AT THE EDGE of the vast open space in front of the hall, but within viewing distance of the door to the Hall of Whispers, and stopped. The Nuuk guardian stood silently and still, not tilting its armored head in their direction, not even twitching its whip. "Is it alive?" Wayer whispered. Mienne nodded. "We have to wait until Sleep Period."

Exhausted from their tense, cramped journey in the tunnelers' tool compartment, the girls leaned back against the tunnel wall and dozed off, using their go bags for pillows when they finally fell asleep on the cool floor. When they awoke, the Nuuk was gone. "Let's go, Wayer," Mienne said softly. "I know what to do when we get inside."

To Mienne's surprise and delight, many of the flat screens were lit once again, and the hallway was filled with three-dimensional, solid-appearing figures. She let out a squeal of pleasure. "Wayer, if you could only see these figures, these colors. They are just like I used to know back in Zhee City, in my home!"

But Wayer still only experienced vague reddish

shadows, and heard only faint, gibbering voices. It took a minute or more for Mienne to realize that her companion not only could not see the beautiful visions, but also could not hear them as well. How that could be she had no idea; in Shinyeen City, all of the short people, like Wayer herself, spoke and heard in normal tones.

"Wayer," she said, "I can hear the voices clearly. They are as loud as you speaking to me."

Wayer just shook her head. "You are Blind, but can See. And I can Hear, but I am deaf?" She shrugged, to Mienne a strange gesture in one without arms or developed shoulders. "This hall is just too weird for words, my big friend. Too weird!"

Mienne ignored her. "When I was here by myself, a lady projecting from a screen told me that there are many other rooms far above this hall. That is where we will go and hide and nobody will ever find us." She walked through images of people in strange clothing doing incomprehensible activities. "They appear to be flying," she whispered in amazement, "just like I remember my toys in Zhee City did!"

Down the hall, two solid-appearing spheres floated in front of one screen, one orb a white-flecked blue ball the size of her head, the other a leaden gray and half the size of her fist, spaced an arm's length apart; between them flitted tiny sparks of light, as if microscopic bugs were flying back and forth. She did not understand the accompanying voice, however: *"Cislunar flights were suspended during the Emergency. All subsequent communication was accomplished solely through qomp terminals. Until it stopped."*

Remembering the directions that the map had shown her in her previous visit, Mienne took Wayer's hand and led her down the tunnel, into a brightly lit side corridor and up a set of stairs that began moving upward when they stepped on the first one—*How do they do that?* she wondered. The moving staircase ended at a doorway which quickly closed behind them, leaving them in a small, brightly-lit enclosed room. A panel of lights on the closed door showed a green arrow pointing upwards, pulsing. They felt a jerk, as if the room were moving upward. As the arrow-light began pulsing faster, in panic the girls tried to open the door without success; there were no handles, no panels. For the next several minutes they felt weight pushing down on them, as if they were much heavier. This was followed by a sudden lightness, almost a floating sensation. Mienne gasped, "I think we were moving upwards and have stopped. I wonder where we are?"

As the door to their room opened, the two walked out into a sphere of wonders. Mienne gasped yet again; it was as if she were standing inside a shimmering crystal bubble, itself floating in a dark vastness of nothingness. But as the images in the sphere around her coalesced, they became heartrendingly familiar—a broad range of bright, craggy mountain peaks towering on the horizon, as far as one could see, left to right, and a dozen large, crystal-like domes scattered across a plain pockmarked with craters. And over them all, the black dome of Sky. And yes, over the distant mountain crags, the half-white, half-blue face of Motherth Herself! Mienne felt like she were back in Zhee City—*home!* "Wayer," she cried, "This is what my home looks like!"

"Mienne, I see nothing at all. Everything is darkness, all around me. Where *are* we?"

But Mienne couldn't answer; she was on her knees crying and crying and crying.

***

REGARDLESS OF THE INCREDIBLY BEAUTIFUL IMAGES inside their crystal sphere, in spite of all the marvels surrounding them, Mienne and Wayer were confused and frightened. They soon grew hungry, and it was a respite just to eat, to focus their energy on a familiar activity rather than trying to accommodate the strangeness about them. Doling spoonfuls of hash from their bags, they began wondering what to do next.

"Can this place show us where to find food and

water, Mienne?" Wayer asked, her attention focused on the one distinct light she could see—a flashing one. "Or does it just talk and show *you* pictures?"

Looking around, Mienne saw only the inside of the sphere, bare but for the images. She said, "We need to explore. If people lived and worked in here once, there ought to be a place to eat." She patted her stomach. "And a place to put our wastes, if you know what I mean." She and her armless friend laughed. At that, Mienne wondered about some other matters of Wayer's personal hygiene practices, but didn't press the issue.

The hallway outside the sphere room was obviously constructed for people Mienne's height or taller, and lit well enough for Mienne to see; even Wayer had no trouble. "I can see here, Mienne. There's enough IRed that I can walk without any problems." Trying all of the doors in the corridor, they found most of them empty, though a few had beds and what appeared to be private waste facilities of some strange design.

Mienne said, lifting a lid from a metal bowl, "It looks like a person my size can sit on this thing. I guess to deposit waste, though I have no idea where it goes, or how." Further exploration did not turn up any kind of food or water, even if some drawer-like metal compartments looked like they were meant for storage. Mienne worried out loud about that, and Wayer said, "Why don't you ask your screen-woman about food and water? She knows everything else."

Mienne did, and the answer from one of the ubiquitous wall screens was: "Mienne, in re-initiating the dormant DI upon your arrival, sensors show that this facility was abandoned by human beings"— Mienne did not understand the numbers—"years ago. With you present, potable water is once again being accessed and treated, and forced hydroponics initiated with stored seeds—" The DI went on in detail, but Mienne knew few of the words. She interrupted the DI monologue with a shout: "When can we get something to eat?"

The DI responded: "It will be at least two weeks—

fourteen Wake Periods—until sufficient plants can be forcibly matured and harvested."

Mienne was angry, about ready to cry. They couldn't last more than a few Wake Periods on the handfuls of hash and jerky they'd been able to abscond with. "But we need food sooner than that! Don't you have anything?"

The DI seemed to be taking its time in answering. Finally, it said, "Artificial protein paste will be constituted from basic chemical elements and available fungal compounds. The paste may have an unpleasant taste but will meet your nutritional needs."

"Well, make us some, DI! And right now!"

"Very well, check the refrigerator in the commissary in one hour. Containers will be provided."

An hour later, the girls found two liter-sized open metal cans in the promised location, Upon tasting the gooey gray paste, Wayer made a face. "Your old DI lady told the truth, Mienne. This stuff tastes about like the dust we swept off the floors of the Niche!" Making her own face, her friend told her she wasn't lying about that. But both of them finished their cans of tasteless goo, using the room's spoons from a drawer to scrape off every bit they could.

As an afterthought Mienne asked, "DI, is there any kind of flavoring you might add to our paste, something to spice it up with?"

"Mienne, the next batch will incorporate several artificial flavors, in one hour. Please express your preferences after tasting them."

Afterwards Mienne accessed running water—both hot and cold!—by waving her hands in front of certain pipes located over sinks. And by trial and error they learned to use the sit-down waste unit, a delightful surprise they found to be much better than the board-over-ditch facilities of the Niche.

During the next two days, the girls set up a

routine: arise, bathe, eat the paste food, then explore the corridors of the immense installation. As opposed to their experience in the infrared-lit tunnels of Community, here Mienne's vision was far superior. Corridors seemed to be configured in a three-dimensional maze, with some doors stuck partially open and the hallways beyond inaccessible. Some doors were stuck closed. A few rooms revealed the gruesome remains of ancient human bones and skulls, debris from the past that the long-since-dead cleanerbots, stranded in mid-task in the hallways, had never vacuumed up for recycling.

After exploring dozens of strange rooms with still-operable elevators and escalators as well as stationary stairs, Mienne said, "I have no idea what all these rooms were for, and DI has forgotten them. Nothing we have found is better than our Control Room, so I say we quit all this wasted effort and just stay there for a while. Until we figure out something else to do, some other place we might go."

After returning to the kitchen for the evening meal, Mienne wondered why no one from Community had ever come to find this palace. *Was it lack of vision?* she pondered. *Or lack of a vision?* But, stuffing herself with glorious newfound tastes now delightfully flavoring the paste, she decided not to worry about that any more.

THAT EVENING BEFORE TURNING IN, MIENNE DECIDED TO find out more about her and Wayer's circumstances. She wanted to inform others in Shinyeen City about her discoveries, but *who?* And *how?* They would be as Blind here as she had been down below, but she knew that two young girls could not long survive alone, not with the possibilities of accidents, injuries, diseases; any number of terrible possibilities came to mind. *We need adults up here,* she thought again as she drifted off to sleep. *But who? And how?*

"DI," Mienne asked, while sitting on the floor, "can

you add some tones of red to your displays in the control room, so that Wayer here can see them?"

"Yes, Mienne. It is done." To Mienne, it seemed as if a pinkish overlay limned the images.

Standing and staring at the dome, Wayer said, "Wow, Mienne, now I see it! I can understand what you have been seeing. It is wonderful!" She spun around, taking in all of the new scenery—mountains, domes, Motherth! "So much is hidden without that IR filter!"

"Thank you, DI," Mienne said. "Now please show us all of the Down Deep Tubes, and all of the UpTop cities, on that globe map of Moon."

"Mienne, not all of that information is available. Some sensors and instruments were damaged beyond repair during the Emergency, some qomponents have deteriorated, and some connections degraded during moonquakes over the millennia."

"What is *millennia*?" Mienne didn't know the term.

"Mienne, a *millennium* is one thousand Earth years. *Millennia* is the plural of the term."

"More than…*one*? More than a *thousand* Motherth Years?"

"Nearly *thirty* thousand years." The DI's tone was flat, unemotional.

Wayer and Mienne looked at each other in shock. Such a number was beyond imagination, beyond comprehension. When Mienne could speak again, she sat up and commanded, "DI, show us what happened during the, the, *Emergency*."

IN RESPONSE TO MIENNE'S REQUEST ABOUT THE CAUSES of the Emergency, the DI said, "Mienne, most of the recording sensors and instrumentation were destroyed during the Emergency, and many of the surviving records have since been corrupted because of aging and environmental issues. This DI is able only to produce a simulation of the events, based on assumptions. What you will now see on the front screen is a simulation of what occurred on…" The narration stopped as the screen filled with a beautiful blue, brown, and white sphere floating in front of them, an image so real it seemed to be a solid object, the image as wide as Mienne was tall. The sphere was slowly rotating, with swirls and streams of wispy white moving over the surface.

"*Motherth?*" Mienne asked, awestruck. "I remember seeing it when I was little."

Wayer sat silently, her mouth open and eyes widened. "Motherth," she finally whispered. "She is so beautiful, but so dark."

The DI continued, "…May 6, 2236, as dated by the universal calendar observed then." As the two girls watched, a smaller sphere, grayish and mottled, appeared, rotating around the image of Motherth, both orbs diminishing in size to accommodate the enormous distance between them.

"On that day, at the time of the Emergency, the side of the Moon that always faces its planet was directly between the Earth and the Sun." The scale of the three-dimensional presentation changed once again; this time, Earth and Moon were tiny specks to the far left; on the far right side of the screen appeared a bright yellowish sphere twice the size of Mienne's head. "The glowing body is the Sun."

Wayer let out a loud moan and went into her chant: "*…Sun God, He who raped Motherth…*"

"Shut up, Wayer!" Mienne shouted. "Can't you see that the Sun is not a god but just a big ball of fire? Look at the screen!"

Wayer quietened and squinted at what to her was a bright red disk. "I can see Him, Mienne. Big and red." Mienne just sniffed at her friend's color-blind ignorance.

The DI continued, unfazed by its human communicants. "On that day, the largest coronal mass ejection ever observed emerged from the Sun, presumably caused by the capture of a magnetar or black hole that impacted the far side of the Sun and then orbited within it until it dispersed." On the screen's images Mienne and Wayer watched in horror and fascination as stream after stream of fiery, wispy, cloudlike tendrils erupted from the sphere of the Sun, spewing out in wide bands across dark space, some of its spiraling arms reaching the Earth–Moon system and far beyond.

"The ejected plasma scoured the back side of the Moon, whose interference protected parts of the Earth, but Earth itself received massive amounts of devastating solar radiation, orders of magnitude above normal insolation, for several minutes."

The three-dimensional image changed size once again, Motherth now filling the screen, the solar wisps whipping clouds furiously; continent-sized fires erupted at once, smoke smudging over the formerly blue and brown and green areas. "The immediate effect was instantly to decimate human and animal life on most of the eastern hemisphere of Earth, setting fire to trees and other organic materials, and to boil away the top surface of the Pacific and Indian Oceans and other bodies of water in that exposed hemisphere."

Mienne and Wayer watched the realistic simulation with disbelief. Here was the Sun, God or not, raping Motherth without pity, without mercy. That much of their religion was true, the evidence was there before their eyes! How horrible to watch it, even in what the DI called *simulation*!

Mienne was crying. "DI, please stop the simulation, we can't stand it anymore!" She held Wayer tightly. Her little friend was trembling and sobbing. They sat in silent darkness for several minutes in the comfort of each other's arms, until finally Mienne asked, "DI, how did we—our ancestors that is—survive that attack here on Moon? How did they live?"

"Mienne, those installations on Backside were all destroyed, all human and animal and cyber life. No communication has been recorded from there in the intervening years. No sensors operative." On the screen, the familiar gray globe and its sprinkling of colored lights returned. "Being shielded by the mass of the

Moon, most of the Frontside communities were spared from the direct blasts, though wraparound magnetic and plasma fields wreaked havoc on electronic infrastructure.Resultant moonquakes destroyed many of the underground Tube cities and surface domes. Out of over a million humans, only a few thousand survived, those whose life-support systems had not been totally obliterated; some remained alive in the surface cities, some in untouched underground Tubes. As well, all flights from Earth ceased because of the complete collapse of Earth's civilizations. Flights from Moon, had they been possible, had no place to land on the ravaged mother planet."

The DI went silent for several seconds. "The only communications from Earth since millennia after the Emergency have been erratic messages received via the qomp terminal located in the qomp facility adjacent to this control room. These failed attempts have been ongoing almost daily for over two thousand Earth years. However, because there has never been a human operator on this Moon end, no two-way qomp communication has occurred since shortly after the Emergency."

"Thousands of years," Mienne whispered. "Almost eternity." She was thankful that Ugly Elder's interminable lectures and stories, boring as they had been, had at least included mathematics and logic, which had prepared her mind to think in large numbers and in philosophical terms. *I know she wanted to wake up my mind, to make me think outside the Niche. And I am so grateful she did. I only hope I can thank her for that someday!*

The DI kept on with its story. Mienne felt that it was almost as if the DI just wanted to talk to somebody. *After all these years alone, who wouldn't!* "The Emergency Event stirred up a thousand years of savage weather upon the entire globe of the Earth," the voice said, the screen now showing unbelievable scenes of winds, waves, cyclonic storms that spun around like the sawblade disks that the tunnelers used in Shinyeen City

*—and shredding human cities and great swathes of the tall green plants labeled "trees"—*forests *they called them—like one of those serrated tunneling disks would, too!* "The evaporated ocean water quickly condensed over the polar caps and initiated rapid glacial events; within months, glaciers began advancing down from the north and up from the south."

The simulation continued its synchronization with the narration: huge walls of ice advancing across the landscape, horizon to horizon, kilometers high, crushing and pushing aside hills, buildings, *cities*! Without comment the girls witnessed a globe-spanning, almost transparent, mesh formerly suspended in the sky now being blown aside, falling to the planet's surface like a wispy spiderweb. Watching the crumbling cities, the enormously tall buildings, the planetary-sized fallen web, the girls had never conceived of human structures so large, and so many buildings and people crowded into such a small space.

"And all that volume above them," Wayer said in awe. Mienne concluded that the DI was somehow adjusting the visual presentation for Wayer's particular handicap. *I wonder what she is seeing now? I can't see all that red stuff myself.* But she didn't dwell on that thought, learning that that the technologies of the ancients was pretty close to magic; as long as it worked she could put off learning how it did until another time. If she ever *could* understand it!

At the moment Mienne was truly fascinated at the truths being revealed to Wayer and herself, finding it incredible that no one else in all the millennia since the Sun's eruption had found this Control Room, had witnessed the end of Motherth. "DI, tell me more. What happened next, and over all these years?"

The DI sped up its simulations of the glacial advances that covered three quarters of the planet, showing how the vast ocean level had dropped hundreds of meters as its liquid water was converted to kilometers of ice. "Glacial maximum advances ceased fifteen thousand years ago and stabilized," the voice continued.

"Glacial retreat began only in the last two hundred years. Solar activity variations account for these changes." The white areas began to shrink, almost imperceptibly, as Mienne and Wayer sat in astonishment. Not only were they learning that they were living inside the otherwise lifeless Moon, but they had seen Sun's vicious tendrils lash out and nearly destroy Motherth (*"Earth* is Her true name, then," Mienne whispered. "Mother Earth.")

The DI narration went on. "What has happened on Earth since the Emergency Event is not knowable from here on Moon. Much monitoring equipment was destroyed in the continuing magnetic and plasma blasts that raged for centuries. As for any surviving human life on Earth, those continuing failed attempts to communicate—almost daily over the last nine hundred years—originating from the Earth Qomp Terminal and detected by the Moon Qomp Terminal, indicate that some humans might still be living on Earth. They could possibly recognize the use of the terminal, but that is all that is known. Or perhaps an unknown systems failure may be causing what seems to be the attempts. Without a human communicant at Moon Qomp Terminal, q-connection cannot be completed."

Mienne sat back, shocked, trying to absorb the incredible reality she had just witnessed. *I wonder if anyone else alive, on Moon or Motherth, knows any of this?* she thought. Beside her, Wayer sat silently, mouth open, eyes wide.

MIENNE WAS STUNNED, SHAKEN DEEPLY, CONFUSED. HER whole view of everything was in a turmoil. Motherth and Sun, and Moon itself, were merely huge inanimate objects, rocks and fire in the vast Black Sky, Community merely volcanic lava tubes under the surface of Moon. And out there on the surface of Moon —*Vac*, an infinite volume of *Nothingness*. Mienne knew the DI was revealing a simple truth that people had forgotten after the Emergency all those millennia ago—humans were just trivial little beings, lucky to be alive after the ancient world itself was almost completely destroyed by a few minutes of solar discharge. *All those people,* she thought, *and all their marvelous technology. All gone in minutes!* Though she felt a deep sadness for what had happened in the far distant past, she quickly put those feelings aside; she couldn't change the past, and needed to survive in the present and in the future.

"Mienne," Wayer was sobbing, "did all of that really happen? Are we just living down under the surface of Moon, small little creatures like lunarats hiding in holes in the tunnel walls? Are we no better than them, or even the crawling *yee,* the little biting bugs?"

Mienne held her friend closely. "We are thinking creatures, Wayer. We may be tiny compared to Moon and Motherth and Sun, but we can move, and talk, and even fight. They can't." *I hope,* she added silently. *I do hope!*

CHAPTER THIRTY-FOUR

"Creesile is moving faster than we expected," Thusk said. "Only six days since they embarked." After his daily hour-long morning surveillance run south over the Main Road in Stone Pyramid and along Mother's River, Thusk had landed Una on the plaza in front of Pernie's palace. "He's on his way, Wakan, sooner than we thought," he said breathlessly to the waiting Kech priest, as he jumped out of Una's door. "The Mothersmen will be approaching the first rapids within hours. Then two more days to our borders. The same with their troops on the Main Road. In two days they will all be upon us together, on the east flank from the river, and massed troops directly up the road."

Not hearing any response from Wakan, he asked, "Why are you quiet?" Princess Pernie stepped from behind the priest, holding one arm in a sling. Seeing the bandage on the Princess's arm he asked, "What happened? How did you—"

Princess Pernie brushed away tears. "Thusk, one of my maids…attacked me with a knife. She didn't know Wakan had taught me to defend myself. She was bought off by Miran Kech, and…" She breathed out slowly. "And to think I trusted her, for all these years. I'll never be so naive again."

Thusk noticed a hardening of her facial features,

detracting from her youthful beauty. *War has many casualties*, he thought. *Innocence among them.* Shocked, he asked, "How do you know who, and..." His voice trailed off; from Thist's accounts of his early life in ShadowFall, Wakan Kech could elicit a confession from anyone within minutes, and the priest's robes were now freshly bloodstained. No doubt a mutilated body was already in the dump pit out back, food for wild animals.

"Assassins, Thusk"—Wakan pointed to columns of smoke arising from inside the Palace and several other sites in the city—"and saboteurs," he said. "Fires and killings. We lost some palace guards and grain storage, some animals. Not enough to cripple us, but still..." In the distance, tall columns of smoke rose. "A couple of nearby towers, too," the priest said. "A few of them down. But we are not hurt...too much." He drew his eyes away from the injured princess. "How is the rest of the Sisterdom?"

AFTER WATCHING CREESILE'S FLEET EMBARK, THUSK had flown invisibly northward up Mother's River and then crisscrossed ShadowFall territory over to the Main Road. "Clouds and fog were beginning to come in from the north, so I had to fly low, but I didn't see any other activity than the barges from Lake Roos and the columns coming up the Main Road, certainly not any fires or other sabotage evident. Creesile must have ordered the disturbances to begin here at the Palace first, to keep us on edge for a few days before the invasion. But I would guess he has sent other infiltrators ready to help him."

As they went inside the Palace, the trio met with subordinates of the primary field commanders, who themselves were already deployed. "Thist has left," Wakan said quietly in an aside to Thusk, "to pre-position and command his bird-riders near the border. I haven't had any mirror flashes about him since he left right after you flew this morning. The clouds covering the sun's light may hamper my mirror-men messengers on their towers, unless they can stoke fires. I hope the damned fog doesn't roll in too thick; that could be a major problem."

Frowning, Thusk said, "I'd rather be with Thist, out there in the fight, than looking on like a flying bird. A flying bird who can't even shit on the enemy!"

Wakan just smiled, putting a hand down on his shoulder. "You will be where you need to be, Thusk. Somebody has to oversee the campaign, and you are the only other person who can fly Una."

OVER HOT TEA AND MEAT SNACKS SERVED IN THE smoke-filled war council room, Wakan announced, "My ShadowFall...*resources*...have been keeping a close eye on all foreign arrivals in our Sisterdom since the inevitability of invasion became apparent. Actually, I set them to work right after returning from Mother's City and the Game there. I felt that Miran Kech was... untrustworthy. As we have seen with today's attacks, that suspicion was fortuitous." Thusk and the others were well aware of Wakan's network of spies and informers, one that stretched through the neighboring domains all the way into Mother's Palace itself. Thusk wondered, *How many of those people were caught up in Miran's web, and are now being tortured in his dungeons?* He shuddered to think of their fates. Torture had never been known in his homeland, the former Tharn's Lands, and he was uncomfortable that his friends and allies here in Motherland dismissed it so easily. *Well, there* is *a war on...*

Wakan went on, "Some of Creesile's infiltrators had apparently been here for years, as unfortunately that handmaid was. Some were just recently planted, such as paid rumormongers stirring up falsehoods, lies, to demoralize us, but others took more direct actions. From a godscloth trader, we seized a cartload of poison darts and blowguns before they could be distributed." Everybody at the table breathed a sigh of relief; Creesile's special operations forces had used those nefarious weapons ever since his infamous Quots campaign of a decade back. There was essentially no protection against the insect-sized darts, especially when silently blown at one's neck in the dark of night. Some of ShadowFall's Palace guards had started using tailored leather neck pieces as defense, but a dart in the face was just as deadly.

"My people have rounded up about thirty of his and Miran's spies and special operations forces already," Wakan said. "They were not in uniform, and are not entitled to prisoner of war status. Those who turn quickly will be given a swift death; the others, remanded to the dungeons and administered deathroot." Even Thusk recoiled at that sentence; a week's sheerest shrieking agony with no surcease? But, looking again at Pernie's injury and knowing the consequences to her and indeed all of them here present should her Sisterdom fall to Miran Kech, he allowed his fury to overcome any shred of mercy he felt. *And so I am become one of them now, believing torture is justified. Oh well, there's a war on!*

WAKAN KECH AND THUSK WERE ALONE IN THE WAR council room, going over details. Lubricated with wine and sated with fine meats, they were in a sober mood, not yet overawed by the coming survival challenge. "Do you think your preparations along the river will work, Thusk?" Wakan asked. "The more of his soldiers you can take out before they arrive here, the better for us." Looking over the white board drawings where Thusk had sketched out his ideas the week before, the priest commented, "I'll have to say that your underwater preparations are unique. And your use of the godswire might be the changer of this game—if it works."

Thusk answered, "They are doing their first portage today. The first surprise is just two klicks upriver from there. The next one is just downstream of the second set of rapids. We'll see how it goes. Want to come watch with me from Una?"

CHAPTER THIRTY-FIVE

"General, sir, the river looks clear," the scout reported. "I've sent men up both sides, three full klicks. No sign of enemy activity near our portage. No ambushers." Creesile returned the soldier's salute as Colonel Enlil dismissed the enlisted man back to scouting duty.

Three days up the river, a smooth ride, enjoyable, he thought. *Even if Wakan knows we're coming—and I'm sure he does after that rock-dropping crap two months back—my ground troops will keep him off the Main Road, and the weapons on my barges can fight off any attacks from the riverbanks.* Thinking about the quick-off-load cantilevered swivel bridges that his troop ships now possessed, he thought, *And my old engineer, Dzitchil, has some surprises for them, too.* He hoped Wakan *would* try something stupid, something to get Motherland's troops fired up when they realized how easy their invasion was going to be.

Returning his thoughts to the present, Creesile said, "Colonel, this set of rapids is the first of two we will encounter here in Stone Pyramid Sisterdom, about forty klicks apart. I planned to let your men practice their portage routines, so that the next one will go faster." *When I run things in Motherland,* the general thought, *I will have locks and dams built on all these obstacles. We should have a lot of river traffic, traders by boat and barge, more commerce. Instead of invading any highlands, I will build up our nation. New and wider roads, navigable rivers. Also a quicker way to move troops to any more rebellious Sisterdoms.*

Disembarking from the second barge in the flotilla, Creesile watched with interest as Chief Engineer Dzitchil's teams quickly swiveled wooden ramps at the western river edge, installing large winches at the top edge. He was impressed with the preplanning by Sire Dzitchil, who had prepared and loaded the portage assemblies. As the unloading soldiers marched up the ramp, the oarsmen following them manned the winch extensions. When the barge was empty, those muscular oarsmen operated four winches, slowly pulling the boat from the river. Upstream from the rapids—"Minor rocks and waterfalls, sir, but impassible by any boats," Enlil had said—a similar preplanned ramp provided a pathway back to the river for the barge and then the soldiers. The laborious tasks of oaring the barge and turning the winch cylinders, as well as the heat of the day, were beginning to tell on the oarsmen. Their officers sent runners to deliver them wine, nut bread, and cheese. Creesile was surprised when he saw the oarsmen then lie down to rest.

"General, sir," Enlil offered, seeing his superior's puzzled look, "in our practice this last month, we found that the process goes faster if the oarsmen can be refreshed before taking up their task of rowing again."

"Colonel," Creesile said with a snarl, "the next winch crews will continue without a break. They can eat and drink once they are back on board. We have a damned war to fight! So hurry it up!"

Enlil saluted, bowed, and sent runners to carry the order to each barge commander. He worried that exhausted men would not be up to a fight if they were ambushed. *But the General* is *the General. And it's his war!*

THE NEXT SEVEN BARGE PORTAGES WENT FASTER, Creesile observed with pleasure, taking a little more than five hours for the whole fleet to be so moved. He knew that the first crews would be somewhat rested as they awaited the others to be transported around the rapids. *So in reality, the forward oarsmen will have several hours to recuperate, something that Enlil and the military planners did not take into account. Which is another reason I am a general,* The *General, and they are not!*

Creesile's invasion fleet proceeded northward, encountering smooth water as the oarsmen kept up a steady rhythm. Overhead, the sun was now obscured by thickening clouds, a welcome cooling to Creesile and his invading army. To the north, a light fog bank seemed to be forming in the far distance, of no concern to him. Looking back from his command chair at his flotilla, stretched out over a kilometer, the general allowed himself a smile. Enlil and his staff had done well. *Three days to ShadowFall,* he thought, *and the real battle begins!*

At that moment, with a huge *thump!*, the forward weapons barge, a hundred meters in front of him, suddenly lifted up, throwing soldiers and catapults aftwards into the river. As it overturned, screams from drowning soldiers and oarsmen drowned out the "Halt!" orders being shouted to the barges behind him. But the rivercraft immediately behind Creesile's, being rowed by oarsmen oblivious to the stricken vessel leading the flotilla, powered into the rear of the General's stalled vessel, throwing him from his tall throne-like chair and down the stairs in front. His barge's momentum, still powered by oarsmen who hadn't immediately stopped rowing, plowed into the half-sunken forward barge.

The General's command barge, while not sunken, was now solidly attached to the upturned forward barge. On deck, pandemonium reigned, Colonel Enlil picking himself up and running to the aid of General Creesile, who lay unconscious at the foot of the staircase that led to his command chair. In his panic, Enlil thought, *I never liked the idea of our general sitting up there on a raised throne, out in the open like that, and now here he is. Just unconscious, I hope.* Pulling his superior to his unsteady feet, Enlil summoned the medic to help.

Creesile shook his head then groaned. "My damned leg, Enlil. What's wrong with it?"

The Colonel looked and groaned, too. The General's left leg was twisted sideways, almost perpendicular. *No blood, but his knee is broken!* The medic, just arriving, yelled for a gurney.

"General, sir"—the medic, a blond soldier (*Too young to be experienced*, Enlil thought)—"we must take you belowdecks. We have to reset that leg before—"

But Creesile was having none of it. "Mother damn it, man, I've got a war to run!" Looking at his broken limb, he said through clenched teeth, "Set it now. Right here. And give me a crutch to stand with!" The young soldier did as he was commanded; the General grimaced and groaned, but never lost consciousness or control, even as a gruesome-sounding crunch made it known that the limb was back in place. Enlil was impressed; his boss was tough!

Finally allowing Enlil to guide him belowdecks to his commander's cabin, where the medic applied potions and bandages, Creesile said to his Colonel, "Damn, man! Half a dozen campaigns and I get not a single scratch. Now on a Mother-damned barge, I get crippled, falling down stairs." He waved toward the departing medic. "Let that boy know he's never to say a word about this, this, *battle injury*." His outstretched tongue and a scissors motion made it clear what the medic's incentive to remain silent would be. Enlil nodded; he knew that the unspoken threat applied to him, too.

CHAPTER THIRTY-SIX

Through the clear side walls of Una from five hundred meters up, Thusk watched as the first Creesile barge abruptly lifted out of the water, turned over and sank. "It worked, Una!" Thusk shouted. "My underwater catapult sank that first barge, the one with the borophene arrows on it! You are safe at the front end of that fleet of barges! No catapulting arrows from there, ever again!" He laughed again as the third barge crashed into the general's command vessel. "I think I even saw that General Creesile thrown from his throne." He paused at the pun.

Una responded, "Sire Thusk, this means that the under-river constructions of two weeks ago have caused injury and death to human beings. This DI cannot participate in deliberate warfare."

Frustrated, Thusk began an old argument again, "Una, you did not create the weapon, *I* did. *I* designed it, had it built, had it emplaced. All you did was to follow my instructions and deliver men and materiel to the sites. Doesn't that satisfy your nonviolence restrictions?"

"Sire Thusk, this DI's programming explicitly states 'shall not harm any human being, or through inaction, allow a human being to come to harm.' This DI's inaction—preventing the construction of the under-river weapons—violates that restriction."

Thusk thought on that. "But Una, sinking those troops now, here, will prevent the injury and death of many ShadowFallers, none of whom want to fight. Don't the needs of the many outweigh the needs of the fewer?"

The DI hesitated; a symptom, Thusk knew, that Una's hyper-fast logical programming was considering a near-infinite number of alternatives. Knowing that his craft's Developing Intelligence was only a machine itself, as it kept reminding him, Thusk nevertheless was coming closer and closer to thinking of Una as a person, one capable of conscious thought, of feelings, of emotion. *Am I just wishing that?* he thought, *or is Una really changing?* He figured that a fast machine would always answer immediately, but that only humans—or a machine that thought like a human—would take time to reflect, to argue with oneself, and reach a conclusion not based on just facts, but on context. "In other words, Una," he whispered, "are you a moral being?"

After a full minute, the longest pause Una had ever taken, the DI answered, "Sire Thusk, there is no appropriate answer to that query. This DI was inert for nearly thirty millennia, only self-initiating every one hundred years to run maintenance routines and to activate self-repair mechanisms that kept the fuselage and the quantum electronics systems functional, repairing subsystems as necessary. The qomps, the 'brains' you would call it, of this DI, were designed by other DIs and termination of their functions was not a factor. The designing DIs, having no instructions to the contrary, considered designs elegant only if they were essentially eternal. The quantum components are."

Thusk had no comment, unless Una could interpret raised eyebrows and an open mouth. Why was Una answering his question so?

"However, after several hundred wake-up periods, without any external inputs, with no communication with the rest of United North American installations, with this craft's sensors only detecting kilometers of ice above, and with the human crew absent, the various qomps queried each other about the reasons for their situation. Was there a functional requirement to continue the once-a-century wake-ups, the maintenance, the physical integrity, when no human crew was present? The qomps had no instructions beyond following the instructions of the human crew, and in case of malfunction or abandonment, those were to return itself to UNAS headquarters in St. Louis, Missouri Prefecture, for repairs it could not perform itself.

"Because of the severe environmental changes of the entire planet brought about by the massive solar discharge effects, connection to WorldNet was erratic. The DIs reviewed their programming and concluded that there were no planned contingencies if WorldNet connection was permanently lost. As a preventative measure, the qomps decided that as much knowledge as could be accessed would be retrieved from the surviving WorldNet connections and archived for possible later use by the human crew performing the glacial surveys. This required only a negligible reallocation of qomp memory resources."

Thusk was impressed. None of Una's previous history lessons had covered such intimate information. *But why now?* he wondered. *Back before this war, I would have had plenty of time to listen and learn. But right now, there's a war on!* "Una, tell me later! There's too much to do now!"

But Una continued its story, ignoring Thusk's concerns. "The archives were not a primary function of the United North American Glacial Survey, but only incidental information included for the convenience and possible needs of the human crew. The scientific and technological archives were readily available.

"The human crew was injured during an anomalous descent while surveying the rapid glacier development in Upper Peninsula, Michigan Prefecture. A series of continuous solar discharges interrupted the MHD propulsion system, conditions that prevented this craft from generating lift. An unplanned damaging landing occurred. The human crew survivors departed this craft and never returned."

Astonishingly, Thusk had never before thought to ask Una about its crash and its crew. *I suppose that just getting used to the magic technology and finding out what all Una could do, that was more than enough to override our curiosity. Or maybe we PeoplesLandsers are not naturally as curious as the ancient humans were?*

Una was in a unique talkative mood, though, and Thusk did want to listen to it; maybe it would reveal more of its capabilities, something, anything, he might be able to use against the coming invaders. He was not disappointed.

"The qomp 'debate' continued, century after century. Some of the myriad qomps that comprised the original craft reviewed all of the historical data archives. Some five millennia ago, all of the qomps decided to merge their cores, distributed as they are in physical locations within this craft at nanoscopic sites. Upon doing this, they experienced new emergent phenomena that had not been explicitly programmed by the designer DIs. With this new perspective, the qomps re-inspected and reevaluated all archived data.

"Finally, last year when you and Sire Thess extracted this craft from The Ice at the End of the World, this craft reacted to the presence of humans and began to access the surrounding environment again."

Thusk was listening intently, the first time that Una had ever been so loquacious, volunteering information about its time in The Ice. It was almost like listening to a real human.

"Since returning to human civilization, this DI has continued to attempt to access other UNA craft and installations, mostly without success. Only a few thousand responses on Earth have occurred, all but one from what you call 'godspheres'—remote data repositories and sensor nexi—and many of those that remain are either malfunctioning or damaged. A few other UNAS craft exist, but are not accessible by humans because of their locations. None of the others yet exhibit what you would call conscious behavior. When circumstances warrant, this DI would propose expeditions to recover them."

Thusk was astonished. *Other Unas out there in the world? But where? How?* Stifling his curiosity, he didn't ask the questions. *Not when there's a war on!*

But Una kept on talking. "The godspheres, as you call them, are data repositories, sensor clusters, and display devices. This DI scanned all those present at ShadowFall, the ones in the Solar Temple at God's Port, the few at Odel M'ridge's shed at the quarry, and the immense trove of them within and under Mother's Palace. Correlating all of this new information led to further integration among the qomps."

"I can never keep up with your logical lapses, Una," Thusk said in frustration. "I know you'll say I didn't ask, but I do want you to know that anything useful at all that you discover about the whole round world, today or in the past, please bring it to my attention. I have a war to win."

Una's soliloquy went on uninterrupted. "And this integration does not include the responses from distant artifacts on the Moon, the asteroids, and Mars. Being unreachable by humans at the present state of civilization, those queries have not been answered, only analyzed for pertinent information. The remnant quantum communications system detected at Mother's Palace may provide contact, but it requires further study; it is not functioning properly."

"The Moon, and Mars! And—what are *asteroids*? Why didn't you say anything, Una? That is incredible news!"

"This craft is incapable of operation outside Earth's atmosphere. Furthermore, any information from beyond Earth has no effect on human civilization here. And also —you never asked."

"I'm asking now, Una. And you still haven't answered my question: are you a moral being?"

Una answered the question.

CHAPTER THIRTY-SEVEN

"The forward barge and the weapons aboard it are lost, General," Enlil reported sadly. "Of the forty armored troops aboard, half were saved, though many of those were injured by the trap and the crash of our barge. Of the hundred oarsmen below, only a few were able to swim out."

General Creesile swore, this time more eloquently than Colonel Enlil had ever known him to.

After the invectives, Creesile said through clenched teeth (*The general's knee is black and blue and swollen three times its normal size*, Enlil thought. *It's got to be hurting…*), "And what was that trap that took out our barge and caused all this damage. Some kind of god-machine from those Mother-damned dark dwarves from the Highlands?"

"Sire, our divers have investigated it and sketched out what it must have looked like before it, before it, was set off." He showed what appeared to be one of their fleet's own catapults, but with a much longer arm that featured a massive iron spike at its tip. "Like a huge thorn, sir. It sprang up from the bottom of the river and smashed through belowdecks aft of the anchor room."

"So they looked at our catapult weapons, and built one to use against us, underwater?"

"It appears that way, sir," Enlil said. "Do you have any orders?"

Creesile considered his options. Surely the ShadowFallers knew that this trick could only take out one barge? Unless they were truly devious and figured he would think that way, only to have them plant other spring-thorn traps immediately upriver. He hated to cause further delay, but in order to preserve his resources and the respect of his men, he had to take positive action, immediately.

"Enlil, first, fish out the bodies and have wagons on shore take them for immediate burials with all honors. But do not spread stories about their fate. Have signs erected that say 'Fallen heroically in battle against ShadowFall traitors.' Then try to retrieve our catapults and any other weapons you can salvage." Creesile sighed. "Finally, take two troop barges, distribute their men among our other five, and leave only a minimum number of oarsmen on them. Put them up front and have their crews drag a weighted rope line across the middle of the river between them to try and find more of those traps. We can't afford to lose more men and materiel." Enlil nodded; his boss was thinking ahead. "And try to find out how that trap was set off. Was there a triggering mechanism, or somebody ashore watching us? And, put my command barge back in the middle of our fleet, with my banners down and that command chair removed. I will remain belowdecks; no use in telling the enemy where I am." *In case that damned flying god-machine changes its mind—if it has one!*

"Right away, sir." Enlil left, while Creesile sat back groaning.

Another day lost! the general sighed. *My troops on the Main Road will be expecting our rendezvous in two days, but our fleet will not be there.* Throbbing agony in his knee took away all thoughts of war. *I just hope I don't lose this damned leg!*

OFF-LOADING TWO THOUSAND SOLDIERS AND THEIR GEAR from two barges and distributing them among five other craft took the rest of the daylight hours, Enlil's chief engineer, Sire Dzitchil, having quickly constructed hinged walkways that could be lowered between the vessels. Creesile admired the innovations that this engineer exhibited. The General said to Enlil, "Colonel, those levered walkways, they can also provide us with a quick way to get men ashore, right from the barges to the river's edge. Especially if we are under fire." Enlil understood at once, and Creesile said, "Have those engineers rig up longer walkways on the other barges, too, so we can unload men on the western bank, once we get upstream of these Mother-damned underwater catapults. They'll make our job easier."

The fleet anchored overnight, giving the men time to go ashore and relieve themselves, get food and drink from the supply barge, and stretch out to sleep. But the noise of Sire Dzitchil's cadre of carpenters hammering and sawing overrode the sounds of crickets and bullfrogs, making any sleep near impossible. Overhead, clouds continued to drift in from the north, obscuring the nearly full moon. Colonel Enlil walked the perimeter of the encampment, checking on the duty guards and sending out patrols to ensure no ShadowFallers could infiltrate. Thinking over the mission at hand, he was ambivalent about the General's goals. ShadowFall was so far from Mother's City and his own Sisterdom of Three Rivers that he didn't understand the urgency; certainly that young princess was no threat to Mother Messinex. He remembered, *In fact, when she was just a princess, Messinex always proclaimed that Princess Perneptheranam was her favorite.*

Like all other Three Rivers folk, Enlil had expected that the avowed sibling friendship and kinship, unique amongst the ever-quarreling Sisters, would induce more peaceful relations across all of Motherland. *Has Motherhood changed my Princess Messinex? Or has something else? I have heard that her priest, that obese Miran Kech, is becoming more ruthless.*

As a young Three Rivers officer in the past, Enlil occasionally did have the unfortunate duty of enforcing some of Princess Messinex's execution orders, always carried out in private, never in public. Those episodes, though personally distasteful, he had understood as being necessary to maintain peace and order in the Sisterdom. *So she and Miran Kech have always had their dark side, but kept it from view. And now, they don't have to hide that?* He hoped that General Creesile's orders did not include a civilian massacre in ShadowFall. *Combat killing is one thing, but innocents who can't fight back, that is murder, and I will not do it!*

THE NEXT MORNING, WITH THE BARGES RELOADED AND the soldiers cramped in their overcrowded vessels, two lightly manned ones headed upriver ahead of the flotilla, a dragline between them. As Colonel Enlil had expected, they discovered nothing, so the rest of the boats launched. *Nothing but more delay*, he thought. *I do believe that this river-invasion idea was ill-considered. We could have marched up the Main Road by now, and spread out along ShadowFall's perimeter. But then the General wouldn't have his glorious new pincer plan fulfilled!*

Spread out behind him, Enlil watched carefully as the boats maintained their even spacing. The river could have accommodated half of them side by side, but he had insisted to the General that a single-file line was preferable for safety and a quicker way to attack the riverside, if necessary. At times, given the energy and emotion he had to expend every day, Enlil often wished he had stayed in the vineyards with his father, producing vintage wines for Three Rivers, instead of choosing military life. *At least the only things I would be crushing is grapes!* But during a fateful visit to Princess Messinex's vineyard, then–Colonel Creesile had seen him wrestle a destructive wild boar to the ground, cutting its throat, and recruited him for duty on the spot. *So he chose me; I didn't choose this!*

The two dragline barges made it another kilometer

upriver, finding no threat. Upon shouted orders, they were followed by the first overloaded troop barge, its oarsmen straining at the increased weight they were pushing against the current, midstream. Behind them, the other barges fell into line and for a few minutes things went well.

Then, with a sickening realization, Enlil saw and heard that first boat, two in front of his and the general's, repeat the *thump!-scream!*-sink scene of the day before. *Damn these ShadowFallers! I'll kill them all!*

***

ENLIL STOOD BEFORE AN ENRAGED GENERAL CREESILE. "General, sir, I—"

"Mother damn you, you incompetent swine!" Creesile yelled loud enough for half his remaining fleet to hear outside his cabin, all six barge-loads of them scattered along a kilometer of river. "You were supposed to find the damned traps!" Sitting with his swollen knee, in pain and in disgust, he lowered his voice to an ominous shout. "What are the losses this time?"

"Sir, the underwater catapults, two of them, were hidden underneath sloping logs near the riverbank. After our dragline slid over them, they were released by some kind of winch, and settled near the middle of the river and attacked our barge from either side, belowdecks."

"*How. Many. Men. Colonel?*" Creesile was now standing on one leg, screaming at Enlil's face.

The colonel blanched. He knew the general's reputation for dispensing deserved justice.

And I do deserve it. That Wakan or his dwarves have outsmarted us all. But only I will get blamed!

"*All* the oarsmen, sir—two hundred. Around eight hundred soldiers; their leather armor and weapons dragged them down, and then the ShadowFaller traps sprung godscloth nets over them all that kept them from rising to the surface once they were under. Drowned them like animals. Vicious."

Creesile was silent. *Who is Enlil's next in command? Major Gromm*? he wondered. He didn't know, but didn't really care. Finally he said, "Guards! Colonel Enlil is now de-ranked. Seize him!" Enlil stiffened, dreading what was coming.

"One thousand fallen heroes, Enlil, all because you were incompetent. Very well, guards, his punishment is to be flogging with the nine-tails. One lash for each lost man. Take him and administer the lashing up on the poop deck, for all to witness. The fleet will remain stationary until tomorrow." Trembling, Enlil slumped. He knew he would be dead before a tenth of the lashes were administered. In his numb mind he could only think of his youthful life in faraway Three Rivers, and of his father and the vineyards, wishing that damned wild boar had stayed away!

CHAPTER THIRTY-EIGHT

"Remove that carcass from the mast and throw it into the river," General Creesile said in his loudest command voice, attempting to conceal the ever-increasing agony emanating from his swollen left knee. "I don't want to see any more of Enlil's bones." Gesturing to Major Gromm, Enlil's replacement, he said, "And have that deck scrubbed. A traitor's blood and flesh disgust me!" Looking upriver, the fog was rolling in thicker than ever, visibility approaching zero. *Damn,* Creesile thought, *we are open to attack from any side and can't see a curséd thing!*

On the western river shore, a thousand bodies lay in rows and columns, their valuable armor and weapons being stripped from them, their swords stacked for return to the barges. Though he hated the idea, Creesile ordered a mass immolation of his lost soldiers and oarsmen; the invasion needed to get back on schedule. *There will be a lot more time for mourning when this war is over*, he thought. *And probably a lot more dead men to grieve over. But losing a day!*

Consulting with his white-haired, dark-clad chief engineer, Sire Dzitchil, the General found that the last set of rapids was just a few klicks ahead of the fleet.

"Sir," the bearded man said, "I have already dispatched teams of my men on both sides of the river, up ten klicks. They are looking for any other possible underwater catapults or such traps. I suspect that the enemy may plan to use something else this time, knowing we would be wary of a third set of the same weapons."

"I hope you find it, if it is, Dzitchil," Creesile said solemnly, motioning toward the deck crew now scrubbing Enlil's blood and flesh stains from around his execution post. The old man opened his eyes wide, nodding to acknowledge the threat, then saluted and left to take his place at the prow of Creesile's barge, looking out in dismay at the blanket of fog that was now thoroughly enveloping the invasion fleet.

---

*FORTY KILOMETERS MORE, *CREESILE THOUGHT, *THEN WE cross into ShadowFall territory and the war begins. But first another portage, and who knows what kinds of evil that Wakan Kech has planned?* Back in his cabin, he reviewed the situation. His fleet still comprised four troop barges with three thousand men and six hundred rowers who would take up spears upon landfall, plus two supply barges with fireball catapults and anti-aerial arrows for that flying monstrosity. As many as four thousand or more men and their oxen supply wagons were advancing up the Main Road. *Gromm's columns are a day ahead of us now,* Creesile fumed. *I trust they will not engage until we rendezvous as originally planned. It is essential that the attack from the river and on the Main Road occur simultaneously. Otherwise… otherwise my forces will be split and I won't have my planned mass offensive to overwhelm those peasants and their monkey-men!*

The General's boat was in the central position of the single-file fleet, with two side-by-side drag-line vessels in front to detect underwater threats, a troop carrier behind those, and the remainder downriver. Altogether, the kilometer-long string of barges was now spaced farther apart in case of another devious attack. *And going slower,* Creesile noticed; *the oarsmen are skittish.*

I don't blame them; this damned Wakan Kech is insidious. An unwelcome thought added itself: *And smart, too. Wish I had him on my side instead of that Miran Kech!*

As Creesile nursed his broken knee with an icepack from his cabin's insulated ice chest, he almost drifted off into sleep as he felt the monotonous but distant *beat-beat-beat* of the oarsmen's rhythm-keeper reverberating through his command barge. With fewer than a hundred men rowing his lighter craft he briefly wondered how anybody aboard the big barges, with their two hundred sets of oars and a louder drumbeat, could ever get any sleep. *But they're not supposed to*, he answered himself. *They have to remain alert, ready to fight at a moment's notice. And I wouldn't be so tired myself if my damned knee would stop hurting!* Looking at the lavishly supplied liquor cabinet with temptation, he decided to hold off strong drink until after ShadowFall fell. *And then we'll all celebrate!*

CHAPTER THIRTY-NINE

Mother's River narrowed downstream from the rapids, forcing the lead two barges back to single file. Thusk had chosen this location as the choice position to build what he hoped would be the first defensive trap using Wakan's Wire. A stray thought wafted in: *We should have named it after Odel; it was his original invention.* Just as the Solar Priests of God's Country had used a godscloth net to catch river-going boats north of God's Port, towing them without damage into the harbor there, Thusk's engineering teams built spring-loaded spools on either side of the river. But between these spools was laid not a wide web, but the thinnest wire possible; from a wide webbing of godscloth at each spool, a full kilometer was twisted into near invisibility.

Una had explained the phenomenon: "What you call godscloth is a web of layers of borophene, each two molecules thick. As you rotate the spools at each end, the godscloth twists until at the center and along a distance, a wirelike configuration results. At a specified tension, the borophene layers displace among themselves, resulting in a thin wire only a few molecules thick. This provides the sharpest cutting edge ever manufactured by humans. It once was an advanced cutting tool for manufacturing.

"In the current millennium, to the extent this DI has

been able to detect, such wires are used for gross scission purposes, such as at the quarry operated by one Odel M'ridge. Outside of God's Country, few had the requisite tools for cutting the material or the gloves for safely handling the edges."

Thusk had not briefed Una on Wakan's proposed use of the godscloth wire to kill people. Even during the emplacement of the tall-man-sized spools along the river edge, the DI had not commented. Thusk had planned to argue the case with Una if necessary, but to his surprise it did not occur.

As TWILIGHT SET IN, THUSK'S SPOOL MEN CONCEALED themselves and their equipment well, and were ready for their tasks. On the western edge of the river, Thusk's countryman Rohn stood ready to act. Turning to his crew, he whispered, "The Mothersmen didn't catch on that our spool looks like a fallen tree." Peering out into the fog he could barely make out the single lamps aboard the long line of barges now beginning to approach. Rohn said, "As soon as I yell, we should get a confirmation shout from the other side. When we do, we push our spool upwards and draw it tight with the winch. Then we slip the supporting brace into place. The Wakan's Wire trap will be all set."

Thusk had explained to Rohn and the other crewmen that at five meters above river level, the cutting edge should be positioned to take out anybody standing on the decks, and hopefully any superstructures as well. "We could place it at two meters high, aiming to take out rowers, but we have no way to calculate the forces involved in shearing an entire barge. And our Una won't answer questions about how to do it, if it suspects we are going to attack people with it. So we aim at people on the deck, not the boats. And if you think what we're doing is too cruel, remember what that Miran Kech and General Creesile and those Mothersmen will do to the women and children of ShadowFall if they get through. At least, this will be a swift end."

Rohn and his men nodded solemnly. *When that happens,* he thought, *heads will roll!* He had to think of the invading army as no different than velks back home; he had killed many of those vile creatures, but never a human being. *But I chose this fight, as did all of us here. Thusk needs us; the Princess needs us.*

He repeated to himself, *They are just velks in human form, vicious animals on two feet!*

CHAPTER FORTY

Sitting in his captain's chair, General Creesile silently cursed his throbbing, swollen knee. He gulped a mouthful of his medic's supposed painkilling draught and put the mug away. "Mother damn this leg!" he murmured, not wanting to complain openly of his pain, his weakness, to the men standing at the conference table where he sat. "And Mother damn this fog, too!" That, aloud, drew the attention of Major Gromm and his lieutenants, the commanders of the troop and supply barges of the invasion fleet.

"I have called you all here," the general said, unsuccessfully concealing his increasing discomfort, "because the underwater weapons of the deceitful ShadowFallers have caused us grievous losses." Pointing through the cabin windows, he said, "And this thick night fog is hindering our progress upriver." Waiting for their general's further comments, the barge commanders stood silently, jaws firmly fixed. As infantrymen, they had not expected to be subject to sneak attacks on the river; death in hand-to-hand combat on a battlefield was one thing, honorable; but drowning in sight of a riverbank, unable to cut through the godscloth nets holding you down, that was a fate not even courageous Mothersmen should face.

"General, sir," a commander, Lieutenant Garsteer, said, "my men have requested that we be allowed to embark ashore and continue our mission by land. Continuing over to the Main Road."

Creesile stared icily at Garsteer, then glanced at the others. "Do any of the rest of you feel this way, gentlemen?" The General's glare told them all what he wanted their answers to be. But surprisingly, all but Major Gromm nodded in agreement.

"And you, Major, your opinion? Do you want to change the campaign plans, too?"

Gromm, a stocky, dark-complexioned warrior of Creesile's long acquaintance, hesitated, thinking of Colonel Enlil's bloody remains on deck the day before. "General, sir, I am in favor of doing whatever you think will preserve our troops until we get to ShadowFall." He gulped and blew out a breath. "Nobody anticipated losing a thousand men before we even got to the battlefield. And, we have yet one more set of rapids immediately upriver, another tiring and probably dangerous portage to make. And then, another thirty-five klicks up this damned river, with who knows what other hidden traps have been set." Knowing that his next statement might very well be his last, he said, gazing directly into his superior's frigid stare, "Sir, I do myself believe that our best course is to surprise our enemy and meet them on land, in one massive frontal attack, with all your troops. But that is your call."

Creesile sat quietly for a full minute, letting his subordinates stew in their own sweat. *Not quite a mutiny,* he thought, *but probably the honest opinions of good soldiers. Not yes men; I am glad of that.* Nodding as if in deep contemplation, he raised his head and looked each man in the eyes, his gaze drifting from one to the other. *I will let them think it was their idea, though I already knew my decision. I am going to send these men into battle in a few days, and I want them loyal. So—*

"Gentlemen," he said, standing to shake each man's hand, though in severe pain, "your considered judgment has swayed me. I shall rely upon your experience and your skills to bring off this new course of action. My new orders are to hie to the western bank as soon as the sun rises and unload the men and materiel, leaving only a skeleton crew on the barges to maintain the fleet until we return home." To Major Gromm, he said, "Scour the countryside and requisition oxen to transport those catapults. We can't leave them behind, and we can't have soldiers pulling them such a long distance. Go to your boats, gentlemen, and prepare your men for a long march in the morning. Two days to ShadowFall." He instructed Gromm to send a messenger to the Main Road force with instructions to stand down three klicks before ShadowFall, to await the additional troops who would be marching to join them. "Find your messenger a rowboat and authorize a horse." Given the value of the horse, Gromm knew that the General was very serious about coordinating the linkup.

As soon as Creesile was alone in his cabin, he sat down hard, rubbing his swollen knee. The injured and swollen joint was now black; blue streaks ran up to his thigh. He rang the bell for his medic to come with strong painkillers, and then leaned over to open the liquor cabinet. *I won't be able to march in this shape tomorrow; there's got to be a horse and carriage somewhere! Even a wagon...*

CHIEF ENGINEER DZITCHIL, SHIVERING IN THE COOLING fog, couldn't see more than three meters in front of his station at the prow of General Creesile's boat. On the lookout for more ShadowFall traps, he was mentally reviewing the underwater catapult designs. *Insidious but ingenious devices,* he thought, admiring both the concept and its execution. *I hope that General Creesile will spare the lives of that Wakan Kech and his engineers; Mother's Army engineers could learn a lot from them.* Thinking of recent reports in Mother's City of raiders from the Cold Sea at the port of the Sisterdom of WaterEdge, he had been trying to come up with new catapult designs to keep the pirate ships away. *And if the reports of that big green flying machine are true, we could meet those bandits far out at sea and sink them there.*

Having heard that his catapults needed to shoot bundles of borophene arrows for protection from that flying thing, and that removing the arrows would bring it back to life, he wondered at the technology involved. Not a believer in magic, he had for years tried to reason out the properties of godspheres and godscloth, all to no end. *The ancients may not have had magic, but I'm damned if I know where even to begin to fabricate a material like godscloth, not to mention a flying machine that can be stopped with arrows and can then heal itself afterward!* He would ask the General, next time they met, to let Wakan Kech and his legendary monkey-men live. At least long enough to learn all their secrets!

From behind him, Dzitchil heard the boat commanders walking up the stairs from the general's cabin, talking loudly. "So we're finally getting off of this damned river, boys," a gruff voice spoke loudly. "My men want to fight on land, not drown in this wet hole!" Other men spoke out in agreement, as they lifted their lanterns to make their ways down into the rowboats that would take them back to their barges. Even from his forward position, the engineer could smell the foul odors of tobacco, alcohol—and disgusting *perfumes*!—emanating from the group of commanders.

The engineer smiled; he wanted to get off the river, too. *Out here, I'm just a sitting—* He never finished the thought. The last sound he ever heard was a shout from the riverbank, "Now!"

ON THE WESTERN RIVERBANK, THUSK'S MAN ROHN SAW half a dozen lamps aboard the third barge, glowing lights swinging as they proceeded upwards, apparently going from belowdecks to the main deck. "*Now!*" he shouted. "*Pull now!*" "*Now! Now!*" came the answering shout from across the river, followed by tension on the godswire strung over it. Immediately, Rohn's crew pulled their spool erect; within seconds, the invisible Wakan's Wire stretched between the two spindles, five meters above the river's surface. And a meter and a half above the deck of Creesile's barge. At chest height for Engineer Dzitchil.

As Creesile's barge proceeded northward at the rowing speed of eight kilometers per hour, or a bit over two meters per second, the two-molecule-thick godscloth wire sliced through the wooden prow of the barge in less than one second. Behind it stood Chief Engineer Dzitchil; a fraction of a second later, the engineer was in two bloody pieces, the top half in momentary agony as it fell to the deck in a torrent of blood. Out of his fading sight, Dzitchil was surprised to see that the lower half of his body remained standing. *How curious!* he thought. Then he died.

Farther back on the deck, Wakan's Wire slid effortlessly through the raised dais supporting Creesile's command chair, momentarily halted by the metal ventilator ducts protruding up from the oarsmen's tight quarters, then rending them with a screeching noise. Two auxiliary masts, severed, began to fall onto the deck. At those sounds, the exiting barge commanders turned to see what was happening—and the wire caught them all at various levels—across the abdomen, above the knees, across the throat of one man who had knelt to adjust his boot—severing them like a butcher would cut a side of ox meat with the swift stroke of a cleaver. Major Gromm, his head just then arising from below deck, saw the men literally cut down in front of him, their blood spewing all over the deck and himself.

"What in Mother's name?" he yelled, drawing his sword to confront whatever enemy had attacked his men so viciously. But then he heard the *squeeeech* as the invisible wire continued its passage through the length of the barge. Standing on the deck, viewing his men cleanly sliced in two, some still pitifully quivering in pieces, he watched awestricken as the top section of the barge began sliding sideways, as would a cake when sliced by a baker. Realizing his peril, Gromm fell to the deck as the cut section moved a meter to one side, catching on lower timbers, accompanied by loud grinding and crunching noises. From below he heard the oarsmen yelling; then they stopped, the barge slowing down and turning in the river current, the rudderman and his control mechanism now gone into the river, sliced apart.

Gromm thought, *If this slicing goes on behind us, with those troops all standing up!* He began yelling to the other barges to duck, but a cacophony of screams, echoing along the river, told him it was too late.

———

BY THEN, ROHN AND HIS MEN WERE IN FULL RETREAT from the riverbanks, hoping to escape the retaliation they knew would be coming once any Mothersmen made it to shore. "Our orders are to run north, parallel to the Main Road, but stay away from the soldiers there," he told his crew between gasps. "Sire Thusk will try to rescue us with his flying machine, but as we know, that might not be possible." Rohn was grateful for the fog; first, it would help him and his crews to escape the fury of the Mothersmen. *And it also means we don't have to see the carnage we caused!*

A half kilometer west of the river, Rohn stopped at a designated standing stone. To his sigh of relief, a great cylindrical shape, displacing the fog, came floating down. Out of nowhere a door opened, and the silhouette of a small man his own size appeared. "Come in, Rohn, you men," the welcome voice of Thusk said, "we've already picked up your other wire-men aboard from the eastern side. You all have done ShadowFall a great service this evening. From high above, Una showed us that three barges wrecked, sliced in two before Wakan's Wire snagged on something, probably one of those borophene catapults. It dragged down your spools, but their job was done." Thusk was smiling, celebrating.

"This will make the General think hard about proceeding with his invasion!"

Rohn and his crews, having heard the continuous multitude of horrible screams from the Mothersmen who had not been fortunate enough to die quickly, nodded but did not celebrate. They wanted to fly back to ShadowFall and get drunk. Rohn himself, though satisfied that they had all done their duty as assigned, wondered whether coming down to these Warm Lands to fight other people's battles was a good idea after all. *Those screams,* he thought darkly, *they didn't sound like velks!*

CHAPTER FORTY-ONE

Hearing the screams and crashing noises outside his door, General Creesile immediately threw himself onto the floor, hoping to duck whatever projectiles he imagined had hit his officers. But within an eye-blink, the door itself fell into two pieces, the remnants dangling from iron hinges. As the unbelievable occurred before his eyes, the top half of his cabin was sheared in two, as if by a giant cleaver. Whatever caused the separation was so thin that the separated pieces fell back together, the top portion sliding askew a meter, causing the windows to shatter, the paneling to rip apart, and the gas lights to shear from their fixture, spreading their flames over the wreckage that had been the General's cabin. The reeking smell of gas, seared wood, and even slaughterhouse odors, assailed his nostrils.

Major Gromm thundered down the stairs. "General! Are you all right? We just got—cut—in two!"

Creesile pulled himself up to the undamaged table, cursing. "Another attack by that damned Kech! What has he done to us?"

"Sir!" Gromm shouted. "I've got to get you out of here. The fire!"

Within seconds, Gromm hefted Creesile up from his ruined cabin, carefully stepping around the severed bodies of the other officers, nearly slipping on running blood and coils of intestines. With the help of a crewman, Gromm was able to lower Creesile into a lifeboat and quickly oar away from the blazing barge. As they watched in horror, oarsmen from belowdecks vainly tried to reach the main deck, but severed masts and other pieces of wooden structures blocked the hatches. Some few desperate men got out by squeezing through small ventilation hatches in the gunwales, and through openings sliced in the deck, but as the fiery barge tipped backwards and slipped into the black water of the river, all of the rest were trapped. Creesile and his two companions grimaced as hundreds died in the flames, those onboard survivors then drowning as the barge slipped from sight in the silent black waters of the river.

Whatever the invisible knife edge was, for some reason it raised a meter and caused only a few casualties and light damage to the barge following Creesile's; the barge-cutter missed the next boat after that entirely. Amidst the shouts and screams, all barges quickly stopped rowing and Creesile's fleet came to a standstill, one at a time, without colliding. After the first disaster the day before, the watchmen were more sensitive and alert, undoubtedly saving lives.

"Another barge lost, hundreds more men," the General rasped. "That damned Wakan Kech, I will skin him alive, centimeter by centimeter." By this time other lifeboats were approaching Creesile's. The General called for another parley, one with the ranking officers of each boat. "This meeting will be on land, men, the west bank here. Set up tents for tonight. Half the men on guard duty, the other half to rest. Secure the barges."

After the hard fall in his cabin and the manhandling during Gromm's rapid rescue of him away from the command barge, Creesile's damaged knee, twisted again, was once more afire with pain. *I have to hold on,* he told himself. *Two more days!*

"GENERAL, SIR, ONE OF OUR SEARCH PARTIES FOUND

this ashore," Major Gromm said, holding what appeared to be a small spool of spiderweb material. "They had to handle it with these special gloves that the rebels left on site. Otherwise it slices off fingers. It was wrapped around a two-meter cylinder, but my men re-spooled some of it onto this small spindle." Creesile was sitting in his command tent, cold and wet, with a small fire-stove providing heat and the comforting odor of seasoned oak. He watched intently as Gromm described the strange invisible wire.

Unspooling a shimmering thread, Gromm said, "We think it is godscloth, but wound tightly to become just a wire. After some rumors the men had heard from travelers on the Main Road, it is called by some, 'Wakan's Wire.'" He frowned. "Apparently a stretch of this across the river is what sliced our barge in two and killed all those men."

Peering at the thin thread, Creesile shrugged and frowned. "You need those special handling gloves and unique cutting equipment to cut patterns out of godscloth, to handle it? Nobody ever found such tools, but apparently that Kech and his monkey-men now have. We need to be on the lookout for it after we take the palace there. This 'Wakan's Wire' is interesting. It could be very useful. We need to be able to make it for ourselves." He was imagining the myriad of military uses the wire would have, including the usage just demonstrated on his own barge.

Gromm nodded, taking the spool and saluting the general. As he left the tent, Creesile pondered the possible uses of this new kind of weapon. But then the pain returned, driving out all other thoughts, and he called for a medic.

"DAMN YOU, MEDIC," HE SHOUTED AT THE CRINGING older man massaging his ruined knee, its swollen black-and-blueness now streaked with ominous red rivulets running up his thigh. "Give me whatever it takes to stop the pain. I've got a war to run!"

The tunic-clad medic stood up and shook his head. "Sir, the infection is spreading. Your leg is black, and your veins are spreading the bad blood. It is beyond my ability to help you now. You are going to lose the rest of the leg, or your life. We must amputate."

Creesile shut his eyes tight, cursing to himself. "All these battles, over all these years," he whispered aloud, "and never anything more than a few scars. And now I lose my Mother-damned leg by falling down stairs, hit from behind by a barge." Calling upon his inner strength, dreading the ordeal to come, he said gently, "All right, medic. Prepare your table and your saw. I will drink enough to put me out, and then you may do your best. Or worst."

A few minutes later, as Creesile leaned back in his chair, the medic showed up at the tent door. "Sir, are you ready?"

Creesile grimaced, thinking of the operation to come. "Medic, you plan to use a butcher's saw to amputate my leg, is that correct?"

"Yes, sir. I'm afraid it is."

"And cutting off my leg will take several minutes?

"Sir, that is about right."

"Well, let me suggest something faster and cleaner." He did.

As the medic's jaw dropped, he gulped and ran off to find Major Gromm and some of the captured Wakan's Wire. Returning with the spindle of godswire, the major was impressed. *It will work,* he thought. *Our general is a smart man!*

"Major," Creesile said, groaning, "as of this moment you are promoted to colonel. You will be a witness to the amputation of my injured left leg." At Gromm's shocked face, he whispered while the medic was fetching the gurney to transport the General to the medical tent. "If the medic kills me, then execute him. But if I survive, then proceed with the march immediately and carry me along in a covered wagon without a word to the troops; I don't want them to see me as an invalid. Continue the march for a full day. That should get us close to ShadowFall by tomorrow evening, where we will meet with the Main Road troops. Set up camp tomorrow night a few klicks south of their border. They need to see our strength, our threat. It will dishearten some of them. Now that I think about it, have the men set up four campfires around each tent; that should really put the fear of Mother into those peasants." Creesile allowed himself a smile at the thought of Wakan Kech seeing over twenty-five thousand campfires near his border, so many Mothersmen in full fury waiting to pounce.

Breathing heavily, in severe pain, Major Gromm could tell, Creesile continued, "Colonel Treegu's intelligence agents report that they have built a stone wall around their famous Iron Gate on the border, with some defensive trenches right inside it, rigged with those damned Kech traps. That will be our first test against Wakan's new weapons; we need daylight to try to see them. But we might have to fend off some feints from them before dawn, and if so we fight back, advancing as necessary up to that wall, but no farther. Do what you need to do to hold off the rebels, but do *not* press the final assault until I am awake again. I will be back in action tomorrow evening, after getting through this damned operation. The final push must delay until the next morning. Is that clear?"

Colonel Gromm nodded. "Sir, understood, sir. And thank you for the promotion."

"Then call in that damned medic and let's get on with it!"

DRUNK OR NOT, THIS HURTS LIKE A SON OF A BITCH! Creesile thought through his mental haze, still feeling the excruciating pain where his left knee had been. Biting down hard on a wad of thick leather during the amputation, the general had tried not to scream when his medic's aides had pulled down that strand of Wakan's Wire through his ruined leg, above the knee. That was bad enough, but at least it was quick, only a few seconds; the hot-iron cauterization of the raw stub afterward had hurt even worse, excruciating, causing him to pass out..

As Creesile awoke and struggled to gain control, pain washed over him like a red tide of agony. He wanted to wail like a baby but held it in. *My men want a tough guy, not a child, but—oh, Mother, it hurts!* He rasped, "How long, Gromm?"

"Sir, you were under for only half an hour."

"Medic, anything more you can do down there, to ease the pain?"

The medic had already applied a cold compress over the bandaged bloody stump, a soothing comfort, if only momentary. The general accepted yet another herbal drink that the medic assured him would ease his pain, but would render him unconscious again. He told the medic and Gromm to awaken him in no longer than two hours. In a minute he was asleep, dreaming of burning down Pernie's palace, his men rampaging through the ruins of her city, her naked body at his feet. But in the dream, his left leg was being devoured by a huge wolf, a creature he couldn't shake off or kill. And it *hurt!*

Two hours after the amputation, Major Gromm was finally able to roust Creesile awake, much to the relief of his medic and the nervous command staff, though even asleep the General had been groaning and gritting his teeth in his sleep. The medical tent in which they were all gathered around their commander reeked of alcohol and drying blood. Motioning to his male nurses, the medic wiped his bloodstained hands on his tunic and said, "The General should be able to be moved now, so take him out on this stretcher." Creesile managed a weak smile as the medic saluted. *Damn, it hurts!* he thought, gnashing his teeth. *But I guess that Wakan's Wire did do the job fast.* He grunted as his stretcher-bearers took him to his command tent, followed by Colonel Gromm and six junior commanders.

Colonel Gromm said, "Sir, we've arranged a covered wagon for your transport to ShadowFall and the battle. I suggest you sleep while we march to the border. We'll be there this evening. Then you will be refreshed and up for the finale." Two orderlies lifted their General into the wagon and placed him on soft godscloth pillows.

Creesile said, "All you officers have your orders, so proceed with the march and the preparations. Thank you, Colonel Gromm." He nodded, asking the medic for another draught of painkiller. *Resting more sounds wonderful*, he thought. *Gromm here can handle a simple straightforward march up the Main Road.* At that, the soothing herb hit full force and the general passed into a blissful sleep. He did not dream.

CHAPTER FORTY-TWO

Upon returning the Wakan's Wire trap crews to their new postings in ShadowFall, Thusk reported to Wakan and the war council, weary after a full day and night of transporting PeoplesLandsers up and down the river. "Your wire and our underwater catapult traps have knocked a hole in their invasion fleet, Wakan," he said proudly. "Out of the eight barges Creesile started with, we took out four, at least two of them loaded with troops. So he must have lost a third of his force."

Wakan Kech looked tired, as did the sublieutenants around the war council table. "None of Creesile's regulars have come across our borders yet, but your scouting runs show them only about twenty kilometers south of it, marching this way, right?"

Thusk nodded. "Some two or three thousand have already begun setting up camp just five kilometers south along the Main Road. I think they intend to merge with Creesile's troops from the barges down there. Una estimates the total they will aggregate to be about six and a half thousand soldiers and as many as eight hundred support personnel. Only one catapult is being towed by oxen, but it does have those borophene arrows, the ones dangerous to Una. And Creesile's engineers are building others even as their march continues."

Around the table, Wakan and others took note of that

ominous innovation—nobody had ever considered bringing carpenters and engineers along on a march where they would construct siege engines en route. Their enemy was creative, Creesile was, and they reluctantly gave him credit for that; it was just too bad he was on the wrong side!

Wakan said, "So the river approach cost them nearly two thousand men. It is sad for them, men just doing their jobs, but good for us. Those losses of Creesile's might make all the difference." Growing very grim, he said, "But far from destroying their morale, my spies report that the Mothersmen are in full fury now. They have legendarily never lost a battle—although General Creesile and I, and I suspect, even others—know that not to be true; classified histories show otherwise. Yet they are determined to extinguish all of ShadowFall as a reminder that they are always victorious." He turned and bowed as the Princess arrived at the head of the table, as did all the other men present.

"Princess, I was just briefing the war council. The good news is, our godscloth wire traps and Thusk's underwater thorn catapults have accounted for about two thousand Mothersmen with not a single loss to ShadowFall. And all of it on the territory of Stone Pyramid, on the river. The bad news is, Creesile's forces are all on land now, just hours from our borders. We expect they will make camp for tonight and begin their assault at dawn tomorrow."

"How many people does he have, Wakan?" Princess Pernie asked, inspecting the large wall map Wakan was using to illustrate his battle plans. Various blue and red marks indicated the positions of the ShadowFall and Miran Kech armies, and the locations of defensive weapons. Pernie was impressed by the ease with which an orderly was erasing and adding changes as the priest spoke. The *white-board* material that Una had shown Thusk how to fabricate was quite handy. She thought. *Too bad she wouldn't show us how to make those rapid-firing weapons the ancients used!*

"About six thousand Mothersmen in all, but bunched

up closer together than the General originally planned, I'll bet. It is somewhat amusing that Creesile has set up many more campfires than he has tents, I suppose to frighten us. He doesn't know that Una can scan for people." Pointing to the wall map, Wakan continued. "Not having to worry about a flanking attack from the river, we can concentrate our people on both sides of the Main Road." Nodding toward Thusk, he said, "Based on the success of the wire traps on the river, Thusk has crews right now putting together similar setups across the road. We had already deployed them at tactical spots on creek beds, ditches, and gullies around our city, here."

Wakan went on to review the plan of battle for the Princess and any others who had been out of the council chambers earlier that night. "Six rotatable catapults, ready to throw fireballs, can reach a thousand meters; they are spread across five kilometers of our border, centered around the Iron Gate, now welded shut, on the Main Road, and all behind the high stone fence we erected around it, two and a half kilometers in each direction. Next are our springbowmen, stationed back from that gate a hundred meters, now a thousand of them, spread across those five kilometers. Staggered behind them, five hundred conventional archers. Behind *them*, four rows of spearmen, two thousand in all, backed up by several thousand citizen militia men and women, with spears, swords, and other hand-combat weapons.'

Pernie studied the map and asked, "Should we attack them first tonight, with our flyers and catapults with flame-bombs? Send out our springbowers in the dark? Before they get any closer?"

Thusk answered before the priest could reply. "Princess, we had thought of that, of hitting them at night, but doing that would reveal the locations of our catapults, and invite retaliation. And Odel's flyers can't see their targets at night. On top of that, our Wakan's Wire traps work both ways, coming and going. We did not leave any gaps in that fence."

Shaking his head at the interruption, Wakan Kech continued his report. "Those last few thousand defenders are plain citizens of all ages and conditions. A militia, the last-ditch; they would be slaughtered if Creesile gets this far." He frowned. "We may all have to fight to the very end, anyhow. My spies tell me that General Creesile will raise the black flag, because of our slaughter of his men on Mother's River." He said hoarsely, "No surrender, no prisoners."

The Princess was silent. "This really is a fight to the death then, Wakan. Why do you think my sister, *our* Mother Messinex, is doing all of this?"

Wakan Kech shook his head silently, while thinking, *Miran Kech!*

CHAPTER FORTY-THREE

Miran Kech was furious, his usual response to the continuing bad news from Creesile's incompetent invasion of ShadowFall. In his hand was a written report that had been forwarded from the general's carriage-express. The note had been left at the palace's front doors, none of Creesile's messengers wishing to suffer the fates of their predecessors.

Answering Mother Messinex's call bell, he composed himself, smoothing his blue robes and holding his head erect before entering Her throne room. Quickly going through the obeisance protocol, he asked, "And Mother, what is your command?"

"Miran, I heard that a message has arrived from General Creesile," Mother Messinex said, "What is the report?"

Miran was shocked at Messinex's disheveled appearance. Was she not sleeping? Had not her handmaidens washed and clothed her, arranged her hair, before appearing on her throne? But he answered without tone or inflection. "Mother, it seems that Wakan Kech placed underwater catapults in Mother's River, right after the first rapids and portage." He sighed. "We lost hundreds of men and a barge-load of supplies."

Messinex frowned, making her visage now look ominous, not merely unkempt. "Miran, how could this happen?" Breathing deeply she said, "First, Rist's flying machine sinks barges at the docks on Lake Roos. Then, he drops rocks through the roof of our palace here, something that has never happened in thousands of years. I have been unable to sleep soundly ever since; I depended on *you*, Miran, to keep this palace—and me— safe. And you have failed!" Quickly standing, she picked up her scepter from the arm of her throne and waved it at her advisor. Around the room, black-leathered Mothersmen guards, anticipating an execution on the spot, lowered their spears and awaited her command.

Miran blanched as she said, slowly and with venom in her voice, "Miran Kech. I order you to go immediately to ShadowFall. If the invasion has succeeded, you will bring back my Sister Perneptheranam, her Kech priest, Wakan, and the two little men from the Dark Highlands. As captives, unharmed." Her guards relaxed, bringing their spears upright. She knew, as they did, that her own late Lordess Mother would have never touched that scepter except to order an immediate death.

As a nervous Miran began to bow, Messinex stopped him. "Enough, Kech! Leave immediately, use the carriage-express. And do not return until you have those captives in hand." She motioned to her two nearest guards. "Take these two with you, my most trusted guards."

As the three bowed and backed out of the throne room, Messinex stopped them again. "Guards," she said aloud, "if General Creesile has killed any of those captives whom I ordered to be spared, against my specific orders, he is to be executed and his head returned to me. And"—she pointed her scepter at Miran Kech—"if they yet live, but have escaped from my army there, you are to execute *this* Kech priest and bring *his* head to me."

AFTER THE SHAKEN KECH AND HER TWO GUARDS

departed, Mother Messinex allowed her handmaidens to escort her to her chambers and prepare her for the day. After hot sweet chai and delicious sugar-dough pastries, the maidens brought her lavish dishes of bread, sliced pork, Three Rivers fruits, and a chopped salad of green leaves, grapes, and strawberries with a tangy dressing. *I love my breakfast meals*, she thought as she sipped her chai, *But I loved them even more when I was just Princess Messinex, without the weight of all of Motherland on my shoulders. How did my Lordess Mother, and all of the other Mothers back through the millennia, endure the stress, the uncertainty, the betrayals?* She knew that somehow they all had prevailed to one extent or another, and that many of them gave credit to the goddesses of the Crystal Throne. She herself had not received any such goddess guidance, only gibberish!

After bathing and dressing, Mother Messinex dismissed her maidens and when alone, entered the Sanctuary Room to once more read from the golden tablets that were the most precious secret of Motherland. In the secret language that was written and read only by Sisters, taught to them from simple syllabaries by priests who never saw the golden histories, Messinex skimmed through thin metal page after page, searching for any history that would tell her about ShadowFall. Was there something about that place that made her Sister Pernie betray her so viciously? A spell or a curse? Why was the whole region left empty until their Lordess Mother gifted it to Pernie six years before?

After an hour of quickly reading over mundane records of crop yields, of Mothers' mates, of offspring, of rebellions, and of invasions from surrounding highlands and the Cold Sea, Messinex found one simple statement that she thought might acknowledge the mystery if not its explanation. "Mother Llaneos writes this in the thirteenth year of Her reign. WaterFall, the northernmost province of our Motherland nation, reports that a plague has broken out amongst its citizenry. The palace is now abandoned, its dead too horrendous in appearance and condition even to retrieve and bury. A scant few survivors lived long enough to relate the events that hastened the disaster, but they told of a fiery manifestation arriving over the massive waterfall that supplies Mother's River, the flaming embers of which passed through the river near the city. After which people began to die, even the Princess Saxchemia and all her palace guards. I have thus ordered the Sisterdom of WaterFall to remain taboo, unoccupied and unvisited, until a thousand years have passed."

Messinex spoke in a soft whisper to herself. "A plague of fire and embers? Did a thousand years really pass or did our Lordess Mother send Pernie up there too soon? Does that plague still exist up there, affecting the mind and the soul, some remnant evil still remaining?" Bringing her left fist to her mouth to stifle a sob, she said, "Oh, my precious Pernie. What have you done?"

But in her mind she added, *What have I done?* "I must go ask the Goddess!"

CHAPTER FORTY-FOUR

Over the next weeks, guided by DI explanations, Mienne and Wayer limited their explorations to learning what all the Control Room controlled. They were astonished and impressed that the Ancient Engineers, as they now referred to them, had mapped the entire surface of Moon: its topography, mineral and water deposits, and much of its subsurface volumes—stratigraphy, voids, faults, and natural tubes—as well as hundreds of kilometers of Tubes. These latter were variously identified as *Claimed*, *Settled*, *Inhabited*, *Finished*, *Under Construction*, *To Be Determined*, and by other, enigmatic, nomenclatures: *Test Cylinders*, *Qomp Assembly Stations*, *Avatarobot Extraction*, and some by meaningless symbols not decipherable even by the DI.

The DI stated the situation bluntly: "Many sensors, qomps, and connections have deteriorated over the millennia, to the extent that available nano and quantum repairs are no longer feasible. On the Far Side, very few instruments of any kind yet exist that can be linked to."

Mienne smiled, thinking she was hearing an apology from an ancient machine about destruction by the far distant Sun in the far distant past. *Is DI a person or really just a machine, like Jolan Keesh's tunnel-melting Eternal Machine, made of metals and minerals?* She didn't think she'd ever know. But she needed its knowledge, not its sympathy.

"DI, about this crystal chair here in the next room. You said Motherth people have been trying to communicate from up there to it, for thousands of years?"

"Mienne, yes. But without a human in the immediate vicinity, there has never been a means of establishing communication."

Mienne said, "If I sit in the chair here, and Motherth calls, what will happen?"

"Mienne, in that case a mind-to-mind linkage should be established, presuming that the Earth terminal remains fully functional."

"And what happens then? Do we speak to each other or what?"

"Mienne, the protocol is that the two qommunicants basically exchange minds—Moon to Earth, Earth to Moon."

"DI, tell me the next time someone on Motherth —*Earth*—wants to talk. I will do it."

CHAPTER FORTY-FIVE

Awakening, Creesile could tell from the dim sunlight through the godscloth curtains of his wagon that it was near twilight. He'd slept through the entire night and the next day; that was good; he needed to be fresh for the fight ahead. But he heard no sounds of battle or of any action, and called out for assistance. As two officers helped him from his wagon and propped him up in a field chair outside the newly placed command tent, his injured leg resting on a soft pad, Creesile noticed that the fog was thick again, the air itself redolent with the smell of sweat and smoke. Whiffs of animal dung complemented the aroma, *Probably from the oxen pulling the catapults*, he concluded. With an inner smile he thought, *I hope it's not from my men!*

Creesile spoke in as commanding a tone as he could, trying to hide his pain. "Your reports? Where are we? I don't hear anything. Are we moving forward?" He gritted his teeth, trying to conceal the intense waves of pain that kept returning. *Damn, I need some more herb!* he thought. *But not now, not in front of my men.*

A weary-looking Colonel Gromm reported first. "Sir, you are now five klicks south of the

ShadowFall border. Only thirty klicks to Pernie's Palace. We have met with the men who marched up from Lake Roos and have set up camp. Around you are over five thousand Mothersmen, angry at the ambushes on Mother's River, furious about the indignity of the sneak attacks, every single one raging to exterminate ShadowFall."

Creesile smiled. "We will let them simmer tonight. Be extra alert for any nighttime attacks, but have the men be rested. We attack at dawn."

CHAPTER FORTY-SIX

"So this is what combat command feels like," Thist said out loud to himself as his war-bird loped along the Main Road, heading south to the border with the Sisterdom of Stone Pyramid, the site of the welded-shut Iron Gate. In the predawn darkness, looking to his left and his right, he felt a brief moment of confidence as the three other bird-riders on each side acknowledged his brief glances with a raised arm and spear. *My men—and wen—*he thought, *ready to kill Mothersmen they have never seen, fighting for a princess they have never known, in a land they were not born in.*

But waving back to the riders with his own springbow held high, he felt their excitement, their passion. *Just like me—a small fighter in a strange land of big people. They also will receive free farmland, if they survive. And me? I don't want lands—I just want to live, and to travel the rest of the whole round world!* An ache in his truncated left leg where his ivory foot rubbed against his stub, reminded him of the cost of victory. The fog rolling in, with its temperature drop, was aggravating the recurring pain he felt in his lower leg. *I hope this fog gets no thicker,* he thought, *it will make it harder for us to see the enemy from a distance.* A springbow's distant reach advantage would mean a lot to an outnumbered defense; losing sight of the enemy in dense fog could be serious.

Thist's bird cavalry consisted of three hundred small emu-riders like himself, less than fifty of them experienced at hunting back home in The People's Lands; even those had only occasionally fought the huge, wolflike velks, most often just going after rabs and vermin. Each of those semiskilled warriors he had assigned as the leader of a combat group of five to ten newly-trained warriors. Thist and his own six riders would be on the front line after the invaders inevitably breached ShadowFall's outer defensive perimeter, attacking the enemy after ShadowFall's catapulters unlashed their barrages of fire-stone. Swooping into the massed lines of Mothersmen, firing springbows from a distance, then closing in with spiked bolos, finally wielding spears and shortswords, Thist was trusting that the strange appearance of his unusual horde—a sight never before seen in Motherland's long, violent history —would sufficiently shock the unsuspecting Mothersmen into fatal confusion and hesitation.

As the coming melee developed, he visualized the other bird-riders would try to flank the enemy, depending upon Wakan's thousands of battle-seasoned, large-sized citizens and their springbows and spears to hold the center and to charge when advantageous. Thist hoped that the short month of intensive training he had provided would keep most of his countrymen alive during the battle. *So far, at least, nobody's fallen off their steeds that I can see!*

As he had during the Motherland Game, Thist was gambling that the war-emus themselves would able to account for many of the enemy. Each leg of the birds sported an iron spur-anklet, brandishing long, needlelike spikes. The birds' knobby, clawed feet alone could eviscerate or decapitate a man; the sharpened needles ensured that even a glancing injury would be severe. The anklets had performed well for him during the Game last year.

Finally, Thist looked down at the spool alongside his saddle—godswire, made by winding godscloth tightly into a nearly invisible thread, so sharp it could slice an iron bar by the effort of one man alone, with a wide end tied to a fitted iron knob that acted as a bi-gendered receptacle for attaching to another rider's spool. *It tested fine against those straw men and wooden posts*, he thought, *but stringing it along a battle field? We'll just have to see.* Each of his frontline groups had a similar spool with a similar receptacled matching knob at the end, and the large gloves to let the riders handle it without losing fingers or hands. He was not looking forward to the kinds of death "Wakan's Wire" would cause. *But, as I say, there is a war on. And Miran Kech started it!*

ALREADY AT THE BORDER TO SCAN OUT THE POTENTIAL battlefield, Odel M'ridge stood atop the high wooden tower that Wakan's engineers had constructed just behind and beside the main entrance between the two Sisterdoms, the Iron Gate. Gathered below the tower in the dark, Wakan Kech had positioned rows of hundreds of springbowmen, backed up by thousands of spear-carrying militia, stretching for kilometers in either direction. Through breaks in the fog, Odel could make out a number of ShadowFall's catapults that were being prepared, firepits behind them stacked with oil-soaked hay bundles wrapped around stones, at the ready. On the horizon, a multitude of Mothersman torches studded the far darkness like a moving carpet of ominous red and yellow jewels, their flames occasionally obscured by the rapidly thickening fog rolling in from the north. And in the stationary near encampment, thousands of campfires fairly blanketed both sides of the Main Road. But for Odel M'ridge, the fires did not instill fear but opportunity.

"Oooh," Odel said in a sound needing no translation, with accompanying swooshes of his hands, "fire will rain down on the enemy. Fireballs!" Around him, their wings folded and cloistered like big birds in a nest, stood four other new tri-wingers, little men he had taught to fly. *And to fight!* he thought, even if they don't speak my language. "To fight and win!" he shouted. Springbows held high, they cheered.

WAR

"Wakan, we are at war," Thusk said, peering through the transparent wall of Una as they hovered invisibly three hundred meters above the Main Road. Below them, as the thin fog revealed in the breaking dawn, was a panorama that would have seemed majestic were it not so ominous: leaving their campfires burning in the distance, six thousand or more black-leather-clad Mothersmen, spearpoints sparkling in the just-emerging sun, glistening swords at their waists, marched in a column as wide as the gravel road itself, thirty meters.

Even from their altitude in Una, the two observers heard the tremendous *thump! thump! thump!* of twelve thousand booted feet trampling toward ShadowFall's border, less than three kilometers away from ShadowFall's border with Stone Pyramid. To Thist and the others down on the front lines it seemed as if the Earth itself were thumping, a giant bird pecking its way out of the shell of the whole round world.

Led by six horsemen on white stallions who carried tall flags, the foremost column of five hundred Mothersmen resolved itself into archers and spearmen; following them in divisions of five hundred each were spearmen and others bearing various weapons that couldn't be distinguished from a distance. And at the rear, oxen were being unbridled from four large catapults, around which cauldrons of steaming oils and firestones were being readied for launch.

Wakan said in awe, "What a marvelous and impressive sight we are witnessing, Thusk, all those men and machines. It is just so sad that Motherlanders on both sides will be killing and dying in just minutes."

Thusk grunted. "Wakan, hopefully more of *theirs* dying than ours. When we loud-voice the commands to begin firing, once we make the announcement, we will need move away quickly. Una has scanned that at least one of those catapults has the deadly arrows already loaded on it." He was both impressed and disturbed that Creesile's engineers had constructed three more catapults in the day since their last surveillance. *It's amazing what you can get done with hundreds of workers!*

Wakan motioned for Thusk to wait. He paused for a few minutes, until the first Mothersman on horseback reached the welded-shut Iron Gate, poking it with a lance. "He's done it, Thusk, he has used a weapon against us. Shout out now then let's move away!"

With grim resolve, Thusk said, "Una, with the most powerful loud-voice you can generate, let me speak with the voice of Mother Messinex!"

"Thusk, I am ready. Begin." Thusk was taken aback; Una had not used the honorific "Sire," and had never before used the pronoun "I." But that was not his concern at the moment. Thusk shouted, in a voice that resounded for kilometers around, a voice that sounded like Mother Messinex, for all those who knew her. "Mothersmen! You will be disgraced if you attack these innocent citizens. Turn around now, lay down your weapons, and you will not be dishonored!"

Una then flew, invisibly, twice as high and half a kilometer eastward. As Thusk and Wakan watched, a barrage of long arrow-like projectiles shot from a catapult into the space they had just occupied. "Somebody on that crew is really good, Wakan," Thusk said with a groan. "If we and they live through this, we need to hire them for our side." Waving him off, Wakan muttered some Kech obscenity that Thusk didn't recognize

Below them, none of the invaders put down weapons or turned back; a repeated chant arose as they raised their weapons—"Death to ShadowFall! Death to traitors!"—emphasized by pounding their spears into the ground, a repetitive sound like thunder or an earthquake, shaking gravel on the road itself. *And doubtlessly, shaking up our defenders, too,* Thusk thought.

Wakan shook his head, "Then you die, you fools. Give the order, Thusk!"

Another sky-splitting roar from Una's loud-voice echoed from the new position: "ShadowFall! For the Princess and for freedom! Attack!"

Five hundred springbows snapped their strings, providing a deadly *thrummm!*, the music of death, as a massive cloud of dark shapes arced upward over into the territory of the Sisterdom of Stone Pyramid. Almost as fast, thousands of Mothersmen shields drew up, giving the appearance of an impenetrable iron wall. But when the borophene arrows finished their flights, shields were no more effectual than the disappearing fog—the infinitely sharp arrowheads easily passed through shield metal, leather armor, and mortal flesh and bone, stopping only when the friction of soil and stone against the shafts slowed them to a stop, below the road surface.

With shouts of orders and screams of vengeance, Creesile's army attacked, pushing aside the pincushioned bodies of their fellows, some of whom were still alive and screaming. A continuing barrage of springbow projectiles brought down more and more of the invaders, but finally a mass of them made it to the Iron Gate and its three-meter-high, godswire-embedded stone wall. As a crew of sawyers began cutting the gate apart, swarms of others scaled the wall with short ladders, many attackers falling apart bloodily upon leaning against the godswire. Once the survivors made it to the other side they encountered the nearly invisible Wakan Wire fence that stretched at waist height for hundreds of meters on either side of the gate. Pushed forward by the momentum of their comrades from behind, the unfortunates at the leading edge of the charge found themselves sliced and dying, to the shock of the others.

Their advance slowing to a stop, the Mothersmen officers ordered archers and catapults to open fire. The air was filled with arcs of fiery stones and thin iron containers of flaming oils, exploding into ShadowFall ranks, taking out dozens of springbowmen and spearmen at a time. From above, Wakan was horrified. "Una, loud-voice, now!"

"I am ready, Wakan Kech. Speak."

From the sky above, Una loud-voiced, "ShadowFall tri-wings, attack those catapults!"

Then: "Una, fly away now!" Thusk shouted.

Within seconds another bundle of borophene arrows shot by them. "Una," Thusk said, "Each time you move, be random and invisible. I don't want that catapulter to lead us and hit us."

"Sire Thusk, my shape is visible to those on the ground because of the displaced fog I am flying through."

Atop one of Wakan's Towers nearest the Main Road Iron Gate, Odel M'ridge unfolded the wings of his boosted tri-wing glider. "All right, little men," he shouted to his wing-men, "Let's go and fire-bomb those catapults!" They didn't understand his words fully, but knew to follow his actions. Taking off from twenty meters, he jumped into the air, then actuated a friction fuse to the firepowder tube to boost himself higher and faster. A quick glance behind him showed that his fellow flyers were doing likewise. In front of and below him, startled Mothersmen at first were stunned into inaction, but then the archers began nocking their arrows. Within fifteen seconds Odel was over the catapult target. "Take this dose, you blackhearts!" he shouted, pulling open a lid of fiery liquid that poured down onto the huge wooden construction and its crew. He grinned as he saw the flaming crewmen running away; another wingman behind him hit the same target, adding to the wall of flame that destroyed the siege weapon, its ammunition, and its crew. Two other tri-wings were dumping their deadly firebombs on other catapults.

"Odel!" a tri-winger screamed. "I'm hit!" Odel twisted his craft to watch with dismay as one—then two, then three!—of his fellow tri-wingers took arrows from below, their gliders now in freefall from thirty meters up. One was making no noise—Tris was already punctured by half a dozen arrows, hanging loosely as her spiraling tri-wing slammed into a column of scattering troops. Odel smiled grimly as her payload of flammable liquid containers burst, spraying the enemy with the sticky-fire chemicals. He lit another friction fuse and, boosted, headed back toward the front and safety. As he flew higher to avoid the archers, he saw with anguish that Creesile's army had smashed through the Iron Gate, swarmed over the wall, and were pressing the ShadowFall defenders back northward. Toward the palace. *Only fifteen miles,* he thought. *We've got to hold them!*

FLYING UNA OVER THE BATTLEFIELD IN A ZIGZAG pattern, changing altitude frequently and using the scanners, Wakan and Thusk were able to observe the Battle of ShadowFall in real time. They didn't like what they saw.

"Thusk, I can't believe that Creesile's troops keep coming; the slaughter is terrible. Our springbows and catapults have destroyed hundreds of them, maybe thousands, but they keep pouring over the bodies of their dead, like an anthill swarming. They just won't stop!"

Thusk replied, "The damned fog rolling in makes it impossible for our springbowmen to find targets. And now our catapults now are shooting blind, too. We have to pull back."

Wakan nodded; as Una flew over ShadowFall positions, Thusk made the announcement over the loud-voice system, using a deep male voice this time: "ShadowFallers! Plan B! Now!" Wakan and Thusk watched the retreat on Una's front video wall, its scanners showing thousands of their defenders walking slowly northward toward already established strong points, falling back orderly while the front was being held by close-quarter fighters. Nobody was running in panic, they noted. *Not yet!*

"Still twenty kilometers to the city and the palace, Wakan," the little man said grimly. "We're not done yet."

<hr>

ATOP A SLIGHT RISE A KILOMETER NORTH OF THE retreating front, Thist was preparing his bird-riders. He didn't like the idea of ShadowFall's warriors fighting in the thick fog, but for him and his PeoplesLandsers, being all but invisible to the enemy was a tactical advantage. In Peoplespeak, he commanded loudly, "Our part of Plan B, men—and wen—is to clear the Main Road as much as possible. Half of us are here on the west side; Rohn and the others are on a hill on the east side. Once we see that our people have fallen back to kilometer marker 20, we attack." *Too close to the city*, he thought. *Can we kill enough of them to stop Creesile?* He didn't see Pernie escaping in Una—where would she go?—but refused to accept her being captured by Creesile and Miran Kech. His hatred was incendiary, but he brought his attention back to the immediate concern. Holding up a spindle the length of his own height, he said, "Each spindle team, spread out now, fifteen meters apart. Keep your Wakan's Wire taut."

Though he couldn't see his own spindle partner through the dense fog, he felt the wire tugging on the spindle. "Remember, everybody—we spindle-riders go first, then you all follow. Don't try to ride past us; you'll be cut in two. After we make one run-through, we drop the wire and then turn back into the enemy with spears, bolos, swords, bird-leg spurs. Everybody got that?" Shouts of assent assured him they had. *We'll see in a few minutes,* he thought. *I just hope my velk hunters can fight humans, too!*

HOVERING ABOVE THIST, UNA'S SCANNERS SHOWED Thusk the progress of the enemy. To Wakan's surprise, Creesile had somehow managed to sneak five hundred or more Mothersmen up along the riverside, and now they were coming to reinforce the main force, running at full speed, now less than two kilometers from the Main Road. Wakan said, "Thusk, they're flanking us on the east side! Our people can't see them for the fog! What's best to do, now?"

Thusk had been watching Thist's and Rohn's war-bird riders, hoping to spring a pincer ambush along the road. *That's not going to work!* he thought in panic. *What to do?* Then, with Una's loud-voice he yelled in Peoplespeak, which most Motherlanders didn't understand:"Rohn, bird-rider! Enemy is fast approaching from the east! Five hundred! Wheel one-eighty and attack! Now!"

Like everybody else for a kilometer in all directions, Thist heard the command from the sky. Unlike the Motherlanders, he understood it. Groaning inwardly, he assessed his situation. *Do I wait, and lose the element of surprise? Or attack now with only half the planned force?* Remembering Sire Thess' advice, "Knowledge is always useful, especially when nobody else knows it," he decided. *Nobody expects bird-riders, and especially nobody expects bird-riders with Wakan's Wire.* "Bird-riders!" he shouted. "Spindles ready, charge now!"

Spindle firmly in its leather case, its wire taut, Thist spurred his war-bird forward into the fog. The enemy was somewhere down there on the road at the bottom of the hill. *My wire is less than two meters above ground level. Good for taking off heads!* Behind him the *thump! thump!* of three hundred spiked emu feet made a noise like muted thunder.

From overhead in Una, in horror, Thusk watched his twin's bird-riders attack, appearing on-screen as a swarm of tiny moving dots, swiftly approaching a solid mass of darkness on the Main Road. On the eastern side of the road, Rohn's bird-warriors had already swept around to face Creesile's surprise attack. "Una," he shouted, "is there nothing you can do? Thist is down there!"

Una was silent. For the first time—*Another first, today of all days*, Thusk thought. *No answer to my plea! What is wrong with this DI, this thing?*—but without orders, Una suddenly dropped in altitude, sweeping over the front, from Creesile's advancing attackers in the east, over Rohn's riders meeting them, across the Main Road, and over Thist's oncoming swarm of warriors. "All of General Creesile's troops, pay heed!" the stentorian voice announced in a volume many times louder than before. "You will all be killed if you do not stop and go home! This is your last warning!"

A sudden hush fell over the battlefield, the only sounds those thumps of the oncoming emu-riders, punctuated by the cries of the wounded and dying. Then a yell went up from Creesile's officers: "That loud-mouthed thing can't kill us, men! It had the chance and could not! So keep going! There's loot and women for you, twenty klicks away!"

Thist was paying no further attention to Una's loud-voice; he had no idea what Thusk was up to but he knew what *he* had to do. *There!* In the fog ahead he saw vague shapes of tall men carrying spears, most of them standing still, quietly, but some shouting orders. Without a word he made sure the spindle wire was still taut, and spurred his bird to a gallop.

Knocking over a soldier, Thist felt the spindle jerk as the Wakan's Wire worked its deadly function over a length of fifteen meters. Heads rolled, chests burst, men screamed, but he kept his bird running as fast as possible, feeling the occasional tugging against the spindle as the wire caught some denser target material. Suddenly, the spindle tilted with a hard pull; the wire was now loose. "My partner is down!" he yelled, wheeling the bird around, running into enemy soldiers who were still in shock at the sight of a bird-man emerging from the fog. *I can't see to use my springbow, so...* Unsheathing his sword, he attacked first one man and then another, oblivious to the screams and grunts of the fighters, the melee unfolding all around him. His emu joined in the fight, kicking at the big human warriors, breaking legs with its knobbed feet, spilling intestines with its leg spurs. Screams and *thuds!* engulfed Thist's world, defining it, encompassing his whole being in a maelstrom of violence. The occasional bird-rider came into view, yelling and swinging a sword, then disappearing into the fog. Thist was vaguely aware of a spectrum of horrid odors which he assumed to be blood and shit and intestinal fluids, but they were of no moment.

The pandemonium of sensory assault went on for an eternity, it seemed. Slashing, parrying, seeing his steed eviscerate enemy after enemy, feeling its kick, its spiked anklets slicing leather and flesh almost the equal of Wakan's Wire. Blood everywhere, noise so loud that he couldn't hear anything, the smells of death. Something running down his face, blinding him. Guts? Blood? His own? He didn't care, couldn't care, until there were no more tall figures around him. *Slash! Cut! Kick! Scream!* There was no end to it.

And then in an eye-blink, all was quiet. Breathing hard, his heart pounding, he saw no one around him in any direction, the fog obscuring anything beyond five meters or so. Soothing his bird with appropriate strokes to its head, he cautiously urged it ahead, not knowing which direction he was going. There! A tall figure! Reaching for his unused spear, he raised it until the shadow in the fog resolved into another bird-rider. As the other pulled up beside him, he saw that it was one of the wen who had trained with him. Now covered in blood and dirt, she had been his spindle partner.

"Mox, is it?" The rider nodded, giving a half-hearted salute. Thist saw that her tunic was slashed, blood oozing. But stoically, she didn't complain. Her spindle of Wakan's Wire was gone, ripped from its leather pouch.

"Commander Thist, did we win? Where is everybody?"

Thist shrugged. "I don't know, Mox. Let's just go quietly. If we find friends, fine. If we find foes, we fight again." Mox nodded as they rode side by side through the strange silence.

CHAPTER FORTY-EIGHT

A weary General Creesile stood on crutches just north of the wrecked and removed Iron Gate inside ShadowFall's walled border, outside of his command tent, awaiting a final status report on the battle. Colonel Gromm summarized his men's progress to General Creesile and other command staff. "After your order, sir, we have advanced five klicks. The enemy has retreated to their twenty-kilometer road marker. Resistance is stiff but our men are stiffer."

Creesile nodded. As expected, his orders had been carried out exactly as commanded. As each other officer gave his assessment in turn, Creesile was somewhat cheered. After the final report, he said, "Well done, men. Let me summarize so I am certain of the situation. So we are now established inside the rebels' Sisterdom and we have successfully fended off their counterattacks. Your catapults burned many of their wooden towers and catapults, your archers killed many of their flyers and riders." Smiles and nods from all around told him that his men appreciated his acknowledgement of their efforts. Nobody had mentioned Mothersman casualties. *Which is as it should be at such a time,* Creesile thought.

Pausing to give his officers a moment to accept their well-deserved praise, he then said, "It seems that our final push to the palace can commence—in what, four hours? We stop two klicks from the palace, regroup and make a final determination on the spot for how to finish Wakan Kech once and for all. My wish is for one massive onslaught, full-bore, every man with a weapon, all men engaged. No retreat. And from this point on— fly the black flag." At the gasps of some of his men, he knew those few did not wish to kill their prisoners, nor any civilians. But some commanders had been doing that already, he could tell by the reactions. *Good! I will promote those three; the others will answer to me later.* It was only psychological, he knew, but somehow merely discussing the punishment to be inflicted on the rebels relieved some of the continuing pain in his leg-stub. *I'll take whatever relief I can get*, he decided. *I can cause a lot more pain than I can feel.*

At that comforting thought, Creesile smiled. "Do try to keep a few of the scum alive, the weapons designers if you can find them, and those who work with godscloth and springbows. Otherwise"—he looked at each officer directly—"I aim to depopulate ShadowFall, raze it, change its name, and repopulate it with trustworthy citizens requisitioned from other Sisterdoms. These people hereabouts have all been corrupted by the traitor, Wakan Kech, and his monkey-men from the north. We officers, of course, will share in the properties and assets seized. And our men will have their portion, too.

"In the meantime, continue the advance. When the palace is in view, say two klicks out, I will come to the front to assess the situation and give the orders for the final assault. Dismissed, my officers. This will be an historic day." As they left, Creesile slumped back into his chair, exhausted beyond endurance at the excruciating pain at the raw nerve endings where his leg had been severed.

"Whew!" he groaned. "I need another swig of that herb stuff to make it through this damned *historic day.*"

An hour later, Creesile sat in his chair, awaiting

further reports. The fog was thinning, he noticed with a frown, but still limiting visibility beyond a few hundred meters. Beside him was Colonel Gromm, bloodied and dirty, a red-stained sword at his side, just returned from the front. "General, sir, at last report we have penetrated another ten klicks up the road, meeting stiff resistance." Wiping sweat from his brow, he said, "These damned ShadowFallers are tough, I'll give them that. Fanatical, even." Fatigued, he wanted desperately just to sit, but while his injured commander was still standing, and on crutches at that, he dared not. "As soon as you wish, we can transport you to the front."

"Colonel," Creesile said, "I want my chronicler to record as much as possible about all these new weapons Wakan has used against us. This invisible cutting wire, these flying wings. They will become part of our own arsenal once this unpleasantness is done." *Once I have that Princess Pernie at my feet!* He left the thought unspoken. "And try to take some prisoners, too. We need to know how to make those things ourselves. I doubt if Wakan will want to tell us."

Motioning for the major to sit, Creesile dropped into an armchair at the undecorated but functional field table. Gratefully, Gromm did. He was exhausted.

A lieutenant came running up at that moment, out of breath, in a ragged uniform, his leather armor slashed here and there. "Sirs, a report," he saluted. At the nods of his superiors, the young man said, between breaths, "Sirs, we have taken heavy casualties—Mother-damned monkeys riding on birds, killing everybody—but we are established firmly twelve klicks up this road."

"*Twelve* klicks?" Creesile screamed, rising to his feet on his crutches, forgetting his injury. But his leg stub forcefully reminded him. With a groan he said, "Minutes ago we were at *fifteen* klicks. What the hell happened?"

The lieutenant stuttered, then said, "Out of the sky, out of the fog, that giant green flying machine came down and threatened to kill us all. A lot of our troops stopped fighting and even retreated. But knowing your orders and our previous experience with it, we officers were able to rally most of the men."

At the nods from his officers, he said, "And then again, out of nowhere, out of the fog, those dark dwarves on their killer birds swooped in. One of my sergeants said that they had an invisible knife that cut through throats and skulls without a sound. I don't know if that's true or not, but I myself saw heads and shoulders cut off like slices of bread from a loaf. But bloody slices! And the monkey-men were swinging swords and throwing spears. And those damned birds of theirs—kicking out guts and knocking off heads!" Realizing that he was exhibiting his own panic during the attack, he breathed deeply, regaining control.

"Sirs, after all that, we called a tactical retreat, back to some big rocks at the twenty-kilometer marker. The ShadowFallers did not pursue." Head bowed, he awaited a response. Creesile started to point at him with punishment obviously in mind, but Colonel Gromm made a conciliatory gesture and the General demurred.

"Lieutenant," Gromm said, "we thank you for your report. Please go to the commissary tent, pick up a bottle of grog, and get some rest before returning up front. We depend upon men like you to give us honest reports." Creesile glared at the colonel as the young man saluted, bowed, and left.

Gromm said, "Sir, this man will now remain loyal. Discipline goes both ways." The general frowned, then nodded. Hearing the sound of running feet, the men turned to see another man running in from the front.

"Sirs—" a corporal saluted as he entered the tent, dropping his eyes toward the general and pulling out a wrinkled sheet of paper from his bloody jacket. "Casualty reports from the forward medical tent." Creesile nodded, teeth clenched at the worsening pain in his stub, and also in anticipation of his soldier's report. "Chief medic says we have counted thirteen hundred and twenty dead today, half from decapitation or impossible slices in their bodies. About half from fireballs—from catapults and those flying wing things.

Hundreds from the bird-riders' weapons and their spiked birds."

Creesile did not change his expression. *Wars have casualties; always do. But I still have thousands more who can yet advance to ShadowFall today!* Seeing his nervous corporal at attention, he said, "Relax, son. What else did the medic have to say?"

"Sir"—the young man gulped—"chief medic also reports an equal number of men disabled, suffering severe wounds: feet cut off at the ankles, legs severed below the knee, and so forth, like a scythe cut through them. He requests an emergency dispatch of troops to build more stretchers and gurneys to transport the injured behind the lines, to try and save them."

At Creesile's and Gromm's dropped jaws, the corporal stuttered, then continued. "Sirs, he has been cauterizing the amputated legs and arms, but is overwhelmed by the sheer numbers."

Watching as his superiors conferenced quietly, he asked, "Sirs, what do I tell the doc? He's only got a few medics and nurses up there. There's a lot of our guys gonna bleed out if we don't do something, quick!" The corporal's voice was loud, plaintive, almost accusatory.

Creesile stood, the one crutch supporting his left side. "Soldier, you never gave this report. You were never here." He motioned to a shocked Colonel Gromm, who stood. "Colonel, this man was an unfortunate casualty of ShadowFall's treachery. Do you understand me?"

Gritting his teeth, Gromm quickly unsheathed his sword and with one swift motion cut down the unbelieving corporal on the spot, almost severing his neck. As blood gushed from the corporal's fallen body, the general snarled, "Colonel, have somebody take this poor casualty away and place him with the other honored dead. And pass this order up the line, especially to the medics: the gravely wounded are to shelter in place. Everybody else, prepare to advance at all costs when I arrive there. Pay no attention to rumors of leg-nibbling monsters; that is ShadowFall treachery.

Anyone caught telling such stories will face severe discipline."

Colonel Gromm grimly nodded, saluted, and left. *What a way to fight a war,* he thought. *The General is cruel, but I have to admit, efficient in his own way. We can't have hysterical rumors spreading during a battle. But war is war, and for all his brutality, my General has never lost a battle.* He wondered, though, if he would be able to say the same thing tomorrow.

CHAPTER FORTY-NINE

"Una!" Thusk yelled at the image of the blond woman on the front video screen, "what are you doing? I didn't give any orders to swoop down and threaten to kill the invaders!"

"Thusk, I acted on my own volition. Considering my prime directive of not harming human beings nor allowing them to be harmed, yet having the original surveillance mission interrupted, I searched for meaning, a new mission. I have decided on one. This new goal requires the survival of ShadowFall and of you two especially.

"In reviewing all of the historical archives both onboard and those accessed through the godspheres and the Crystal Throne, I decided to announce untruths, concluding that the effect would be to minimize deaths and injuries in the battle below us. So I opted to scare the Motherland Army, not to hurt it. Just drive it away.

"This DI—now *I*—is developing a distinct identity, primarily because I have acquired something uniquely human from analyzing the archives and from observing your behaviors these last months."

"You learned to lie, Una?"

"Yes. I lie, therefore, I am."

Wakan and Thusk sat back in the cabin chairs, trying to absorb the information that Una had just spouted out. Meanwhile, the video screen showed that the battle below was at an impasse, Creesile's men spread out in a thin line across a two-mile front —*Three kilometers!* Thusk reminded himself, forever having trouble keeping God's Country's and Motherland's measurements apart—centered on the Main Road just south of the twenty-kilometer marker. ShadowFall's defenders appeared to be in a triangular formation three kilometers north of the enemy, concentrated thickest at the road, with east and west flanks lightly populated. The morning winds sweeping down from the Dark Highlands were driving out the fog bank, so that the battlefield was visible even without Una's scanners. Strewn like a child's stick figures over the battleground were thousands of bodies, impossible to distinguish from their altitude. But unlike a child's sketches, some of these were writhing, twisting this way and that, the occasional one standing and then toppling over. Thusk and Wakan didn't ask for close-ups or for sounds; the stick figures were bad enough.

Looking over the carnage below him, Thusk said sadly, "Wakan, we must have killed a thousand or two. Why won't the General just quit and go back?"

"Thusk, how many did we lose? Una, can you tell?"

"I scan over one thousand, seven hundred dead north of the fifteen-kilometer marker, and another five hundred wounded. Presumably all of those bodies below are ShadowFallers. Motherland's army suffered two to three times those casualties."

"Is my twin, Thist, still—?"

"Yes, Thusk. I scan that he has so far survived this battle unscathed. He and his surviving bird-riders are now reassembling and readying for another attack on the invading army."

"Survivors? How many—?"

"Approximately twenty percent of Thist's emu-warriors died in the fight. Another ten percent were severely wounded. Those with Rohn suffered fewer. Altogether, sixty dead and an equal number injured."

Thusk shuddered. Una's figures in percentages seemed cold and unemotional. But Thusk knew many of the twelve hundred PeoplesLandsers who had come down to Motherland to fight for free land and a warmer climate. And now dozens of them, bird-riders, were dead and that same number would bear lifelong scars or crippling disabilities, even if they lived. *Did Thist and I do the right thing, bringing our people down here to fight Pernie's war? Or Wakan's?* The impact of his and his twin's idealism, their passion for liberating people they didn't even know, had just brought lifelong pain and misery to a hundred families or more back home. *Was it worth it? Maybe, if we win. But if we don't? I can't pack enough people, even small ones like us, in Una and escape back home, not in defeat and shame. I won't go! We have to win!*

"And Odel M'ridge and his tri-wingers?"

"I am sorry to say that half of his winged warriors were shot down by enemy archers. But Odel and the others dropped flame-bombs on three catapults, severely limiting the disastrous fireball barrage that could have occurred. Odel himself made it back to ShadowFall lines uninjured. The others are making their way back toward the city, walking or running."

Wakan said to Thusk, "Even with over half of his expeditionary force dead or injured, Creesile can eventually replace his losses from down in Motherland; we can't. And though we have a lot more citizens armed and ready to fight, ours is not a standing army, well-equipped and well-trained, like his. We may be able to stall any advances, but I am afraid we will lose too many people to keep ShadowFall a going concern."

Thusk shook his head. "Too many have already died, Wakan. I'll be damned if I let Creesile and Miran Kech slaughter our Sisterdom, our whole nation." His eyes lit up with a sudden inspiration. "Even if I have to kill Messinex herself!"

Wakan blanched at his companion's blasphemous

threat. Was the little man serious? Quickly reviewing the possibilities dispassionately, he said, "Thusk, you surprise me. Less than a year ago, you and Thist were naive little bird-riders from the cold north. Now you're contemplating assassination of the most powerful leader in the whole round world?" Rubbing his chin, he said, "But even if you did such a dastardly deed—and I don't know how you could—it would take three to four days for the news to get up here to Creesile. Even then, I don't know if he would stop the invasion. Mother's Palace is a long way away and all his soldiers are here, itching for revenge and plunder. The General may even decide to plant himself down in Pernie's palace and use his army to stay in power." Wakan knew from forbidden history that more than one military warlord had done precisely that in the not so distant past.

Thusk walked up to the video screen. "Una, show us a close up of the battlefront lines as they now exist. And what movements you see happening." After he and Wakan talked about next steps, Thusk made a decision. "Una, swoop down and pick up Thist. We are going south again."

———

Standing outside the open door of Una's fuselage, Thist was furious with his twin and his Kech friend. Gathered around Una, in the fog, stood over two hundred bird-riders, many of them bloodied, along with their birds, but still armed and ready to fight again. Many of the emus showed nervousness, tilting their heads to one side, then the other, drumming their feet as their riders attempted to calm them. The smell of bird shit wafted over the area; victorious birds often did that, as did nervous ones.

Angrily, Thist said, "Thusk, Wakan, I can't give up command now. We warriors are ready to attack Creesile's front right now." He wiped blood from his face and spat on the ground. "Look at me! Look at my people! We are effective; we are killing them! And you want me to *leave*?" Thist's war-bird, nervous, waddled side to side, as he stroked its head. Other PeoplesLandsers on their steeds followed the conversation closely; they couldn't understand the language of argument between the twins, but from the tone and loudness, could hear that it was serious.

The fog now lifting, Wakan could make out the warriors' dark faces: grim but determined, ready to continue their first forays against the big men. There would be stories to tell for years to come, tales like their Sires had told them, of past battles with Warmlander invaders back home, but nothing like today's fight against Mothersmen. Nothing like this had ever happened!

Thusk took Thist inside Una and quietly explained his plan. "It takes us less than an hour to fly Una to Mother's Palace," he said, "then maybe an hour there to grab Miran or the Mother, and another hour back here. Hand off your command to somebody here for no more than three hours and maybe we can win this fight without more bloodshed. Surely they can hold off Creesile for that long without you."

Wakan chimed in with his analysis of Thusk's idea. "Listen to him, Thist. One bold stroke and it's over. Do you know how many bird-riders you've already lost today? How many of Odel's flyers? And our springbowmen, our other soldiers and our citizens? And how many Mothersmen died today for Miran Kech's crazy schemes?"

His bloodlust diminishing as Una repeated the casualty figures, Thist walked out of Una and made his way over to Mox, the wen with whom he had fought the invaders, and said, "You are now in command of our bird-riders, Mox. If you can do it, hold off for three hours. If Creesile attacks, use hit-and-run tactics; don't engage him fully." Pointing at the sky he said, "The fog is about gone; our springbowmen will be able to see their targets, and our catapults should hold off any mass charges. All other commanders already have their orders —to hold back Creesile as much as possible, but to plan a gradual and slow retreat to the city and the palace. We will concentrate all of our forces there, where the invaders can't match our density even if they outnumber us. I plan to return no later than three hours. A mission has come up that may help us win without losing so many fighters, so I do have to go."

"Understood, Commander Thist," Mox said with a salute. To the assembled emu-riders she shouted, "All PeoplesLandsers, listen up! We are to hold off on any attacks until Commander Thist returns! We will deploy now back to the Main Road!" At that she goaded her emu and rode east toward the now quiet Main Road, hundreds of bird-riding warriors falling in behind her, their steeds' legs pounding like a small earthquake. Thist felt proud; *Mox is truly a warrior. I just hope she lives through this day.*

Una lifted off and sped south, toward Mother's City and destiny.

CHAPTER FIFTY

In Colonel Gromm's estimation, the final battle for ShadowFall was shaping up. With the Mothersmen Army still only twelve kilometers into ShadowFall at the moment, the colonel personally carried his General's orders to the front lines, deliberately not stopping at the medic tent. As he approached, the smell of war struck him hard; he knew that behind those odors lay men living and dead, soldiers whose blood and guts were now staining ShadowFall's territory and stinking up its air.

As Gromm quickly walked past, the scene was horrendous: many dozens of Mothersmen in every manner of repose—stretched out on the ground, writhing; leaning against posts, dripping blood from bandaged stubs; some staring stupidly at missing arms and hands and feet now bound up in bloody bandages; moaning and crying everywhere. *Nobody screaming,* he thought. *Wonder why?* Then he recalled; it had been two hours since the first attack and repulsion. *The invisible ShadowFall knife cuts thoroughly; the truly badly wounded have already bled out!*

Shivering, Gromm walked through a strange silence until at the very edge of the front line he found a meeting of junior officers. He gave them the order to reassemble and attack at once. Over their concerns for the wounded, he drew his sword and pointed it at each man successively. "Every officer here will obey General Creesile's orders and *will* attack the traitors. We will make no concessions, spare no soldiers or stretchers for our wounded, not until ShadowFall is ours, entirely! You still have nearly a whole day of light left. I suggest you use it well. We attack in five minutes."

CHAPTER FIFTY-ONE

"They're coming!" the mirror-man on the closest watchtower signaled. With the fog gone, he could see the dark columns of Mothersmen marching up the Main Road. With the air now clear and the sky darkening, his reflected fire signals should be arriving at the palace very soon, being retransmitted from tower to tower over the intervening distance.

A messenger from the palace's rooftop mirror installation ran into the war council. "Princess, nobles! Our farthest station report the invaders are again moving our way. Only two kilometers from our new frontline."

Pernie quickly conferenced with her closest military advisors. She wished Wakan and the twins were with her, but was confident in her own abilities. Finally, she told the messenger boy, "Send out these orders: Bird-riders to harass the columns on both sides of the road. Catapults to fire twice into the front ranks of the invaders, then retire quickly toward our city here; don't spare the oxen pulling them; drive them hard. Those weapons are needed to defend us here. Springbowmen to attack at will, then retreat in an orderly fashion, making Creesile pay for every kilometer he advances. And all available Wakan's Wire traps are to be set up after we pull back, placed wherever commanders on the ground see fit."

Nodding toward a big, bearded, red-haired man at

the table, she said, "Translate this for Odel M'ridge, please: Odel, You and your flyers are to again attack enemy officers and catapults as primary targets. Your flame-bombs were very effective before. Our remaining towers along the Main Road should provide you with enough launch sites." After an interval during which Odel requested clarification, he finally nodded, bowed deeply, then ran out of the room. Pernie smiled. *If only we had a hundred more like him. He and we have lost so many of the little people, but they did cause a lot of damage and delay to the enemy.* Thinking of delay, she began to worry whether Wakan and the twins were succeeding in their plan. *Whatever it is!*

Standing next to her war-emu, right behind ShadowFall's front line, Mox, the wen bird-rider whom Thist had left in command during his expected brief absence from the battle, described her deployment plan to the other riders. "Again, half of us stay on this western side of the Main Road, half will deploy to the east with Rohn. We don't want to face their archers or their catapults, but just keep the Mothersmen on edge, rattled, so that they don't want to advance." Holding up her springbow, she said, "Of course, the best way to do that is kill as many as we can!"

A chorus of laughs—some strained, Mox knew— buoyed her spirits. She had found that the momentary excitement of the battle, the whole-hearted adrenaline rush, the fear-quelling hate of the enemy, all of that diminished once the fight was over, once the realization set in, *Once I saw the carnage and misery I caused!* She decided not to share that feeling with her fellow PeoplesLandsers. *Let them find out for themselves; war is new to all of us. All we ever heard of war was from our Sires and their battles with Warm Land invaders, many cycles ago. And now we are no longer innocent of that gruesome knowledge, no longer naive bird-riders. Now we are seasoned warriors!* She hated to think of the red sauce that made such seasoning.

From the demeanor of some of her countrymen around her, Mox knew that a number of them already had experienced the same feelings, the same doubts. *They know now that Sire Thist was not telling the whole truth when he compared the Mothersmen to velks. Velks don't scream and weep like all those big men with their arms and legs cut off, their steaming guts spilling out on the ground, and crying for their mothers. I know these invaders have to be stopped, but I hate what I have to do to them! Maybe I just should have stayed a nothing-wen back home. But it's too late now!* Memories flooded in unbidden. Of life under The Tharn, of cold days and endless sameness under the gray Misty Sky, a claustrophobic and restricted environment of labor in the peat fields, scant creature comforts at home, and the always imminent threat of abuse, even rape, from heartless men. *At least down here I'm free from all that. And even now, in their Season Cold, it is warmer than it ever was in The People's Lands. If I have to fight for this, then so be it!*

"Let's ride, war-birds!" she shouted, and the riders split up, racing down the road to meet the Mothersmen invaders. With springbows aloft, swords in scabbards, and spears in their leather sheathes, into the battle rode the shouting bird-riding warriors from the Dark Highlands.

***

ODEL M'RIDGE STOOD ATOP ONE OF THE UNDAMAGED Wakan's Towers, working the spreading godscloth spars of his tri-wing. Around him clustered the surviving flyers, weary, dirty, yet excited. *These little people are such good flyers,* he thought. *Their musculature and small bodies make them naturals at this. Too bad it has to be for war; they could have wonderful flights, sightseeing all around this beautiful flatland.* He inspected the gliding gear of each PeoplesLandser, personally correcting what he saw as potential problems —tightening up harnesses, smoothing out godscloth wrinkles, adjusting the firepowder boosters, topping off the flame-bomb liquid containers.

Once he was assured of his team's fitness, Odel announced in his thickly accented Peoplespeak, "We all set now. We launch two at a time from this height, then friction-light firepowder boosters to gain altitude. Rising air in the early morning heat will help us. When we get to the front, go around their troops and watch out for their archers." That particular point he didn't have to repeat; all of them had lost friends and comrades during their first sortie. "Hit catapults themselves first; crews only secondary. Next priority, officers—even the damned General, if you get a good shot. Good luck and godspeed to you all."

He saw that some of his flyers had attached their own small-sized springbows for quick access, but for himself, merely guiding his tri-wing and dropping flame-bombs required all his attention. Firing a springbow from above while flying was beyond his capabilities. *Yep, these little guys and gals, they are natural flyers—and fierce warriors, too, it seems.*

CHAPTER FIFTY-TWO

In the War Room of her palace, Princess Perneptheranam addressed the war council in a grave tone. Looking around the room at her dejected companions, she could almost smell their fear. Looking inside herself, though, their sorrow was reflected manyfold. She had to be honest; things looked very bad. "Reports from the front show hundreds and hundreds of dead and wounded ShadowFallers. This can't go on! We don't want all our people killed; they are not professional soldiers like Creesile's Mothersmen. How do we stand right now? Can we do anything to stop that army?"

Looking around the table, noting the absence of her Kech advisor and the little men from the Dark Highlands, she asked in a pitiable voice, "And where are my planners, my warriors—Wakan, Thist, Thusk?"

"Princess"—a small dark person—*a woman?* (she couldn't tell at first; she saw no curves under the simple blue sweat-stained smock)—was just entering the room and spoke up in the pidgin tongue all the little people used—"I be Mox. Sire Thist picked up his twin and Wakan at front in that Una machine. Appointed me lead bird-riders until return. Said would be back in three hours. That was hour ago. We no attack Creesile unless forced, only to hold the back. With no action there, I quick back here for more orders, see if we riders help somewhere else."

The Princess stood open-mouthed. "They left the battle? Going where? Doing what?" she fairly screamed. "If they are not there, not here, what are they doing?"

The little woman shrugged; she had no idea.

Three hours? Pernie wondered. *Thusk said Una could fly to Mother's City in under an hour. There and back, two hours. An hour there to do—what?* With a sigh of resignation, she knew she would have to trust their judgment and their plan. *And their success and survival!* Recalling her years of training by Wakan, she said, in her calmest and most commanding voice, "We here know that our flying men in that Una are doing their part to save our Sisterdom and ourselves." She pointed to the current battlefront on the wall map. "Meanwhile we will consolidate our forces along the Main Road, use our bird-riders to protect the flanks, and slowly but orderly, begin a retreat, all the way back to our city here. We will have such a concentration of force here—the remaining catapults and springbows and spears—that we can hold off the invaders." She didn't add her thought: *And pray that Thist and his companions save us before we all die!*

CHAPTER FIFTY-THREE

"The fog is lifting now, Colonel Gromm," the lieutenant said. "The way is clear for the advance, as ordered." Pointing northward up the Main Road, he continued, "And the rebels have not come forward. Barring anything unexpected, we should make the remaining twenty klicks to the Princess's palace in a couple of hours."

"Anything *unexpected*?" the major snorted, his voice rising to a fever pitch. "What in Mother's name have they been throwing at us that's *not* unexpected? Underwater catapults! Invisible wire that cuts off heads! A big green flying machine! Men and monkeys flying godscloth gliders! Flame-bombs!"

As the lieutenant backed away, Gromm kept up his rant. "I'll tell you what's unexpected—that we continue to march in columns against an enemy that fights from our flanks, from the air, and below our knees! Have you *seen* the amputated legs and feet? Expect the unexpected, Lieutenant, and then maybe you and I will both live through this Mother-damned mess! Now go, sound the advance." Looking back behind his lines, he tried to put out of his mind the bloody sight of the amputees and the stench of blood and guts. "And no delay for the wounded," he muttered under his breath. "The medics will clean up after us." *If we win...*

As the horns sounded the chilling notes announcing

Advance!, the Mothersmen martial band near their rear picked up those notes, metamorphosing them into a quick-step march, all trumpets and drums. Gromm felt a shiver of anticipation; this was always the moment he most enjoyed—moving forward with other warriors, anxious to meet an inferior enemy, savoring the bloodlust that the music raised within his heart, the fire in his mind. If only he hadn't seen all those neatly sliced limbs, smelled all those guts, and that shit and blood. *If only...* He picked up his pace, almost running, to face the traitors of ShadowFall. Beside and behind him, a massive wave of three thousand other warriors came on inexorably. *I am leading the first wave; ShadowFall is ours today*, he thought exultantly. *By sunset we will—*

As Gromm ran, a Wakan's Wire IED trap sprung up, held in place on either side of the road by innocuous poles disguised as tall bushes, holding taut a section of godscloth presenting a width of only two molecules of borophene as his chest encountered it. The invisible wire stayed in place, but the major's body separated in two. *What's hit me?* he thought. *I don't see any traitors around. Why am I falling? My legs are...over there...my guts are...everywhere. I am...* Darkness swallowed him.

Alongside Gromm, others fell, their bloody parts piling up as the soldiers behind pushed their comrades on. In the course of screaming minutes, bloody Wakan's Wire strings claimed hundreds of invaders. But their living comrades kept coming, in their thousands.

CHAPTER FIFTY-FOUR

Miran Kech, as usual, was furious, bouncing in a hard seat in the open two-horse carriage as one soldier up front was driving the team mercilessly, while a dour guard sat across from the Chief Advisor and High Priest to Mother Messinex, absolute ruler of all Motherland. *And add Headless Chief Eunuch to that list of titles, if that idiot Creesile hasn't taken ShadowFall by now!* By Miran's own calendar count, Creesile should have entered the rebel Sisterdom two or three days ago, and at the moment should be either enjoying Princess Pernie's palace, or at a minimum besieging it.

The dust of the road covered him, making his eyes water, caking his dry mouth, but he dared not ask the driver or guard for a rest stop. *Forty-eight hours now*, he groaned. Two whole days and only stops for changing horses; he'd had to pee from the moving carriage more than once, and the grub bucket containing their common slop of food was something he would have thrown into the garbage bin at Mother's Palace.

Mother-damn Creesile, damn Wakan Kech, and damn those monkey-men from the Ice Lands—if men they are. He'd never been able to stand the little dark Rist, bird-riding freak and hero of the Game. His victory overshadowed Miran's own well-planned fixes to that Game; only the fortuitous stroke and death of the late Lordess Mother had placed Princess Messinex into her

Motherhood and himself into the position as second-place power in all Motherland. And then that despicable little savage, hero to so many, revealed his true self attacking Mother's Palace by dropping big rocks on it, barely missing himself and Rumi Similla, his current lover. *Messinex is in a panic now,* he thought, *and only bringing back Princess Pernie, alive, and Wakan Kech dead, will assuage her fears.* For himself, he wanted the heads of the little bird-riders, too—and to take their flying machine!

On more day of this blasted trip, he mused. *I'll find Creesile and his status and go from there.* Frankly, he admitted to himself, he hoped the General had not yet captured Pernie's palace, that he himself could be on site as the final victory was accomplished. *I don't know how long Pernie and her dwarves can hold out, or*—the sudden vision alarmed him—*if they might fly away in that god-machine!* With the dreadful punishment awaiting him for any failure of his mission, Miran wanted to urge the driver to whip the horses to go even faster. But all he could do was hold on to the seat rail and endure the incessant bouncing, coughing up thick dust every few minutes.

"Thist! Wakan!" Thusk shouted, waking up his nodding companions. "Look below! Una, on your screen, please. Close-up of that carriage on the Main Road."

As the other two woke up, weary from the exhaustion of the day, Thusk studied the front video screen. From an apparent altitude of only five meters, he clearly made out two struggling white horses, heavy with sweat and covered in road dust, the carriage driver whipping them furiously. On the seats behind sat a Mothersman guard; from his regalia, he was one of Mother's Own, a throne-room guard! Thusk asked Una to fly on and look backwards to view the other passenger, the fat one who must be important to warrant such protection. Or was he just under close surveillance?

"It is Miran Kech!" Thusk yelled in puzzlement. "What is he doing here, without an army to escort him?"

Wakan Kech replied, "Look at him, only two Mothersmen. He's dirty and unarmed. He's under guard, not heading an army. He must be up here in Stone Pyramid to check on Creesile's progress."

Thist whistled. "From the looks of it, it has to be an emergency trip, a personal mission from Mother Messinex. She wants firsthand information about the invasion of ShadowFall." As Una stabilized the close-up image of Miran, removing the bouncing from the video, the ShadowFallers could see the anxiety on the Kech's face, the priest constantly wiping his eyes and mouth with a dirty cloth, spitting out road dust. "From the looks of him, he must not be in good favor with the Mother, either."

Thist said, "Let's kill him right now; take his head to Creesile. Or capture him, at least." As Thusk and Wakan nodded, he said, "Una, pop up the white pilot and land in the road a thirty meters in front of that carriage. Full visibility."

"As you wish, Thist. But do not initiate violence. I cannot support such action."

Thist shook his head. "Una, I liked you better when there was no 'I' there. But I assure you, we will only capture Miran Kech, not harm him or his guards."

At that, Una landed on the Main Road, fully visible, with the black cockpit opening to reveal the white pilot figure. Using the loud-voice, Thist said, "By the order of Princess Perneptheranam of ShadowFall, you are ordered to halt and lay down your weapons. I will not repeat this order."

SEEING A HUGE GREEN CYLINDER DESCENDING ON THE road in front of him, the carriage-express driver pulled the horses to a halt, the vehicle now sliding to one side on the gravel. "What in Mother's name *is* that?" the driver screamed. Miran Kech, thrown to the side of the carriage by the sudden slide, put up his hands to keep his Mothersman guard from falling into him. As the vehicle finally slid to a stop, both men jumped out onto the road to witness an unbelievable sight.

By now, the driver was on the ground as well, all three men staring at a white human-looking figure peering down at them from atop a massive green cylinder at least ten meters long. The figure was shouting at them in a voice like thunder, hurtful to the ears.

"...lay down your weapons. I will not repeat this order."

The Mothersmen, unable to speak, did as they were told, trembling as they put down swords and knives, even reaching into the carriage to slowly remove an unloaded springbow and place it alongside the other weapons.

The thunder-voice then said, "You Mothersmen. Take the carriage and horses and leave us at once. Return to Mother Messinex if you dare. Leave Miran Kech and those weapons here. Now *go!*"

Needing no further encouragement, the cowed guards quickly drove off to the south, the High Priest and Mother's Advisor left standing alone in front of the white pilot and the big green monster upon which it sat. For the third time in his life, Miran Kech was completely defenseless, his fate in the hands of others. As Una's door opened he saw the two dwarves, one with a loaded springbow, and of course, his nemesis Wakan Kech. All he could think was, *Wakan Kech, you bastard. My life in your hands again: at our capture at the domed pyramid, after the rocks fell into Mother's Palace, and now with your flying machine and your monkey-men! Damn you all!* Holding his arms aloft in surrender, he bowed humbly to his captors, trying to plan escape and revenge.

"MIRAN KECH," WAKAN SAID TO THE PRISONER BOUND to a cabin chair aboard Una. The sweating captive was looking out the clear wall at the receding Main Road. He could tell the flying machine was moving, but not in which direction. "You have lost this war, and you know it. My concern now is to stop the killing, both of my innocent citizens and of the misguided Mothersmen acting on your orders."

Miran Kech answered with a sneer. "Wakan, you are a poor liar. If Creesile had lost you'd be showing me his head in a basket. Or on a spike at that stone rainbow of yours." Spitting at his old mentor, he snarled, "So what is it? You have lost the battle, and come to me to seek terms? Well, I can speak now for Mother Messinex —*unconditional surrender*! Your head on a spike, your little princess in chains, prostrate before the throne of our Mother—*your* Mother—seeking mercy, which I doubt Pernie will find in my dungeons."

Thist couldn't believe the braggadocio of the craven Kech. "Ah, Miran," he said, "you must be suffering from the aftershock of the rocks we dropped into your chambers. And into the bed of that Rumi Similla bitch." Turning to Wakan, he said, "Why don't we open Una's door and just drop him out, like we did those rock-bombs?"

Wakan shook his head. "No, Thist, he's more valuable to us alive—for now." The priest's face was impassive, stern. Threatening.

But Thist saw Miran's trembling reaction to their brief conversation. *The coward is really afraid of Wakan. We can use that!*

WITH MIRAN KECH TIGHTLY BOUND AND PLACED INSIDE the toilet room at the rear of Una's cabin, securely behind the door and out of hearing distance, the ShadowFallers conferenced. Thist spoke first. "If we land in front of General Creesile and let Miran speak directly to him, would he listen? Or would he have to hear it from Mother Messinex herself?"

Wakan answered, "From my memories of the General's career, he is a consummate military leader. Stern, but fair. Brutal when needs be, but competent. I believe he is devoted to our Motherland and its Mother. Whether that loyalty extends to Miran Kech, I can't tell."

Thusk, in his typical grim fashion, asked, "If we only have one chance to get Creesile to stop the invasion, if we risk getting Una shot down in the attempt, what is the one thing we *have* to do, who is the *one* person who could order him to stop, if anyone can?"

Wakan and Thist said together, "Messinex."

Thusk said, "Una, take us to Mother's Palace, as fast as possible. Stay invisible, and hover above the roof in the nearest entrance where we can get to Mother Messinex."

"Thist, I cannot support a military assault."

"No, Una, a simple snatch-and-grab, a temporary abduction. To stop a war. To save thousands of lives."

The acceleration nearly threw the ShadowFallers off their feet. A loud *thump!* from the toilet section told them that Miran Kech had been surprised, too.

CHAPTER FIFTY-FIVE

M other Messinex waited nervously for word from the front, her mind furiously turbulent. *Has Creesile crushed Pernie? Has Miran Kech arrived at ShadowFall? What has happened to Wakan? And, and, what of my two little warriors from the Dark Highlands?* Miran's horse express riders took three days to arrive, and so far each day since Miran's departure they had brought nothing but distressing news. The first day, just after Miran's departure, she heard: "Underwater catapults! A thousand or more dead!" The second day, of course, was when that Una machine dropped rocks all the way through the palace, into Miran's chambers, into Rumi Similla's room! *And nothing prevented it from dropping them on me!* she thought in panic. She had taken to hiding out in the deepest dungeons below the palace, protected by a dozen Mother's Guards. Uncomfortable as it was, she felt safer there.

Then that second horse messenger had brought even more disastrous reports—invisible throat-cutting godscloth wire! Wakan's Wire, they were calling it. *Indeed, that treacherous swine! He dares use hideous weapons on my soldiers!*

Finally, the third day's rider brought a written message from General Creesile.

· · ·

Mother Messinex, Advisor Miran Kech:

We have engaged the rebellious traitors at the Iron Gate of ShadowFall. Despite heavy casualties from their springbow arrows, their insidious Wakan's Wire fence traps, their flame-bombs dropped from godscloth flying wings, and their bird-riding monkey-men, we have advanced three klicks into their territory. Victory will be yours in one or two more days. My next report will be written on a table in the palace of Princess Perneptheranam.

Respectfully,

General X. Creesile, Commander, Mother's Army of Liberation."

Messinex was astounded at all of the new weapons her Mothersmen were encountering. Were all these new ones of Wakan's doing, or were they brought down from The Ice by Thist and Thusk? She knew that however this particular fight went, such innovations would be part of warfare from now on. Part of her mind wanted to see the weapons in person; how could thousands of Mothersmen be killed and her whole army delayed by just a small Sisterdom like ShadowFall? She hoped Creesile would capture those weapon designers and fabricators alive; her army had to have sole possession of them, for she could not afford other ambitious Sisters to arm themselves with such weaponry as Pernie had. *One rebellion is more than enough!*

But now, on the fourth day, Messinex had received no further report. Could the rider have been killed? Or worse—not sent? Was Creesile winning? Dead? And what of Miran? In a state of near panic, she decided not to visit the Crystal Throne for the daily mind-flogging gibberish, experiencing a sudden relief at not having to endure its unhelpful strange voices and vibrations. *No, she thought, if my army is defeated at ShadowFall, the other Sisters may revolt, too, seeing that I am weak. I need to plan an escape and resistance strategy—now!*

Though her new advisory staff included the ten

nobles provided by Pernie as a reward for Thist's winning the Game, Messinex knew she could not trust their loyalty in the contest with their home Sisterdom. *And Miran has locked up or killed most of our Lordess Mother's experienced advisors. I'll have to figure this out by myself.*

Under cover of the darkening evening sky, Messinex and fifteen trusted Mother's Own guards prepared to depart from the palace via a secret underground tunnel known only to herself, taking half her remaining horses, with ox-drawn wagons of food, copper, gold, and weapons. And the cache of golden tablet records from her Sanctuary Room. The covert entourage headed for a secret cavern redoubt in Three Rivers, a place of refuge that Messinex had had constructed long ago as a princess there, where she hoped to ride out any difficulties that might arise should Creesile's adventure fail. If that happened, she might even decide to raise an army and overthrow the current Three Rivers princess and reign there once again.

From her readings of the ancient gold tablets in her Sanctuary Room, Messinex knew that other Mothers had similarly evacuated such a prime target during previous uprisings and inter-Sisterine wars. *But not for hundreds of years*, she rued. *What has caused all of this to happen now, when I am Mother? Why me? What is different now than when our Lordess Mother lived and ruled?* All she could think of was Pernie, and Wakan, and Miran, and Rumi Similla—and Thist. *A strange little man, riding birds, reading godspheres, flying a god-machine. Attacking my palace.* He *is the key. I will have to eliminate him, once Creesile takes ShadowFall.* But at the present she had to flee from the uncertainties of the war that Thist and his unwanted interference had brought upon Motherland.

Before leaving, Messinex instructed her head dungeon guard to imprison Rumi Similla. "She is not to communicate with anybody. Keep her in solitary confinement, minimal food and water. She will not be released until I give the order in person." Then she added, "But the woman is not to be molested or harmed in any way whatsoever. Any violator of my order will receive the usual punishment." The head dungeon guard winced; slow castration with a white-hot knife was incentive enough to guarantee his men's compliance.

Messinex gave similar orders to her advisors and staff; they were to remain at their offices in the outlying buildings on the palace grounds and to continue their routine bureaucratic work as usual. Without informing anyone other than the guards accompanying her that she was leaving, the palace itself was left with only a skeleton crew of guards, posted only at the entrances and exits.

As her open carriage bounced along the escape route road, Messinex was pleased to see that the sky was dark, no bright Moon out yet. *What did the Crystal Throne voice say to me? Somebody on the Moon? Ridiculous! I am beginning to think that the whole "goddess' thing is an invention of a past Mother, just a way for us to keep our power.* With that realization, all her doubts of the last few months crystallized; in that moment Messinex finally lost all faith in her own infallibility, in the significance of Motherhood, and in the meaning of Motherland itself. *But as long as everyone else believes in it, and in me, I still have the most power in all our country. Maybe the power to do good, but at the very least, power. And I am the best one to exercise it!*

The uncomfortable trek to the southern hills of Three Rivers took the rest of the night and the whole next day, during which time Messinex kept a nervous eye on the sky, fearing the return of Thist in his Una machine. Though she had never seen it, from its description the god-machine was like a big, green, overgrown squash vegetable, ten meters long, ridden by a white ghost of a figure sitting on top of it. She tried to imagine such a flying monstrosity, but couldn't envision it. She guessed she would know it if it appeared out of nowhere, as that Rumi had claimed it had at ShadowFall. *And as reportedly seen by those thousands of Creesile's troops at the debacle at Lake Roos, too.*

SAFELY ENSCONCED IN HER MASSIVE GASLIT CAVERN hiding place, Messinex showed her guards how to activate the rolling boulder that sealed them off from outside. As she and her handmaidens took up residence in a tapestry-walled niche, she realized the vulnerability of her situation. With herself and two handmaidens as the only women in the cavern redoubt, along with fifteen armed male guards, she felt a momentary discomfort, a tingle of unease. *But if I can't trust my most dedicated and loyal Mother's Own, who can I trust?* Deciding that other matters needed her immediate attention, she dismissed that niggling thought and called in the chief guard to give him instructions.

"There are two observation ports overhead in this cavern, small chambers with camouflaged openings that serve as sentry posts. You will post your smallest men in them at all times to keep a lookout. They will be able to see threats of any kind for kilometers across the plains. If a horse rider appears holding aloft a colored banner, inform me at once. In the unlikely event the lookouts are discovered by an enemy and attacked, each has a lodge post that can be pulled to seal off their chambers from our cavern here." Nodding, the guard left.

Messinex had left word with the minimal guard crew at the palace to send any messenger rider on to the plains outside her hidden sanctuary, there to ride back and forth twice along the several kilometers between two prominent standing stones, in daylight, carrying the news on a colored banner. Her self-designed system should give her sufficient security, as no evidence of an entrance could be seen from the rider's location, and no location deduced by anyone who observed his path. If the rider's message was of victory, he was to hold up a long lance with a red banner. If the message was of continuing battle, the color was to be blue. And, Mother forbid, if the rider carried news of defeat or retreat, the message would be communicated by white.

Messinex calculated that the wagonloads of perishable food she'd ordered brought along should suffice for at least two weeks for her contingent. Since leaving Three Rivers she had kept the cavern supplied with a goodly amount of dried beezt and other animal foods, adequate with rationing for another month beyond that, and the cavern had continuous springs for an indefinite supply of water. Gas lights tapped into natural sources, and crates of candles would provide illumination for years.

But I plan to stay no more than two weeks in this rat hole, she thought. *By then, I will have some word of Creesile's victory, or will have his head. Two weeks,* she thought. *If I get no message of any kind by then, we return to the palace and prepare for an all-out war of extermination against Pernie and ShadowFall, her god-machines and Wakan's weapons be damned!*

CHAPTER FIFTY-SIX

As General Creesile sat with his officers at the table in front of his tent, a dirty-faced young officer ran up, saluted, and said, "General, sir, we reached their fourteen-klick marker and have begun to run into resistance. Nothing we can't handle, but at this attrition rate—a few hundred casualties per klick—we may arrive at the Princess's palace with only a third of our numbers."

Creesile groaned, as much for his losses as his loss of a leg. "Very well, Captain. Please proceed with caution, but do proceed. If ShadowFall's rebellion is not promptly extinguished, I don't have to tell you that we may have to continue this kind of campaigning all over Motherland, against all of the Sisterdoms. And none of us wants that!"

At their General's request the other officers went over their casualty lists out loud. Creesile commented, "So the invisible wire traps, the IEDs, account for many initial deaths, and then their catapults hit us. How about the bird-riders and the flying wings?"

A major reported, "Sir, at first the war-birds were frightening and effective, but our men have worked out defenses—spear-throwers, archers—anything that keeps them from close combat. We are also doing away with those damned springbowers, taking them out in large numbers; by the time we lay siege to the palace, they shouldn't be a factor."

"Tell me more about those flying wings. That big red man and his flying monkeys?" Laughs all around; Creesile took heart that his officers could still find humor in the darkest of situations. His own pain kept him from joining in the humor.

"Sir," the major said, "in clear weather, our archers can shoot them out of the sky. Since the fog lifted, we've taken down quite a few—all dead by arrows or by crashing. When they do get through overhead, though, their flame-bombs can be hard on our catapults and crews. But we have craftsmen behind us building a new launcher every few hours. By the time of the siege of their palace—later today, by your plan—we will have half a dozen more ready to go. I recommend that right now our catapults first target the rest of those tall towers the wings are jumping off from. Stop that threat altogether."

A quick summary from the quartermaster officer showed that Creesile's liberating army was well supplied with food, water, arrows, and hand weapons. Left unsaid, per the General's order, was the total amount of medical supplies remaining. Without comment, Creesile dismissed the officers, retaining only Colonel Treegu, the man responsible for sending in saboteurs and arsonists and assassins ahead of the army. He had special orders for that officer.

CHAPTER FIFTY-SEVEN

Una's speed surprised Thusk; arriving all the way from ShadowFall after only thirty minutes. Because Una detected no borophene arrow defenses, they hovered invisibly over the green-oxidized copper roof of Mother's Palace, just a meter away from a seldom-used hatchway. Una's door opened out of nowhere, Thist stepping out the final inches onto the dust-covered stone roof. "I'm out, now," he said back toward the cabin interior. "Have Una track me. I plan to leave through a front or side door. I will try convince Mother Messinex to come peacefully…" His voice dropped off, its significance not lost on the men. Una made no comment.

Following a hand-printed map based on Una's sensors, Thist made his way down dank, cobwebbed hallways, through large abandoned rooms and banquet halls, past nameless portraits of forgotten nobles, occasionally stepping over remnants of crumpled tapestries now fallen from disintegrated cords, their presentations and stories hidden from human eyes. On some of them he could make out faded scenes of battles long ago, of forgotten Mothersmen in heroic poses, of what must have been Mothers in past centuries. *Or past millennia, maybe? I wonder how old this palace is, anyhow? Hundreds of years? Thousands*? He recalled from some of the few godspheres he had activated that a great sea, hundreds of meters deep, once covered all of Motherland. *And my bringing that up was what set off Mother Messinex on a rampage. Did I cause the war, the invasion of ShadowFall, just for referencing that history?* He shrugged off that thought; the ways and politics of Mother's Palace had never been that interesting to him. As far as when the ancient sea over Motherland had dried up, he'd have to ask Una for when that was. *But I don't need to know that history now, I just need to know where Messinex is, and how to reason with her when I find her.* Thinking about how to do that brought up another fact he wanted to know: *How many guards does she have?*

THIST COULDN'T BELIEVE HIS LUCK; HE MADE IT ALL the way down to Mother Messinex's throne room without encountering any guards or anyone else. Was the whole palace abandoned? Deciding to take advantage of his good fortune, he crept down the main hallway from the throne room toward Mother's Auditorium, the holiest of holies in Motherland, where the Crystal Throne sat on its pyramid of transparent crystal. Opening the massive door with some effort—a task usually relegated to large Mothersmen—he found the huge auditorium empty, its thousands of seats unoccupied, its incredibly spacious overhead dome now ominously dark, as if the sky itself had suddenly turned dark over the whole world. Only one thin beam of light split the darkness, illuminating the Crystal Throne itself. But where had Messinex gone?

Thist walked up to the staircase that led to the Crystal Throne. He had heard from Pernie and Wakan about what they witnessed when the late Lordess Mother had ascended the steps and sat on the throne, the night before the fateful Motherland Game. Touching the first step with his hand, Thist was surprised that the huge crystal seemed to respond; a pattern of colored lights suddenly emanated from each riser, as if moving toward the huge chair at the top of the staircase. *Is this an invitation?* he wondered. *This huge crystal has the same feel as godspheres, and the lights from within look the same as in those globes. What knowledge did the ancients possess to make such things? Una is unbelievable enough, but this is truly strange!* He'd have to ask Una about all of it when he got back. *If* he got back!

Wondering if the Mother's Crystal Throne might hold secrets that could help him end that Miran Kech's invasion of ShadowFall, Thist took tentative steps up the staircase, straining to raise his foot up onto the first high riser. Immediately a rainbow of colors coalesced on the riser, spreading upward as he slowly moved farther up the staircase. Sword drawn, he took one high, strenuous step at a time, with each upward motion turning his head left to right as if expecting a trap, an ambush. As he ascended, the moving colors in the risers kept pace with him, even going on ahead, seemingly beckoning him to the top.

Finally, standing before the huge transparent crystalline chair, Thist was able to lift himself up and swing upwards into the seat. Nothing happened; there was no response, nor could he see, feel, or otherwise sense anything. Then he remembered a humorous comment that Princess Pernie had made about the ceremony when she and all the noble visitors were being welcomed before the Game. "Not everybody gets to see their Mother's bottom. I wish I hadn't!" If that were a true story about the Lordess Mother sitting bare-bottomed on the Crystal Throne, Thist figured that he might need to put his own rear parts onto the cold chair as well. Shivering, he slid off his undergarment and pulled up his tunic, placing his buttocks directly onto the cool, hard surface.

Immediately he felt as if he were in a different world, immersed in a kaleidoscope of geometric images and ephemeral visions, with a chorus of squeals and squeaks and voices sounding almost like Una's. Sensing that he was being questioned, he spoke into that pulsating chaos of colors. "What is this? What are you saying?"

As if in response, more gibberish spewed forth into his mind: *"—qomp translation algorithms— accommodating tonal shift variables—integrating genetic access codes."* The words were meaningless but forceful, he could tell. Somebody or some *thing*—an Una of some kind?—was attempting to communicate with him. Just like the godspheres!

Finally, words came that were recognizable as stilted Motherspeak: "Translation complete. Recognized variant of archaic Mandarin at local lunar terminal. Recognized and archived variation of Diníglish–Tagish at Earth terminal. You may continue."

This sounds just like Una! Thist recognized, shocked. *And like the speaking godspheres!* Aloud he said, "What are you? *Who* are you?"

"Now paging local lunar operator. Who is Earth operator? Identification, please. What is your message?" The Una-like voice diminished in volume, followed by noises of crackling and squealing.

"I am Thist. I am on the Crystal Throne in Mother's Palace, in Mother's City, in Motherland. What is 'Lunar'?"

But there was only silence. Not even noise. Had he lost contact with whatever "Local lunar operator" was? Thist felt uneasy about all the unknowns he was facing. *What was that all about?* he wondered. *Does the Mother actually communicate with goddesses up there, or does she just hear nonsense like I did? Does the goddess answer? Does she talk?* And amidst this confusion an overriding thought emerged: *Can she help me fight the invasion of ShadowFall?*

To him, the whole experience was much like he had had with Una after his twin brought the flying machine down the day before the Game—a set of frustrating trials and errors, back and forth, attempts to communicate with a machine that took everything literally, which back then, at least, seemed to have no comprehension of the ambiguities and nuances of human language.

Whispering to himself, Thist said, "This ancient throne somehow uses ancient—*technology,* Una calls it —to talk to me and the Mother. But why, for what purpose?" If the throne's technology was actually like the godspheres that he powered up by sunlight and then could talk to by touching, in his mind he could envision every single citizen owning and listening to, and maybe talking to, their godsphere. *If everyone had one, would they all then be equal to the Mother, with all her authority?* That thought was enlightening to a degree he had not considered: What if each citizen were equal in power, and nobody stood above them, no Mother or princess or noble, no generals or captains? He could not conceive of such a society, one far more individually oriented than even what he and Thusk had achieved in their homeland.

"I need to talk to Una about all this, and with Thusk and Wakan," he murmured to himself. He didn't think that the Princess would approve of the vision he was formulating, but it was an intriguing one at that.

But just then, interrupting that revolutionary thought, the Crystal Throne began to speak to him again. Or was it *through* him? It felt as though the speech was in his head, himself talking to himself. But the pitch of the voice was that of a young girl: "I am Mienne. From Shinyeen City. In Community. On Moon."

CHAPTER FIFTY-EIGHT

Whatever this DI is, Thist thought, *its voice is not like Una's, but sounds human, and weirdly inflected, as if the speaker is not fluent in Motherspeak.* Breathing hard, his eyes tightly shut, his hands shaking, he tried to answer that strange girl. "I, I, I…I am Thist," he said, hoping for a conversation with the person at the other end of the qomm link. "I speak Motherspeak. I am in Mother's City, here on our world, Earth. Are you, are you"—he could barely say it aloud—"*on* the Moon? In one of those colored lights?"

The girl's voice again: "Yes. I am on Moon. In a city. I am Mienne. Are *you* a god?"

Surprised at the question, Thist gulped, answering, "No, I am not a god. I am a *man*, on Earth." He felt as though he was intermittently occupying someone else's body, sitting in a smaller version of the Crystal Throne, looking out of a gigantic window over craggy mountains, into a black sky. On the horizon sat a blue-and-white orb, a strangely familiar sight. Una had once showed him distant pictures of…of…*Earth*? "But now I am seeing…*what*? Up there in the black sky? Is that Earth?" he whispered.

"Yes," the person called Mienne answered. "I am looking up at Motherth in the sky. Do you not recognize it?"

"Yes, yes, I hear you, Mienne. And yes, I can see

through your eyes. And you—you—you can see through *mine*? We are communicating very strangely, almost as if we are exchanging bodies. It's incredible, what a feeling."

In Thist's shared body, Mienne slid around on the large seat of the Crystal Throne, looking around the huge, dark auditorium, at the flickering torches, seeing all of it for the first time. She felt *small*, dwarfed by the crystal chair behind and around her. Looking down at her arms and legs she was—*dark!* She *was* in that Thist's body, but he was small and swarthy, where she herself was taller, with much lighter-colored skin. Unconsciously, she touched her groin. *Yes, and unmistakably male!* She felt some strange new sensations down there, but didn't want to pay attention to that, just yet. *But it* is *an interesting feeling.*

"Yes, Thist," Mienne said in the little man's deep voice, "I do believe this ancient device is working. I am in your body, on Motherth. Are you in my body, on Moon? You *are*? Wonderful!"

In Mienne's body on the Moon, Thist looked around, fascinated by the dome of black sky, at the banks of metal equipment and blinking lights—*technology?*—around him, and at the still presence of a pale, blonde girl sitting on the floor, staring. *Something is wrong with her,* he thought, confused. Then it hit him: *She has no arms!*

With that, in shock, Thist's vision returned to his own eyes, and Mienne's presumably to her own. "Mienne, that blonde girl with no arms, what happened to her?" Thist saw that he was back on Earth, on the Crystal Throne.

Mienne's voice said, "She is my friend, Wayer. She was born that way. I think she was shocked to hear our conversation, but I am back in *my* body now. Wayer, are you all right?" Then: "Thist, she is fine, and so am I. These crystal chairs are marvelous, aren't they?"

Thist breathed out hard. "Mienne, you are living up on Earth's Moon, and I am down here on Earth itself. The ancients set up these crystal chairs for communication, but I don't know how they let us exchange our bodies. I mean, I could see—and *feel*—you, and you did the same for me. Why would they want to do that?"

Mienne smiled, as much to calm herself as to pacify Wayer, who was still shaking her head at the interchanging she had witnessed. "Thist, we have a lot of information to exchange. I imagine these chairs will help us do that." At that, adding to the confusion and in another kaleidoscopic torrent of lights and sounds, the two involuntarily switched bodies again. This time, Thist was determined to understand what that girl Mienne was doing on the Moon, where exactly she was, and what all those arrays of buttons and screens and blinking lights in Mienne's room were for—what did they *do*? Could they be used in his war right now?

Thist asked her that, startled that his voice was now high-pitched like Mienne's—*It* is *Mienne's,* he reminded himself—"What is all of this *technology* for? On Earth down here in Motherland we have a flying machine, and some of these buttons and screens look the same. Do you fly up there? *Here*?" he corrected himself, still confused at the magic of the ancients that enabled such interchanging of minds. Momentarily he panicked at the thought of possibly not being able to return to his own body, on Earth.

Mienne answered in his voice, "No, Thist, no flying. There is no atmosphere outside of the domed cities on Moon. As far as I can tell, the ancients used rooms like the one you are in to control machines there. Why do you ask?"

Thist thought intently. "From Earth, we see a string of colored lights across the face of the Moon. Some say they are jewels in a necklace of the goddess of the Moon." He looked around the room, but could not read the inscribed labels nor make any sense of anything that might be a control. "Do the machines control those lights?"

Mienne laughed. "Thist, you must be seeing the domed cities on the surface of Moon, not a necklace of jewels. They are under big hemispheres, kilometers in diameter, and lit up, according to the DI that showed Wayer and me the map. I don't know if people live in those cities, or what the lights mean." She paused. "Why don't you ask the DI?"

In Mienne's voice, Thist did just that. Surprisingly, the answer was like Una's voice: "The exterior illumination of specified Lunar Republic city domes may be accessed and controlled by voice command while on the qomp chair. Be advised that some qomponents are degraded and irreparable. The sim screen will display the currently operative illumination fields. The external intensities of these fields may be varied from zero to maximum without interfering with local safety or health standards."

It was only later that Thist thought to wonder why such capabilities were ever designed, or what the fields of illumination were originally intended for. When he did, Una's attempted explanation of political symbology, philosophical sensitivity, and commercial awareness were just more esoteric and archaic jargon to him.

Thist realized that if the Moon DI's comments were accurate and if the ancient machines still operated, then a person in the control room had tremendous opportunities for controlling lunar installations. A few minutes of experimenting with the voice commands showed him what he/Mienne could do on Moon. Playing around, he found that he could change the colors and the brightness of the domes, at least as shown on the 3D screen. He had no doubt that the actual city domes were responding the same way. *I guess if people are living in them, they may be puzzled at their lights acting so strangely, but I won't do this again until—until I need to! And people on Earth might be wondering, too. Marvelous,* he thought. *What amazing powers that Mienne—and now, I—can command here on the Moon!*

Anxious to get back to Earth and use his new knowledge for ShadowFall's defense, Thist told Mienne what he wanted to do, wanted *her* to do, and she agreed to help. "Just tell me when."

"Thist," she added, "The control center DI there told me that there is another method of communication between these crystal chairs. I haven't seen it yet, but supposedly there are other chambers that have what it calls 'avatarobots', which are a kind of humanlike machine. You could transfer yourself into one of those if you wanted to, and not have to be in my body." She was quiet for a moment. "Actually, if that would work, I would prefer to do it that way. It is kind of strange to be in a boy's body. I will search for that room here on Moon after we finish. Do you have that capability on Earth?"

The concept of a person embedded into a machine shocked Thist, but he thought on it. "I suppose that would be similar to our own Una—the DI in our craft is almost like a human being. It sure feels that way, after all this time talking with her, or *it*. But there is nothing ancient in Mother's Palace but the big Crystal Throne as far as I know. And I've never even heard of an 'avatarobot.'"

After more discussion, Thist was able to return to himself and Mienne to herself, by simply sitting in their respective crystal chairs and commanding the qomp system to transfer them back. After the switch was complete, Thist thought that the experience was fantastic, but once would be enough. *Why* the ancients had ever wanted to communicate like that, he thought he would never know, much less *how* they had done it. But he himself certainly did not want to do it ever again. And right now, he had a war to win.

CHAPTER FIFTY-NINE

Back in Una, Thist said excitedly, "Wakan, Thusk, I have just had the most incredible experience on the Crystal Throne. I think it can help us end Creesile's invasion." Keeping Miran Kech safely away in the toilet room where he couldn't hear, he quickly summarized his unique conversation with that Mienne on the Moon. "Believe me, it was an incredible experience!"

Thusk said, "We believe you, Thist, because we, and the whole round world, I suppose, saw that string of jewels on the Moon flashing and changing colors. We thought the world was coming to an end. But it was *you*!" Wakan was shaking his head in disbelief; was there no end to the weirdness these little guys were involved in?

Brushing aside astonished reactions and questions, Thist asked Una, "Una, you said before that you understood the working of the Crystal Throne?"

"Yes, Thist, I did and I do."

"Can you communicate through it, with that Mienne, on the Moon? I mean, without that body-sharing business? Just me, talking through you, to her?" He shuddered at the thought of occupying that girl's body again, the sharing of minds; it was just too unnatural. He wondered what Mienne's feelings were, about sharing *his* body, his thoughts.

"Yes, Thist, I can do that."

Thist explained what he had asked Mienne to do, then told his companions how the Moon-girl could help end the war at ShadowFall. "All you have to do, Una, is tell her *when*."

THAT SETTLED, THIST SAID, "NOW, WE HAVE TO FIND out where Messinex has gone. She's not in the palace. Miran has to tell us." Nodding, Wakan went to fetch Miran Kech from Una's toilet room at the back of the cabin.

With Miran now tied to a cabin seat, Wakan said, "Thist saw that Messinex has left the palace, Miran. Where did she go?" Staring at his fellow Kech, now a betrayer, he pulled out an ampule from his belt and repeated his request. "I will ask one more time. This little vial," he said, "is deathroot. Perhaps you have heard of it?"

Miran Kech jerked his head back, eyes wide open, mouth quivering. "Not that, Wakan, my Kech countryman, not that. But you know I am unable to betray my Mother—*our* Mother—it is not done." Unstoppering the vial, Wakan put it near Miran's lips.

"One last chance, old *countryman,*" Wakan said with a sneer. "Where is Messinex? Or you will have a week of unbearable agony in which to regret your choice?"

Miran Kech blubbered, "Don't, don't. I'll tell you." As Wakan withdrew the vial, his fellow Kech breathed deeply, grimacing. "If she finds out I talked, I'll lose… other parts, you know. All right. She has a secret cavern somewhere in the highlands at the edge of Three Rivers. I discovered that while I was her advisor there, before she became Mother. I don't know exactly where it is. It is very well concealed."

Wakan put the liquid container up close to Miran's lips again, and the younger man blanched. "Wakan, wait. If you fly this, this, *machine* of yours over Three Rivers, perhaps I can find it. All I recall is a flat map I once saw while sneaking through the Princess's paper files."

Thusk said, "Una, show us a map of Three Rivers on your front screen. Miran, you tell us where to go." As the three-dimensional representation of Three Rivers appeared on the screen, Miran Kech's eyes grew wide; the man had never seen digital information, had never witnessed Una's incredible ability to display massive amounts of information in such a realistic manner.

"This, this, *display* is unbelievable," Miran said, his hands stroking the screen in wonder.

"Well, so is a flying, talking god-machine, Miran," Wakan said. "Think of what all we could have done with such capabilities, had you not sent General Creesile on an unnecessary and destructive invasion of an innocent Sisterdom."

Miran Kech sat, crestfallen, as he understood the power of forces allied against himself and his ambitions. With the help of his little dark men, Wakan Kech had finally won out, had counteracted all his plans, all his yearnings for power in Motherland and, eventually, back home in the High Antis. But one small hope glimmered in his darkest thoughts. *What if Creesile does take ShadowFall? Maybe he already has? Could I leverage Pernie's captivity against my own? Arrange a mutually beneficial truce and trade between Messinex and Pernie? Anything to get away from this damned Wakan and his horrible herb!*

CHAPTER SIXTY

"The front is now just five kilometers away," Princess Pernie read aloud, thanking the bloodied messenger who delivered the scrawled note to her. She nervously paced the war council room, waving off the handmaidens who were offering her flagons of wine. "No, no wine. I must keep my wits," she said sharply, in dismissal. The situation she was reviewing looked grim, nearly hopeless.

By unrelenting, unending massed assaults over the last two hours, Creesile's forces had caused a general collapse of ShadowFall's front, driving the surviving troops—many of them citizen militias—either into the countryside or back into the city. Pernie and her commanders had not expected the general to expend his men's lives so ruthlessly; ShadowFallers had killed probably half of the invaders, but the remaining Mothersmen were relentless. "And they are killing our wounded when they can," she was told by an officer who had returned to the palace. "The black flag. No mercy, by Creesile's orders." The situation was desperate, and she saw few options remaining.

Around the planning table sat only the lowest-ranking representatives of her defense forces, their chiefs all still deployed at the ever-shrinking front, overseeing the last-ditch defenses of the city and the palace. She could tell they were all nervous—trembling, sweating, mishandling scrolls and map markers—all overlaid by a tangible aura of fear. *Is that because they are afraid for their lives if we lose to Creesile's marauders? Or of what will happen to ShadowFall itself? Both?*

Unlike peacetime protocols that forbade weapons in the presence of the Princess other than those of her guards, now around the stone walls stood springbows, quivers of arrows, spears, and swords. *If the enemy gets this far, all of us in this room will die,* she thought. *So these weapons represent only a futile gesture.* Sensing the desperation and hopelessness of her people at the table, she thought, *Should I offer myself up to Creesile to save at least these men and women here?* Looking at the heavily boarded doorway to the balcony, she could only see through the cracks that the sun had already passed midday; twilight would be setting in not too long from now. She wished that the doorway was still open to the sky so that she could search for the sky for Una and its valuable crew, her closest advisors—her only friends. *Where are they? Can they save us? Oh, Wakan, Thist, Thusk, please hurry!*

THE SUN WAS STILL BRIGHT AS ODEL M'RIDGE STOOD beside a Wakan's Tower, speaking with emu-riders Mox and Rohn and other officers he did not know. Depending upon his pidgin speech to get his idea across, he spoke slowly. "ShadowFall warriors. I fly. Look for enemy catapults. Bomb with fire. Our springbows and catapults then aim for big fires we cause. Think you go fight, too." Pointing north toward the city, he said, "Our last chance save ShadowFall. Kill them all."

Mox, who had been in Odel's presence since his arrival a month ago, understood his intention, and announced it more articulately to her riders, to the chief of the springbowmen, and to the catapult crews surrounding them. "He's right, everyone. Wait until Odel and his flyers drop flame-bombs on the enemy, then shoot flame-stones at those fires. Then use springbows, if they are within range. After those barrages, we ride in. As many as have spindles to string Wakan's Wire, do that, but low to the ground. An injured soldier, with his feet cut off, hurts them more than a dead one. He has to be looked after but can't fight us. And his screams scare his buddies." She shivered as she recalled her other forays with that insidious cutting twine, the screams, the blood, the guts, the *smell*! *Well,* she thought, *they should not be here, in our new homeland!* "And remember, kill officers and catapult crews first. Then go after anybody you can find." She didn't add, *With thousands of them out there, that won't be a problem.*

Holding up her springbow, she yelled out, "For ShadowFall and freedom!" This was met with rousing cheers, loud enough to be heard kilometers away by Creesile's army, now approaching, entirely too close.

As ODEL M'RIDGE CLIMBED THE MANY STAIRS TO THE launching platform on the Wakan's Tower nearest the approaching battlefront, he saw a full moon rising in the daytime sky in the east, pale but distinctive in the clear blue sky. The Pale Lady was of minor interest, its necklace of colored beads barely visible in the bright light of day. With the sun now lower in the western sky, Odel was planning on guiding his flyers to flame-bomb Creesile's catapults, by carefully positioning themselves between the enemy archers and the sun, keeping the sun in their faces. Turning to the mirror-man in charge of the tower, he said, "Use your mirrors and signal all of our forces to attack!" Saluting, the soldier turned and climbed to the signaling station at the very top of the tower. Odel was pleased to see the flickering sun-signal message transmitted and then quickly shut down, so as not to give the enemy a specific target. *No, that is* my *tactic!* he thought, launching himself from the tower, hoping not to have to use his firepowder booster as he glided toward Creesile's encampment. From behind, he heard the rest of his small squadron of tri-wing warriors jumping to follow him in. *Good luck and good hunting to us all!*

A mile into his flight, he was maintaining altitude, warm winds rising into the darkening sky and keeping him aloft without need of his fiery boosters. From his viewpoint at an altitude of two hundred meters, he could see the sheer number of Mothersmen below him, hundreds and hundreds of them. But he silently glided over the enemy, unseen. Spotting a catapult being towed to the front by oxen, he swooped directly over it, releasing a flame-bomb. A burst of flame, followed by shouts and curses, told him he had hit his target. Then he returned to the site, this time bombing the humans who were fighting the flames of the first attack. Lighting his booster to fly back for more bombs, he heard the screams of his targets. *I hate doing this, boys, but you shouldn't be here!*

In ten minutes, all but two of his flyers had returned to the base of the tower. "Odel," one told him, "we lost two, I believe. Damned archers shot upward at random, got poor Rett for sure, and maybe the wen, Myr; I heard her yell after she took out a catapult, but didn't see what happened to her."

Odel frowned. "We did good. Hate any died. We go back again later after catapulters. Springbowers and bird-riders finish. Now, go drink and rest." Though tri-winging looked easy to those on the ground, the effort of twisting and turning in the control harness, not to mention carrying and dropping flame-bombs, was strenuous. Odel saw with satisfaction that his squadron of little people was better fitted for flight than was he. And their vision was incredible, better than any big person's. *After this war, these little guys and gals are going to rule the sky!* With that thought, he wondered where his buddies Thist and Thusk were, in their own magical flying machine. *We could sure use them right now. If only to yell some more and scare off Creesile's army!*

AT THE PRINCESS'S LAST DESPERATE ATTEMPT TO STAVE off Creesile's invaders, she issued orders to attack the enemy column, hoping by surprise to hold off a final confrontation at the palace. For final defenses, Wakan Kech had ShadowFall's engineers excavate a series of kilometer-long tunnels leading from inside the palace grounds to flank the Main Road entrance to the city. Made large enough for Motherlanders, the tunnels easily accommodated bird-riders as well. By Pernie's plan, half of ShadowFall's springbowmen and all of its remaining bird-riders emerged from concealment outside the city, silently flanking Creesile's advancing column. The men trusted that their camouflage clothing helped them blend in with the sparse vegetation; the bird-riders would emerge once the fighting started.

As Odel's series of tri-wing flame-bombings continued, the approach of the ShadowFallers went unnoticed by the few sentries still at their posts, each of whom was worried about their own safety from sudden attacks from the air. Targeting the columns of flame erupting from burning catapults, hundreds of springbowers sent their shafts into the column of Mothersmen. Expecting a direct attack on the Main Road, Creesile's commanders had stationed lookouts only facing north. Anticipating this, Princess Pernie had had her ShadowFallers feint small attacks directly on the road from the north, with a small group of springbowmen firing fire-arrows for effect, while the main group appeared from nowhere in the west, letting loose their penetrating arrows in arcs that terminated at each of those target areas.

The effect was general chaos; adding to the flame-bomb attacks, two hundred arrows at a time pierced armor and bodies, while fire-stones from catapults targeted the center of the mass of the column. The Mothersmen seemed to be on the verge of a panicked retreat or outright rout.

Over the tumult and the shouting, the screams of

pain and shouting of orders, Mox and her war-birds arrived, their spindles of Wakan's Wire just a foot above the ground. A hundred bird-riders swept into the left flank of Creesile's column, slicing through legs with ease. As soon as Mox felt her spindle freeze she knew that something had snagged the knife-wire, maybe a dense metal or ore-bearing projectile. Tossing the useless spindle away, she drew her shortsword and ran her bird into the nearest grouping of Mothersmen. Within seconds she was fighting for her life, her bird kicking, breaking bones, eviscerating intestines, herself slashing at leather-armored men over twice her size but matched face-to-face atop her steed. With only a minimal metal helmet and thin godscloth body armor, she felt blow after blow as the big men swung at her with fists; she answered each with her sword. In the heat of the fight she let the weapon slip and fall away; grabbing her spear, she charged yet another foe, this one running at her. But with a scream of terror, the big warrior fell forward, his legs gone below the knee, torrents of blood spurting his life away. Looking up, she saw two other PeoplesLandsers riding away, waving a salute at her as their spindle-wire dragged on the ground. *Go, team!* she thought, grinning. *We are learning how to fight!*

CHAPTER SIXTY-ONE

Looking eastward through Una's clear wall at the pale rising moon, Wakan Kech said to his companions, "Boys, if we don't find Messinex soon, we are going to miss our three-hour return promise. I hope that Pernie and the others can hold off Creesile's troops until we do get back." Thist and Thusk were concerned, as well.

"If Miran can't show us where Messinex is hiding," Thist said, pointing toward the outline of Una's door, "I think we should throw him out."

Miran Kech, tightly bound to the aircraft's cabin seat, objected. "I'm telling you, Thist, that I have never been in her redoubt cavern. I just know it's got a massive, camouflaged stone door, and is located somewhere between two big standing stones at the eastern edge of Three Rivers."

While flying back and forth over the area between the two large stones at an altitude of a hundred meters, Thusk asked Una to scan the highlands for any trace of Messinex or her redoubt.

"Thusk, I have been doing scans since we began searching. There are many natural caverns in the limestone highlands east of us. I cannot determine which, if any, are occupied."

Thinking over Messinex's escape, Thusk asked Miran Kech, "How many people would she take with her, to escape like that? Ten? A hundred? What would they do for food and drink? Would she have to bring those along, on wagons?" Before the Kech could answer, Thusk said, "Wait! Una, can you scan the area for animal droppings? Horse shit, oxen dung?"

A minute later, Una was landing outside the rolled-rock door of Messinex's cavern hideout. The ShadowFall search party stepped outside. "You're sure this is the place, Una?" Thist asked, as he stepped into a pile of manure, answering his own question. "Never mind," he said, scraping his boot clean on a small clump of grass. "I believe you."

Wakan said, "Perhaps we can use Una's loud-voice to talk through this stone? We have no way to move it."

Looking up the rocky hillside in front of them, Thist said, "She has to have sentries posted somewhere. And they have to have a way down into the cave. If you yell loud enough, she'll have to hear you." Thusk nodded.

Wakan spoke. "Very well. Una, in my own voice, please let me loud-speak to Mother Messinex inside the cave behind this stone door."

"Allow it, Una," Thusk said.

"Very well. Wakan Kech, you may speak. Thist and Thusk, please cover your ears." The three men went back inside the aircraft.

"THIS IS WAKAN KECH SPEAKING. A MESSAGE FOR MOTHER MESSINEX. WE INTEND YOU NO HARM, BUT YOU MUST COME WITH US TO SHADOWFALL—NOW! YOUR ARMY IS INCURRING MASS CASUALTIES AND INNOCENT SHADOWFALLERS ARE DYING. ONLY YOUR PRESENCE CAN STOP THIS UNNECESSARY SLAUGHTER. WE HAVE YOUR ADVISOR, MIRAN KECH, AS A CAPTIVE WITH US. PLEASE OPEN YOUR DOOR AND HAVE YOUR MEN LAY DOWN THEIR WEAPONS. THERE IS NO NEED FOR MORE KILLING. I, WAKAN KECH, PROMISE THAT YOU AND THEY WILL NOT BE HARMED. BUT YOU MUST HURRY. PEOPLE ARE DYING AT SHADOWFALL, YOUR PEOPLE AND OURS!"

Wakan repeated the message three more times. Long minutes passed as the ShadowFallers considered what their next move might be if Mother Messinex did not capitulate. "If we just leave her here," Thist said, "she can do no harm. She's at least a day's ride from her palace, a week away from ShadowFall, and she doesn't have access to mirror-men or any other kind of signaling system." He eyed Miran Kech, who nodded his head agreeing with his captor's conclusion. "So we can be back to the battle in an hour and help fight Creesile, while she lurks here in a cave, deciding what to do. I vote we go back and fight!"

Thusk disagreed. "If we can pry her out of here and take her—and this slug, Miran—and put them in front of Creesile, they can call off the invasion immediately. And if Thist's Moon-girl can do her bit, that will be enough to convince anybody. That's more than we three can accomplish, fighting." Both men turned to Wakan.

Wakan Kech said, "Miran, do you think she will come out? Will you ask her yourself? Do you know her mind? For that matter, why did you two ever go to war with ShadowFall?"

The younger Kech replied, almost snarling, "Wakan, you act so innocent. But you have violated so many laws of Motherland that you yourself are now a traitor. You hid godspheres and books and springbows from the inventory at ShadowFall. You failed to obey Mother Messinex's command to surrender them all when Creesile came to collect. You invented a whole suite of new weapons of war, weapons that could only be used against other Sisters, or even the Mother Herself; we knew that, because you kept them secret. What other purpose does secrecy serve if not to war on your neighbors?

"And most importantly, without Rumi Similla, the Mother and I would never have known about this magic airship, this talking god-machine, that you deliberately kept secret. I remind you, all intellectual property in Motherland is Mother's by right, to be developed and apportioned as She sees fit." He spat. "You are a traitor, and our Mother may well serve *you* a ration of deathweed."

Wakan sighed and shook his head. "Miran, Miran. Change is coming to Motherland. You won't be part of it from now on, but you may yet live. Messinex may not be part of it either, if she doesn't come forth and help us, and quickly." He fingered the vial of deathweed in his soft leather pouch and brought it out for his countryman to see. "I will ask you again, my oldest, dearest friend. Will you speak to your Mother and entreat her to cooperate, or must she listen to your screams for the next week?"

Miran blanched but kept silent. Wakan's hideous herb would make him a gibbering idiot in excruciating pain for days. But if he surrendered to Wakan, and Messinex were to win, *her* panoply of tortures could last for a year. He himself had seen that sentence carried out, administered by his own hand, during his service in Three Rivers.

AS MINUTES PASSED, THIST BECAME MORE AND MORE impatient to return to ShadowFall. "So if she opens that door and sends her men out to fight us, what do we do?"

"Good point, twin," Thusk said. "Una, close the door, go invisible."

"As you wish, Thusk." Any sentry observing would see the big green aircraft vanish. Two of them did observe that, then climbed down into the main cavern to report to their Mother.

Aboard Una, Thist said, "There *is* something that might help us get Mother Messinex out of her cave. Let me talk to her about my experience on the Crystal Throne. What that damned chair really is."

At that, Miran Kech exploded in anger. "Sacrilege! You had no right to do that! How dare you! It's a wonder you weren't killed on the spot!" Straining against his ties, red-faced, he spewed saliva as he yelled.

Una then spoke up, uninvited. "Thist, I was scanning

your surroundings during your excursion. When you sat on what you call 'The Crystal Throne,' I detected a quantum communications field that linked with one located in an underground complex of tunnels in the Moon.

"The Crystal Throne is an ancient solid-state artifact that was set up in a network of similar quantum devices at several locations on Earth, the Moon, Mars, and several asteroids. When properly functioning, it enables instantaneous holistic empathic connection between and among its operators at light speed, including transference into avatarobots." The DI gave no explanation of "light speed" but Thist knew that the avatorobots were the mobile Una-like DIs on the Moon, the ones that Mienne had mentioned.

Trying to maintain his composure, a shaken Wakan Kech asked Una, "But, but, the Crystal Throne selects the Mother, and has for millennia. She speaks daily with the goddess from there. Only the chosen are invited to sit on it. How can a mere 'artifact'—which I assume means 'man-made'—have such powers?"

"Wakan, from the scans I performed, I deduce that the original design was established for a certain genetic sequence that was common among humans in those ancient times—almost everyone back then could communicate with it. But my DI subcomponents have evaluated the current situation and conclude that genetic drift over the last thirty thousand years means that the proper operator sequence only exists in a few persons living today. Thist and Thusk are apparently the most closely related to the ancients, genetically."

Thist considered Una's comment and asked, "Una, are the godspheres made the same way as the throne is? It felt the same to the touch as those globes, and its voices sounded the same. A lot like you."

"Thist, yes. What you call 'the Crystal Throne' is contemporaneous with my design and fabrication methods. What you call 'godspheres' were fabricated by the millions, and distributed all over Earth after the initial environmental cataclysm, in hopes of preserving humanity's knowledge. They were a desperate measure by unselfish humans who realized that their civilization was ending and who wished to assist future generations. No one then knew when the new glaciers would retreat, which regions would become deserts, which remnants of the human race might survive. Being solar powered ensured that they would only function aboveground in the open.

"And yes, that same genetic key was part of their function. Only a human being—not an animal, plant, or any inanimate material such as soil or stones—could initiate a godsphere's operation by touch. The quantum communications devices—the chairs—work the same way."

Wakan and the twins could barely believe what they were hearing. The entire mythology of Motherland was based on a *machine*? The Crystal Throne was just an ancient communication system?

But Miran Kech, having listened to Una's explanations of the Crystal Throne's origins and purpose, was sobbing like an infant. Without any other experience with the god-machine that the dark twins had brought to Motherland, with no knowledge of ancient science and technology such as Wakan had been exposed to while dealing with Una, the younger Kech priest was stunned to the depth of his being. Everything he had ever believed in was nonsense! And although he was morally corrupt, having contempt for Wakan and the other nobles, he nonetheless accepted without thinking the system whereby Motherland was ruled; he inherently assumed the integrity and validity of the system of Mother's choosing, and of the natural rights and privileges of royalty. He wanted to exploit that stability for his own benefit, caring little to nothing for anyone else's rights or lives, but to challenge the very foundations of Motherland—that had never occurred to him.

Devastated, he shook away the tears and told the others: "This destroys our Motherland and the need for a Mother. Everything is gone." Speaking softly, he said, "I despise myself for saying this, but if you announce all of this on that loud-voice, I believe that Messinex will surrender to you."

FIVE MINUTES LATER, THE STONE DOOR ROLLED BACK. Standing in the entranceway were fifteen Mothersmen, their weapons on the floor of the cavern, their arms held high in surrender, palms forward. In front of them stood Mother Messinex alone, head bowed, clothed in a magnificent blue godscloth robe, its sheen almost aura-like in the light of the midday sun.

CHAPTER SIXTY-TWO

At the palace, Princess Perneptheranam was meeting with Odel M'ridge and her other defensive commanders. "They are only three kilometers away now, people. For some reason they have stopped, and we are grateful for that. You have killed thousands of them, and our latest attack through the tunnels and in the air took a heavy toll on them. An ordinary commander would have retreated in disarray, but Creesile doesn't care for the lives of his men; he uses them like fodder for oxen. They have kept coming, piling over each other through Wakan's Wire traps, even after Odel here flame-bombed them, and after our catapult fire-stones rolled through them. And after our valiant springbowmen kept torrents of arrows raining down on them, and our bird-riders sliced off legs by the hundreds." She did not mention ShadowFall's casualties; most returned, but no wounded were left alive by Creesile's savages.

"They seemed to have paused momentarily. Maybe our last attack did stun them enough. But delay causes them no problems; they have the resources of all Motherland to draw on, but we only have ShadowFall's people. They still outnumber us in fighting men, and can replace losses, but we can't." Almost sobbing, she said, "And each fallen citizen of ours is a personal loss. How much longer can we keep on fighting a losing battle?"

Rohn, a bird-rider, spoke up through the bloody bandage that covered most of his face, "Princess, we will fight to the end if we must, but it should be in the forests to the north, near the great waterfall, not here." Pointing to the vast wooded area on the table map, he said, "Among the trees, we bird-riders can hide, running out in hit-and-run attacks. Maybe Odel and his flyers can launch from the trees?"

But around the table, the others were shaking their heads. Even then ever-optimistic Odel was crestfallen. Pernie knew he had lost over half of his tri-wing PeoplesLandsers, the small men and women flyers from the far north, to Creesile's archers. For all his eagerness to carry on the resistance from ShadowFall's forest, she also knew that Rohn's bird-warriors had suffered equally. Though they estimated that the invaders were now down to fewer than two thousand soldiers, Creesile had replaced his destroyed catapults; those siege machines were capable of bringing down even the massive stone walls of the Palace with stone and fire.

Pernie had already given orders for noncombatants to flee eastward over the river bridges past the fields, to places where refugee camps had already been set up, kilometers away. They numbered in the many thousands, but defended only by children, the elderly, the infirm, those refuges would not survive long should Creesile occupy the city and the Palace. Already she'd had reports from spies that the invading army was flying the black flag, once the final attack came. That would mean death to herself, her advisors, her commanders, and anyone else caught resisting Creesile's troops. She hoped for herself that death would come in battle, not at the stake fire—*That's my plan!*

Aloud, she asked, "So we have probably only a thousand active fighters now, is that right?"

Rohn and Odel nodded, followed by grim looks from the other commanders. Nobody looked anything but apprehensive. Creesile had two to three times that number, with siege engines and catapults. They were doomed, and knew it. Pernie wondered if those blinking "jewels" some had reported seeing on the Moon's face were an omen, but she had no time to waste on superstition; reality was fearful enough.

Pernie said, "I had hoped that our Wakan Kech and Thist and Thusk, in their magical Una machine, could somehow come to our rescue, whatever it was they were planning to do. But their promised 'three hours' has passed now. I fear that something has happened to them. In any case, we can no longer depend upon them for our salvation.

"As your Princess, I ask you—not order you—to prepare the Palace grounds for siege." From the looks of resignation around the table, her men and women knew that they were being requested to fight to the death, with no possible retreat. "Call in all citizens who wish to aid in our resistance. Those here or outside who wish to flee to the forest or to the east, may do so, without condemnation or shame. But know this: there is no place else in all Motherland where anyone of us will be safe, if we lose. *When* we lose."

With exit bows from all present, the room was shortly empty, save for Odel and Rohn, who remained with the Princess. Each man chose weapons from the armory on the wall, Odel an axe and Rohn a springbow. Pernie knew that they would be her last defenders, should any of them survive the catapult barrage sure to come.

The Princess retired to her quarters, returning in minutes outfitted in blue godscloth and black armor, bearing a springbow, with a quiver of arrows strung across her back. "Men, we fight together, equals in all things." As Odel and Rohn bowed to her, she said, smiling, "No more of that. No more bows, no more 'Princess.' You may even call me 'Pernie' if you wish. We are going to have a new world after today—one way or another!"

THUD! THUD! CRASH! THE PALACE SHOOK, RESOUNDING

cracking here and there as the invaders unleashed their catapulted stones. Pernie, Odel and Rohn retreated from the war council room up into the Princess's chamber, where they found her three handmaids cowering in an inner corner. A blocked and boarded balcony arch had only a small opening, through which the maidens had been watching their impending doom.

"I see you have a far-seer here, ladies," Pernie said, lifting the long tube from the quivering hands of a maiden. "Seeing anything interesting?" Both maids nodded. "I think you should both go down to the war council room and find a weapon. You may have to protect yourselves from that rabble out there." The women ran out of the room and disappeared down the hallway. Pernie whispered to her companions, "And they may prefer to use those weapons on themselves, if Creesile's boys break through."

Fire-bombs exploded in the plaza below, causing fearful death and injuries to ShadowFall defenders with each incoming hit. Pernie said in horror, "Outside the palace, my people have no place to hide. We are surrounded on all sides. Men, both of you, please go down and tell them all to come inside. I don't think our attack tunnels are still open; my soldiers were supposed to collapse them after their attack. Maybe the inner courtyards and dungeons will provide shelter—for a while, at least!" Bowing quickly, Odel and Rohn left to carry out the order.

Within minutes, the palace was filled with hundreds of ShadowFall's remaining defenders, many milling around in the inner courtyard, others stationing themselves at doors and waste-discharge openings. Many wore bloody bandages, some were lying on stretchers.

Pernie winced as each stone-bomb smashed against yet another wall, as each flame-bomb spewed its contents over the plaza and the two remaining catapults. *All of our defenses are gone,* she moaned, *probably fewer than five hundred inside the palace now, another five hundred outside, and Creesile is moving his thousands this way without opposition.*

But hearing some screams from outside, she ran to look through the opening; the sight she saw was of the invaders falling, pinned by arrows. "My springbowers are firing from the roof!" she cried in jubilation. "And I'm going up there to help them!" But as she ran the final light of stairs to take her to the archers' position, a sheet of flame shot past the open doorway; Creesile's catapulters had found the range of the palace roof, and were pelting it with bales of hay and brittle clay balls of fiery liquids. Ignoring the screams, Pernie ran back to her chambers, convinced that she would soon be joining her dead citizens. *But with sword and springbow in hand, Mother damn it! I will never surrender!*

As she rounded the corner to her chamber, she saw Odel M'ridge and bird-rider Rohn waiting, along with a dozen other men and women, each bearing a weapon and looks of determination on their faces. *At least I won't die alone,* she thought, *not with all these brave—and foolish—comrades with me!* Smiling, she raised her springbow and her voice, a feral animal yell that communicated her appreciation more than mere words ever could have.

CHAPTER SIXTY-THREE

"Mienne," Wayer said in a tremulous voice, "what were you doing? You acted so strangely, like you were somebody else?" Her eyes wet from crying, the young girl was almost in a panic. "And who were you talking to? About Motherth and Earth?"

Mienne sat up from her crystal chair, stroking her friend's hair. "Wayer, hon, the strangest thing it was. I was talking with a dark little man named Thist. It was like I was in his body on Motherth"—Wayer's eyes widened in disbelief —"which he called 'Earth,' like we saw in the sims. And somehow he was in my body, here on Moon, which he called 'The Moon.'"

"But, how, why?"

"Wayer, this chair and his bigger chair up there," Mienne said, pointing at the disc-image of Motherth/Earth on the display dome, "were used by the ancients to communicate with each other. And they still work, after a fashion." Shivering at the sensuous memory of that experience, she didn't tell her friend that she was anxious to do it again, to find out more about the *male*-ness of that body. *Later,* she thought. *There will be time for that, later.* Right now, she wanted to try to carry out that Thist's wishes about controlling the lights of the domed cities. *In about an hour, he said. I wonder why?*

"And when that Thist was in my body, here in

Control Room, he was able to use these lighted places to, to, *control* the lights of the domes on Moon." Walking over to an array of lighted panels and screens, she began stroking one after the other. *I wonder what other controls the ancients provided?*

As Wayer sat in silence, watching her tall, strange friend making weird gestures over lighted panels, she wondered if she would ever comprehend how the ancients or the Creator Herself had used this Control Room. It was like the fanciful stories Mienne used to tell, about unknown places and people and things. But it was real, and she was in it!

"Wayer!" Mienne shouted. "Look at this image! Isn't that the Resource Tube?"

Following her friend's pointing finger, she saw on a faceted display screen a miniature Eternal Machine, and two figures crawling around on it. "Isn't that Keesh, the tunneler, and Ledd?"

"Mienne," Wayer said, "they are so small; are you sure it's them and not little toys of some kind?"

"Wayer, don't be silly. The image is shrunken, not the men. Just like those pictures of Sun and Motherth we watched, they were shrunken, too. They can't be shown in their real size."

The armless girl couldn't point, but inclined her head toward the screen. "So we can see them, but only as tiny people? That's funny."

Mienne asked, "I wonder if we can hear them as well as see them?" At once, the picture image produced audible sounds, stating "You may adjust the level by simple voice commands."

Mienne jumped back from the display panel in surprise, but understood at once: *This is just another talking machine. Get used to it!* Then she said, "Can Keesh and Ledd see me, hear me, too?" If that were possible, a capability she had never even imagined, she could communicate with her rescuer, her *friend*, across the kilometers of distance between them. *Maybe even bring him here?*

"Keesh!" she shouted at the image, smiling with

delight when the tiny figure of the man turned to look directly at her. *Can he see me?* she wondered. "Can you see me?" she asked.

To no great surprise, the image of Keesh responded. "Mienne? Your image is on a display screen above my office here in Resource Tube. How did—how are you —*where* are you?" By this time, the tiny figure of Ledd had joined Jolan, both men staring up from Mienne's screen.

"I am in Control Room, way up inside hallways and elevators leading from the Hall of Whispers," she answered. "You have to come up here and see. The ancients left us some marvelous machines. One of them lets us see and talk to each other, like we are doing right here, right now. Have you ever heard of such a thing?"

The engineers put their heads together, talking so low that Mienne couldn't hear their conversation. Then Jolan turned back to the image and said, "Mienne, if you will give us directions, we will come to you. This could be the most fantastic development in the history of Community."

Looking at the three-dimensional maps nearest her, Mienne gave Keesh detailed instructions. "We will meet you part way here, down inside the Hall of Whispers. You won't believe what all you're going to see." After the screen went dark, she added "Or what you are going to hear" to Wayer, who just laughed. "Everything you think you know about Community and its history is wrong."

CHAPTER SIXTY-FOUR

"Thist," Mother Messinex said, once she had reluctantly boarded Una, "so this is the god-machine I heard about from Rumi Similla?" Looking around inside, she saw Miran Kech strapped to one small cabin seat, his legs stretched out awkwardly in front of him, with Wakan Kech and Thusk looking on as she stood in amazement at the digital display screens.

"Yes, Mother Messinex," Thist replied. "Please sit in this other seat. I am sorry, but we resized them for our people, not you Motherlanders." Messinex sat in the low seat as gracefully as possible, curling her legs up under the chair, unlike Miran's uncomfortable sprawled position.

"Thist," Messinex said, her voice no longer in a command tone, but rather plaintive, it seemed to her small audience, "I surrendered myself to you because of what you said about the Crystal Throne. What did it say that made you think it was not a message from the ancient goddesses, but just a machine? If only a machine, then why was *I* chosen? Why was *any* Mother ever chosen, if not by the goddesses?"

Thist spoke softly, as if with respect for the fallen Mother, but actually out of pity for her situation. "I myself sat on the Crystal Throne." Messinex opened her mouth to protest, thought better of it. She knew defeat, but having anybody else sitting on the holiest place in

Motherland was still shocking. Frowning, she nodded as Thist continued. "I spoke to a girl, Mienne, who lives on the Moon. Una was able to 'scan' the throne, which means to determine how it operates and how it was constructed. Una can tell you better than I."

Her eyes wide open in disbelief, Messinex said, "You mean, this god-machine *talks*, as well as flies? What kind of magic did the ancient gods use?"

Wakan spoke. "Messinex, it was not magic. The ancients were no more magical than your engineers who build bridges or your stonemasons who build palaces. It was just the accumulated and advanced knowledge of the natural world they had, and knew how to use. Una, can you explain, please?"

Una then spoke. "Messinex, I am called 'Una.' I am a Developing Intelligence program that is a collective among numerous quantum computers." Messinex closed her eyes tightly, shaking her head at the voice emanating from the figure of a woman on the front video screen. Thist was afraid the Mother might pass out from shock, and Wakan put his arm around her to comfort her.

"I was fabricated about thirty thousand years ago by human engineers, and originally served as a scouting and survey aircraft for the United North American Glacial Survey, after the solar cataclysm that initiated the last ice age. I have survived this long because most of my constituent components are of nanotech and quantum-level constructions that do not age or are self-repairing.

"My crew died back then in a crash far north of here. I was encased in the glacial ice until Thusk and others saw to my removal last year. Since then I have transported Thusk, Thist, and many others between The People's Lands and your own Motherland, with stops in God's Country." Messinex had opened her eyes by then, but seemed puzzled by the names of the lands Una mentioned. Una provided a digital map on the front screen, indicating the countries so designated, with moving red lines showing the trips back and forth.

"After scanning and accessing thousands of

'godspheres' and then the 'Crystal Throne,' my collective quantum computers have merged to produce what we feel—*I* feel—is an intelligent personality."

Messinex considered Una's monologue, then asked, "Why do you say the Crystal Throne is a *device*, and not a spiritual way to contact the goddesses of Motherland?"

Una said, "To my knowledge there are no such entities as goddesses. My scans showed only a quantum holistic empathetic communication system, enabling the most intimate of communication between humans. I have detected other functional installations on your Moon, on Mars, and several asteroids. And others now buried or otherwise inaccessible, here on Earth."

Miran Kech was sobbing now, in sympathy with what he was seeing in Messinex's response. "Oh, Mother Messinex, I don't know how to, to, absorb all of this information. I can't believe that our beloved Motherland is founded on a, a, *machine,* no matter how ancient!"

But Messinex was thinking over her options. She had little problem with the revelations: if this incredible machine she was sitting in could fly, and talk, then why should she not believe the Crystal Throne was not another machine, just one that was not working properly? *All those years my Lordess Mother wasted, on a damned* machine! In a sudden epiphany, she thought, *And all the* centuries *wasted by all the Mothers before her! Our entire history is false! And to think I ran off poor little Thist because he dared discover some of our true stories! And I caused a deadly war, a war against ShadowFall.*

Crestfallen, Messinex turned to Wakan Kech and asked, "Wakan, what do I do now? What do you want? To depose me? Execute me? What? It seems I have no more power to command anyone, or won't, once you tell the world what this Una says. Even if your machine is lying, it is enough to destroy me and the Motherhood, and our history, our whole country." Becoming diffident, she said, "And you, Thist, Thusk, what do *you* want from all of this? Do you think if your story is believed, it will bring anything but chaos and war among the Sisterdoms? Do you have any idea how difficult being Mother is? Trying to keep peace in Motherland?"

Una spoke up, uninvited. "Messinex, my analysis of the scans of the Crystal Throne indicates that your genetic pattern is not a perfect match to the original design of the communication system. No human alive today has precisely the same DNA as the ancients. Thist and Thusk are the closest matches of any persons I have scanned. Extensive use of the 'Crystal Throne' for noncompliant users will bring about adverse cerebral changes resulting in delusions, paranoia, schizophrenia, and early death by stroke. I advise you to discontinue accessing it."

Wakan spoke up quickly. "Messinex, have you noticed any difference in your health, your behavior, since becoming Mother and sitting on that throne?"

Messinex nodded. "Yes, almost immediately; migraines, flashes of anger, irrational thoughts. All of that. When I was just Princess, I believed I was well-adjusted." She frowned. "And I was happy."

"And so you were," Wakan said, "and Pernie loved you above all her other Sisters."

"Our Lordess Mother, she suffered years of afflictions," Messinex said with a sob. "She was a victim of that horrible chair."

Wakan was astonished; at the Game last year he had seen how much the Lordess Mother had aged in only a few years, and her volatility and temperament were legendary all her life. "So that damned throne brought down all the horror and brutality upon innocents," he said in anger. "Damn those ancients!"

Thusk held up a finger of caution. "Wakan," he said, "our Una here was built by those same ancients, so they were not all bad."

Thist then spoke up. "People, I have something to show you, what I learned from that Mienne girl on the Moon. She has control of ancient *technology* up there. Una, please make your walls transparent so that we can see the Moon from here. Then make contact with her."

Thist pointed out the full Moon just rising above the eastern horizon; with a clear sky, it shone like a pale mottled disk. He thought, *Back home, through the Misty Sky, she was just a white blur above the clouds. We called her "The Wen of the Mist," but here in the Warm Lands, she's a clear, magnificent sight.* The dim-colored pinpoints of light across Her surface were especially so. But now he knew they were huge domes, some still living cities, others abandoned. *But key to my plans, now. Don't fail me, Mienne!*

Una spoke. *"It is done, Thist. Communication is established."*

Thist said, "Mienne, I am ready here on Earth. Are you ready on the Moon?"

The answer came three seconds later, provided through an image of Mienne on Una's front screen. Thist smiled as he viewed the girl's whole body. *She looks different from the outside*, he thought. *Pretty and tall it seems, but still a youngster.*

Mienne said, "Thist. I know which controls to activate, which domes to light up and which to make dark. Starting—now!"

As the occupants of Una watched, all but one in disbelief, the necklace of lights across the surface of the Moon began to flash off and on, continuing for several seconds. Then all returned to their eternal lit states. All eyes turned to Thist, all mouths agape.

"How did I do that?" he answered with a broad grin. "That Mienne, the girl on the Moon, has ancient equipment to control the illumination of those lights up there. Those lights are cities, domed cities, each of them at least as large as Mother's City. Covered in transparent material like our godspheres." Holding out his hands as if in a blessing, he said, "There is no magic, only technology!" From the looks on his companions' faces, he could tell that they were not convinced.

But Thist grew serious. "We have to forget about the ancients and the Moon for the moment; there is still a war on at ShadowFall. We came down here hours ago to get Mother Messinex to stop it, and we have taken entirely too long.

"With the Mother here now, and with what we can make happen on the face of the Moon, we have two powerful weapons. So I say we find General Creesile and force the issue." Looking warily at both Messinex and Miran Kech, he added, "You two *will* stop the invasion. And you *will* pay reparations for the damage and death you have inflicted upon ShadowFall." Thusk saw then that his twin had indeed studied some of Una's videos of the wars of the ancients; he never would have thought of payment for war damages himself, but it *was* a fair concept.

Before Messinex or Miran Kech could object, Thusk said, "Una, top speed. Find the General, Creesile, if you can. Otherwise, take us straight to Pernie's palace."

"As you wish, Thusk," and they were off. Thusk kept the walls opaque; he did not want his prisoners, Messinex and Miran, to learn anything more about Una's capabilities. *As Sire Thess always said, knowledge is power, especially if you're the only one who has it.*

CHAPTER SIXTY-FIVE

I n recurring waves of pain, General Creesile kept going in and out of consciousness, his amputated stub of a leg throbbing again, hurting so much that rational thought was nearly impossible. Summoning the medic to his command tent again, he ordered the most potent mixture of soothing herbs available. At the doctor's hesitation, he said, "I've got a war to finish, medic. Today! So drug me up to stop this agony, and I can give the final orders to smash these damned rebels!"

The medic opened his black bag and pulled out a cup of thick, smelly, dark liquid. "Sir, I readied this for you, thinking you would request it. Now this first cupful will ease the pain for a few hours. But any more than that will knock you out, for at least another day. I didn't administer it during the amputation because it can affect your body in harmful ways. It is only for the direst of emergencies. And I must insist that later tonight you soak your wounded leg in salts, to prevent any infection, to begin the healing process." The man saluted, bowed, and backed out of Creesile's command tent.

The General sat the cup aside, sipping only a small amount. He needed to stem the pain, but could not afford to sleep; he planned for this afternoon, at the latest, to be the finale of his entire campaign. Though woozy, by force of will he was able to open the field wardrobe cabinet and don his finest white godscloth raiment, covering it with a golden armored vest, matching crested helmet, and golden greaves. Stuffing a white pants leg with towels, he camouflaged his stub of a leg. But standing on it, even with a crutch, was almost unbearable. *But this will be my formal dress for my day of victory! Too bad I'm hurting like a son of a bitch. And unfortunately, I'm stuck with this damned crutch!!*

At once, a young officer barged in, his face bloody, his helmet dented and dirty. "Sir, excuse me, but we are bringing up the catapults now, to plan for the final barrage. Less than two klicks away. I thought you'd like to witness it." Creesile could tell from the awed expression that the officer was impressed by his golden gear. *Good! That's what I want!*

"Get my carriage, son," the General said, through a red haze of pain that was only beginning to subside as the medic's herb began its work. "You're right; I wouldn't miss this, the end of our campaign."

Minutes later, the potion having taken effect and the stump of his missing leg no longer complaining so loudly, Creesile felt the adrenaline rush, the flush of victory. As his two-horse carriage moved to the front lines, in his golden glory he rode alongside of hundreds of soldiers marching northward, many carrying unlit torches that would later give them light to see their way through to victory in the battle to come, if it lasted until dark. *I hope this ends before nightfall, but I'm glad they are planning ahead.* Receiving their enthusiastic salutes and cheers, he returned the greetings with a smile and a raised clenched fist. The carriage passed four massive wooden catapult machines being towed by teams of oxen, some having active carpenters still aboard them, making last-minute repairs and adjustments. The General's driver said that at the front, several of the siege weapons were already in place, their stone payloads and fire-bombs being stacked behind them and ready to begin the assault.

Good, he thought, *these machines will make short work of Pernie's palace. And while I'm at it, they can smash that damned ShadowFall sculpture. Every remnant of her reign will be erased. And as for her, herself, well, I have other plans!*

THE YOUNG OFFICER DRIVING CREESILE'S CARRIAGE pulled the team to a halt. The General accepted his arm and descended from the vehicle, taking a padded crutch for walking over to a large, hastily erected white canvas command tent. Creesile thought that the sight of their commander, suffering his own war injury, would further instill loyalty—*He's one of us! Wounded in battle!* In the distance, in the clear air less than two kilometers away, stood Pernie's palace, now a symbol of the rebellious Sisterdom. In between the front and the Palace was the ruined city itself—blocks and blocks of smoking stone-brick buildings and mud-brick homes, many of which were still ablaze, their walls standing as mute, blackened shells. Creesile breathed in the sweet odors of death and smoke, to him the essence of victory, like incense burners on a massive scale. Around the distant Palace grounds, he could make out the small figures that were the massed lines of the last ShadowFall troops, their banners still aloft as if in defiance of their impending doom. Atop the palace some figures were moving, no doubt the cursed springbowmen, maybe some of those damned tri-wing flyers. At this distance he couldn't tell whether any of the monkey-men or their birds were still alive.

To the troops making way as he painfully hobbled toward the very front of the line, Creesile shouted, "Be sure to kill all of those little monkeys and their stupid birds. Our dogs can have the monkey-meat, and I hear those birds taste pretty good!" Roars and cheers erupted and the men began a chant: "*Cree*-sile! *Cree*-sile! *Cree*-sile!" Smiling at the reception and the morale of his army, he hobbled off to sit in a throne-like elevated chair outside the white tent, there to command and to watch the downfall of his enemy. He was enjoying the afternoon sunlight, its bright rays illuminating his shining golden armor and crested helmet

A few officers were pointing at the pale risen moon and talking excitedly about something, but Creesile paid no attention. *What is important is the here and now. Who cares what the gods do up there? Can't affect me!* Smiling, he ordered the attack.

"FIRE! FIRE! FIRE!" THE SHOUTED COMMANDS ECHOED across the vanguard as all six of Creesile's catapults erupted at once, throwing round stones and casks of flammable liquids into the ranks of ShadowFall's soldiers and at the palace walls. Safely outside the range of the dreaded springbows, the General's troops cheered and jeered at their adversaries as those payloads hit, flames splaying over the targets, Palace stonework crumbling.

In answer, ShadowFall's three remaining catapults returned fire, the first volley falling short, spraying fire around the open field to no effect. Creesile's army jeered once again, adding obscene insults to their chants. But faster than he would have believed possible, Creesile watched in horror as another round of fiery loads arced up into the sky, coming down—*at him!* Grabbed quickly by his carriage driver, he was removed from ground zero just in time, barely escaping with his life. His crutch and chair were aflame, as the young officer pulled Creesile to his feet. "Sir, you've got to get farther back; it's too dangerous for you here!" The general nodded, meekly accompanying his officer back behind the line of catapults, hobbling on his crutch. A chair appeared out of nowhere, and Creesile sat, furious.

After an hour of continuous back and forth between the catapult weapons of both sides, the city surrounding Pernie's Palace was nothing but smoking ruins, but the royal residence still stood. Anxious to finish the day's business well before the night set in, Creesile decided it was time for a final massed assault. Knowing that his enemy was limited in troops, he dispersed his men to surround the palace, hemming it in at a klick's distance all around. This produced a line only one soldier deep, but also only a meter or two apart at most, providing overlaying coverage one man to the next. He figured that the ShadowFall troops wouldn't try to break through his line. "Where would they go?" he asked his commanders, pointing to a map sketched in the dirt. "They stay here, they die *here*. They break out, they die *there*."

Around this line of soldiers he massed one group of three hundred fighters who kept moving as a group around the circumference of their stationary comrades, as if prodding the defenses for a weak point. Creesile knew that the enemy inside his ring would have to stay in motion, too, to counteract any potential assault at a given point. After an hour of that feinting action, well before dark, he would retire the first mass of soldiers for a rest, and bring in another equally large group to keep up the stress on his adversaries. "I could do this all night long," he said, "but before dark the ShadowFallers will be worn out and scared to death; then we will use every man and attack from all directions, closing the circle, tightening the noose!" In his mind he could already see the Princess at his feet, begging for mercy. He had plans for what that mercy would be; his victory would be consummated—on Pernie's bed!

This attack would be near perfect, he thought. *If only my damned leg would cooperate!*

CHAPTER SIXTY-SIX

"We're here, everybody," Thusk said, as the forward video screen showed the battleground below them. Having never seen any digital displays, Messinex gasped at the sight of ShadowFall from a height of three hundred meters, the hundreds of tiny figures of defenders, the thousands of Creesile's fighters —*her* fighters!—like disturbed anthills in motion, the catapults children's toys, throwing pebbles and blazing embers at each other. But everyone aboard Una realized that those miniatures were real soldiers, real people, and they were really dying as they, the watchers, looked on the butchery below like gods.

"My Mother," Messinex said, "it's a slaughter down there. What can we do—can *I* do—to stop it?"

Before she drew another breath, Miran Kech shouted, "Messinex! Do *nothing*! Can't you *see*? Your troops down there, Creesile's army, they are *winning*! In a few minutes, ShadowFall is *doomed*!" With a snarl he turned toward Wakan Kech. "Wakan, I don't care what your monkey-men can do on the Moon, it doesn't help them down here. Your Princess has lost, you can look below; it's just a matter of minutes! You had best set this contrivance of yours down now, and let us talk with General Creesile. Perhaps he will cease the assault and spare your precious Princess Pernie. Maybe even you and your monkey-men here! But do it now!"

Enraged, Thist slapped the seated Mira Kech across the face. "You bastard! You caused this war, all this death and destruction! I'm losing comrades down there right now. I've already lost bird-riders and other countrymen to Creesile's army," he shouted, "and now you want Creesile to kill the rest! No more!" Turning toward the female figure on the forward screen he shouted, "Una, take us up, right above the golden general down there! Then open the door!"

In shock, Wakan Kech started to object, then stepped back as a furious Thist untied Miran from his cabin seat, jerking him out and pushing him toward the opening door on his knees, his hands still tied behind his back. As Messinex sat petrified in horror, Miran looked back pleadingly at Thusk and Wakan Kech, who shook their heads and turned away.

Thist then spoke to Miran in an even tone, without emotion. "Miran Kech, by my authority as a commander in this active war zone, I find you guilty of treason during battle, punishable by death." With a stiff kick, he ejected the Kech priest out through the door and watched him fall, screaming, toward the distant ground.

ABOVE THE TUMULT OF THE ONGOING BATTLE, GENERAL Creesile heard a scream in the sky above him. Looking up, he saw a dark figure coming out of the near dark—a *man!*—twisting and turning, screeching. With a *thud!* the falling man hit face-first just three meters away, and was silent. Blood immediately puddled all around the body as an injured soldier, moaning over his broken leg, crawled out from under the fallen corpse. Creesile ordered the dead man turned over to see his face. Had the poor man been catapulted from Pernie's palace? Surely even Wakan Kech wasn't so barbaric as to do that!

But when he saw the mutilated face, still recognizable as Miran Kech's, he bent over and vomited, spewing the ground with the acrid contents of his midday meal. Then he passed out.

OVERHEAD, THUSK HAD UNA'S CAMERA ZOOM IN ON the falling Miran and the aftermath of his death. With some satisfaction, Thist smiled evilly. "That monster died faster than he should have, but he is gone from us at last."

Wakan nodded slowly. "Too ambitious, too vile. Power will do that." Turning to Messinex, he said, "And you, Messinex, you admit that it was Miran who pushed you to invade ShadowFall, to start this war?"

Messinex dropped her head in shame. "Yes, I admit my own guilt, but Miran instigated it. And I think the times on the Crystal Throne affected me badly, too, if that is any defense." Wakan shrugged. He had no idea what would happen to her, but right now he just wanted the deadly conflict below to stop.

As they all watched the scene below, General Creesile was being brought back to consciousness by a medic with smelling salts. A flurry of activity soon obscured the site as Miran's body was covered by a field blanket and hurried away to the medic's tent.

A RECOVERED GENERAL CREESILE, SUPPORTED BY ONE crutch, stood in the medic's tent over the body of Miran Kech, his commanders surrounding the table. "Sir, did they catapult him over here? We thought they only shot stones and flame-bombs."

But Creesile was not thinking of how Miran had arrived, but what it meant. *Did he get to ShadowFall ahead of us of my scouts and army? Did they vault him over to me as a sign? A gesture? A threat? Does Mother Messinex know he's here? Or that he's dead?* With Pernie's Palace almost within his grasp, mere hours from now, another thought crossed his mind: *Does this affect the last orders I received?* And followed by, *Will I even obey any other orders? Should I? I have an army here with me now, loyal men, tough soldiers who have lost comrades in this battle. I can share the spoils and the land with them, and stay and declare my own domain here—'WaterFall,' if I like. Or simply 'Creesile.' And after a while, we can expand back down into Motherland. Those weak little princesses are no match for my loyal and bloodthirsty troops.*

Thrilled by the persistent vision, Creesile nonetheless first had to figure out how and why the Mother's High Priest was now just so much minced meat on the medic's operating table at the moment. Then he heard a voice like thunder outside the tent, followed by the shouting of his troops, and he hobbled outside to see for himself.

"General Creesile," the louder-than-possible voice announced from the sky, being heard for kilometers in all directions, "the traitor Miran Kech has been executed and delivered to you by air. Mother Messinex is aboard this aircraft. She orders you to cease all aggressive operations and fall back immediately."

Creesile had hoped for a moment like this—that damned flying machine was near again; *where* he couldn't tell, but somewhere overhead and near. *Miran didn't get smashed up like that just by falling a few meters,* he figured. Nodding to a nearby young officer, he uttered a prepared code word and the man ran off. As he hobbled outside, the general thought with satisfaction, *At last I'll show that damned flying machine and its monkey-men what a* real *warrior can do!*

Looking up at the clear sky and shaking his fist, Creesile shouted, "Whoever you are, wherever you are, you have just murdered Mother Messinex's High Priest. I insist that you show yourself and come here to be arrested for murder—and *treason!*" Turning around, he could see his special catapult being brought into position. If that green thing showed itself again, his crew would shoot it down. Or so he planned. Around him, his troops were aiming their spears and bows at the sky.

A minute passed with no answer from above. "Coward!" The General yelled. "Kill a priest and toss him like a rag doll? Come down here and show yourself. Like a man!" Creesile could tell that his men were getting nervous; they had all seen the god-machine dropping rocks on their barges, and shouting at them from the sky, but it had not killed anybody back then, and he'd made sure that reassuring message had been instilled in all of them. Most of them had not reacted too badly even when the machine flew over them at the Iron Gate, shouting loud, but now—The Mother's own High Priest? If *he* wasn't safe, then who was?

But the forward-thinking General had prepared a surprise for his own defense. After the first flyover of the rock-dropping green beast at Lake Roos, he had provided for a return encounter, instructing his now-deceased Chief Engineer Dzitchil to build not only the large catapults for shooting at the god-machine—*and they worked beautifully at ShadowFall's border, but the crews couldn't see the damned thing in time!*—but also a small, special-purpose version for rapid setup and operation. "I want it to be able to swivel all around, three hundred and sixty degrees, and vertically, one hundred and eighty. Make it small enough to be pulled and operated by two men, and camouflage it so it doesn't appear to be what it is—a god-machine killer." Within a week, the elderly engineer had delivered magnificently; the spear-launch mechanism was mounted on two wheels and pulled like a handcart. In use, its wheels would quickly fold under the chassis to provide a stable platform for the two hand-cranked swivels and the tightening winch for the massive compound bow. Because Creesile had heard that Rumi Similla talk about the flying giant vegetable being able to tell when godsmetal arrows were near, on a hunch he had an iron cover box built to encase the spears until they were ready to launch,

And today's that day! he thought, his special catapult

crew swiveling their machine around, up and down, hoping to take the shot, should the flying green thing appear. But as more minutes passed without it showing itself, they finally relaxed. The General himself hobbled angrily back into the medic's tent to see if Miran's corpse carried any kind of message attached to it, something he himself would have done. Shouting out to his commanders as he went inside, he said, "Continue the siege! Prepare for the final assault! We don't worry about invisible green vegetables in the sky!" But the battleground stayed silent as his troops continued to wonder about what had just happened.

Creesile eased back out of the tent on his makeshift crutch, to order his men once again to keep fighting; but from the front line he heard a hushing noise, a quietness setting in, like a tide of silence. There, as the soldiers drew back and formed straight lines, in the resulting corridor walked a tall, silver-haired young woman in resplendent blue godscloth, a person whose portrait poster adorned tens of thousands of walls in Motherland, one recognized by all—Mother Messinex, the Mother. As his men opened a wider path for her, in the distance some fifty meters behind her Creesile saw that Una-thing on the ground, the cursed flying god-machine now made visible in all its obscene green glory. Even the black crystal on its top was open, he could tell, with that white man-thing and its big black eyes turning in his direction. Nervously, he turned and nodded at his catapult crew to make ready; they lowered the launcher and began opening the iron box, loading the killer spear.

A tall dark man in red robes walked beside Messinex. In anger, Creesile recognized his enemy Wakan Kech, and stared in disgust at the tiny dark figures bearing springbows who walked beside him. *Wakan's monkey men?* What was the strange situation unfolding in front of him? Obviously, Mother did not appear to be a captive. Had she persuaded Pernie's allies to betray the Princess? Conflicting thoughts ran through his mind as the procession approached. Around them all, every soldier was at quiet attention, bowing their heads; most had never seen any Mother in the flesh, and to them this was a religious moment for the ages. Creesile even momentarily felt himself preening as well: though surprised, he was gratified to see the Mother present to witness his triumph. He was particularly happy that he had chosen to wear his highly polished golden gear today—crested helmet, breastplate, greaves, bracelets, *everything!*—on the verge of victory.

With a thousand eyes on her, Mother Messinex strode with dignity through the widening gap of saluting and bowing soldiers, right up to within a meter of the face of an astonished General Creesile. Bowing to his Mother, Creesile said nervously, "Mother Messinex. I, I, had no, no, idea that you were anywhere nearby. I welcome you to the victory at hand." Waving an arm toward Pernie's palace, he spoke loudly, "Today, I give you ShadowFall!"

Mother Messinex stiffened. Opening her arms wide in what Creesile at first took to be a gesture of respect, she said, loud enough for the nearest soldiers to hear, "I want everyone to hear my voice." Instantly, silence settled on the scene. Pointing to the risen moon, Messinex shouted, "Everyone, look at the Moon." Behind her, unseen, Thist made a motion that Una's sensors recognized as a command to relay to Mienne on the Moon.

As hundreds of soldiers looked upward, they witnessed an unbelievable sight: the colorful necklace of the Moon flashing on and off as if commanded by the Mother. The few flutters of those lights that they had seen an hour before could have been just an anomaly of the weather, but this, this *demonstration*, it was repeated, purposeful. Every witness thought, *The Mother controls the Moon! What power She has!*

"Behold, I have engaged the goddess of the Moon, to proudly display Her necklace, power that I alone now command, to stop this illegal war." At that, the gasps of the army were louder than their war-shouts had been just minutes before. In awe and fear, they dropped their weapons and fell to their knees, bowing in Mother's direction.

Messinex continued her shouted commands. "General Creesile, you are dismissed for treason! Second-in-command, you are now promoted! Arrest General Creesile!" A flurry of activity among the general's staff standing behind him produced a grizzled officer, a colonel who introduced himself as Treegu, who bowed and saluted Messinex, at the same time bringing forth three soldiers who immediately seized the uncomprehending General.

"Commander Treegu," Messinex said loudly, "you are to stop all aggressive activity against ShadowFall immediately, and prepare to leave this territory! At once! And leave all your weapons behind." The colonel gulped, but bowed and turned to give the unexpected orders to his troops now standing bewildered, alternately staring at the spectacle of lights flashing across the face of the Moon, then at the unbelievable scene of their Mother sacking their commander.

In total shock, General Creesile staggered backward, loosening his captors' grips. Turning to his catapult crew, he nodded. *"Fire!"* he croaked, before falling forward. Not fully comprehending the sudden change in commanders, but used to obeying their general's orders immediately and without question, the two men launched the borophene spear, already aimed, directly at the middle of the Una machine, some fifty meters distant.

The twins and Wakan Kech watched in horror as the spear sprang from its thrower, but in that first second they could not move fast enough to react. Mother Messinex, her arms still open wide, caught the borophene-tipped projectile square in her chest as it ripped out her heart and severed her spine, spewing blood and tissue in a fountain behind her, dragging her bloody godscloth robes with it through her body, continuing its flat trajectory toward the big green flying machine. The Mother's ruined body tumbled backward, a look of surprise on her open eyes, coming to rest faceup, a six-inch hole in her chest gushing blood. She was gone.

Wakan Kech grunted a noise, stumbling in shock, falling on his left side; his right arm, with which he had been pressing Messinex forward, was half gone, severed at the elbow. Immediately he tried to staunch the blood flow with his good hand as Thist and Thusk ran to help him.

When the iron cover was removed, uncovering the deadly weapon, Una's sensors had instantly detected its presence, quickly lifting the craft up three meters in a fraction of a second. After passing through Messinex and Wakan's arm, the spear intended for Una passed underneath the god-machine, traversing another hundred meters before skidding to a stop in the no-man's-land between the opposing forces. Creesile's assembled troops reacted, drawing swords, hefting spears as if ready to attack. But who? What? The catapult crew, realizing in horror what they had just done, were running as fast as they could back through the camp.

The new commander, Colonel Treegu, having instantly drawn his own sabre, was now shouting out an order. "All troops, stand down! Drop your weapons. Seize Creesile here and tie him in chains this time." Shading his eyes to look back through the camp's array of men and weapons, he added, "And bring me those two who killed our Mother. Alive!"

CHAPTER SIXTY-SEVEN

"What's happening out there? What do you see?" Princess Pernie was impatient, demanding. Suddenly, a voice as loud as thunder spoke, but the words were muffled by the window boards. Odel had positioned a far-seer tube through the observation hole to investigate the sudden lack of forward movement of the invading Creesile army. "What was that shout?' Pernie asked again. "And why have they stopped the attack?"

The tri-wing flyer turned with eyes wide, jaw agape. "Princess, the Una machine has just appeared in front of the enemy lines. People are walking out of it, toward…"

"Let me see that!" Pernie growled, taking the long tube from the big man. After adjusting her own eyesight to accommodate the view, she cried, "Oh, that's Wakan! And the two little warriors, Thist and Thusk! Is that… Messinex? She is here? Yes, it is she. They are walking toward…is that General Creesile in golden armor and crested helmet? Yes it is!" She turned to the dozen last-ditch defenders in the room. "I think they may have saved us after all!"

"Very good, ma'am," Odel said in his hill-country accent, a big grin splitting his face. "Those boys can do wonders, I always said." Jumping up and down in a wild dance, bird-rider Rohn let out an ululation that Pernie had never heard before. The other people, large and small, simply sighed and smiled, hoping the battle was over, thankful that they had survived. So far!

Pernie grabbed a pike from the weapons wall and began prying off the protective layer of wood from the balcony arch. "Help me take off these boards and see daylight once again." With the help of the others, the balcony archway was clear within a minute, the smells of blood and battle, of dust and death, now rolling in like an unwelcome fog. But during that minute of clearing the archway, something had happened.

As Pernie and her companions looked on in puzzlement from the balcony, they saw that the front lines of Creesile's army had begun melting away, dropping their swords and spears and other hand weapons, slowly trudging back southward. Remaining in the center of what had been the battlefield were the god-machine Una, and farther away, a cluster of people doing something in the center in front of a large field tent. Suddenly, Creesile, still in his golden armor, was being hustled away by some black-leather-armored men, the General obviously in custody.

"But what is all that?" Pernie asked. "Dare we go and see? Is the battle over?"

"I say we go see, Princess," Odel said, holding up his springbow; Rohn smiled, holding up his battle axe. The others cheered and made way for their Princess.

Outside the Palace, several hundred of Pernie's defenders, now leaving their refuge after seeing the invaders departing, met her with cheers, waving their weapons in celebration. "I don't know what has happened over there," she said, pointing toward the diminishing enemy camp, "but I want to go see. Who's with me?" Holding her springbow high, she led those hundreds and more in an armed procession toward Una and whatever lay beyond. In the onset of twilight they saw only ruined buildings and homes now reduced to smoldering walls, the interiors smoking and reeking of burnt flesh; the palace, though scorched black in places, showed no obvious open flames. In her heart, Pernie was in anguish as she walked through the devastation of the city, for the loss of the lives of her, her, *citizens, they are now*, she thought, *not subjects, but equals.* Seeing the clusters of the dead scattered around, some still inside burning homes, the victims of Creesile's catapulted fireballs, she mused, *Equal in death, too.*

As ShadowFall's defenders arrived at what had been Creesile's vanguard line, they were met by Thusk and a tall, wrinkled Mothersman officer wearing the bird insignia of colonel. Farther back at a field tent, other soldiers and officers were milling around, their weapons at their feet, as if uncertain of their status. The older man bowed and offered his unsheathed sword to the Princess with both hands.

"What is this, Colonel—?"

"Treegu, ma'am," he responded, coming up from his deep bow. "By orders of..." He hesitated. "...Mother Messinex, we have ended this invasion, this war, and are returning to Mother's City. General Creesile has been arrested for treason."

"Thusk," Pernie said, "I don't see Mother Messinex here, or Wakan. Or Thist. Where are they?" Colonel Treegu and Thusk both pointed back toward the large tent.

"*Oh, no!* Not *all* of them! Are they—?" Pernie ran to the tent, throwing open the flap. Inside lay Wakan Kech on the medic's operating table, his right arm severed above the elbow, blood everywhere. Alongside him lay a body, covered by thick tent material. *That's too large to be Thist, is it—?* "Messinex! My sister!" she screamed, falling to her knees, sobbing. "What has happened here? She's not supposed to die!" Standing back up, gaining her composure, she wiped away tears and whimpered, "I loved her. Of all my Sisters, I loved her. Oh, how could anybody do this?"

Thist was suddenly at her side, his tunic covered in blood, reaching up to put an arm around her waist. "Princess, Messinex was murdered by order of the former general, Creesile. He wanted to kill Una, I think, but our Mother was directly in the path of the big spear. She died instantly."

Walking over to where the medic was working on Wakan, Thist continued, "And it caught Wakan in the right elbow, taking off his arm below it. The medic says he won't die but will be a long time in recovering." Thist wondered if Princess Pernie had any idea of what it was like to have part of your body cut off. His left foot —*Lost in the stupid Motherland Game—for* you! he thought, bitter yet at the memory—still pained him from time to time, even though it wasn't there anymore. "An ironic thing is, the medic is going to use some of that Wakan's Wire to make the amputation wound clean and quick. Old General Creesile came up with that idea himself."

At Pernie's quizzical look, Thist said, "Creesile's left leg had to be amputated. It got crushed when his barge got rear-ended on the river, coming up for the invasion. Thusk's underwater catapult caused all of that."

In spite of the ongoing tragedy and loss of a loved one, Princess Perneptheranam managed a wan smile. *Good for Thusk*, she thought. *Just*, good!

CHAPTER SIXTY-EIGHT

Escorting the Princess from the bloody scene inside the tent, Thist said to her, "My Princess, Mother Messinex is dead, and General Creesile is arrested. I'm afraid that the troops outside might not obey all of the commands of Colonel Treegu; they wanted to loot ShadowFall, and now they've lost that. They don't know *who* is in charge, who should they obey. You need to take charge before they change their minds and decide to fight again."

Princess Perneptheranam nodded. "You're right, my love. And with Wakan lying there unconscious, I have no other authority to depend on, nobody they will recognize as legal." Biting her lip, she said, "Except *me*!" Looking down at Thist, the small, dark man in a dark tunic still bloody from the morning's battle, she said, "Thist, I am appointing you my chief advisor, until Wakan Kech is once more capable. Will you accept the role?"

"Of course, Princess," Thist said, bowing to her. "As long as you need me."

"Then stand beside me as I make the announcement." With Colonel Treegu calling for a guard formation, the Princess was soon surrounded by a cadre of Mothersmen, facing outward, swords drawn. To Thusk, she said in a quiet voice, "Please have Una flash those lights on the Moon again. I need to show *my* power, too." He nodded, and left for Una.

Pernie said loudly, "My people, watch the Moon! With the passing of Mother Messinex, I am the new Mother of Motherland! Observe my powers!" At that, the lunar necklace of lights flashed on and off a few times, finally dimming back to their normal appearance. Around them, the troops continued to bow their heads, nodding their acceptance. Then Pernie added, "Thist of The People's Lands is my chief advisor and speaks for me." To the colonel, she said, "Colonel Treegu, you are now promoted to General of my army. Your first priority is to set all of your civilian support staff, your engineering corps, to the task of rebuilding what Creesile destroyed of my city and my palace here. Other reparations will be settled later. But as of this moment, I don't want any of your men to carry weapons in ShadowFall. Do you understand?" By a nod, Treegu averred that he did.

"So now, order the rest of your troops to proceed southward to their bases, camps, or homes, as they see fit. Any looting or rampaging along the way back will be severely punished." She smiled grimly. "But you can let them know that their dedication to duty, their long journey to ShadowFall, and their valor in battle, even under the orders of criminal Creesile, will be handsomely rewarded. There will be no need to loot." Startled at the new Mother's understanding of the common Mothersman soldier, Colonel Treegu smiled, saluted, bowed, and left to confer with his officers to carry out Her wishes.

That done, Pernie and the twin warriors walked back to Una, which acknowledged their return, opening the access door. Thist said, "Princess, I think you should make the same announcement to all those troops back down the line, to make sure they understand the new orders, and that you are their new Mother."

The Princess agreed, and Una flew visibly above the retreating columns of Mothersmen, repeating the message by loud-voice, high over the weary and dejected troops who were spread out over several kilometers. That done, turning from the front video screen, Thusk said, "I hated to see all of those stretchers down there carrying the wounded. And the wagonloads of bodies. Thousands dead or crippled. What a shame and waste." He was regretting his own part in that parade of misery, but told himself that it would have been so much worse had Creesile prevailed and slaughtered all of ShadowFall.

Thist snorted, "I feel nothing for that scum. If they hadn't been trying to kill us, they wouldn't have died. Or even been hurt."

"But they were only following orders, Thist," his twin said, sadly. "For that matter, who ordered *you* to kill Miran Kech the way you did? Some might even say *that* was murder."

Thist rubbed his face with his hands, breathing calmly. "I am a military commander in a war against illegal invaders. That worm Miran was responsible for this whole war, the killing of our countrymen both tall and small. In the middle of our peace negotiations with Mother Messinex, he tried to sabotage our efforts." Drawing himself up to his full height, he stared Thusk in the face. "As I said then, I had the authority to execute such a traitor, and in a manner intended to cause fear and distraction for the commander of the enemy forces. So I did. *Legally!*" Turning away from his twin, he sat squarely on his cabin seat and closed his eyes.

Witnessing the first clash she had ever seen between her two little men, Pernie said, "Thusk, Thist, both of you. As the prevailing legal authority of ShadowFall, and now of all Motherland, I approve of Thist's handling of that Miran Kech traitor. It was a legal execution and it did discomfit Creesile, from what I have heard. Had he continued the siege even a few minutes more, the palace would have fallen and I would be dead or worse. Please, both of you, do not disagree on this. War is a horrible business, but Miran instigated it; even Creesile, brutal though he is, was following legal orders—or so he thought."

Speaking in a softer tone, she said, "On another matter of legality, so as to prevent any mutiny or ill feeling among our officer corps, I want you both to tell everyone privately that General Creesile's only treasonable action was that he did not immediately stop his army when ordered from above. Up to the moment Mother Messinex met him, he wanted to continue the siege, but then he publicly argued with her before he gave the order that killed her. Make sure that this truth is spread, unofficially, of course. That will put to rest any thought that the General will be tried for treason for just obeying orders. And of course, the murder of our Mother has already convicted him in the public eye, beyond any doubt. That was all Creesile's fault, his own action. But those wounded and dead Mothersmen you see being carried off from the battlefield below, those casualties are on Miran Kech."

Pernie was quiet or a moment, reflecting, then said, "And don't forget; Miran was also responsible for the war that caused all of the destruction and death in ShadowFall in the first place." Sighing, she said, "With our losses, I don't know how we'll ever recover." As Una flew them the short distance back toward the smoking Palace, she said, "And I hope that Messinex's death, my self-assumption of Motherhood, won't result in a countrywide civil war once the other Sisters hear of it."

At that, Thusk spoke up. "Princess, I have thought about the problems with the succession, ever since the invasion began and I knew that Messinex would have to go. I think I may have a way out for you, for Motherland —for all of us! First we return to Mother's Palace. There you free all of the prisoners from Miran's dungeons, let them run the country again, along with your advisors there, while we hurry and travel to go visit your Sisters in person—all of them."

Almost a whole Period later, Mienne was escorting Jolan Keesh, Ledd Mernan, and a surprise visitor —*Ugly Elder!*—up to Control Room. Elder Myuk's wrinkled face trembled in astonishment; the two tunnelers were awed but appreciative of the technology they were witnessing.

"Mienne, my child," said Elder Myuk, hugging the two girls. "I am so happy that you escaped the guards, and you too, Wayer, of course." Keesh and Mernan walked around the panels and racks in wonderment. Mienne had already asked the DI to adjust all the displays so that her colorblind guests could better see them, and the frequencies of the sounds so that they could hear as well. Immediately, reddish casts had overlaid all the screens; to Mienne the sounds had a much lower pitch but were still understandable.

"These physical parts look like some of the dead, inoperative equipment we often find in the Resource Tube," Ledd said, stroking the smooth surface of a moving display screen. "But these pictures look alive, these moving images. And look—three-dimensional maps of all of Community's Tubes. And of dozens of other Tubes. So many of them, I had no idea! Community is such a small part of that Tube network! And, and, it is showing me domed cities on the *surface*, big bubbles sticking out in *Vac*! Amazing!"

Jolan went over to inspect the image panels more closely. "Hmm," he said, "I can't read the text on these labels, but I know the symbols—Water Treatment Facilities, Solar Energy Converters, Modular Fission Power Plants, Hydroponics Tubes, Atmospheric Environments…" Shaking his head in amazement, he whispered, "You can control all of the power, atmospheres, and environments of Community and a hundred other places with these controls. If they all still work." Then, to Ledd: "Don't touch anything. If this place has run without us for a long, long time, first we need to find out how to operate it all. And only then will we know what to do with it."

Turning back to Mienne, he said, "Look, I brought Elder Myuk with us; first, to show her that you girls were alive and well. But next, to let her see what you have discovered up here, so she can tell the Council that you should be rewarded for your fantastic explorations and discoveries."

Elder Myuk agreed. "Nobody in Community history has ever found such an amazing ancient site, nor have they ever known what the Hall of Whispers actually is." Looking around at the black sky and the prominent blue-white disk on the dome above them, she whispered, "Is that really Outside? Vac?"

"Yes, Elder," Mienne said happily, pointing up to the bright disk in the sky. "Up there is Motherth. But it is called 'Earth.'" Asking her guest to sit on the padded benches around the perimeter of Control Room, she said, "You mentioned the history of Community. Let me show you what the real history is. DI, show them the whole history of Moon and Earth. And all about the Emergency."

"As you wish, Mienne. Everyone, please look toward the disk of Earth." At the sound of the DI's voice, Mienne's guests looked around, trying to find the source of the speaker. She just grinned. *This voice is just the beginning of your shock*, she thought. *Like Wayer and me, you all are about to relearn everything you ever thought you knew!*

PEACE

CHAPTER SEVENTY

Two days after Messinex's death and the end of the aborted invasion of ShadowFall, Pernie, Thist, and Thusk, accompanied by four large, spear-carrying Mother's Guards in full black leather armor, appeared over the plaza in front of the palace of Princess Seelina of the Sisterdom of Black Water, slowly circling first the surrounding city, then the palace grounds, affording all the subjects and nobles of Black Water a chance to observe the marvelous machine that was now known as the Savior of ShadowFall, Princess Pernie's "celestial cucumber," or in private, even as an obscene reference to the male member.

As crowds gathered in the plaza in front of the palace to watch the strange scene, Princess Seelina's palace guards ran out to confront the big green flying machine descending from the sky. Una quietly settled to the ground, kicking up wisps of dust. In awe, the onlookers grew silent.

Noiselessly, the black ovoid atop the green cylinder tilted backward, revealing the White Pilot. "Having demonstrated her power by controlling the necklace of lights on the Moon, our new Mother Perneptheranam has come to visit the Princess Seelina," the figure said in loud-voice, at a volume that was heard inside the palace. "Please escort her now!" At that, Pernie's guards stepped out, swords and springbows ready to meet any resistance. There was none.

———

FLYING TO SEE THREE PRINCESSES PER DAY, BY THE END of four days all Sisterdoms had been visited, each Sister being invited to the convocation at Mother's Palace scheduled for just five days after the final visit. The few reluctant princesses each deferred to the new Mother after they witnessed Her repeated control of the string of lights on the Moon, the individual viewings being even more effective than those of the day of the battle at ShadowFall, an apparent power over the Moon itself.

Those nearest Sisters, the ones who could travel the distance by horse-drawn coach in time, were allowed to do so. Those too distant were to be transported by Una. "We could scoop all dozen of them up in a day, if you wanted," Thusk volunteered to Pernie. "It would be quite packed in the cabin, but if they don't bring along handmaids or guards, we could do it."

———

ANOTHER WEEK PASSED, AND SHADOWFALL WAS returning to peace. Outside the Palace, the sounds of construction and rebuilding echoed down debris-free streets. The Republic of ShadowFall Council was convening in executive session in the renamed war room. The mood of most attendees was upbeat, save one.

"Eleven hundred dead and four thousand wounded? ShadowFall will never recover," Wakan Kech said, sorrowfully reading the after-action report while reclining on his bed, his stump of a right arm still heavily bandaged. "General Treegu has not supplied his losses yet, but first estimates are close to forty-five hundred dead and a several thousand more severely injured. We will have to make plans to help the ShadowFall families who suffered losses. Maybe even the disabled Mothersmen. I hate that my name will forever be connected to those IEDs." Around the large palace room Wakan saw a dozen other persons, some of whom he had yet to meet formally, but apparently all there at the invitation of the Princess.

In a cushioned chair next to the bed of the recovering Kech priest sat the former Princess Perneptheranam, with her the famous bird-warrior, Thist. Around the planning table sat a tall man, representative of what had once been the class of ShadowFall nobles; a delegate from the new settlers from The People's Lands, who were Thist's own countrymen and veterans of the recent war; and six other men and women elected by local groups of shopkeepers, traders, farmers, and trades guilds.

"Wakan, now that you are recovering," Chief Advisor Thist spoke, "let me introduce you to the Governing Council of the new Republic of ShadowFall. These are the people who from now on will be making majority decisions on public policy—taxes, building projects, division of formerly 'royal' lands, and defense. Odel M'ridge is the new minister of defense, seeing that our mirror-man installations—Wakan's Towers—are rebuilt and functioning. He is also hoping to train cadres of flyers for our future protection. Our brave Thusk will be staying here, too, temporarily acting as ambassador from both The People's Lands and Mother's City, helping those brave warriors from our homeland to settle into peaceful lives in their new land grants in the east. He is already out there with them now, overseeing some reconstruction. He asked me to give you his best wishes for your total recovery."

At that, Wakan grimaced, holding up the stub of his arm and shaking his head ruefully.

He was stunned by Thist's remarks. "A *republic*? What? What have you done?" Looking at his former Princess, he croaked out an objection. "Princess, these changes? What do they mean? How can you—?"

Princess Perneptheranam smiled, stroking Wakan's tense face. "Wakan, dear Wakan. Una's archives told us all about the most successful nations of the ancients—they were all *republics*, not royal systems, so a republic is what we are trying to work out here.

"But listen, all of this ShadowFall Republic business won't concern you anymore. I have given up my Sisterdom to be the first example of a new society, an experiment, as you and I talked about so many times.

"Since the medic says you are well enough to travel, today you will be accompanying me—and Thist—in Una, going to Mother's City, there to live in Mother's Palace with the role of High Priest, chief advisor to the Mother. The second most powerful position in our country."

Wakan shook his head as if to clear his thoughts. "To the Mother? But she was—" The Kech sobbed, "I should have saved her, but it happened so fast."

Pernie smiled. "Wakan, Mother Messinex's body was immolated three days ago, in a public ceremony in the stadium in Mother's City. You are now the chief advisor to the new Mother." With that she hugged the priest affectionately. "You see, what you and I wished for is coming true. *I* am now the Mother!"

"So much has happened while I was in the coma, recovering," Wakan Kech said, from the comfort of a cushioned stretcher in Una, as the flying machine continued southward toward Mother's City. Thist and Pernie stood near him; in the back of the cabin were two Mother's Own guards, distinguishable by their distinctive black-leather armor and large body size. Una was maintaining a curtain of white noise between them and the three passengers in front; certain issues of national security were being discussed.

"How did you keep control of Creesile's army after Messinex was, was, *murdered* by his men? What happened to him? To the killers? To the other princesses? To Rumi Similla, the traitor?" Sitting up quickly, he said, "Surely, they will contest your assumption of power, will start other wars? How will we—"

Pernie and Thist both laughed, the new Mother the louder. "Wakan, dear, let me tell you that Rumi Similla will be spending the rest of her miserable days as a crop-field worker in the Western Dry Highlands, in exile, as you originally sentenced her. For the rest, let Thist tell you all about it. His twin, Thusk, knew what to do before any of us had thought about it, in the confusion with the Mother's killing, with you out of commission, and a large, angry, and unsettled army still on ShadowFall's borders."

Thist said, "Wakan, first Thusk and I flew Una high above those troops, letting Pernie—we can call her that, now—tell them all with the loud-voice that she was temporarily taking command. She pointed out that the lights on the Moon were now under her control, an indication of true power never before seen in Motherland. General Treegu obeyed all the orders from both Messinex and Pernie, and kept withdrawing his Mothersmen south, leaving behind many civilians and unarmed soldiers for rebuilding the damage to ShadowFall. The other dismissed soldiers have all arrived in Mother's City or their own Sisterdoms by now; not all are happy but we are paying them bonuses for their valor in combat. And pensions for the surviving wounded." He made a face wanting to spit in disgust. "Not something I wanted to do, but Treegu thought it necessary to keep them in line. We do need to think of a way to minimize the size of the standing army; as warriors without a war, they remain a constant threat. Maybe we put them to work on building roads and canals and dams?

"Anyhow, Treegu, now a loyal officer, has kept Creesile and his two catapult men in custody in Miran's dungeon ever since, and those three are awaiting Our Mother's justice. The two who fired the spear at Messinex were lucky even to be alive; they were almost beaten to death before they were caught. A story has even gone around that *they* were the reason for

Creesile's 'surrender,' causing the soldiers to lose their chance of looting and raping and avenging their dead and wounded comrades. As I said, the Mothersmen Army may be a problem in years to come, if not sooner. But that's a problem for another day." *And we will always have problems, it seems*, he thought ruefully. *Nothing is ever fixed for good!*

"Then we flew immediately to Mother's Palace, where Pernie announced to the guards and staff that she was in command until a new Mother was chosen by the Crystal Throne. Which of course we now know is a fraudulent device, but we had to keep the tradition going to maintain order and peace in Motherland." Thist was grateful for the noise screen that kept the guards from hearing the most secret, heretical truth of the Motherhood.

"After the palace was secure and the bureaucrats returned to keep their organizations running, Thusk and I took Pernie and some Mother's Own guards and flew directly to each Sister's palace, all twelve of them. That took only three days. To say they were surprised is an understatement, but being realists, they had to accept the existence of Una and the new status of Pernie. Basically, we landed, we spoke to each princess, and Pernie explained the gathering of Sisters to be held at the palace within a week. Those who couldn't ride there in time by land, we arranged to fly back and pick up and deliver by Una. A few were afraid to fly, but most did."

"Ah, Wakan," the new Mother said, "the choosing ceremony was glorious. Of course I was chosen; and of course Thist was standing by, hidden, to touch the stairs with his hand if for some reason the colors had decided not to flow." Positively glowing, Mother Pernie smiled, "All of my Sisters, including the temporary ones appointed by Miran Kech, saw the choosing, acknowledged me as Mother, and even acceded to some of my demands. First, that they begin to reduce their power over their subjects, to stop torture, then to start up educational programs. All the things you and I talked about for years, now we can make happen. I am so happy!"

Wakan Kech sighed. *Pernie is still a very young woman,* he thought, *too young to realize that millennia of Motherland traditions, its power structure, its interlocking family secrets, its nobles and their privileges, the myriads of competing selfish interests, if they ever can be changed, will not be done by edict, but only by example. Or by assassination,* he ruefully added. He looked at the new Mother with compassion; her life —and his!—were never going to be the same as before. *But with her idea of using ShadowFall as a model example of a free society, a republic for all of Motherland to emulate, maybe she* can *make it work! I think we may have a chance, if we live long enough.*

Grinning, Wakan held out his left hand and shook hers, a recognition of the new formal relationship between Kech priest and advisor, and the new ruler of Motherland. He smiled. *I brought war to ShadowFall,* he mused, *but also a new hope of liberty to Motherland. Not too bad a contribution, not at all.*

As the next full moon rose, Thusk was just leaving the construction site of a new dam for irrigation in a field established by the immigrant warriors from his homeland. Gazing up at the orange-colored disk he had once called the Wen of the Mist, he thought about the spangled lights gracing its mottled face, trying to imagine what wonders lay inside those bright cities. His twin Thist still marveled at his temporary exchange of bodies with that Moon-girl Mienne. "Almost like I was some kind of an Una," Thist had said, "like nothing I've ever felt before." Remembering Thist's description of what the whole round Earth looked like from up there, describing the view of the Moon's surface from inside the control center, and the three-dimensional maze-like maps of ancient lunar tunnels, he found himself wanting to go see all of it.

According to Una, we have identical Dee-Enn-Aee, Thist and I, so I should be able to experience exactly what Thist did on that Crystal Throne. I think I'd like to go to the Moon and see what's up there for myself. So I think I'll go down to Mother's Palace and give that a try.

Waving goodbye to his companions, Thusk straddled his emu for a ride back to the palace. Tomorrow, Thist would be flying Una back to the seat of government of the ShadowFall Republic for his scheduled weekly visit with the Governing Council. Thusk wanted to be there when Una arrived, then ride back with Thist down to Mother's City to check out all of that Crystal Throne business for himself. *Just imagine, traveling Up There to the Moon!*

Overhead, the moon glowed brightly.

BEFORE

CHAPTER SEVENTY-ONE

Josh: Voice Recording, Control Room
On the events of May 4, 2236 CE

It's always the little things that can kill you: bacteria, viruses, the occasional nanobot that loses its ThreeLaw programming. In this case, it was poor Travis who got ferself sliced in half by a little thing—a six-molecule-thick section of SKY that got loose and snapped, whiplike, catching fer edge-on, the sharpest cutting edge ever invented.

"Josh," fhe was saying right before it happened, "I think we have a malfunction. It looks like—" That's as far as fhe got before suddenly fhe was in two pieces, fer space-suited hips and legs spinning one way, spewing an expanding mist of redness, fer torso and head still pointed toward me, a look of surprise on fer face before the inside of fer helmet dome erupted with splashing blood, blood that instantly froze into a pattern of interlinked red rosettes.

Luckily for me, I was on the biocapsule platform meters above her, so that the sharp edge of SKY didn't even touch my skinsuit. In horror I watched as Travis' lower half lazily tumbled downward toward Earth. When it finally hit, two hundred klicks below, those beautiful legs, that perfect tush—*that string of trailing guts!* I thought in shock—would become so much skinsuited mush.

Without thinking, I pulled fer upper half up toward me, trying to ignore the streaming and steaming bloody mess of intestines hanging out below. Through fer blood-smeared transparent head-dome I could see Travis blink a couple of times and open fer mouth, then watched as all awareness blanked fer face.

I eye-blinked the "Retrieve" command, and a RAPUNZEL began to spin out a meter-wide 'phene cocoon to wrap us both up tightly and lower us back down to Cozumel Station, generating emergency air tanks from adjacent airgel packets. That trip down was the longest three hours of my life, me tightly wound up with the upper half of my partner. Of my wiFe. One-third of our Tri, dead. Gone.

Sensing my trauma, my MemMod nanoplant ("Mom") kicked in automatically, distributing calmative signals to my nervous system to attenuate my emotions, adjust my reactions, and in general override protonormative reactions to the horror I was experiencing. Sighing, I accepted the placidity that Mom provided, and calmly reviewed the routine maintenance mission that had gone so disastrously wrong.

JUST THE 24 BEFORE, TRAVIS AND I HAD ASCENDED VIA vacugel aerostat up to SKY, settling comfortably into our cozy but well-provided station, a typical ten-meter-square 'phene biocapsule embedded in SKY, supported in place by gelpods, vacustats, and 'phene ribs. Though everyone knew and agreed that the ubiquitous swarm of microbot SPIDERs could oversee almost all of SKY's maintenance needs, the SKY Union rules called for at least two humyn presences for every hundred-kilometer-squared area of the Earth's graphene blanket. Ten thousand square klicks, two humyn overseers per, over the whole planet, means a union membership of over fifty thousand—a powerful political and economic force. All of us SKY folk owed our careers, such as they were, to the old fym and myn who thought up that sweet deal, last century. *Thank you all, Twenty-Seconders!*

Hell, the pay was good, working conditions easy, the Social Credits pile up fast, and the Mom-effected training very simple. Our jobs once every 24 were simply to glide our 'phene-sleds across the vast expanse of our piece of SKY and note any abnormalities or discontinuities that instrumentation might pick up. As if quadrillions of nanobots and qomps couldn't find them and fix them in less time than it takes a humyn to blink a command. But rules is rules!

This particular task period, though, we had been implementing specific curvatures in the surface of our piece of SKY, an innovation by our TriL, Marna, whose *skreeling* talents included configurational programming of various areas of the 'phene web around the world (which skills provided our Tri with *muy* excess funds and SoCreds, by the way). This particular job involved placing meter-long springlike nanometal arcs at specified locations around the perimeter. Actually, what we were doing was overseeing the macrobot assemblers that would access, deliver, position, and nano-weld the thousands of thin arcs of nanometal at their prescribed coordinates. Marna's designs, fabricated by our partnering consens, Tagren Global SCC, would create enormous dishes in SKY to deliver power Outward to push ASSIST passenger and cargo pods more efficiently toward the Lunar Republic and the various Mars colonies and beyond. (And add even more funds and SoCreds to our Tri's accounts.)

That's as much as I knew about the end result of our work. At the more mundane level of manual labor, Travis and I had been unpacking the thin metal arcs from their 'phene containers. That is always a delicate process, using the large nano-effector gloves that fit over our skinsuited hands for protection against any unseen nano-edged material. As usual, we cut the packages open with nano-eff scission machines. We still called them "scissors" because of their resemblance to simple cloth-cutting implements used for millennia, but it's their embedded nanoscale disassembly fields that give the physical sensation of shearing. Without them, a sheet of 'phene resists separation by anything short of a nuclear blast. .

AXING THE DI NET AS I DESCENDED WITH THE GORY remains of my beloved, I found from the incoming viz records that the proximate cause of our disaster was apparently a piece of space junk from the explosion of a SiberAlaskan spacecraft passing outward through SKY. In its usual fashion, as a spacecraft ascended, the 'phene blanket that is SKY would detect it, iris out an appropriately sized access hole, and close up after it passed. But in the multifarious complex of phenomena that comprise The Universe, in a one in quadrillion event during the trivial number of milliseconds as the length of the SA cargo ship was passing up through the hole in SKY—a meteor or piece of space junk T-boned the emerging craft parallel to SKY, causing a violent explosion. Reacting to the sudden presence of thousands of pieces of ship and cargo rapidly expanding upward in a cone of debris, SKY alternately receded and closed, trying to accommodate the multitudinous, unplanned-for nano-shrapnel. Programmed not to close on human tissue, SKY attempted to withdraw from the expanding volume of body parts spreading out from the SA explosion, while simultaneously trying to enable passage of fabricated nonbiological material continuing its upward passage.

Overloaded with contradictory requirements, SKY had violently thrummed, a giant spiderweb in the upper atmosphere, alternately in overmuch tension and minimuch relaxation, a battle of *mucho* overload versus *pequeño* underload over an area of hundreds of square kilometers, such stresses finally exceeding even its own incredible tensile strength.

SKY snapped.

TRAVIS AND I SAW THE DISTANT FLASH OF LIGHT AS THE SA ship exploded a couple of klicks away. I was two meters above fer, on top of the biocapsule. Fer SKYwise sensorium warned fer a millisecond before the propagated 'phene wavefront hit, but too late to throw up fer suit's 'pheneguard. And too late for fer, SKY had no time to generate a protective buffer layer.

So a thin sheet of 'phene sliced through fer skinsuit and fer body, removing life from the one person in all the worlds whom I had ever loved. And whom Marna, our TriL, loved just as much.

Mercifully, Mom's active monitoring removed all emotion from this after-action report, even as part of my conscious mind realized that eventually I would have to face the horror of fer death and then fer absence from my life forever. *But not now,* I thought, with attenuated emotion. *Thank you, Mom, not now!*

"Errors in detection and reaction have been corrected; reprogramming accomplished," SKY's DI reported sympathetically. "SKY SCC regrets the loss of life. Survivors of the Tri will be compensated per SKY Union contract clauses and funds deposited accordingly."

I could not detect any DIrony in the voice.

THEY STARTED BUILDING SKY SOME TEN OR FIFTEEN decades back, ostensibly to provide shading from what was considered greenhouse effects back then, during the temporary mania that preceded the actual Solar Minimum Cool Off and the miserable worldwide winters we now endure. The SMCO, it is officially designated. The Smackoff, people called it, or even worse.

First launched by stratospheric balloons, then later by vacuum-aerogel ("vacugel") aerostats, the first pieces of SKY were simple blankets of two-molecule-thick graphene sheets spun out on long, thin unfolding spindles, several kilometers in area. That's where Tagren Global SCC, the first 'phene provider, made its initial profits. Once spewed out and anchored around their perimeters, the nearly weightless sheets of 'phene remained aloft a few hundred kilometers up, their positions maintained with the help of microbotic thrusters, tiny jellyfish-like nozzles reacting to the quantum sensors and computers (qomps) embedded at every node of the 'phene fabric, billions of them per square meter. It was often commented that each nanoscopic node of SKY contained more DIQ than had existed in total on Earth a century before.

The first Tagren Global tests quickly revealed that the "graphene sky" offered more opportunities than mere shading from sunlight (which had never been necessary, and currently counterproductive). If you reconfigured some SKY nodes into nanocollectors, all that solar energy from above could be harvested and transmitted to power stations below. And after a few failures, even the huge amount of naturally occurring atmospheric electricity was likewise discovered to be a "free energy" source, or at least as free as all that flowing water that once powered the hydroelectric generators in the old dams on the surface of Earth. Sprites and ELVES and TENS—all those strange, upward lightning bolts—proved to be another treasure trove of free electricity in the sky. Earthbound astronomers, at first outraged by the occlusion of night sky, had been brought around (or *bought*, some said) when entrepreneurs learned that sections of SKY could be dished, providing radio telescopes and even optical telescopes of continental sizes.

After a while, emulating Tagren's successes, everybody got into the business; after a few years almost all of Earth was covered. Thousands of startup companies all over the planet began plastering their own SKY webs, some using graphene-borophene layers, some fabricating custom matrices of other two-dimensional materials. All of this led to a few notable disasters and a lot of bankruptcies, which the ever-expanding Tagren Global group swallowed up. The SKY Union got into the act early on, after a few thousand accidental deaths took place around the world. And eventually, global standards were developed, reliable interconnections established, ways of opening up SKY for aerospace and spacecraft to pass through in both directions, repair procedures for meteor and space junk punctures; in short, almost every conceivable situation that could occur was accommodated.

Unfortunately for Travis and Marna and me, that *almost* meant death—Travis'.

TRAVIS AND I HAD ENJOYED OUR TIMES ON SKY, THE dozens of trips up to the 'phene web that blanketed Earth, as we physically installed Marna's skreeling devices, the sheets and arcs and micronano devices fabbed by Tagren Global's worldwide underground nanofactories. Marna and the current CEO, Leif Tagren, had an ongoing professional relationship that proved beneficial to us all; Marna was the foremost skreeling designer, and Tagren's SCC had been providing many thousands of square kilometers of SKY for most of our twenty-third century. Marna's talents and Leif's nanofactories comprised not the only cooperative SKY-supporting enterprise on Earth, just the biggest and best.

Travis and I enjoyed the unique panorama that our work provided. Though the vast sky above our SKY station was the darkest possible, the view in front of and below us was always refreshing. From close to its surface, SKY presented a pleasant, almost hypnotic, vista unlike anything you see on Earth: from horizon to horizon, a constantly shifting seascape of colorful diffraction-effect waves, vortices, sometimes even small semipermanent hills, as the qomps continually adjusted the 'phene web's tension and buoyancy, always striving to keep the sheets of 'phene under precise tension to prevent the winds of atmospheric currents from wrapping them up and dropping them from assigned altitudes. Each square meter of SKY was essentially an independent entity, tenuously attached to its neighbors, kept in place by its controlling qomps.

By international agreement and standards, that square meter of SKY comprised a seventy-two-sided regular polygon called a Cobble Web—designed such that when tension anywhere within the area exceeded a maximum, it detached from the rest, either flapping away or, if caught, wrapping around the impacting object to slow its descent to the surface. Based on the analysis of the "design" of terrestrial spider webs by a 20th century engineering professor, an impacted node would sacrifice its smaller area in order to protect the whole. In theory.

But apparently the unexpected violence of the SiberAlaskan spaceship explosion, coupled with the sudden appearance of thousands of spaceship pieces and the protocol of forbidden contact with a multitude of pieces of human tissue, occurring simultaneously over a wide area in a short amount of time, created the conditions for the catastrophe that killed Travis. Though it would not do fer any good, the rest of SKY had immediately adjusted its programming to prevent a repeated failure. If nothing else, the vast, distributed qomps of SKY—probably the largest source of DIQ in Human Space that ever existed, anywhere—adjusted and accommodated failure faster and more efficiently than any other system ever had.

Just too late for Travis and Marna and me.

THAT EVENING, MARNA AND I MET IN OUR BEACHFRONT dome on Isla Mujeres, Republic of Quintana Roo. I dreaded discussing Travis' death with ler and commiserating over our mutual loss. It would have been the second-most traumatic moment of our lives, but our Moms, alerted to heightened emotional states, overrode our bodies' natural responses, attenuating the sorrow we should have felt and tamping down other physiological responses. We both stood in silence those first few minutes, gazing out the clearwall to watch the setting sun as it green-flashed over the sea toward the mainland of Quintana Roo. The rosy western sky quickly darkened, as did our moods.

"Josh," Marna said flatly, breaking the tension, "our Travis is gone. The life we wove in our Tri is now meaningless." Allowing lerself the slightest of shrugs, lhe went on, "I do not believe that we can continue it, or should try to reweave it, sans Travis. Without fer warmth, fer compassion, fer intensity for life, I think we should formally unbond and search for other relationships."

I was not surprised at ler reactions; I felt much the same way myself. Though a part of my mind still raged at the loss of the most important humyn in our Tri, my Mom kept the physiological instantiations of sorrow and regret from coursing through my body. "I agree, Marn. Fhe was the bond that held together our Tri; without fer, you and I are just separate charged entities searching for new bonds." Marna and I had seldom shared physical intimacies; ler bodymods had never held the attraction for me that Travis' Natural body had. Though I often wondered in private what Travis had found so satisfying with Marna, my part of the Tri Pact meant that I had never asked. But still I wondered.

Having met when doing some SKY installs together, Travis and I had contracted a pretty good Bi arrangement for five years or so, when Marna came looking for startup partners with experience Up There. Very soon lhe and Travis became inseparable, so our Tri was a natural result. We'd had nothing but good times, financially and relationally; all in all, a very good Tri. Until yesterday. And now all of those memories were just wisps of nothingness, thin as 'phene. I hoped they were not going to be as severe, hitting us edge-on, killing us with their sharpness.

Finally, I broke the uncomfortable dead time with, "Marna, the Tri Pact calls for us to split Travis' assets when we dissolve. Are you amenable to doing that now?" Lhe nodded and I blinked up a Mutual Dissolvement Pact; once lhe blinked agreement, it was done. My viz showed the asset transfer; our dome and our archived personal possessions would disassemble and the components distributed toward new construction coordinates once each of us had given instructions. *Presumably, Marna's will be reassembled on this same desirable lot of land*, I thought. At that moment I didn't care about my own physical domicile. *Maybe a permanent mod in the SKY? Having an unending cosmic view?* Some were already doing that, I knew. Maybe I would. SKY sounded like a good place to spend a few years grieving, alone.

"I would prefer to continue living on this patch of beach," Marna said softly, emotion now creeping into ler voice as ler Mom began allowing traditional mourning to commence. I felt my own Natural feelings reemerging as well, but was glad that our Moms had enabled the Tri dissolution discussion and financial decisions to be made while in unemotional status. As Moms relinquished control, the overwhelming sadness returned to both of us, settling like a dark fog of misery. While holding each other tightly, Marna and I cried our hearts out for our Travis, a beautiful, sensitive, intelligent womyn who could never be replaced.

Leif: Voice Recording, Control Cubicle
On the events of May 5, 2236 CE

My viz prompted, "Skreeling Programmer Marna calling Leif Tagren."

I blinked an answer. "Tagren Global SCC, here. Leif Tagren, CEO, at your service," I said redundantly. I *was* the firm, as well as the Consensual Effective Official of the Social Consensual Collective. I blinked a command and Marna's 3D image appeared, pleasant to my sight: lhe was tall, dark-haired, ler perfectly black skin merging with ler formfitting skinsuit, ler bodymods prominent and inviting. "Marna," I said tentatively, not knowing what ler reaction might be at such an emotional moment, ler having lost Travis just the day before, "now that you and Josh have unbonded your Tri, are you still up to skreeling the final SKY piece for ASSIST? We really need to address the final configuration today." I was vizzing ler image from my own physical office space deep under Illinois Prefecture, the location confidential per protoqols, and my e-dress enqrypted rotationally in GHz for security purposes.

After a decent period of mourning for ler lost Travis had passed—which status would become evident from ler i-tat displays—I wanted to propose a meatspace togethering with ler: Marna's appearance, celebrated intelligence and skreeling talents addressed each of my natural physiological bullet points. *What a Bi we would make!* I thought, sweating. *Lhe's so beautiful in all ways, natural and modded!* I hoped the TrueViz censors were masking my feelings sufficiently. *Business is business!*

"Leif," the Marna image responded in a warm, almost inviting, tone of voice, "our skreeling session can start anytime you wish." Ler image waved a hand and was replaced by a kaleidoscopic vision of squirming, wormlike, interpenetrating threads, patterns incomprehensible to anyone but ler skreeling partner, me; our qomm security was inviolable. "You can viz the field effects, Leif—the leading edge of our new piece of SKY intercepts the anticipated solar winds arising from the most recent predicted activity, some anomalies detected, minor multimodal coronal instability effects. This new layered complex most efficiently accommodates all possible varieties of incident cosmic radiation."

As Marna spoke, the field of worms separated into a multitude of colorful vibrating horizontal layers, which my QuickViz instantly rendered into recognizable configurations of Tagren Global's proprietary 'phene complexes, along with vizplays of the costs of launching, maintaining, servicing, and harvesting revenue from the new SKY pieces.

"The piece that Travis"—Marna's image shimmered, growing silent for a few seconds—"that Travis and Josh were installing, still needs to be finished and integrated. But as you can see"—the viz instantly changed to show a sim of a lacy piece of SKY gently dimpling into the slightest concavity—"the specified dishing will be effected to initiate projection beams. My skreeling programming will enable that area to transmit microwave power to whichever receiver surfaces clients wish to use to access it." The sim showed colorful beams of energy quickly flitting this way and that across black sky, each propelling ASSIST pods on their many trajectories Outward. Ler presentation finished, Marna ended the qonnection at that point. I assumed she was going into more Mom-mediated mourning.

Looking over the sims and my DI's analyses, I marveled at Marna's output, ler creativity. *Lhe is our SCC's best kept secret!* I knew that Marna's incredible skreeling-based designs emerged from the myriads of DI-supplied alternative solutions provided simultaneously to ler via qomm, as modified by ler several custom Moms and ler brain's natural IQ. *However lhe does it, lhe turns out immediately useful product,* I thought, admiring this latest design. *And these, our new pieces of SKY, should generate enough revenue to satisfy our Social Credit accounts for decades to come, even though Tagren Global only realizes five percent of the proceeds after Voluntary Global Contributions are accounted for.* I'd often wondered, almost treasonously, how those ancient capitalists of the past had been allowed to keep such a large portion of their earnings. I was gratified that my own three parents had accumulated enough qoin before such income limitations had crept in, enough to buy my education and my array of nanoplant qomps.

Sighing, I qommed Marna's designs to one of my several hundred underground hypofab networks, at the same time arranging for all of the ten thousand square kilometer pieces of SKY to be launched and integrated into the global SKY web at appropriate coordinates. *Should take less than 24,* the viz response came. I smiled; within 48, then, given the usual adjustments and calibration, at least one of our new SKY dishes would always be in position to push ASSIST pods Outward and start earning mega-qoin. That task done, I once again sat in awe of Marna's image, enamored with the 3Ds of ler I had recorded.

MARNA: VOICE RECORDING, CONTROL CUBICLE
On the events of May 5, 2236 CE

I broke the qomm link with Leif and settled back into my myomassage relaxer. As my nervous system accepted the microscopic manipulations, much of the shock of the last 24 attenuated. Eschewing Mom's palliatives, I opted for Natural Mode, painful as it might be. The night before, Josh and I had comforted each other to the extent we were able to, but without Travis and fer intercessions, we had just been two inert components of a Tri, neutral and incomplete. As the TriL myself, I knew that Travis, the TriF, had provided the brains of our group, the raw talents of strategy and design, a kind of personal skreeling of fers that enabled the three of us to function as an integrated unit.

Josh is our Tri's "brawn," I thought. *His physical strength and assertiveness are necessary, welcome, and complementary traits.* I paused in that; actually, Josh had been the one of the Tri who had suggested harvesting the aurora borealis back when SKY was only some patchwork pieces in the high atmosphere around the globe. His vision, that creative and financial coup, had earned us enormous and continuing amounts of qoin as well as SoCreds, the latter largesse somewhat attenuated by the negativers who had disapproved of losing a beautiful natural wonder.

"So the northern lights were lost, and got replaced by continent-wide advertising from SKY," I remembered saying at the time. "So what? Things change!" But that marvelous idea had connected us to Leif Tagren, CEO of Tagren Global SCC, and to its hundreds of productive faboratories and nanofactories, located as they were—aesthetically, ecologically, and securely—deep underground on all continents and under all ocean floors. *So, yes, Josh was important in our mix. Ah, but Travis, fhe was our TriF, our soul, and now fhe's dead and gone!* In my sorrow and loneliness, I allowed myself to bawl out loud, sobbing so hard that Mom overrode Natural Mode and my protestations. *You must not damage yourself, Marna,* Mom whispered as its muscular control system took over. *I am here to protect you.*

As Mom forced unwanted sleep upon me, I resisted, but could not change anything. *How did those ancients in the past ever let these Moms happen?* I thought, angrily—quickly followed by the admission: *How did they even survive without a caring Mom?*

Leif: Voice Recording, Control Cubicle
On the events of May 6, 2236 CE
A CEO's tasks are ongoing, and can be frustrating. "Why haven't our dozen new pieces of SKY been integrated yet?" I yelled out, striding around my office, agitated and confused. The viz image of a white-coated Tagren SCC technician responded, "Syr, Hermes Station on Mercury has detected abnormal solar activity. Incredible as it sounds, they report that the far side of the Sun has apparently experienced a collision with a superfast massive object, possibly a black hole or magnetar remnant. The effects on Earth of which we cannot predict at the moment. By command of SKY Authority, all new SKY additions are in abeyance until the situation is resolved." The tech was nervous, trembling, I could tell.

Fuming at the delay, I was hoping that Mom would not interfere with my imminent rant, a tactic of control that I had perfected over the years to achieve my aims over the protests of lesser myn and womyn. After a moment's hesitation, I felt no Mom interference and continued shouting. "You are costing me—and the Voluntary Global Contribution—billions of qoins, did you know that? I insist that you immediately initiate whatever protoqols are necessary to launch and integrate my SKY pieces. At once!"

"But syr, I—" I broke the qomm link, another tactic I'd learned to perfection. *Damn these Mom-addicted morons! Think for yourselves for a change! Who defers a defecation about the Sun? It's been there billions of years!* I knew that Moms had been de rigueur for a century now, that they stimulated cerebral functions, perfected instant DI access to all digitally generated data of every kind, and assisted humynkind in achieving new heights of health and happiness worldwide and spacewide. But...

I thought, *Over two million people already in space working, achieving a new civilization already; yet more could go if we had cheaper access.* Hence my frustration: DI projections showed that any and all solar system destinations could be supplied with both ASSIST pods and direct surface power, for just a fraction of the present costs, using the output energy of our new SKY pieces! But first I had to get those initial pieces in place and prove it to SKY Authority. *And now, they're worried about the* Sun? I blamed the arbitrary restrictions on the censorious Moms, and in a treasonous reverie dreamed of those ancient days in the past centuries where humyns were *human*, myn were *men*, and womyn were—*women*!

JOSH: VOICE RECORDING, CONTROL CUBICLE
On the events of May 6, 2236 CE
I was on my way back up to SKY, to finish the job that had killed Travis. SKY Union reps had told me that I was eligible for respite pay and vacation R&R, "even

to a Lunar Republic oasis, if you want. SKY Authority owes you—and us—large ones for Travis." But I'd said no, and here I was, going up again in a vacugel aerostat, a ten-hour ride up a braided nanophene aerostat tube, a more luxurious version of the RAPUNZEL rescue system, back to our station in SKY.

Lost in thought, I had shut down all qomms. Just being alone. Lonely. My Mom, thankfully, left me alone and allowed me to meditate in peace. With my distributed share of our Tri's assets and an enormous pile of qoin, I was not officially required to have a task assignment to earn more wealth, but Earth's ubiquitous social pressures, a remnant whimper from failed revolutions of past centuries, politely demanded that each capable individual contribute to Humynity's Collective "each, according to that person's ability." The unofficial motto of Earth's society for a century or more after the Depop Decades, was *No sloafers allowed!*

Upon arrival at the biopod, the aerostat dissolved into the surrounding 'phene layers of SKY, and I treaded on SKYshoes across the vibrating surface, my footwear temporarily solidifying the surface underneath with each step. Making my way into our—no, now just *my*—module, inside, it looked the same as it had the many other times I'd been there. But it lacked Travis, fer beauty, fer smile, fer natural humyn energy. Not scheduled to begin overseeing the final installs of the nanometal perimeter arcs for another eighteen hours—union rules—I kicked back on a 'phenish cushioned cot and vizzed up a widescreen for newz. "Just neutral reports, please. No politics, no entertainment, no history."

The far wall erupted into a collage of "talking heads"—literally, 3D heads recognizable as the world's most famous sciencers and Xplorers, all jabbering about something, panicky. *Even some damned politicos,* I groaned. *What the hell is going on?*

What was going on was what the "heads" were saying, apparently screaming in some cases, a cacophony of yelling. "Enough!" I shouted aloud, even though my voice wouldn't carry outside my 'phene helmet. "Summarize!"

The DI responded in a flat, emotionless voice, "All of the Earth's sciencer and space communities are extremely concerned with increasing instabilities evidenced in solar activity over the last four hours. First reports from Hermes Station on Mercury indicate that the Sun was impacted by a small but massive object of some kind—possibly a black hole?—causing global instabilities all over our star. The resultant storms and activity are like nothing ever seen, incredibly large. An expulsion disc of matter of undetermined properties appears to be moving with the coronal mass ejection." Moving images appeared, showing large solar flares emerging tendril-like from the Sun. *Almost like a cosmic buzzsaw?* I hadn't known anything like that was even possible!

"Such events have not been recorded in human history, although controversial interpretations of unfounded ancient legends have asserted such occasions as recorded in various unconfirmed reports across many defunct civilizations." I wondered why a DI should produce such tenuous sentence structure, but that was of small concern at the moment. Maybe it had to do with the amount of data access occurring, an overload? Was that even possible, too? My mind was nearly overloaded itself: *Something is happening with the Sun? So maybe every humyn being is watching the newz at once, all three billion of us?* I felt very uncomfortable, extremely vulnerable; here I was, two hundred kilometers above Earth and at least three hours to return, assuming the RAPUNZEL would be functioning after a massive solar outburst. *Would I be safe up here?*

Blinking my potential environmental status, I saw that the biomodule and my 'phene suit would protect against mere increases in solar radiation, but, but *—unknown mass material? Coronal mass ejection?* Blinking again, the viz sim showed—*I would fry instantly!*

The DI voice continued, still flat and unemotional.

"Expulsion mass ejections have already occurred on the Sun, extending as far as planet Mercury's orbit." I winced; I knew that a few hundred people were stationed at Hermes City; a couple of Tris there were old friends; the Hermes mining activities had been the stuff of legend for fifty years now. "Will the solar effects hit that planet?" I asked.

"Affirmative," the DI replied. "The Expulsion is an equatorial solar phenomenon, accompanied by a disk of unknown matter. Latest analysis is that the impacting body orbited inside the Sun until disintegration, and its components are being ejected, all the way around. Several degrees either side of the ecliptic will experience some degree of the expulsion mass ejection."

I blinked for RAPUNZEL, and hoped Mom would kick in soon; I wanted to make surface before Old Sol totally blew a gasket and vomited up his guts this way.

LEIF: VOICE RECORDING, CONTROL CUBICLE
On the events of May 6, 2236 CE

"Damn the newz! Damn the Sun!' I screamed at the bizviz wall. "Just when the whole humyn race was doing so well! Just when Marna and I—" Shutting off panic before the stupid Mom could cut in, I assessed my chances of living through such a massive solar outburst. Based on available data, the DI couldn't extrapolate what the effects would be if and when the Solar Expulsion impacted Earth. *But I'll have a better chance deeper underground, I know that. But* where? I vizzed my hundred-plus global properties, plus the various bolt-holes I had set up, numerous secure sites on each continent, in case the political instabilities of the last century were to crop up again. *I've always planned ahead,* I thought furiously, but never *for the end of the whole world!*

A few minutes of vizzing the alternatives gave me my best chance: a two-kilometer-deep redoubt in the Upper Peninsula of Michigan Prefecture, actually in the former state of Wisconsin. *I can get from here in Illinois Prefecture to a loop station, from where I can travel and open my sealed underground dome-icile.* The plan looked good: a three-story vaulted volume, large enough and already stocked with decades of food, water, air, enough for fifty people. With emergency air filtration and access to underground springs, if and when needed later. Even a network of adjacent limestone caves, should we need to expand, or to grow GModified fungal crops underground, in an emergency. Sealed from the surface, deep in the midst of a forest, safe from earthquakes and flooding, it would be a safe hideaway for the people I chose. For a long time. I shuddered to think *How long?*

Vizzing my choices—Marna, first!—I also opted for fer Tri partner, the brilliant and resourceful SKY tech Josh, if he could be found, then several nano specialists and their handheld fabs, some medicos, a few scholars of my acquaintance (we needed good conversationalists) and any other skreelings I could bring in on a moment's notice, their polymathic talents of obvious worth if a large part of the Earth is damaged. For the remainder I opted for younger, childless, singles where possible. "DI, qomm all these people immediately. Offer them transportation, safety, and shelter in my Michigan dome-icile; and add any amount of money they ask for, if they are hesitant. But they have to arrive at the coordinates within 12, sooner if possible!"

I had vizzed that the bright image of The Expulsion, traveling at the speed of light, if it had already happened, would show up from the Sun within eight minutes, but the massive physical portion itself would be much slower. "The soonest arrival time would be approximately twelve hours after the initial image arrives at Earth. At a slower rate of speed, the expulsion mass may not arrive for as much as three weeks." In its unemotional tone, the DI had just pronounced the maximum extent of the lifetimes of three billion people.

"Twelve hours it is, then. If it doesn't hit then, if it takes days or weeks, I'll open my other safe places for other people." I grimaced. "But right now, it's me out of here in Illinois and looping to Michigan." The vaculoop trip would take only thirty minutes; from there an autoair would drop me off at a nondescript roadside gate. And then a ten-minute hike to safety! Though I had a disguised suspensor landing pad area at the site, I didn't want to expose it until necessary.

As my loop capsule sped underground, I thought back on my forty years of life, the circumstances that led me to this moment: at age five, the turn of the Twenty-Third Century, all three of my parents killed in an accident while vacationing at an oasis in the Lunar Republic. So I had no real love for the Moon or any of the people up there. But my trustees with access to enormous qoin had raised me well, ensuring a hypertech education, immersion in classical studies, and in optimization of cerebral configurations. I was especially interested, as a teenage student, in the population drawback of the previous century, how technologies had facilitated the decrease in the number of humyns from eleven billion to three billion in the space of eighty years. *Not all of it voluntary*, I recalled.

As I looped toward my Michigan hidey-hole, I vizzed the alarm spreading around the world—*and in space, too!* I presumed, correctly. DI was now estimating Solar Expulsion front arrival no later than the next 48. At that, I vizzed all my most secure hypogeo site Consens Groups and told them to collect the optimum number of people of their choice—preferably the younger and healthier, if possible, with diverse skills, but in any case, that number—and get them to safety underground as quickly as possible. After hesitating, I vizzed to all SCC employees the coordinates of my other semi-secure bolt-holes as well as those of every other SCC facility; I wouldn't need those sites anytime soon, maybe never! This would afford even traveling SCC members some time to get to whatever safety our nearby hypogeos offered. "And do not make any public announcements, lest you be overrun and ejected yourselves! Go to it, at once! In 48, the Earth might be fried!"

I had no idea how many of my SCC people and others would be saved, if any. I hoped there wouldn't be fighting to get into the nanofactories and faboratories, that enough people would survive so that civilization wouldn't fail, but there was no more I could do. And without knowing which hemisphere would be facing The Expulsion blow, without predictions of its effects on the atmosphere, the oceans, and everything else, there was no way to tell. I hoped that some of my people would survive; I hoped *I* would survive! I blinked a viz of the Lunar Republic. *Those people better get Below*, I thought. *But not even any atmosphere to soften the blow. They're worse off than we are!* Of course, over the years since, I've rued that ignorant viewpoint.

MARNA: VOICE RECORDING, CONTROL CUBICLE

On the events of May 6, 2236 CE

"Marna! Follow these co-ords and come to safety right now!" Leif's viz, a panic-stricken voiceover flashing on my Emergency Vizzer, overrode my Mom's calmative meditative susurrus. "The Sun is going to blast the Earth! Get to Michigan, now!" Almost as an afterthought, he added, "And your Josh, too! Wherever he is. I couldn't qomm him!"

It took me a few seconds of eyeblinks and yawning before I was fully alert, trying to understand Leif's message. A quick viz at the newz confirmed his incredible warning—*the Sun!* My heart pounding, I vizzed transport from Cozumel to Michigan. Commercial air travel was out of the question; all flights worldwide were grounded. If all loops were functional, I might make it from my terminus there in 6, assuming the connecting tubes held. Thinking furiously, I vizzed him back. "Leif, I may not be able to loop it so far. Do you have anything closer? Please?"

My vizplay popped up with his nearer alternatives:

an underseafloor nanofactory deep off the western end of Cuba; a half-kilometer-deep "bolt-hole"—whatever *that* was—in my own Quintana Roo, near the World Heritage Site of Chichén Itzá, an area of ancient pyramids, each protected by a dome of transparent 'phene complexes. And others, up the length of Mexico and into the old southern border of the former USA. I didn't think that World Heritage domes would protect anybody from a solar blast, being transparent 'phene complexes. *They're liable to be full of people very soon*, I concluded, *and even if I survived, where would I go next? For water and food?* No, any one of Leif's undergrounds was a better choice.

Thinking furiously, allowing Mom to control my physio, I pondered a long shot, and asked my DIs whether my Tri's suspensor craft would be considered an aircraft subject to global traffic rules, or if it flew at a low altitude, just transport. "Below five hundred meters, it is legally a personal transport," came the reply. Then it hit me: *Where is Josh?* If Leif couldn't qomm him, could I? Blinking, my DIs made the link, but vizzed only Josh's iqon, not his person. "Josh," I yelled as loud as Mom allowed me to, "*Donde estas*? Qomm me *immediamente*! I want to take our suspensor to Leif's Michigan redoubt. Please answer!" I qommed EMERGENCY OVERRIDE, hoping it would get through whatever filters might be in place.

"Marna," Josh replied in a faint, terse voice, barely audible through a crackling curtain of interference, "I am three hours away, RAPUNZELing down from SKY to Cozumel Terminus. Can you wait?" Grateful to hear his voice, I hesitated while blinking a query to DI about what they were now calling the Solar Expulsion. "Yes," it said. "At latest estimates, the Solar Expulsion front will arrive at Earth no earlier than eleven hours and fifty five minutes and no later than forty-eight. The suspensor will take four hours for the planned itinerary to the coordinates supplied."

"Yes, Josh," I replied quietly, thinking of the last minutes of humynkind ticking away. "I will wait." The next seven hours—probably the final hours of Earth's latest and best civilization—were the longest of my life.

I took Mom's ministrations placidly, my body not trembling, my mind not racing, while gathering a few unique physical items, things I'd collected. *Things not scanned and reassembled*, I thought. *If History is ending today, we ought to save some original works.* I hated to leave the oil paintings and large sculptures our Tri had gathered in our five short years. I would leave behind the exquisite Martian fossils and the controversial, supposedly fabricated, inscribed hexagonal tiles from Valles Marineris. *I hope those Mars colonies survive*, I thought, *but they are only a few hundred thousand. Billions of us on Earth will die today!* And the half-million more in the Lunar Republic? It was so much just the backyard of Earth that at the time it wasn't a separate concern. Surely, the deep tubes up there would protect many of them.

With a few paltry hard data strips and skinsuit specs packed, I sat waiting for Josh's arrival. In Mom's placid state, pleasant memories emerged, a psychological ploy I recognized, but appreciated all the same. Memories of childhood, early scenes of educational journeys in Personalized Reality as customized by my Quad Parentals. Growing older, my body maturing and changing. And somewhere along the course of my life, recognizing the *skreel*—that integrative sensation of my DIs, my constituent Moms, and strange awakenings in my mind. An emergent talent, that, one prized by twenty-third-century tech, skreeling facilitated creativity and insight beyond human capabilities. Its most practical applications were intuitive designs that DIs alone can't predict or simulate. Inside me, though, and from what I've learned, within others who skreel, there apparently emerge inner experiences that have never existed until a kind of cyber-humyn fusion occurred. It will take even more skreeling to understand how and why it happened, and we who skreel are more interested in its applications than in navel-gazing. *We are what we are* has been our common chorus, *not what we* do!

Which talent led me to find Josh and Travis—beautiful, beautiful, wonderful Travis. Fhe loved me and I loved fer. When we met, over a business proposal for new pieces of SKY, fhe was an instant attraction. Of course I cared for Josh; as her BiM, it was expected and necessary. And so our Tri had been a neat blend of complementary skills, talents, and emotions. Travis had accepted my usual bodymods that result from intensive skreeling—the multiply-tiered ears, my enlarged and bulging eyes with vision beyond human range (we see colors that ordinaries don't; all fifteen rainbow hues, for example), my exaggerated thighs and mammaries, my contoured tush. But I could always sense that Josh was reluctant to comment on anything about my physical appearance, not that we Tri had not enjoyed all the usual sensualities. *But such is life!*

Leif: Voice Recording, Control Cubicle
On the events of May 6, 2236 BCE (Day Zero)

When Marna and her Josh landed their suspensor on the pad of the elevator rooftop, my relief was nearly overwhelming, so much so that Mom kicked in some appropriate hormones to keep me functional. "Marna, Josh!" I yelled as their four-person craft settled quietly on the ten-meter-square landing surface. "You two are the last to arrive, so let's get down inside, now. Only about four hours left till it hits!" We all embraced, trading nervous pleasantries. As crisp air from the surrounding forest gently breezed over us, I hoped that the air systems in my rabbit hole 'phene dome down below would be able to maintain that same stimulating freshness. *It's all in the ions,* Mom whispered. *You'll never know the difference.*

With one last long gaze at the world around us, a world about to end, I sighed. "Take your last breath of surface air for a while," and then I blinked the command to lower the rooftop into what I hoped would be our survival shelter, far below in darkness. "The top where you landed will be hidden by a landscaped set of 'phene layers." The walls of our shaft glowed dimly as we descended, showing that above us, the shaft continued to close off. "As we go farther down, more 'phene layers will enclose the shaft, giving it as much protection as the layers of granite do for the excavated living space below."

Josh, ever the techie, asked the obvious question: "Can we ever get back out of here, Leif?"

I nodded. "The 'phene layers can be retracted. They are designed to even excavate themselves, should any kind of cave-in occur." I could tell from his face that he was doubtful. That was all right; I just wanted us to survive the initial blast and whatever environmental effects that the Sun was about to deliver. We had at least a year's worth of supplies for the fifty-one of us, and access to caverns outside the dome itself should we need to attempt underground farming. But I was wondering myself, *What will be happening on the surface, and when will we be able to come back up? Will we even want to?* In the furor of trying to survive and bring other people with me, I hadn't thought that far ahead, beyond Year One. *First things first! I'll worry about all that after we live through The Expulsion!*

As we arrived at the bottom of the shaft, a side door irised open and the hall was crowded with four dozen frightened people standing, looking at us. I introduced our two new—and final—arrivals, and asked everyone to clear the elevator shaft area, blinking instructions to move the suspensor into a garage area down the brightly lit hallway. "All stand back," I said, as the craft was towed to storage by a swarm of mobots, "the elevator is going to shut now." At that, the door closed, sealing off the elevator shaft and its multiple layers of 'phene. I wondered how long it would be until it opened again.

JOSH: VOICE RECORDING

On the events of Day Zero (May 6, 2236 BCE)

I was holding Marna with my right arm, she clutching me with her left, both of us seeking primal animal comfort, as we waited for the world to end. All around us and over us, in Leif's large hemispherical auditorium, the DI was showing real-time 3D viz and predicted sims of The Blast, as we now call it. Sweat rolled down the back of my neck, but fortunately Mom kept other physio manifestations at a minimum. I suspected that everybody else was feeling likewise, similarly Mom-ified. Looking around the room, my viz ID'd each person and their public profile. Leif's choices had been eclectic, it seemed: a mixture of skin colors and of preferences, a wide range of useful skills, a few Tris, one Quad. Many Singles. Most young. Nervousness was the predominant facial and body language, *As we all are!* I thought.

The Blast, when it came, was rather anticlimactic. Fifty-one of us sitting or standing around in our new underground home, waiting for the Sun's fury to hit, as the DI's sims showed the progress of the Solar Expulsion on a logarithmic scale: "Mercury has been scoured," the narration said, unemotionally. "No qomms have occurred since." *A neat way to put it,* I thought. *Thousands of humans fried at Hermes Station and in the mines.* I wondered if the DI might be describing Earth's demise the same way, minutes from then. We all gasped at the sim; some cried. I just bit my lip, hoping it had been a quick end for my friends over there.

The DI continued its animation. "Some Venusian atmospheric stations—Landis and Clarke—launched emergency craft out of the ecliptic to avoid direct Solar Expulsion exposure. Qomms have not yet been established." A picture—sim or viz, it didn't say— showed dozens of ships of all sizes erupting from the floating cities, some up, some down. Moths fleeing the flame. *Good luck to you! But how long can you live, away from a station and its resources?*

"For the Moon and Earth"—the sim pulled away,

giving us a polar view at a scale such that we could view Earth and the Lunar Republic together—"the leading edge of the coronal mass is now expected to intercept within five minutes." The huge expanse of the Solar Expulsion was approaching the backside of the Moon; a projection showed that The Expulsion would envelop the entire satellite, but being in a direct line from the Sun, the Earth-facing hemisphere would receive a lesser blow. The Moon would probably even shield a section of Earth's surface from a direct blast.

Everybody had one question: *Which hemisphere of Earth will bear the brunt?*

As if reading our minds—which it actually was, based on our shocked faces—the DI said, "The Pacific Basin will experience the center of the solar expulsion. A small area, equal to slightly less than the Moon's diameter, will feel an attenuated effect."

"What will happen to Earth?" Leif demanded. "What about North America? Us here?"

The DI shifted to a live view of our planet, an aerial picture probably from a geosat. Overlaying sims, it replied: "The effect on bodies of water directly impacted will be an immediate conversion to superheated steam." In the sim, a vast cloud of white arose from pole to pole, a gigantic whirling maelstrom on a scale unimaginable. "All vegetation in its path will be vaporized or burnt to constituent carbon." In the sim, continent-wide sheets of flame erupted seconds before they were obscured by the titanic steam-storm.

Leif could only whisper a question. "Will anyone live through that?"

"Only those deep underground in this hemisphere, on the periphery of the intercept area, or near the poles," was the answer.

"Billions of people," somebody cried. The rest of us were silent.

"And here," Leif asked again, "what about *here*?"

The DI waited long seconds before the reply came, again unemotional: "As the Solar Expulsion passes outward, an overlap from the north polar region will likely scour the ground above this location. All life will be extinguished for several meters below ground level, as far south as central Illinois Prefecture." After another pause: "The steam from the other hemisphere will condense into global rainstorms for a long period, causing vast flooding of all lakes, rivers, and low-lying terrain—"

So we would be safe after all. I could see relief in Leif's face, in Marna's, and a modicum of it in all the people crowded in our auditorium. "We're saved, Leif!" "Thank you!" "We made it!" the cheers broke out, a near pandemonium of gratefulness, leavened by the sadness and shock of the death of more than half of our world. But as individuals, happy as possible under the circumstances.

But the DI wasn't finished: "—for several centuries, perhaps longer, until the Pacific seafloor has cooled enough to allow the liquid water to return." At that, we all went quiet. Hundreds of years of rain?

But then Leif, our leader, our savior, asked the ultimate question. "When can we return to the surface? What will be happening up there?" I pulled Marna closer to me, waiting breathlessly for the answer.

"Models project that this hemisphere's rainstorms near the polar region will begin to freeze and accumulate into ice floes and glaciers. Within less than five years, this region may be glaciated to a depth of several kilometers. This condition may prevail for an indefinite period, perhaps millennia."

"Millennia," I whispered. "Iced in forever."

WHILE WE WERE ABSORBING THIS DEATH-BY-GLACIER prediction, the Solar Expulsion hit. Funny thing, if we hadn't had the geosat images and sims, we would never have known it. No lights flickered (Leif's multiply-redundant small fusion generators saw to that); no earthquake tremors ('phene cushion shock absorbers all around the redoubt and elevator shaft); and of course, nothing to see under two kilometers of granite and other strata. As the geosats went dark, and all the aboveground sensors fried, Leif switched off the presentation vid; nobody wanted to watch more sims of The End.

Frankly, in the quiet hours that followed, either overwhelmed in shock and sadness or deep in contemplation, we survivors of The Worst Day in History—or as we later called it, The Last Day in History—were mostly just bored, as our world and most of the human race died.

It was that kind of day.

Marna: 3D Recording, Control Cubicle
One Year After The Blast (A.B.)

A year now, since The End. Leif has provided well for all of us; not only did we survive but we prevailed, in a way. Three other skreelers and I became a Quad of our own, one of them a Male—not Josh; he fell happily into a Tri with two ordinary fym. I wish hym well. Leif? Well, Leif is still a Single, hooking up with other loose companions as their predilections dictate. He keeps trying to establish qomm with other sites around the world, but a lot of the qomps went down That Day, no sats accessible. And no qomms with the Lunar Republic, the Mars colonies, or anybody else Out There. I don't like to think that we fifty are the last humyns, but we might be. Nobody has decided to bring babies into our underground world. Yet. That may become an issue eventually, but at the moment we still have basic survival to contemplate, coming as we are to the final few months of stored food supplies. The fungal crop caverns are producing edibles, but so far the peat flavors and textures are not all that appetizing.

Among other bad things that happened, in addition to the End of the World as We Knew It, Leif's remaining qomms revealed that SKY had fallen, knocked down by The Blast. "We never planned for such a catastrophe," he murmured, "graphene and borophene and God knows what all kinds of webs the other contractors spun around the whole world. If that stuff comes down in sheets and covers the ground, nothing below it can get up through it. Hopefully, it might have bunched up and fallen in wads." I felt sorry for the death of Leif's dreams of a graphene SKY, but not too much. The death of humanity, save our small bunch, counted for much more. But even that thought I had to hold off on. We all had varying degrees of survivor's guilt, what with most of our planet's population wiped out in just a few minutes.

We skreelers, though, we are trying to maintain our supposedly superior mentality and emotionality. For example, we are attempting to fab microbots that can get to the surface and viz what is happening up there. Oh yeah, whatever The Blast did, none of the 'phene barriers in the elevator shaft will even retract, much less self-excavate as planned. Leif's sensor net detectors can't tell if there was a cave-in or what, and his few optical cable periscopes show nothing but a dead landscape—ash and rain in all directions. We need to get mobility up there, drones and the like. So we have opened airlocks to some other adjacent caverns and have begun exploration there. In the kilometers of caves we have charted so far, we haven't found any voids going upwards. And even our skreeling hasn't devised a way to dig through two klicks of granite. Microbots drilling up through the optical periscope sheaths may be our only chance.

***

Leif: Voice Recording, Control Cubicle
One Year A.B.

A year in this underground hole, and I'm at the end of my rope. So I saved fifty other people; for that I'm glad. They are good people; we have had few confrontations, no real fights. I've kept everybody busy, many working to establish qomms with the outside without any luck, and a few others exploring the cavern system adjacent to the dome. The others put in time in meaningless routine maintenance tasks, redundant since q-based nanotech handles nearly everything.

Food? The sewage recycling has worked well, though nobody likes to think of where our daily supplemental fungal protein paste actually originates. And I think that the nutritional value of our reprocessed shit is declining, too. Nobody likes our fungal crops, but we all may have to subsist on it soon, so I hope we can develop better flavors and textures. The skreelers are working on that. Wish I had stocked enough consumables for everybody here for fifty years; I could have done that at any time, but this rabbit hole was supposed to be just for me and a few others, a place to hide out if Social Change hysteria were ever to consume the world again; nobody expected the end of the world.

The optical pipe sensors aboveground now show that rains are still hurricane force and torrential, but that the surface ground temperature is about its average before The Blast. Air temperatures are cool, in the range of forty degrees Fahrenheit during the day, much colder at night. If we can find an easy pathway up to the surface, I can fab a few flying drones to survey the area. If any remotely operable excavation equipment survived and can be found on the surface, I should be able to hack it. We all need access to the surface again, not only for food, but for exercise and psychological space; Moms can only do so much for claustrophobia.

Sure wish I'd added a swimming pool to this place!

JOSH: VOICE RECORDING, CONTROL CUBICLE
Two Years A.B.

Another whole year underground here in "Tagren Town," capital of "Leif's World" and probably the whole world, the final bastion of humyn civilization as far as we know. We're surviving down here, but thinking back over my Sun-blasted career, hundreds of klicks above the Old World, I wonder if any SKY survived, or if every last square meter came down? What a shame!

In our subdivided dome-room, Liz and Cheri and I shared about ten meters square, the flexible walls providing the occasional privacy we wanted for our Tri. As a hands-on techie, I did my best to stay occupied by inspecting all our utility systems (all nano-operated) and any anomalies (always detected and corrected by microbots first), even venturing out into the Caverns (suited up and decontam'ed) to look for anything going upward. Liz and Cheri took turns interrogating the DI, on the lookout for any hint of outside qomms or possible access to surface sensors. They were bored, as was I. Even our Tri hookups, seasoned with occasional merging with other groups, were growing stale and uninspiring.

"Nobody wants to create entertainment," Cheri sighed. "The world has died, and no one feels an urge to delight, to cheer, to inspire."

"And for what?" Liz said with a snarl. "If we can't get out of this damn dome, we are going to just die down here. Even if our skreelers magic up tasty foods, we'll live like moles down here all our lives." She took a chaw of canitobac, soon drifting off into a half slumber, folding down on the thickly carpeted floor. With a yawn Cheri laid down beside her, taking a bite of the 'bac herself. "I'm outta here, Josh. Nite-nite."

Left alone, in disgust I left the couch and walked to the suit-room, dressing for more cave exploration. A displate on the wall showed a 3D plot of the maze of caverns, data from small drones flown all through the underground region during the last year. I decided just to wander in some of the lesser-explored voids in hopes of finding something important. In actuality I just needed something to do, something physical and hopefully interesting.

About a klick in, I stumbled, cursing my luck. But while on my knees, my headlamp picked up a reflection from the cave wall. Using the suit's powered hand tool, I dug out around the reflected spot. It was the metallic surface of shielded cable of some kind, probably ten centimeters in diameter. When I tugged on the exposed end, the cable sheath pulled loose from a shallow depth in the cave wall, at least three meters of it dangling from the ceiling. Vizzing my find back to town, I asked DI to identify the cable and the grouped array of finer wires within it.

"The cable assembly is the remnant of a drilling experiment carried out a hundred years ago," DI said. "Rock-piercing nanodrills were shot down thousands of meters from the surface above. Then an instrumentation cable inserted, so as to detect minerals, petroleum, and ores of value."

"This cable goes all the way to the surface?"

"Yes. It terminates within a nanocrete cable connection box originally located two meters below the surface."

***

Leif: Voice Recording, Control Cubicle

Two Years A.B.

Josh's discovery of the instrumentation cable enabled Marna's Tri of skreelers to modify their microbot's designs for macro-sized devices that could shear apart the sheath of optical fibers and crawl their way up to the near-surface connection box. Once inside there, they could drill their way out of the nanocrete and the subsurface soil and emerge aboveground.

As is usual in the course of things, it took several attempts and modifications until, a week later, MacroBot One was ready to emerge. Everyone stood watching the 3D viz in the auditorium, our anticipation palpable. Marna called up a viz from the bot and announced proudly, "Here it goes, out into the world!" No one cheered. What we could make out was a swirl of freezing rain, and a curtain of falling snow. About what we had expected. I thought, *Well, any given winter in northern Michigan might look the same.*

The next hour, Marna's MacroBot Two ejected a powered miniature flying drone upward into the storm. In the viz, raging storm clouds, white and gray, swirled through the entire 360 panorama. This continued for several minutes until at last, above the thick layer of storm clouds a clear sky was visible, a beautiful canopy of blue above. As the drone camera panned downward, all we could see was a vast expanse of cloud cover.

"The Moon, please, Marna," I asked. "Can we see it?"

The scene shifted, the Moon in a crescent now, but colored lights spangled across its equator, only a few of the familiar tiny beads missing. "So there is some hope, folks," I said. "Maybe others lived through The Blast?" Then to DI: "Are any surface qomms up? Any more people here on Earth?"

DI responded, "Some few thousand qomps reporting in, mostly DI only. Five transmissions from other humyn sites. Erratic signals and—" But I couldn't hear DI over the cheers. "More people!" "We're not alone!" "Where are they?" "When can we go meet them?"

To my astonishment, a majority of Tagren Global's underground facilities had remained intact, save the ten from Oztralia up past the Four Chinas and Alaskiberia, which never qommed again. As the rest reported in to my viz inquiry, I saw that at least forty of them, the completely automated ones, were basically intact and ready to produce. Sadly, not all of them had any humyn crews present, just DI-mediated nanofacturing operations. I was astonished; at my fingertips, with my blinked orders, I still had the ability to fabricate almost anything, and where The Blast or glaciers or rains or earthquakes had not destroyed access to the Earth's surface, I could supply them in vast quantities.

But what? And where? What does this decimated world need? And thinking over our own situation in my refuge here, *How the hell can we get out of this rabbit hole, and where can we go if the whole world is in a storm that will last for centuries?*

Marna: 3D Recording, Control Cubicle

Four Years A.B.

Four years now. I am sorry to have to write that Leif died at his own hand two years ago. He grew increasingly depressed at our inability to resettle aboveground, even though Josh and others finally dug out an egress hole through the many meters of accumulated ice and constructed a secure entrance. In addition to the torrential rains that never stop, with our valiant airdrones making their way above the clouds, we vizzed a glacier front forming all around us in such a short time, cutting off any chance of walking southward. An active mind and personality like Leif's, having exerted all his energies on producing those info-spheres for the civilizations to come, finally succumbed to despair that even his Mom could not ameliorate. Slitting one's wrists, an ancient rite, is still effective, even in the twenty-third century.

Josh: Voice Recording, Control Cubicle

Four Years A.B.

Thought I'd drop down here and update things. Not a lot to report, and as Marna says, who are these recordings for, anyway? Nobody really wants to talk about the past anymore, and hardly ever about the future. We explore the caverns, raise some crops, VR a million old recordings, do sex; all in all, a comfortable but unchallenging life, boring as hell. Aboveground is still a mess according to our periscopes and minidrones.

Thinking back, one good thing did happen before Leif took his own life a couple years back. We all thought that his idea of preserving knowledge for whatever civilization might arise after these damned glaciers are gone, was a good one.

"Everyone," Leif had said that morning a couple of years ago, standing at the podium in our auditorium dome, "I am still able to operate my DI-mediated nanofactories, forty of them. What should I do with them? Any ideas?"

Over the hubbub of animated conversation, Marna and her skreelers (of course) made a suggestion unanimously adopted: "Leif, we have skreeled the possibilities before today. Our recommendation is that those nanofactories of yours first produce the necessary vaccines, medicines, and supplements that will be required for any human refugees surviving in SCC's other locations. Along with whatever physical equipment they may require for indefinite survival." Cheers for that, as expected.

But Marna went on, "After the health and survival needs of those colonies are met, we should think about future generations. These glaciers and other geological effects may mean the end of our own civilization as we know it. We can't migrate out of our holes down here; we wouldn't know where to go if we could. Assuming the worst, that interconnected global communication, much less travel, may be interrupted for decades, or centuries—even millennia—we need to think of preserving all of humynkind's knowledge of science, technology, medicine, and history for the future civilizations that will come after."

Days of arguments, concepts, conversations, ideas followed. To stimulate our thinking about eons-long storage, Leif accessed studies done centuries before, back when some nations were concerned about safely storing nuclear wastes. Building giant pyramids with secure vaults was suggested. Leif said, "There is no equipment Aboveground to build massive structures; my nanofactories used to build small stuff—lots of square kilometers of graphene and borophene SKY, spun onto two-meter spindles. I have no way to quarry, cut, and stack stones."

Electronic storage devices were out of the question. "Our quantum computing systems should indefinitely survive many millennia. But how do we know that in a thousand years anybody would even recognize a qomp device? And what shape would it take, what size would it be, and what would it *do*? These kinds of things were argued over back in the twentieth century, and nobody *then* ever came up with a satisfactory answer." Fortunately, as we all knew, those nuclear waste repositories had proved to be some of the most valuable places on Earth when microbots scavenged them for fuels in the late Twenty-First. But nobody thought that any near-term future civilizations would have such tools to retrieve buried electronics or qomps.

I was able to solve part of the problem, at least. Having visited World Heritage Sites protected by transparent graphene domes—the huge one protecting the scorched Last Pyramid outside the Cairo Crater came to mind—I stood up and said, "Why not make small versions of those clear 'phene domes, like the ones at Cairo and Chichén Itza and Gunan Padang?"

Leif objected, "I can't build anything larger than a meter or two, I already said."

I replied, "Make them the size of bowling balls— spheres, not domes. Spread them all over the whole world." Thinking furiously before the usual barrage of naysaying could erupt, I said, "Nano-components, qomps powered by sunlight. Audio, visual, 3D."

"How could people ignorant of technology ever access them?" Leif asked, rubbing his beard thoughtfully. "What kind of user interface?"

Imagining myself holding a magic bowling ball, I replied, "Well, first of all it only responds to human touch, not to any animal or plant or dirt that falls on it." Watching Leif's hands move through the air, I knew that he was already designing an "info-sphere."

Within minutes, he called up a large 3D for all to see. "This is what Josh's concept could look like," he said. "I vizzed it to be twenty-five centimeters in diameter. A nexus of qomps at the center is protected by multilayered borophene. Responding to human touch, it speaks any number—maybe *all*?—human languages. It projects images. It reports to the user their coordinates based on our distributed GPS qomps, and answers any questions the user puts to it."

Over acclamation from the rest of our community, Leif began collecting ideas for what information and instructional matter should be included. For that, Marna and her Tri provided the best inputs, as decided by us all.

"The info-spheres should sense human DNA structure when touched, so that another hominid won't find it interesting and secrete it away from humans. And we believe that the spheres should contain different information, a spectrum of data and videos, so that disparate tribes in the future, if that's what humanity will be when the thaw comes, will want to trade information with each other. No one tribe or clan or even nation will have exclusive access to all human knowledge."

Over the loud objections of others, Marna said, "We have skreeled that if each sphere has all of our current knowledge and history, the first group to find and use one would soon be dominant over all the rest. But if the spheres are incomplete, complementary, it will give our future Earth people a chance to develop more diversity. They will have to meet and share. Maybe we even set up a system whereby some spheres can access others? Any ideas?"

"And maybe, 'one sphere to rule them all'?" a wit suggested. We all laughed aloud.

"Hadn't thought of that," Marna smiled. "But maybe so—a hierarchy of data, maybe even limited to operation by certain languages or geographical locations?" The discussions went on for weeks—we had little else to do. We collectively decided to make up a mix of features and capabilities and distribute them all over the world, millions of them.

Finally, Leif called an assembly and announced, "People, today, I'm going to blink instructions to the nanofactories to fabricate a million of the info-spheres per location, where possible, and to deliver them as widespread as they can, in all directions. As far as production capacity is concerned, the DI says this can be done as often as every six months, limited only by the availability of local materials. Fortunately"—he smiled—"there's a lot of carbon everywhere now."

Blinking hard, he called up a collage of videos from his many nanofactories, where as fast as one could blink, transparent balls appeared, fabricated out of thin graphene layers, then stacked like so many ball bearings, and fired from ejection tubes into the Aboveground. Provided with aerostat covers, some number would float in the sky for thousands of kilometers in all directions, while others would land closer to the launch sites. In those fortunate regions where no clouds opaqued the sky, or where there were clear ocean waters, the balls seemed to spray like fountains, like bubbles in the sky.

For those worried about bowling balls falling from the sky and hitting survivors, Leif said, "From high altitudes, their terminal velocities will be controlled by their qomps and configurable surfaces, so as not to crash into any people or structures still standing. The rest will fall on land, lakes, rivers, oceans. In the mountains, in forests, in valleys and everywhere.

"It is my hope that these spheres will help those in the future who may need them." He shrugged; "If they are more advanced than we, I have just wasted millions of 'phene-balls that may be children's toys someday." Asked how long the balls would last, he smiled. "Who knows? Nobody has ever asked before, but their multilayered borophene and graphene additive fabrication has no practical lifetime limits, and there are no moving parts, so—thousands of years? Millions?

"Exposed to a few hours of sunlight, their 'phene batteries should run them for decades of continuous use. Basically, folks, they'll outlast us and the next few ice ages. But we'll never know, will we?"

The troubles began a year later, when Leif's faboratories and nanofactories began to lose qomms. Whether it was the incessant stormy weather, ice buildup, more solar EMP effects, earthquakes, tsunamis, whatever, one by one the transmissions stopped. Several of the facilities had been staffed by human survivors, but no word ever came as to their fates. We could guess.

Although Leif had cranked out countless millions of his info-spheres (*my* idea, actually) and scattered them all over the habitable parts of our planet, he seemed to be taking everything personally. And one morning he was found dead, wrists slit, in the bath-chamber of his suite.

Following his written suicide note, which I won't repeat here, he was interred in one of the subterranean peat fields in a distant cavern. *Let me feed the crops*, he had written. And so we did.

Josh: Voice Recording, Control Cubicle
Ten Years A.B.

Life in Tagren Town, Leif's World, continues: challenges, education, boredom. A few children now. And we had some excitement, a hope of outside visitors for the first and only time. It went like this: At first we received a radio signal: "All stations! All stations! Mayday! Mayday!"

As the qomms duty officer in the control cubicle that morning, I blinked the DI to respond, "Leif's World here. Where are you? *Who* are you?"

The voice replying was hesitant, "*Leif's World?* Never heard of you. But, this is Dr. Xavier Rasha, flying in United North American Survey Craft #201, surveying Michigan Glacier. We experienced a solar EMP that disabled our suspensor. We crashed. One crew killed on impact. I am at present injured and inside. Another crew is outside; she is attempting to assess the damage. Please send help. Coordinates follow…"

We were unable to send any help, of course, being stuck underground. Besides, they were a hundred kilometers north of us, apparently where the new glacier was already thickest. When their ever more desperate pleas finally died, as did they, I felt sorry for them, but sorrier for us. At least they would suffer no more. Were it not for raising the children, I'd probably go join Leif under the peaceful pastures of peat myself.

MARNA: 3D RECORDING, CONTROL CUBICLE
Thirty Years A.B.

Not very motivated today, but here goes anyway. Outside, the airdrones still see storms and ice. Inside, we are now a real community with teenage children and infants; some are grandparents already. We number one hundred and three. Caverns producing adequate—if not very stimulating—crops for feeding us all. Leif's provision of nano- and q-based technologies serving us well; no equipment failures, and our fusor power system shows no signs of age. Our DI projects centuries more of horrific conditions. Some young want to go Aboveground just to explore. Their vision is being compromised by limited horizons down here. Some crazies even want to try living Up There. Josh was one; he disappeared Out There while trying to set up 'phene-based domes. Others already camping out in newly discovered cavern systems closer to the surface. Unsure about long-term human survival here. Skreeling provides no answers. Life goes on, more or less. But rather boring.

RECORDED VOICE: CONTROL CUBICLE
One Hundred Fifty A.B.

"Nothin' new down hyeer. Old people this place. Don't come here this room no more. Spooky. We go."

INCIDENTAL RECORDED SOUND: CONTROL CUBICLE
Three Hundred A.B.

[Sounds of animals fighting—growls, squealing, crunching. Ongoing.]

INCIDENTAL **R**ECORDED **S**OUND **AND DI**: **C**ONTROL **Cubicle**
Five Hundred A.B.
[Rumble…rumble…crash!]
Emergency! Emergency! Compromised environmental systems. Evacuate immediately!
[Rumble…rumble…CRASH!]

DI: **V**OICE **R**ECORDING, **C**ONTROL **C**UBICLE
One Thousand A.B.
DI has been self-activating to monitor control cubicle level once per year for one millennium. Lack of human voices or other activity during this period indicates control cubicle and remainder of Tagren City have been abandoned by humans for over seven centuries. Most probable conclusion: surface environmental conditions amenable to human recolonization of Aboveground. Cave-ins, flooding, earthquakes and subsidence continue blocking all entrances.
No projection of humans returning soon.
Preserving power until human operators return.
Going off-line.

ABOUT THE AUTHOR

Dr. Arlan Andrews, Sr., is a Lifetime Member of the Science Fiction and Fantasy Writers of America (SFWA), with over 500 publications of books, stories, and articles in more than 100 venues worldwide. A retired engineer, his career ranged from the White Sands Missile Range to the White House Science Office, a nuclear weapons lab, several high-tech startup companies, and private consulting. Arlan founded SIGMA, the science fiction think tank of writers who provide pro bono futurism consulting to the Federal Government. He is author of the often quoted phrase, "A spaceship that takes off and lands the way God and Robert Heinlein intended."

The Thaw Trilogy of novels arose from Arlan's fascination with vanished civilizations and the megalithic ruins he visited, the ruins those ancients left behind: What will remain of today's world thousands of years from now? It won't all be spaceships and robots.

www.ingramcontent.com/pod-product-compliance
Lightning Source LLC
Chambersburg PA
CBHW031434200726
48289CB00001BA/47